WHILE ANGELS DANCE

WHILE ANGELS DANCE
The Life and Times of Jeston Nash

Ralph W. Cotton

St. Martin's Press ◆ New York, N.Y.

Production Editor: David Stanford Burr

Design: Basha Zapatka

Library of Congress Cataloging-in-Publication Data

Cotton, Ralph W.
        While angels dance / Ralph W. Cotton.
                p. cm.
        "A Thomas Dunne book."
        ISBN 0-312-11098-7
        1. United States—History—Civil War, 1861–1865—Fiction.
        2. Outlaws—West (U.S.)—Fiction.   I. Title.
        PS3553.0766W45 1994
        813'.54—dc20   94-2346
                                                                              CIP

First Edition: June 1994

10 9 8 7 6 5 4 3 2 1

For Mary Lynn . . . of course; and for Floyd C. Trexler.
What times we've spent understanding angels.

He that sitteth
in the heavens shall
laugh: The Lord
shall have them
in derision.

　　　—Psalms

Part I
A Killing Frost

◆✳ 1 ✳◆

. . . They greatly influenced my early years.

When I first took up with my cousins, Jesse and Frank, and the Youngers, the Millers, and that bunch, I was on the run same as them. We were all young, full of spit and fire back then; but they'd thrown in with Quantrill's guerrilla forces and already learned to slip around by the skin of their necks, while I still worked with Pa, tending the fields and handling horses. By the time we met up, they were miles ahead of me when it came to living on the run.

Riding under a black flag had taught them some hard lessons. Getting caught meant death, stretching rope with their toes pointing to the ground—no trial, no nothing. It was a plain and simple fact; knowing it kept them sharp eyed and lean.

Myself, I'd had the misfortune of killing a Yankee soldier over a horse swap, and though the killing was self-defense, I didn't stick around to explain. Since Kentucky was a neutral state, that is, being kicked back and forth between Sherman's Yankees and Hunt Morgan's rebel forces, you could stumble into more trouble in two minutes than you could crawl out of in a hundred years.

So I lit out of Kentucky late at night on a freight train in the dead of winter, with a broken jaw, four copper pennies, and a wrinkled up letter in the pocket of Pa's old mackinaw. Had it not been for killing that soldier, I would've played out my life helping Pa turn forty acres of dark earth into corn and tobacco. I would have done so proudly, but it just wasn't meant to be.

I never knew that young soldier's name or much else about him. He was a big ole Irish boy, bad tempered and dumb as a stump. The truth is, I had cheated him a little on the price, but that's just horse trading. It was nothing worth killing or dying over, and I knew it. When I saw he wasn't happy with the trade, I even gave him back his money and the receipt for his horse just to avoid trouble. But then as I turned to walk away, all of a sudden he jumped me from behind.

There was just the two of us in that livery stable, and he wasn't fighting like a man out to settle a dispute. I knew right off that he meant to kill me, and he would have . . .

But the next thing I knew, a woman screamed at the sight of me staggering out covered with blood, and my pa came running, looped my arm across his shoulder, and pulled me into an alley beside the mercantile building.

"Listen to me," he'd said, helping me out of my bloody coat and into his warm mackinaw. "It don't matter where you go . . . just go! If they catch you, they'll hang you." He took off his slouch hat and shoved it down on my head.

I needed to think, but my thoughts were addled. All I could picture was a blue uniform and hard knuckles pounding my face. I remembered wrapping my hands around a pick handle somehow, and to this day I recall the sound of it slicing through the air as I swung it again and again.

From around the corner of the alley, voices split the darkness, and I heard horses jolt noisily to a halt near the livery stable. "Who did this?" I heard a soldier yell in rage. "Where is he?"

"They're coming," Pa said. Steam gushed in his breath like smoke from a bellows, "Get out of here!"

"My horses!" I said, and my jaw made a sound like rocks crunching together. The pain nearly blinded me.

Pa shoved me away that night with tears in his eyes. "Damn them horses, that's what got you in this mess," I heard him say, as boots pounded across wooden planks, and I took off through the alley out of town.

I glanced back once, saw Pa slip into my blood-splattered coat, and I wondered why he did it. It was only when I'd reached the woods outside of town and heard the volley of rifles that I realized Pa had given his life to save me.

The letter in Pa's mackinaw was from my Aunt Zerelda Samuel, Frank's and Jesse's mother, and the only kin who'd kept in touch since Ma's death. She'd written to Pa to tell him they'd moved to Nebraska Territory because of the war. All I could think of that night was to find my kinfolk as quickly as I could. I needed help, my jaw being broken, and I needed a place to settle in and put the violence behind me. I knew nothing else to do but hop trains, sleep in haylofts, and suck eggs when I could I steal a few here and there.

I must've been a sorry sight the day I showed up in the Samuels' front yard, but Aunt Zerelda, or "Ma Samuel" as she asked to be called, took me in and cared for me like I was one of her own. "Look here," she said to Doc Samuel, after I'd cleaned up and gotten some hot stew in my belly, "he looks enough like Jesse to be his brother."

Old Doc, Jesse's and Frank's stepfather, was a good hand at mending and healing, and as soon as I got my strength back and rested a couple of days he went to work, cutting, cracking and realigning my face. When he'd finished, he carved a small chunk of wood, fitted it between my teeth to hold my jaws slightly open, and tied a strong sling around my face from under my chin to the top of my head. I went three weeks bound that way, but it was worth it. Except for a lump of crooked bone that still pains me in cold weather, old Doc did a fine job repairing my jaw.

"It ain't perfect," he'd said, the day he removed the sling. I spit out the chunk of wood and worked my jaw carefully. Doc tipped my head back, studying my face through his spectacles, "But you'll soon be able to chew, cuss, and spit tobacco. Can't ask for more'n that, can ya?"

"Reckon not," I'd said, touching my jaw carefully while examining it in a hand-held shaving mirror. I glanced up at Doc and managed a stiff grin.

Living on stew, tea, and molasses until I could bite down on something solid, I lay around like a sore cat for another five or six weeks before I ever met my cousins. With the war pressing hard on the Southern Regulars, guerrilla forces shouldered more and more of the fighting. Quantrill's men were so heavily pressed along the border that Jesse and Frank only slipped home now and then.

I could tell it troubled Ma Samuel, her boys off fighting and she and old Doc forced off their land in Missouri because of the evacuation order, Order Eleven. They called Order Eleven "The Devil's Prayer," for it ran decent folk out of Cass, Bates, and Jackson counties, and left their homes and holdings at the mercy of red-legs, Yankees, and thugs. But the Samuels were a strong family, closely knit. And hard pressed as they were, they never whimpered; they hung on and made do.

I have a soft spot a mile wide when it comes to my kin. I always did. So no matter what's said of the James brothers, in their defense, they were just what times turned them into—no better, no worse. True, they could be cruel as a killing frost outside our own circle, but to our own kind, our brothers-in-arms, Frank and Jesse James were the kind of friends you'd willingly die for, because you knew they would do the same for you without batting an eye. And that's the long and short of it.

Until news of my being at the Samuel farm reached Jesse and Frank through the grapevine, they had probably forgotten they had a cousin over in Kentucky. When they heard of my presence they approached me cautiously. I didn't know till Frank told me about it months later: they'd watched the house for days, leery of a trap. When they did venture in, it was sudden and silent.

I'd been drawing a fresh bucket of water from the well; the only sound in the stillness of morning was the squeaking crank handle and the clucking of chickens scratching in the dirt. Then all at once behind me, a horse nickered low, and the single heavy thud of a hoof jarred the ground. I froze, felt the skin ripple on my neck, and wondered in that split second how the hell a rider could've slipped in without them chickens raising a fuss.

"Let me give you a hand, Cousin," said a voice at my shoulder, and I spun around facing Frank James. He stood so close I could see the tiny veins in his eyes.

Frank could lock on to your eyes like a coiled viper, and though I learned to overcome it in time, that day at the well, off guard, I just stood there staring, dumbfounded by the sudden appearance of this stranger with a friendly smile and a voice like gravel wrapped in silk. And behind him . . . less than fifteen feet . . . not one rider . . . but six! They'd slipped in as quiet as smoke, and sat there atop their horses, looking hard eyed and evil.

There was not enough room to look down between Frank and me, but had I been able to, as I learned seconds later, I would have seen his gun poised an inch from my heart. "You seem a little tense, Cousin," Frank said. He reached past me and hefted the bucket in his left hand without taking his eyes from mine. "They're not working you too hard here, are they?" When he stepped back with the water bucket, I saw the brass framed Colt come down from my chest.

I couldn't answer; I just stared back and forth between Frank and the others, truly stunned. Either I'd gone stone deaf, or this bunch had just materialized out of the morning mist.

The riders sat watching me with eyes like gun sights; nothing stirred but their breath in the chilled air. Then behind me, once again I heard a hoof thud against the ground, and without turning from Frank and the others, I knew that someone else had crept in. Knowing it, I felt like a lapdog stalked by a pack of timberwolves. Apparently this bunch could slip around as they pleased.

Frank smiled as his pistol disappeared beneath his frock coat. "Come around here, Jesse," he said. "Meet our cousin."

"So you're Jeston Nash," said a quiet voice, and I watched Jesse circle the well and rein his bay gelding between me and the others. His eyes shifted about the yard as he spoke. Unlike Frank who could stare in your eyes till your nose bled, I noticed Jesse couldn't keep his eyes still for a second. His eyes searched everything around him, pinned everything in its place, and checked back like a schoolmaster to see what'd changed. "I hear you've been hiding out here a while," he said.

I hadn't thought of my being there as "hiding out," but that's what I was doing. Once that woman saw Pa's body, she had to say it wasn't he who killed the soldier; and that being the case, I was on the run and hiding out, no different than Jesse, Frank, and these others. I just hadn't heard it put that way, and it took a second of consideration before I answered. "I reckon so."

Jesse leaned down slightly and stared me straight in the eyes. I noted our striking resemblance and wondered for a second if one of our fathers hadn't jumped the fence some years back. "That makes you an outlaw . . . don't it?" He reached down a gloved hand and smiled. I glanced at the others; they sat silent as stone. Beside me, Frank nodded his head as if settling something of great importance.

"I reckon it does," I said, reaching my hand to Jesse's.

Behind him, the others seemed to ease down in their saddles. Jesse saw how closely I watched them, and he nodded toward them over his shoulder. "They're kind of a loud bunch, ain't they?" His smile widened.

"Yeah," I said, feeling a little red-faced. Frank reached over and slapped me on the back, and in a second we all laughed like fools.

It might seem strange that after taking the precautions of watching the house and checking me out before making their presence known, once they rode in, looked me in the eye and shook my hand, they took me at face value, no questions asked.

But that's how it was in them days of bitter madness during the great civil conflict. You learned to size a feller real quick. If he was a friend, you could tell it in his eyes; and if he shook your hand you could tell if he meant it. I reckon Jesse and Frank must've seen all they needed to know about me that day by the well. I was young, inexperienced, and without a friend in the world; but I was blood kin, at a time when being kin meant everything.

And I learned a lot about Jesse that day by shaking his hand. Jesse's handshake had been strong, but cautious, as if any second his hand might disappear, leaving you holding nothing but air. Over the years I'd come to learn that's how it was with Jesse; his handshake fit him from the ground up.

✦❋ 2 ❋✦

"Ring it on there, Cousin," Frank said, as I eased forward a step and let the horseshoe slide up from my hand in a low arch.

We'd driven a long spike in the side of the barn, six feet off the ground, and laid a plank twenty feet away for a pitching base. What time we weren't fishing along Giddle Creek or mending fence around the cattle pasture we gathered by the barn and bet on horseshoes. "Goddamn it!" Cole Younger shouted, when my pitch spun around the spike and hung there. "This is bullshit! I hate a son of a bitch that lies—"

Frank and I had suckered Cole and Jim Younger into a game and beat them four in a row. "Pay up," Frank said, "and quit bellyaching."

Cole pointed his finger at me and spoke to Frank, "Your cousin lied, by God. He said he never played wall-bangers."

"Don't blame me." Frank grinned. "He's your cousin, too. Any lying he does must've come from your side of the family." Frank took a deep draw on his long-stemmed pipe, blew the smoke straight up, and said, "Everybody knows the Jameses don't lie."

"Yeah," Cole said, snatching the horseshoes off the wall, "and fish don't shit underwater . . ."

In the weeks before joining the squad, I'd met my other cousins, Cole, Bob, and Jim Younger. Cole rode with another squad, but when he heard Frank and Jesse were at the Samuel farm in Rulo, he rounded up his brothers and came to visit. Four of the six riders who'd surrounded me at the well drifted back south once they saw everything was on the up and up; the two who stayed were Ed and Clell Miller, longtime friends of Jesse and Frank.

Of an evening, we sat on the front porch, passing around a jug of whiskey, and talked way into morning. Listening to Jesse and Frank,

I soon realized they were fairly well educated, but they never showed off their book learning like some fellers might. I reckoned the war had taught them a confidence of mind that was beyond any need for fancy trimmings.

Frank had a way of studying a situation and molding it to suit his purpose, like a potter working heavy clay. Jesse was the opposite, headstrong and forceful. He would rather knock something down than figure how to go around it. Watching them, you could tell that either of them would be missing *something* without the other. Yet together, if you looked real close, you could see their minds clicking as one, like two wheels in a clock.

One morning in early spring, Jesse stood behind me in the barn while I wrapped a liniment poultice around his horse's hind leg. "Think that's the problem, huh?" he asked.

I'd tapped a rising on the horse's leg with a sharp knife and squeezed fluid and pus into a small bucket. I stopped when the yellow fluid turned red with blood, and pressed on the poultice. "No, Jesse," I explained, "this horse has a crooked spine. His leg is just swollen from the pressure."

Jesse stepped around and examined the horse up close. "I hadn't noticed, but I think you're right."

"I know I am," I said, feeling kind of cocky. "I can look at a horse and tell you what he had for supper."

"So you're that good with horses, huh?"

I smiled and pushed back my hat. "I know horses like the devil knows sin."

"Is that right?"

"Damn right," I said, turning back to the poultice. "Before I got in trouble, I did pretty good, buying and selling. I even picked and delivered them . . . for a price, of course." I finished the poultice and patted it with both hands. "Fact is—"

I stopped talking, noticing the silence behind me. When I glanced around, Jesse was gone.

Three days later, Jesse, Frank, and I watched the mended horse run in the corral. "I don't see a thing wrong," said Frank.

"You have to look real close," I said, "and know what you're looking for."

"Come on," Frank said, "I don't believe it. There ain't a thing wrong with that horse's back."

"No," Jesse said. "Cousin is right. I never noticed it myself till he pointed it out."

"So, Cousin's a horse-man?" Frank grinned.

"He's a hell of a horse-man," Jesse said, his expression as solemn as a preacher.

"I bet he knows horses like the devil knows sin," Frank added. Both of them stared straight ahead. I eyed them up and down, knowing I was being set up.

Jesse nodded. "He can smell a horse's fart and tell what it had for supper . . . for a price, of course."

Frank turned to me grinning, "Want to show us how you do that, Cousin?"

"Both of ya go to hell," I said. The joke was just their way of telling me not to overestimate my own importance.

One evening I rode with Clell Miller to pick up a jug of whiskey over near Rulo. Folks called the place the Three Torches Tavern; it was nothing more than a plank shack in a clearing, sitting beside a barn and a water trough. We'd heard pistol shots earlier, but thought nothing of it till we neared the clearing.

"Don't go in there," said a voice coming from a brush pile. Clell and I swung our horses off the road as the owner of Three Torches came crawling through the brush. His face was chalk white; a wet streak circled his crotch and covered most of his pants leg. "It's a slaughter," he said in a shaky voice.

"What's happened?" Clell asked. His hand went to his holster.

"There's a crazy man in there! Thank God you came along. He's killed one and is about to kill two others. They've got him trapped in the barn, but they won't hold him long."

Clell glanced at me, then back to the trembling man. "One man's dead? That's the slaughter?"

The man chafed his hands, hugging them to his stomach. "I mean it, mister, it's terrible." Two shots rang out in the distance.

"Who has him trapped?" I asked, getting a little concerned.

"Two fellers that was with the one he shot. I don't know none of them. They just drifted in—"

"Shit," said Clell. "I'll handle this."

"Think it's all right?" I said, not wanting to get caught up in a ruckus.

Clell laughed. "Sounds like just a drunken brawl."

We galloped a couple hundred yards and stopped at the edge of the clearing. I didn't even have a pistol. Clell drew his rifle from his scabbard and we eased our horses forward. "I don't know, Clell, maybe we ought to—"

"You worry too much," he said.

In the clearing, a shot came from the barn and thumped into the water trough. Two men with rifles lay hunkered against the trough and an arm hung over the edge dripping blood. At the other end of the trough two boots stuck up, bobbing in the water. When the men heard our horses nicker, they spun toward us for a second, then took off running. "I'll be damn," Clell said, "sure is a shy bunch around here."

"That's close enough," said a voice from the barn as we eased toward the trough. We were close enough to see the dead man swaying in the water, water turned red with blood. His eyes were open wide and severely crossed, as if trying to stare into the bullet hole between them.

I'd stopped when the voice told us to, but Clell ignored it, walked over and propped his boot up on the trough. *"Ummph."* He looked down shaking his head. "I've never seen a man's eyes opened this wide or crossed this bad in my life." He motioned me in with his finger, "Come here," he chuckled, "you gotta see this."

"I can see from here," I said, ready to ease toward the shack but afraid to make a move. Hoofbeats pounded away from the rear of the shack and disappeared deep into the woods.

"You can come out now," Clell called to the barn. "They've gone."

From the barn: "Where'd they go?"

"Hell, I don't know," Clell answered. He shrugged and looked back down at the cross-eyed corpse. "Texas, I guess . . . if they've got any sense."

A slight laugh came from the barn as the door opened slowly. "Don't try any far-handed shit," the stranger in a boiler hat and a buckskin shirt warned.

"We're just here for a jug," Clell said. He leaned his rifle against the water trough. I opened my mackinaw slowly to show that I had no weapon. The stranger watched us as he walked to a horse tied beside the shack and brought it back with him. "Why'd you cross his eyes?" Clell asked.

"He was a card cheat," the stranger said, nodding down at the corpse.

"That's a lie!" The owner had ventured back and stood partly hidden around the corner of the shack. "You-all wasn't even playing cards."

We glanced toward him, then back to the stranger. He hooked his thumb in his belt near his gun handle. "Well, if we had've he would've. He just looked like a cheat." A smile moved across the stranger's face, then vanished. "So why take a chance."

"Good point," Clell said, glancing again at the pale-faced corpse.

When we'd gotten our jugs and headed back to the farm, we sat atop a low rise and watched the stranger disappear into the woods. He rode along with us three miles and ate some dried shank that Clell took from his saddlebags. He wolfed it down, poured a long drink of whiskey behind it, and let out a gurgling belch. "I'm obliged," he said, wiping his sleeve across his mouth. He told us his name was Jack Smith, but that his friends called him "Quiet" Jack. When I asked him why, he didn't answer.

"Ask around for Cletis Avery," Clell called, as "Quiet" Jack headed off into the woods. "Tell him I said to find you something to do till we get there."

"Think he'll do it?" I asked as we stared at the woods.

"Aw, yeah, he'll show up. I know his type; he's on the run from something. He'll think about it a while and figure he's better off with us than on his own." We turned our horses. "He'll fit right into the border fighting."

I watched darkness creep into the night sky, and considered Clell's words as we reined our horses away from the woods. "What's it like down there, the war?"

Clell answered in a low voice without facing me, "You know how to find out, don't you?"

On our next trip to the Three Torches Tavern, Jesse, Frank, Cole, Clell, and I reined up at the edge of the clearing as Jesse held up his hand and nodded toward two finely trimmed horses hitched to the front of the shack. "Damn it," said Cole, glancing away from the horses and out across the woods, "my pardifus needs attending. I think I'll go lie under a tree and take care of it." He slipped away silently and disappeared into the woods.

I thought about Cole's words for a second. "Does that work?" I asked Clell, as we coaxed our horses across the clearing.

"No," he said in a quiet voice, studying the pair of slick, well-kept horses, "but it takes his mind off it."

"The hell's a pardifus, anyway?" I asked, slipping down from my saddle and half-hitching my reins to the porch post. No one answered.

Inside the Three Torches, the owner's finger came up, pointing at Clell and me as I closed the door behind us. "There's who you need to talk to," he said, nodding his head, looking nervous. "They was here that day . . . shore was."

Two well-dressed men wearing dusters and boiler hats turned toward us from the bar, eyeing the four of us with disregard, the way big stags size up a string of young bucks. Even with Frank, Jesse, and Clell wearing sidearms in full view, I reckon to these two, we looked like farm boys on a night out. "You, boy," one of them said to Clell as we sidled down the bar. Clell leaned back from the bar and put his finger to his chest.

"Yeah, you." Then he glanced past Clell at me. "You, too—both of you—step over here, right now. We wanta talk to you."

I started to walk to them, but Clell put his hand up, stopping me. I heard Jesse whisper something to Frank, and Frank chuckled under his breath. "We can't," Clell said, "our feet won't reach."

"I don't want no trouble in here," the owner said, wringing his hands. The two men looked at each other and walked toward us.

The taller of the two stopped less than three feet from Clell. The other stood back and flipped his duster behind his holster. "No trouble," the taller one said, "not if you tell me about the man doing the shooting here the other day."

Jesse and Frank leaned against the bar. "Bring us a jug," Jesse ordered, rapping his fingers on the bar top. Frank stared down, picking his thumbnail. I stood next to Clell, tensed and watching.

"What about him?" Clell asked, with a broad grin.

"You know him?"

"No." Clell shrugged.

"Ever see him before?"

"No."

"Seen him since?"

"Huh-uh." Clell shook his head and turned away as the owner set a jug and four wooden cups on the bar.

"That ain't true," the owner said. "You-all rode out'n here together."

In a flash, Jesse's hand shot out, caught the owner by his hair, and slammed his face on the bar three times, quick as a whip. In the same second, Clell and Frank spun around with their pistols drawn and cocked. Clell's long-barreled Colt jammed up under the taller man's chin. Frank held his pistol at arm's length, the end of the barrel an inch from the other man's temple. The two men froze. "Don't you wish you was home right now," Clell said with a crazy grin. With his free hand, he reached out and flipped the taller man's gun from his holster and pitched it to me. Not sure what to do, I cocked it and pointed it at the man's chest.

"You young men are making a big mistake," he answered through clenched teeth, staring down the barrel of Clell's forty-four. "We're trackers, manhunters. There's three more of us in the woods. They're mad dogs. You don't have a chance."

Jesse turned the owner loose. He slid back off the bar leaving a smear of blood and broken teeth. "You couldn't track shit if it was on your shoes," Jesse said. Outside, the woods exploded in rifle fire. We heard a scream, then silence. "That's our cousin out there." Jesse grinned. "He eats mad dogs. He's taking care of his part-of-us." He glanced toward me and winked. "Why don't you go help him with the horses?"

I hesitated a second, uncocked the forty-four, and laid it on the bar. I wanted to say something, something about these two men. I knew that after I left, they were going to kill them, and I felt I should stop it somehow. I looked at the men and felt a sickness crawl across my chest. "What's the matter?" Clell asked, glancing at me over his shoulder. "Can't you handle your pardifus?"

When Cole and I returned with a string of three horses, the tavern was ablaze. Through the smoke and fire, I caught a glimpse of two bodies lying on the floor and had to turn my head from the sight of it. "Christ, Jesse, why?" I said. I looked at the drawn faces of my cousins and watched the flames glitter in their eyes. They stood silent, expressionless. Near the water trough, the owner lay huddled in the dirt, his hands trembling against his bloody face.

Jesse walked to the finely trimmed horses without saying a word. Taking down a feed sack that hung from a saddlehorn, he walked back to where I sat watching from atop a gray gelding and turned the bag upside down. In a cloud of blowflies and bloody sawdust, a human head fell to the ground with a thud, and I jerked back so quick the horse almost bolted from under me. "Holy God!" I shouted, leaning back on my reins as the horse veered away from the terrible stench.

"This is how they take in prisoners," Jesse said, gazing up at me through hollow eyes. "Before you judge us, Cousin, get to know the enemy. That's Curly Hayes and Max Dupre in there. Today they were looking for somebody else, tomorrow it might've been us."

Jesse stepped up into his saddle and gigged his horse to the water trough. He stared down at the owner of the Three Torches Tavern. The man sobbed behind his raised hands. "Be out of here before the smoke clears," Jesse said, "and learn to keep your mouth shut the next place you settle." He swung his horse around and motioned us toward the woods. We fell in behind him, single file. As Clell passed the man huddled against the water trough, he spit a stream of tobacco down on his chest. "You're lucky we don't kill you, too, you loudmouth son of a bitch. You just caught us in a good mood."

The day Jesse, Frank, and the Millers left the Samuel farm, I turned gut-restless and caught myself walking about the yard kicking at dirt clods. They'd simply vanished before dawn without saying a word. Instead of fishing or pitching shoes, I spent the day sharpening plow blades while old Doc Samuel stayed busy at the grinding wheel. If I started toward the toolshed where he worked, he would meet me at the door, politely blocking my entrance.

By suppertime I sat on the porch step feeling lonesome, restless, and left out. When I finally heard the door of the toolshed open, I looked up and saw Doc Samuel walk toward me with a sawed-off shotgun hanging from his hand. At the same time, as if planned, past him and past the shed, I saw Frank come riding out of the woods leading a tall chestnut gelding.

Frank rode up at an easy gallop, stopped, and handed me the gelding's reins. From inside his duster, he pulled out a .36 caliber pistol and pitched it to me, butt first. Catching it in surprise, I studied it a second and looked up at him. Then, old Doc came up beside me and handed me the sawed-off. The barrel felt warm from the grinding wheel. When I took the shotgun, Doc just turned and walked away.

Frank folded his forearms across the saddle and spit a long stream of tobacco juice. "Clell says you're wanting to ride with us." His expression was like a cat watching a cricket. I'd never said a word about it to Clell; he must've seen it tugging at me that first night near Rulo.

I'd thought about it since then, but I'd never brought it up. After what'd happened in Kentucky, I'd surely seen enough death and violence to last a lifetime. Killing that soldier and losing my pa bore heavy on me, and before I met Frank and Jesse, the Youngers, and the Millers, I'd gone around in fear, expecting something terrible to happen at any second.

But somehow when Frank and Jesse arrived, my fear disappeared as if overcome by their great air of confidence. If my cousins feared anything between heaven and hell, it never showed, not in their sharp and watchful eyes or their calm and easy manner. Around them and the Millers I felt bold, and once they were gone I wondered if fear would return. I hated what'd happened the other night at the tavern, but after seeing that severed head, I felt it was justified.

"Don't let it tug at you," Frank said, like he was inside my head listening. "Before I joined Quantrill, I pulled a hitch with the regulars." He spit a stream and pushed his hat back. "After Centralia, I was a year blowing the smell from my nose. All I wanted to do was come home and read Shakespeare." Frank shook his head with a weary smile, "But the killing's all around us. It came and found me, same as it found you, way the hell in Kentucky."

I watched a lazy column of smoke curl up from the chimney, as the gelding tugged at the reins.

I knew what Frank was saying. I could stay here and hide for now or forever, but it served no purpose and it fit no reasoning. Whatever was waiting to find me would find me here or in the deepest, darkest crevice on earth. I had to get over losing my pa; I had to get over my fear.

For the first time in my life I was free to my own choosing, and other than these people, no one on earth would give a damn if I lived or died. That being the case, what did I really have to fear? What did I really have to lose?

"I'm no soldier," I said quietly, glancing away from Frank, out across the north timberland.

"Nobody is, starting out." He grinned and spit another stream. "But I hear you're a hell of a horse-man. That'll get you a long ways."

The big gelding tugged restlessly at the reins in my hands, shaking out his mane and gnawing at the bit. Taking hold of the saddle, I swung up easy, facing away from Frank and tilting my hat down on my forehead. I felt like a young pup being weaned, torn between the nurturing comfort of hearth and kin, and the heart-thumping pull of the open road. I felt at home here, but it was not my home. It was a peaceful place, a place to rest and heal; but if I stayed here, this place would haunt me forever in remembrance of something I'd lost.

I looked toward the farmhouse again as the gelding rippled his muscles and thrashed against the reins. The chimney smoke streaked into a rose-gray twilight and faded like old memories.

I nodded to Frank and pulled my pa's slouch hat lower on my forehead. Near the barn, crickets strung together a lonesome harmony as we cantered our horses through the front gate, with the sawed-off across my lap and the evening air feeling cool against my mended jaw.

Frank spit out his wad of tobacco. "Big world, ain't it, Cousin?" he'd said, wiping the back of his hand across his mouth. I hooked the gelding forward without answering and we swung south at an easy gallop. I never looked back that night, not once, not until we'd disappeared across the creek, deep into the woods, headed for the Missouri border.

◆✳ 3 ✳◆

"Dingus! Goddamn it!" Old Cletis reined up hard from a dead run, his spotted horse rearing sideways and kicking up chunks of earth. I had to swing my horse away to keep him from sliding into us. "Jesus, boy!" he shouted. "Are you *trying* to get killed?" The echo of gunfire popped across the flatland amid the screams of the wounded and dying. Ahead in the distance, Southern Regulars fought the Yankee infantry hand to hand. "What the hell are you doing out here?"

"I'm looking for the Maddens," I yelled above the distant melee.

"Maddens, my ass. C'mon, goddamn it!" yelled Cletis, as a rifle ball thumped into the ground near his horse's hooves. I bumped his horse and made a quick turn. My gelding reared high. I'd seen two men spring from behind a maple tree and run toward us firing. My shotgun was up and cocked as my horse settled. I let off a round right across Cletis's chest and, not seeing what was going on, he nearly flew from his saddle. "Aw, shit!" he bellowed, then seeing one man hit the ground with a faceful of buckshot, he swung his pistol and emptied it into the other.

Now the woods to our right came alive with dark figures in long black coats. They yelled and fired as they moved from tree to tree, closer with each volley. A slug tore into Cletis's horse and it went down with a pitiful scream. A stream of blood spewed from its throat like a Roman fountain. I'd caught Cletis by his coat sleeve as the horse fell, and he swung up behind me still cussing, his pistol in the air, his clothes flapping like loose rags.

Bullets spit past us like hornets as I hooked the gelding out across the stretch of flatland and up across a low rise. Cletis leaned near my ear. "Where you going?" he yelled.

"The Maddens are pinned down over there! They've got our string of horses," I yelled above the din of rifle fire and horse hoofs. We topped the low rise and headed down, momentarily protected from the rifle fire.

"Forget 'em," Cletis yelled, "and damn the horses. Frank said get you and get your ass back before he pulls out."

I reined up, turning the gelding in short, wild circles, searching in all directions, unsure of my next move. "Do something, goddamn it!" Cletis bellowed. The gelding thrashed against the reins as I jerked back and forth confusing him. "I mean it!"

Fifty yards behind us on the other side of the low rise, the Jayhawkers had mounted and the sound of their horses roared like thunder. My gelding reared high, almost spilling over backwards, and then came down bucking sideways. "By God!" Cletis swore, "I'll get off and walk!"

"Hang on!" I threw my arm back around him just as he was ready to slide down. Kicking the gelding forward, we bellied down toward a creek bed thirty yards ahead. Shots slapped at the ground as we slid over the edge and down the steep bank. In seconds we pounded along the creek bed, kicking up rock in a spray of water.

"Yee-haw, goddamn 'em," Cletis yelled, waving his floppy hat. I glanced back over my shoulder, then leaned low against my horse's neck as coarse mane slapped at my face. "Pull out near the woods," he yelled. "I'm *hoping* the bastards follow us in."

"The squad in there?" I yelled back, slapping my hand on my hat to keep it from flying off.

"Goddamn right!"

The riders must've sensed a trap; they had fallen away by the time we topped the creek bank and slipped into the woods. The gelding was winded and lathered, foam dripping from his bit as he snorted, cantered, and slung his head. Ten yards in, Cletis let out a whistle—a night-bird call we used—and we drifted in among the members of our squad.

"You've got some tall explaining to do, boy." Raymond Claire stomped forward as Cletis slid down from behind me. Before I could speak for myself, old Cletis turned quickly and slammed hard into Claire.

"Not to you he don't," Cletis growled. Claire staggered back and threw his hand to his pistol. He looked dumbfounded by the speed and strength of old Cletis. "I'll shove it up your ass," Cletis hissed through clenched teeth, and Raymond Claire's hand jumped away from his holster.

"Hold on," I said, sliding from my saddle. I grabbed Cletis by his coat sleeve, but he slung me away. I saw killing in his red-rimmed eyes; Raymond Claire saw it, too. He backed a step with his hands chest high as Cletis leaned toward him like a stalking wildcat.

"I'm trying to hold things together here," said Claire, "that's all."

Cletis let out a breath as Claire backed away. "The Maddens are dead," he said. "Dingus was gone to help 'em. I stopped him."

"Good enough for me," said Claire, his hands still chest high as he backed farther away. "I'm just looking out for all of us."

"Yeah, I bet," Cletis said. He hiked up a gob of snot and blew it out near Raymond Claire's feet. Claire turned tail back into the woods. Old Cletis scratched his white beard and raised a bristled eyebrow. "Sumpin bad wrong with that sumbitch," he said in a lowered voice. "You watch him, Dingus, watch him close." Then his voice kicked up a notch as his brother Parker came out from behind a tree, letting down the hammer on his rifle. "And don't ever grab my arm when I'm fixin' to kill a sumbitch." He pointed a thick finger at me. "You got that?"

"Yeah," I said. I saw him wink toward Parker. He slapped my hat from my head. "You got that?"

"Yeah, goddamn it, I got it!" I bent to pick up my hat and Cletis slapped the side of his boot against my ass, knocking me forward. I heard him laughing as I got up dusting my hat against my leg. "You old bastard," I shouted, but Cletis and Parker had already turned and started off to the coffee pot.

"That little Dingus sumbitch saved my ass out there," I heard Cletis say to his brother loud enough for me to hear. He glanced back over his shoulder and said, "I'll never live it down."

I was lean as a waxed rope when Jesse and Frank took me into the squad. Like any farm boy I was broad handed and foot-thick from hopping clods and wrestling a plow, and plain dumb in some ways from staring at a mule's ass from daylight to dark. But when it came to horses—picking, breaking, training, and even stealing them—I had what you call a natural talent. I *did* know horses like the devil knows sin and, be it a blessing or a curse, it was my gift for riding stock that carved me out a place among the guerrilla forces.

For a long time they called me "Dingus," an unknown. Cousin Jesse bore that name before I joined. He didn't mind giving it up; it no longer fit him anyway. By that time, he and Frank were well-known squad leaders in the guerrilla circle.

I still wore my pa's slouch hat the day I joined the squad. It was two sizes bigger than my head, and Ma Samuel had sheared my hair clean to the scalp right at brim level before I left the farm. I reckon my age and appearance said little for me.

"Where the hell'd you find this scarecrow?" Raymond Claire asked the day I rode in with Jesse and Frank. Every group has an asshole; ours was Claire. I saw it right away, and bristled up like a yard hound. But he just glared at me, and laid his hand on his pistol.

"Go easy," Jesse warned him, "this is my kin," and Claire's hand slipped away from the pistol.

"Yeah," said Frank, leaning in with a dark grin that looked more like a panther showing its fangs, "and you ain't."

Claire backed away with a nervous smile. Even then, my cousins had a reputation. They could turn cold as blue steel and dangerous as a skillet full of dynamite.

Like any young man new to a job, I'd been nervous and overeager at first. Aside from handling horses, most things I did, I did with uncertainty. The first Yankees I shot caused me to puke up my guts, and I was squeamish about stripping belongings from their bodies. Seeing all this, Raymond Claire right away took me for either a coward or an idiot . . . but I was neither.

Two weeks after the death of the Maddens, I sat in the shelter of the woods and watched mosquitoes swarm above the backwater swamp of Dog Creek. Spring had swollen its waters up across the low land nearby, and now, though summer had forced it back within its banks, the creek had left the ground sodden and the wild grass twisted in limp swirls.

Cletis and Parker Avery stood watch thirty yards out. I dozed against my saddle on the wet ground, half-hearing the distant thunder of cannons, knowing that after the battle we would slip in, gather arms, ammunition, and horses, and disappear like ghosts. We would deliver our spoils back to the Southern Regulars or use them ourselves on our next raid.

The sound of the battle must've tangled with my dreams, and I heard Pa scream for the thousandth time since the night of his death, and I felt myself running out of the alley across dark fields as rifles exploded.

I bolted up from the ground, my knees trembling same as always from that terrible dream. Shaking my head, I glanced around the campsite and saw Raymond Claire standing beside the fire with an ugly grin. I rubbed my face, ignored him, and walked to the fire. My mouth was dry and bitter tasting.

"What's the matter," he sneered, "soldiers chasing you in your sleep?" I bent down without answering and drew a cup of coffee. Whatever Raymond Claire had against me ran deeper than I could fathom. I'd written him off as a rotten son of a bitch and stayed away from him, best I could. But with Jesse and Frank away from camp and the Averys out on watch, it was just Claire and me, and I wasn't going to take a nickel's worth of his bullshit.

I stood up with my coffee as Claire circled the fire toward me. I tried to go around him and walk back to my saddle, but he stepped in front of me, laughing. "You've got boogiemen chasing you, don't ya, boy?" He made a stupid face, and I felt a dull throbbing in my head. He shoved me backwards. "Don't ya, huh?" he taunted, and shoved me again. Then: "Huh, boy?" and that did it.

I dropped the coffee and swung as hard as I could. "I'll kill you, you son of a bitch," I shouted. But I was off balance from his shove. He stepped aside and caught me by my wrist as I lunged forward. Twisting me backwards in an arm lock, he threw his arm around my throat. He had me, had me cold. With my wrist jammed up between my shoulder blades, all I could do was rear back in pain as he choked off my breath.

"Killing a few 'Hawkers at Goose Creek don't make you nothing in my book." He tightened harder around my throat. "I'll gut you like a goddamn hog."

He threw me to the ground and I lay there heaving, trying to stand, my feet scraping the ground. I tried reaching for my pistol but my right arm was so weak and twisted it wouldn't move. I gasped for air as he started drawing a ten-inch dagger from its sheath, and I struggled, pulling myself across the ground, trying to roll away and run. Then I heard a rifle cock from the other side of the campfire and we both froze. Jesse and Frank had slipped into camp without making a sound.

As Claire spun facing them, I looked past him and saw Jesse's rifle pointed straight at his chest. Frank stepped to the side and walked a wide circle around the fire. "Hope we ain't interrupting something here?" Frank's voice was soft and cold, like the updraft from an open grave.

Claire swallowed hard, letting the half-drawn dagger slide back into the sheath. He tried to sound like a schoolboy pulling a prank, yet his voice was like that of a man counting steps on a gallows. "Having a time funning with the new man here, that's all." He shrugged. "Hell, Frank, you know how I kid around."

Cletis and Parker Avery came running in. Frank glanced at them and they stopped suddenly. Old Cletis's eyes shot toward Claire, glittering in the firelight like warning labels on a bottle of poison. Jesse stood bone-still with his rifle leveled and cocked. Frank spoke down to me without taking his eyes off Claire. "Anything to it, Cousin?" he asked.

Up on my knees now, my arm throbbing and numb I said, "There ain't nothing to it, Frank." My voice was sand across hot metal. Struggling to my feet with my hat in my left hand, I slapped dust from my shirt. "It's settled," I said.

Frank studied my eyes. "It's *settled?*" There seemed to be some question on his part. I knew what he was ready to do.

I stared back, nodding real slow. "It's settled," I said firmly. The sand in my voice cleared some, but the metal was still hot. I didn't want it to cool; I just wanted it under control.

Frank nodded over his shoulder. Jesse tilted the rifle up and let down the hammer. I sensed an air of relief from Raymond Claire. I knew that one word from me and he was a dead man, but at that second if Jesse had pulled the trigger, he would have had to kill me, too. That's how bad I wanted Claire, and as Frank stared into my eyes he must've read my intentions without me saying another word. As far as I was concerned it was settled; I'd just signed Raymond Claire's name on the waiting list to hell.

◆✳ 4 ✳◆

Inexperienced though I was, I'd already learned that all it took to kill a man was a strong resolve to do so. I made that resolve, seeing the look on Claire's face when he drew his dagger. I would be justified in killing him. It was only my respect for Jesse's and Frank's command that kept me from doing it right then.

My arm still ached as we broke camp and headed out across the flatlands. Seeing how bad I wanted Claire's hide, Frank sent me off with Cletis Avery to gather fresh horses. It was good thinking on Frank's part. I was under control but just barely, and Quantrill had a low tolerance for fighting among his troops. Had Frank or Jesse shot Claire when he was about to knife me, it would have been a different story. But if I threw down on Claire right now after saying it was over, I would be the one at fault.

"That's how Quantrill will call it," Frank said. "Should've had us kill him right then."

"No, Frank," I said, letting out a breath. "When the time comes, I'll call him out on my own, face to face, and I'll kill the son of a bitch. What will Quantrill think of that?" I sounded like a hot-headed schoolboy; I couldn't help it.

"Face to face, huh?"

"Damn right," I snapped. Frank pointed his finger at me as if it were a pistol, clicking his thumb up and down.

"Guns blazing and blood flying, right, Cousin?" Frank twisted his lips in a devilish grin. I couldn't stand it.

"I ain't afraid, goddamn it!"

"I know you ain't, Cousin." Frank pretended to blow smoke from the tip of his finger. He nodded toward Cletis, letting me know it was time to go. His grin faded, and he shook his head as he turned his horse. "Quantrill will be real impressed," he said.

William Clarke Quantrill was no saddle trash like some guerrilla leaders I could mention. He was strict but fair. As soldiering goes, guerrilla style, that is, there ain't been a better group of fighting men ever assembled than those of his command. Most of them were like I was coming in, greener than goose shit. But learning Quantrill's hit-and-run methods of warfare turned us into crack troops: We were able to wreak death and misery on the best fighting force the North threw at us.

The people of Missouri and the Ozarks proudly called us "The boys," and for the longest time we shouldered the war along the Kansas-Missouri border on our own. Even when Southern forces pulled back, we fought on like demons, foraging food, stealing ammunition, eating, sleeping, and fighting on the run, living on horseback no different than wild Indians. Enemy forces feared us worse than a blanketful of rattlesnakes: we asked no mercy . . . and showed none in return.

Cletis's and my job that night was to pull up fresh mounts and meet the squad at Dant's Mill the next evening. We sat atop our horses and watched the rest of the squad disappear into the woods. "Don't let Frank get you rattled, Dingus." Cletis grinned. "Listen to him and you'll learn something. You might even stay alive long enough to know why you learnt it." He laughed and spit a long stream of tobacco. While the rest of our squad lit out across the flatlands, Cletis and I turned our horses and crept back through the brush country into Cass County.

I stayed in the woods as Cletis rode down before daylight to contact our supplier and pay for the horses. Twenty yards out, he disappeared into the silver mist that shrouded the bottomland. So thick was the morning mist had a regiment of soldiers been there, I wouldn't have known it.

I slipped down from my saddle quiet as a ghost and searched the mist till my eyes blurred. I couldn't see a blasted thing. I kept my ears peaked like a watchdog's, but all I heard was dew dripping through the leaves around me.

I don't know how to explain the difference between the sound of a man leading a string of horses and the sound of horses carrying riders. It's something your mind learns without you knowing how. But I hadn't learned it well enough to know the difference that morning. Leastwise, when I recognized the difference, it was too late to make a move.

The second I sensed something was wrong, I took hold of my saddlehorn and started to swing up. Circling me less then ten yards out, I heard what sounded like crickets chirping with steel legs, and realized I was surrounded by at least a half a dozen cocked rifles. It was the first of many times I would meet up with Daniel Zanone, then captain of the Kansas Free Militia. His voice was a growl that seeped out of the mist from all directions. "Stop right there," he said, and I felt a sickening ripple in my belly.

I heard ground cover break behind me as he walked up and drew my hands behind my back. There was a clinking sound, then a cold bite of steel as shackles clamped my wrist and tightened up like a ratchet.

A sweat-crusted bandanna was pulled over my mouth and drawn tight. Something hit me from behind, slamming me to the ground. Rolling onto my back, I looked up at a rifle barrel and the bearded face above it. "Lay real still," the face whispered, "and I won't kill you just yet."

Lying there under the gun, I heard the soft rustle of footsteps moving away through the brush. They moved back up the trail Cletis and I had ridden in on. In minutes I heard their footsteps coming back, this time louder and muffled by voices and laughter. Above me the man who I'd later know as Zanone stepped back, and called out across the woods, "Is this all?"

"That's all we get, Captain," said a voice from up the trail. "No sign of any others."

Zanone called down into the mist over the bottomland. "Bring him on up."

In minutes Cletis Avery was thrown to the ground six feet away. His hat was gone. A swipe of gray hair hung down between his eyes. Blood trickled from a knot on his forehead. It ran down, spreading into his white beard. "You little sumbitch," he rasped. I glanced around to see who he was cussing. "Don't look away," he said, glaring straight at me. "You no-good bastard, you sold us over."

Right then a boot kicked him in the chest and he rolled into a ball, gagging. I lay there stunned, not believing my ears as the group of riflemen closed around us. I thought Cletis had taken too hard a blow on the head, making him talk crazy.

Zanone had walked away from the group, then returned about the time Cletis caught his breath and started cussing me again. One man raised a rifle butt ready to bust Cletis in the head. Zanone stopped him.

As Cletis ranted and raged I decided he'd truly lost his mind, but as I listened I began to see he was up to something. "You take these bastards to that money and you'll rot in hell. You'll never see a minute's peace, you Judas bastard."

Somebody dropped two ropes on the ground, both tied in slip knots. This kind of noose wouldn't break your neck; it would choke you to death slow, in half an hour or more. I tried to figure what Cletis was getting at about the money. At that time, you couldn't shake enough money from our squad to fill a tea cup.

Two pairs of hands raised me to my knees and I got a glance at Zanone's eyes. I could tell he was studying what Cletis said. He reached down and jerked the bandanna from my mouth. Cletis managed to lunge at me. "You'll burn in hell for telling them."

He did real good. It took two men to hold him back. "What money is he talking about?" Zanone demanded. He knocked the hat from my head and grabbed me by the hair. I stalled. He backhanded me across my mouth. I felt my lip split and go numb. "What's he talking about, boy?"

Zanone busting me across the face gave me a couple of seconds to choke and spit while I tried to think. My mind raced across a dozen lies as I tried to calm down. All that stood between me and death's dark tunnel would be the words from my mouth. If my tongue slipped or my voice wavered, I wouldn't get a second chance. This was for keeps.

Staring at the ropes on the ground, knowing one of them would soon squeeze me out of this world, I went blank for just a second. Cletis must've seen it. He lunged at me again. "You tell them *nothing*, boy," he hissed fiercely, and he took another boot in the ribs.

He was convincing as hell. When Zanone asked me about the money, Cletis looked genuinely surprised that I hadn't already told. Now Cletis's expression was one of regret. It appeared he was the one who'd spilled the beans.

Zanone looked at Cletis with a smug grin. "Thanks for your help, Old Timer." Then he looked back at me. "What about that money, boy?"

I had stalled as long as I could. My hands were shackled and eight gunmen stood around me. Zanone had reached down and picked up a rope. He slung it over my head and drew it snug. I pictured myself swinging from a tree, and that picture soured in my trembling stomach.

"Don't tell him a goddamn thing!" yelled Cletis. "They're going to hang us anyway."

Something told me that there was no way in hell I could get both Cletis and myself out of there alive. If I bargained for us both, it was going to look like what it really was, two desperate men trying to save their necks.

If Cletis hadn't started the scheme I would have died beside him without a whimper. I'm sure of that. But he did start it and I could only figure he meant for me to play it the way it fit. Whatever his reason, he was giving me a shot at staying alive. I had no way to ask him if I was playing it right. I went for it as best I could.

"He's talking about twelve thousand dollars we pulled loose from an army payroll yesterday over near Finley," I said.

"That's a damn lie," yelled Cletis. "He's lying to save his ass. I made it up about the money."

For a second I thought Cletis had turned back on me, but judging the curious expression that swept Zanone's face, I realized Cletis knew this game, knew exactly what to say to make my story believable.

"Shut up, you old son of a bitch!" I yelled. "I ain't dying so that Missouri trash can keep my part of the money."

Zanone let go of the rope and kneeled down face level watching me close. His breath smelled sour of salt pork and tobacco. "I heard nothing about a payroll robbery," Zanone said, testing me.

I stared him straight in the eyes and didn't flinch. "We killed them all," I said. "You'll hear about it today when they send riders out to see what's happened to it. All they'll find are six bodies rolled off into a gulch." I shut up and waited. Zanone stood up slowly and paced back and forth a minute, scratching his beard.

"Let's string them up, Captain," came a voice from the gunmen. Zanone quieted the voice with a glance then looked down at me again. "So you're wanting to lead us to the money, is that it?"

"I don't want to lead you anywhere," I said, "but I don't want to hang either."

Nodding his head, Zanone looked at the riders then back at me. He took the rope again and shook it. "I can smell an ambush a mile away, and I think that's what this is."

"That's what it is," yelled Cletis, playing it to the hilt. "Don't believe this yeller liar." I heard him grunt as a boot hooked him again. Zanone was teetering on the edge of hanging us. My next words would push him one way or the other.

"Suit yourself," I said. "You saw how many horses he was bringing up. There's only six horses and two of them was for us. There's only four men waiting not more than half a day's ride from here. They're worn-out and wounded, and sitting on twelve thousand dollars. All I ask is that you give me part of it and turn me loose for taking you there." I hesitated a second just to make it look good. "And your word that you won't shoot me in the back when I leave."

At that time in my life, I was unfamiliar with the game of poker, but in a way that's what we were doing. For me and Cletis this was a high-stakes game with all the odds in Zanone's favor. We opened on a bluff while Zanone held all the cards. Now that the pot had grown to twelve thousand dollars, Zanone was getting curious. It would cost him nothing to play the hand.

"What about the old man here?" Zanone stared at me.

There it was. If I bargained for Cletis, Zanone would see right through it. That was his last try at calling my bluff. If I gave up Cletis, I must be halfway telling the truth.

Zanone had nothing to lose. He knew it. He could kill me any time, or use me to lead him to the rest of the squad. If I was lying about the money it was no big deal. If I was telling the truth, twelve thousand dollars was a good day's pay.

"If you let him go he'll track me down. Give me a gun and I'll shoot him myself before we leave."

As much as my words sickened me, I was honest about that part. Whether I made it out of this or not, Cletis was going to die. It would be better me shooting him than leaving him hanging from a tree, that's if I could make myself do it. I wasn't sure, nor will I ever know, because Zanone honed in on my statement and turned over the last card of the game. "But you wouldn't care if we hang him or shoot him? I mean, knowing he would kill you, given a chance." Now he waited, watching for any hesitation on my part. All I could do was play it out, hard as possible. "I don't give a damn how he dies, long as he's dead before we leave here."

I tried to look at Cletis, to somehow let him know I was sorry. He just stared at the ground. I reckon he knew if our eyes met, Zanone would see right through us.

Zanone laughed as he pulled me to my feet. "Boys, I don't know if this kid is a liar or a coward or just one greedy son of a bitch, but for twelve thousand dollars, let's find out."

They pulled Cletis to his feet and he lunged at me before they could grab him. "You rotten bastard," he snarled, "it's you who killed me."

As they dragged him away, our eyes met for a split second. As he cussed and spit at me, deep in his eyes I saw his message. I saw it clear as day. The last I remember of old Cletis, his eyes were telling me, "You done good, boy, you played it all the way."

Then within minutes, instead of shooting or hanging that poor old man, they hoisted him upside down from an oak branch and built a fire under him. For nearly an hour they made me stand there watching him burn, and I couldn't dare let on that it bothered me.

All I could do was grit my teeth and try not to look straight at the grisly scene. Instead, I focused past it onto the rising mist across the bottomland. I thought of my pa and our mules, Buck and Hazel. Plain as day I could see them standing in their stalls, smelling wet and warm from the day's work, cracking grain, and thrashing their hoofs on the straw-piled floor. The thrashing and cracking came from Old Cletis above the raging fire, but I refused to hear it as such.

I'll say this for that old man. Hanging over the crackling flames he never once yelled out. He jerked and quivered and even bounced up and down some toward the end, but he let out no more than a long, rough growl. It was like he was straining to keep from screaming his lungs out. God love him, I believe he thought I would break down if he carried on, so he hung there and cooked to death.

Leaving the woods, we rode right past him. From the corner of my eye I saw a piece of him drop off and sizzle in the fire, and I heard a heavy thud as the rope burned through and dropped him into the fiery coals.

My knuckles turned white as frost from gripping the saddlehorn and I stared straight ahead, grateful to leave that hellish place. The sight of old Cletis jerking and wiggling above the fire, and the smell of his flesh burning and dropping off the bone, is something I'll never forget. Never.

I had no plan when we rode out for Dant's Mill. I only knew that I was still alive and kicking instead of swinging from a rope. If there were any order on the "waiting list to hell," Raymond Claire's name had just dropped a notch. Right then my only purpose in living was to find a way to kill Zanone, as slowly, as painfully, and as gruesomely as possible, same as he'd done old Cletis. This was big thinking for an unarmed kid under shackle and guard.

◆✱ 5 ✱◆

What happened that morning in the woods, and what was to happen that evening at Dant's Mill would affect my life for a long time to come. Until that evening, nobody had ever heard of Jesse or Frank James, leastwise, not outside our circle of guerrilla fighters and sympathizers. As for myself, had it not been for Daniel Zanone, I might've drifted away after the war and never been heard of again. But fate was busy that day, dabbling with the strings of our lives in a way that would take years to untangle.

As I said, Daniel Zanone had nothing to lose that day, and I knew he wasn't completely taken in by my story. The number-one rule of guerrilla fighting is to never give up the location of your squad. Why old Cletis started such a scheme could have only been for one reason. He did it to save my life. He must have figured that if I was slick enough to pull off the story, I would surely be smart enough to work it to a favorable end. Either way he knew he wouldn't be there to see it.

Zanone knew if there was twelve thousand dollars waiting at Dant's Mill, so much the better; he would claim it as his own and he and his men would keep their mouths shut. If there was no money, he would still get the jump on a squad of Quantrill's men. This was the kind of situation that could turn a cutthroat like Zanone into a popular statesman.

If he hadn't been so full of himself, he would have pulled in some other forces before riding in. But that would have meant sharing the glory and turning in the money if there was any. I reckon if there's one thing you can always count on, it's a greedy bastard's instincts to work toward his own interest and screw everybody else. However the chips fell, I knew there was nothing waiting for me at Dant's Mill but a bullet in the head, or worse.

*   *   *

Rounding the bend less than a mile from Dant's Mill, I knew that any move I made, I had to make soon. Up ahead, the road would swing down in a wide turn for two hundred yards, then double back through the valley beneath us. The mill lay down in the valley. If I could get past the rider on my right and over the edge of the road, I might roll down out of sight and make it to the squad.

This was my day for long shots. The edge of the road turned into a steep rock slide that descended twenty yards, then became trees and thick brush. If a man searched for a place to break his neck, he would find none better. But I was desperate.

I'd rode docilely all the way, looking whipped and submissive, hoping to catch them off guard. I was still shackled and gagged and I'd lost Pa's old hat somewhere along the road. There were two riders before me, four behind, and one on each side. The one on my right had a rifle laying across his saddle pointed at my belly.

My reins were lashed to the saddlehorn snug enough for no more than a steady trot, but I knew this chestnut gelding was quick out of the hole. He would jump past a tight rein if I gigged him hard enough. All I needed was to be a little to the right of the animal in front of me.

I was tensed and ready even though I looked like a cowering dog. Watching the side-to-side sway of the rider in front, I waited till he veered slightly left at the same time as my gelding veered right. I knew at that second if I busted forward, my horse would shoot to the right to keep from hitting the horse in front. Just before the horses swayed again, quick as a hornet, I braced tight and nailed the spurs to him.

The gelding bolted forward so fast, he ricocheted off the front rider and plowed up onto the horse beside me. Barely keeping saddle, I put the hooks to him again just as the rifle shot blazed past my face. Digging away from sharp spurs, my gelding reared up, bellowing like a bull. For a second we were on top of the horse and rider, then the four of us went off down the rock slide end over end.

We tumbled and bounced like a bucket of bones. I heard guns going off behind us and I heard a horse's leg snap like seasoned hickory. I was in midair, sailing straight for a tree, when the horse and rider bounced over me and slammed into it first. Glancing off the horse, I rolled another ten yards into the woods through briars and downed timber.

Rifles barked, spitting holes through leaves and branches. But I was free and moving. Deeper down the hillside I realized the gunfire wasn't just Zanone's men shooting at me. Now the road above sounded like Armageddon. Without knowing it, I had led them into a trap and jumped out right as it snapped shut.

I clawed and dug my way back up the hill. Still working against my shackles, I got to where the rider lay half-pinned under his horse. His head lay twisted at a broken angle. He pitched and quivered in pain; across him, his horse whinnied in agony, thrashing its bloody head against the tree trunk.

I jerked my own single-shot pistol from the rider's waist belt and a six-shot revolver from a holster under his arm. I have never been able to watch something suffer, so I fired a shot between the horse's eyes at close range, fanning my hand behind the hammer to guard my face. As for the rider, I left him there frothing blood. He could work it out with God, for all I cared.

Dropping my spent single-shot pistol, I cocked the six-shooter and headed up toward the road. I pictured Zanone hanging upside down over a fire with his ears melting like hog fat. I had him. By God, I had him good.

Two of Zanone's men came backing over the edge of the road firing at the other side. They didn't look behind them and they didn't get another chance. I popped each of them twice in the back and they tumbled down the rocks like bundles of rags. Then, before I could get another ten yards up the hill, Zanone backed over the edge the same way. "Captain!" I yelled, and he spun facing me. I wanted him alive and kicking, somewhere deep in the woods overlooking a foggy bottomland.

Still young, learning—learning the hard way—I'd figured wrong. Seeing I had him covered, I thought he would give up and drop his gun. It was my first mistake. When he turned, his gun was up and ready to fire. Realizing I couldn't take him alive, I pulled the trigger three times, but heard the heart-sickening click of empty chambers. My second mistake was not checking the gun when I grabbed it.

The firing up on the road lessened as Zanone stepped down toward me wearing a crazy grin. At ten feet, he raised the gun level to my head and took aim. I squinted my eyes shut and told my soul good-bye. I could sense where the bullet would hit me, almost feel it tearing through my forehead.

I heard the blast rock heaven . . . but I was still alive. Something warm and wet stung my face as Zanone slammed past me and rolled downhill into heavy brush.

I blinked, caught my breath, and saw Raymond Claire sidestepping down the hill. Smoke curled from his double-barrel shotgun as he stopped five feet from me. He bent down, taking up Zanone's pistol. I stood dumbfounded for a second trying to get a hold on what was real and what wasn't. My face was splattered with Zanone's blood. I wiped my shirtsleeve across my eyes. Claire pitched me the shotgun and motioned toward the brush. "Go in there and make sure he's dead."

Not wanting to make another mistake that day, I hesitated a second. Breaking open the shotgun, I glanced down, checking the chambers. From one, a gray haze seeped out into the air, in the other a shell glinted in the evening sunlight. I looked up at Claire and saw him smiling. It was the first time he'd ever been friendly toward me. He glanced at Zanone's pistol in his hand, checking the chamber. "He nearly got you," he said.

I nodded. A slow, heavy pounding started in my head. "If you hadn't come along he would've killed me," I said. "You saved my life."

Claire shrugged and glanced back over his shoulder up the hill. "You'd have done the same for me." The pounding grew worse, I wondered for a second if he could hear it. I almost asked him.

He stepped forward and nudged me on the shoulder like an old friend. "Get in there and make sure he's dead." Then, seeing my stunned condition, he asked, "Are you alright? Can you hear me?"

"Yeah," I said, blinking my eyes and snapping the shotgun shut, "I'm alright." The pounding grew even louder. It was like the beat of a large funeral drum. "I just wanted to thank you first."

Claire nudged my shoulder and said, "Think nothing of it." He grinned and started to say something else, but just as he opened his mouth, I squeezed the trigger and blew most of his head off. The drum fell silent behind the ringing in my ears.

I'd made two mistakes in a row, and something told me that turning my back on Raymond Claire would be my third and final. If I'd misjudged him, it was a mistake I preferred to live with and wonder about than to die of and know for certain.

There was no reason for him to have changed toward me that soon after wanting to carve me open like a Christmas goose. Something told me, when he reached for Zanone's gun and checked the chamber, that he planned to roll me over and say it was Zanone's doing. Right or wrong I'd think no more about it; he could sort it all out in hell.

I picked up Zanone's gun and stuck it down in my waist belt. My gelding was up from the fall and shaking dirt from his mane. I walked over to him, took up the reins, and checked him out good. He wasn't hurt from the fall, but I could have laid half my little finger in the gash I made with my spurs.

From the road Parker Avery called down to me, "Hey, Dingus, how are you making out?"

"I'm alright," I said, "tell Frank everything is settled."

I would not know until months later, but while I stood there yelling up the hill to Parker Avery, Daniel Zanone listened as he crawled through the brush like a wounded rat.

I was bone tired and so glad to be alive and back with the squad, I forgot about Zanone for a second and begin working my way up the rock slide to the road.

By the time I topped the edge of the road, four corpses had been propped up against each other, back to back. Parker stepped in beside me and handed me Pa's old hat. "We found this five miles back, that's what put us onto you." He had the strained look of a man asking for news he dreaded hearing. I must've looked like a man with news I hated to tell.

Still shackled, I dusted the hat against my leg and dropped it on my head. I spoke without stopping or facing him. "Bad news," I said. "Your brother Cletis didn't make it."

"How did he get it?" Parker's voice trembled. Frank rode up hearing the conversation. I stopped in the road and gazed from one to the other, then rested my gaze on Frank. He studied my face for a second, then spoke to Parker. "Go down and help bring the other bodies up. We'll talk about Cletis later."

The two of us watched Parker Avery disappear over the edge of the road, then Frank stared back down at me. "How bad was it?" he asked.

"Damn bad," I said. "If Parker has to know, I'll tell him, but I'd sooner not talk about it."

Frank studied the long-stemmed pipe in his right hand. Reaching down, he tapped the bowl against his boot heel, dumping the ashes to the ground. "You'll have to tell him, but you decide when."

I nodded and stood there silent for a few seconds. Frank inspected the pipe before slipping it into his pocket. "Old Cletis saved your hide, didn't he?" I didn't answer, I just looked away.

"You came close to bringing that bunch down on us," Frank said.

"Yeah, but I didn't, did I? After what they did to old Cletis, I would've done anything I could to spark a gun battle. But I wouldn't brought them in on you, that's a fact."

Frank locked his eyes on mine, searching for any flaw or hesitation on my part. I held his stare without batting an eye. Finally he nodded and glanced away. "You did good, Cousin, you showed bold."

When he said that, I looked away across the evening sky and thought of old Cletis hanging over them flames. All of a sudden I felt shame at being alive while that old man hung from a tree and burned to death saving me.

Long after dark, we quit searching the briar thickets for Zanone's body. I didn't like thinking he might still be alive, but we had tarried long enough in a patrolled area. With the full moon rising high, we rode out single file, ten yards between us, just inside the woods line. I remained shackled. Apparently Zanone carried the only key.

6

A light came on in my head at Dant's Mill, for after that day I became a different person. Among Quantrill's riders I'd felt like a bastard child at a homecoming; though everybody did their best to make me feel welcome, I didn't think I belonged. But after being captured and nearly hanged, after seeing old Cletis spill open like a steer on a spit, and after head-popping Raymond Claire with that ten-gauge, something in me changed overnight.

When my shackles fell to the dirt at my feet, I stared down and felt a shiver go up my back. I rubbed my raw wrists, felt cool air against them, and vowed the only shackles to ever go around me again would be after my heart stopped beating.

"I'll die first," I said, kicking the shackles away. They rattled across the ground raising a wake of dust.

"Welcome to the war," Frank said, with a grim expression.

"I mean it," I said, looking up at Frank and the mounted squad. Right then, I felt sadness mixed with anger. "Goddamn them all. They'll catch the devil by the horns if they catch me again."

Swinging up into the saddle, I pulled my hat down low to avoid the faces of the squad. Something inside me died at Dant's Mill. Frank and the squad must've seen it. I didn't know what it was—innocence, gentleness, something like that, I reckon. Whatever it was, it left a hollowness I would be a long time in filling, and even longer in understanding.

I glanced at Frank and saw the strangest look on his face, as if there was something he felt he needed to say. But Jesse must've seen it too, and he jumped his horse between us before Frank could speak. "Let's move out," Jesse called out to the squad, and as we swung our horses toward the deep woods, he stopped beside me before riding up front. "It's dog-eat-dog, Cousin," he said, his face shadowed by the brim of his hat. "God help us . . . may the meanest dog win."

* * *

Over the next few days, I noticed a difference in how I was treated by the other riders. Before, if I was placed somewhere on lookout, the squad would spend half the time explaining what to do and how to do it. Even then, they would keep coming back checking on me. Now it seemed that when it came my turn to watch all they needed to do was nod and I was in position.

Every night for the next week, Parker Avery managed to be beside me any time we stopped for more than a few minutes. Finally, I sat down beside him and told him the whole story about his brother Cletis. He never said a word; he let out a deep, painful breath as if the fire that killed his brother now raged in his own chest.

When I was through, he got up and patted my shoulder without speaking. He took a canteen of whiskey and went into the woods. I started after him, but Jesse stopped me. "Leave him be," Jesse said. "It's between him and old Cletis." For the longest time that night, we heard the solid thud of his fist against a tree trunk. Next morning his hand was swollen and wrapped in a rag. In all the rest of the time I knew him, Parker never mentioned his brother's name again.

Nobody mentioned Raymond Claire . . . ever again. Frank knew I'd done him in; maybe nobody else cared one way or the other.

Being from Kentucky, I never really had a calling or purpose in fighting the war. For the people of Missouri and Kansas, the killing and hatred had boiled to such a point that had it not been for the war, and the uneasy peace that followed, they'd still be fighting today. Me? I was just following my cousins at a time when I had no direction of my own.

I'd overcome my fear at a high price; twelve months of killing had turned me as hard across the chest as drawn cable. I became skilled in using a ten-inch glades knife I'd taken off a dead man near Memphis: I not only kept our squad fitted with the finest riding stock, I'd learned to sneak up on a Yankee guard and kill him as quietly as a vengeful spirit.

That whole year with the Southern Regulars pulling back in defeat, we followed the bluecoats so close you could smell their feet on a warm night. We slipped around in Cass, Bates, and Jackson counties almost at will, taking what we needed from their camps and burning what we left behind.

When we passed wounded columns of Southern Regulars along the road, they stared at us in awe, in fear and disbelief, as we rode into the fury they'd left behind. "The boys," they whispered under their breath, as if saying it aloud would conjure evil upon them. To acknowledge them in their pitiful state would have brought them shame, so we stared past them knowing, as well as they, it was their blood and severed limbs, their dying screams and lost hope and honor we would wade through in the fields ahead.

"Crossed anybody's eyes lately?" I asked "Quiet" Jack, the night he slipped through a red-leg patrol and joined us near Bent Creek. I hadn't seen him since that day near Rulo, but I'd heard he was one of the best of "Bloody" Bill Anderson's battalion. Clell Miller sent him to us after we lost most of our squad in an ambush.

"None that didn't need it," he said, finishing a plate of beans. "You the squad leader?" Cannons thundered along the distant border; orange fire streaked and disappeared from the horizon. From the sound of it, we'd be waiting all night for the battle to end.

"Yeah," I said, "till Jesse or Frank gets back."

"Last time I saw you, you wasn't even wearing a gun. Now you're a squad leader?"

"It's been a busy year," I said. "You got a problem with it?"

"No offense; I just like to know who I'm working for."

From across the low campfire, Parker Avery took a drink of whiskey from a canteen, then passed it to "Quiet" Jack. "Dingus is straight-up," Parker said. "If he wasn't, Frank wouldn't put him in charge."

"So you're old Cletis's brother," said Jack, after raising the canteen, and passing it back. Parker just nodded and cut another shot from the canteen. "I rode with Cletis a while when I first came down here. I hated hearing about him burning up."

I gazed into the fire, picturing Cletis and smelling his roasting flesh. "We all hated it."

"I heard you shot the man that burnt him."

"No," I said, "I didn't shoot him, but I was there when he got splattered by a shotgun."

"You saw his body?"

"No."

"Then he might still be alive?"

"I don't see how," I said, and I turned facing Jack. "Why're you asking?"

Jack shrugged and leaned back against his saddle. "I liked old Cletis. If the man that killed him is still alive I'd love to gut-hook him."

"I figure he's dead. But even if he ain't, I doubt you'll ever run into him."

"Never know." Jack tilted his hat down across his eyes; and for a second the cannons paused and the earth settled, as if to let God catch his breath. "You know what they say," Jack said, as the ground trembled under the renewed pounding. Sparks stirred and swirled in our low fire. "They say all demons meet on the road to hell."

By the end of the year, the Yankees had thrown a strong blockade along our border making it difficult for us to duck out through the "back door," a strip of Arkansas that opened into the Indian Nations and on down to Texas. They had us trapped, and knew we were tired and dragging. When rumors of Lee's surrender circulated along the border, a lot of fellers just bowed their heads and went home; but we stayed on, and those of us who didn't die in the saddle became the most vicious bunch of gunmen to ever plague the earth.

"Leave him," Jack said, "that's all we can do." Lightning flashed across our faces. Rain beat against us in blinding sheets.

"No, goddamn it!" I yelled above a clap of thunder. "We'll stay together—die together if we have to; but we ain't leaving him."

Quantrill, Frank, and a handful of men had lit out to Kentucky to lay low and make plans. Jesse and Cole were down in the Nations. I'd been in charge for the past week, and we'd lost over half our squad. "That's crazy," Jack said, shaking his head as I gigged my horse past him and up the mud-slick trail.

We'd been fighting on the run for three days. Parker Avery, "Quiet" Jack, and myself were all that remained of our old squad. We had two new men; one had taken a slug through his chest. I blamed myself. "That's how it is," I yelled over my shoulder above the wind and rain. "We're staying up here till morning."

I topped the hill and ran my new bay mare into the shelter of a pine forest. She reared high, slinging mud as I spun her around beneath the pine canopy. Seconds behind me Parker and Jack came splashing in;

their coattails flared out behind them. "Jack's right," Parker shouted as they reined up beside me. "Even if he lives, he'll slow us down." I started to swing my mare away, but Parker grabbed her bridle. "It ain't your fault, Dingus. You gotta let it go."

"No!" I yanked loose as Floyd Nix came up off the trail leading Kenny Ellworth. I let out a night-bird whistle and he splashed toward us. "He's one of us: I ain't leaving him to die alone."

Poor Kenny lay shivering on his horse's neck. Wet mane clung to his face like a shroud, and his left arm hung lifeless down the horse's side, pouring out blood. "Thank God," Floyd said, "I thought you'd left us." I glanced at Parker and Jack in a flash of purple light. They looked away.

We formed a circle under the towering pines and Parker dragged Kenny from his saddle and over to a tree trunk. We huddled there, with the wind whipping our coattails and cold rain stinging our faces. Parker cradled Kenny in his arms, and above the pounding thunder yelled, "He's bleeding awful, Dingus. We've got to plug him up."

I slapped my drenched hat across my mare's rump to move her out of my way. Shouldering in between Jack and Floyd, I bent down next to Kenny and Parker. Kenny's face was pale and drawn. His sunken eyes flickered between this world and the next. When lightning wavered across his face, it exposed the gruesome handiwork of man against man.

"Stay with us Kenny." I leaned in close. "I'll get you through this . . . *just hang on.*"

Tearing open his coat and shirt, I ran my fingers through the dark paste until I felt the bullet hole. With each breath, I felt blood bubbling against my fingers. His chest was cold as ice.

Floyd Nix tore up a wool shirt and handed me a pile of rags. I took the longest strip, rolled it into a tight point, stuck it into his chest and twisted it deep. Kenny gagged and trembled, but soon the bubbling stopped and his breathing grew stronger, more regular.

Floyd cut a piece off Kenny's coattail and laid it over the wound. I bound him with strips of rag as tight as I dared. "He might make it," I said in a whisper, glancing between Parker and Floyd. "He just might."

"Quiet" Jack had taken some chopped tobacco from inside his coat. He sheltered the fixings under his hat brim and rolled a smoke. Running the cigarette in and out of his mouth to firm it up, he stood up and splashed toward his rifle scabbard. "I'll watch the trail a while," he said. His voice sounded unconcerned. "Let me know when he dies."

Kenny Ellworth was just a good-natured country boy who should've gone home when the war ended. He'd taken up with Quantrill's riders after Jayhawkers hung his pa and raped his mama to death. I'd trained him myself, and he followed me like a kid brother. As for "cause" and "purpose," I reckon nobody had more reason to thirst for blood than Kenny, but I should've sent him home—and I didn't.

Floyd Nix worked up a small fire near Kenny and Parker—Parker never let that wounded boy out of his arms—and I sat staring across the low flames most of the night, running things through my mind.

Here was old Floyd Nix, a backwoods preacher pushing fifty. He should've been somewhere thumping a Bible and eating free Sunday dinners instead of wading mud and fighting for a cause that was already lost.

There sat Parker Avery holding Kenny against his chest as if he were his own son, though he agreed with Jack and knew the boy wouldn't live the night. Since his brother's death, Parker had slipped deeper and deeper into the mindless warmth of alcohol. He was a gone-down drunk, lost in a sea of blood.

I shivered and drew closer to the fire.

Near the woods line, Jack Smith leaned against a tree watching the valley below. "Quiet" Jack looked like the son of the western frontier, but he'd grown up in New Jersey in the heart of a city. What had brought him here was anybody's guess. Like myself, Jack said little about his past. I only knew that sometimes he was sharp as a briar, and other times he seemed dumb as a chunk of coal.

I huddled near the tiny fire and stared across at Kenny for the longest time, watching his soul slip away little by little. I had some dark thoughts about living and dying that night. I knew it was God's business, but I sure questioned his bookkeeping.

Lightning twisted and curled, as if God had it by one end and the devil by the other. Somehow, I felt like poor Kenny's soul—maybe all our souls for that matter—was nothing but a small trophy in a great tug-of-war. I wondered if any of our lives amounted to more than the quick purple flashes that flittered across our faces and disappeared into the dark.

Near dawn, Kenny Ellworth stirred a few seconds and gazed over at me. His voice was a torn whisper. "Jess . . . that you?" The rain had let up some. Fog crept into the forest like swirling spirits come to claim one of their own.

I circled the fire and leaned down close to Kenny's face. Parker had dozed off with Kenny in his arms. Floyd leaned in with me. Jack Smith walked up behind us cradling his rifle. "It's me, Kenny," I said. "You lay still and rest a while longer."

"Did we get a bunch of them, Jess?" His voice seemed to come from a long way off.

"Yeah," I said, going along with him, "We got a whole bunch, now be still." Kenny coughed deep and his body quivered in pain. "Reckon I'm gonna die . . . ain't I, Jess?"

I glanced at Floyd, who reached out and put his hand on Kenny's forearm. I looked back at "Quiet" Jack standing behind me. He rolled his eyes and looked away. Turning back to Kenny, I placed my hand against his cold jaw. It was smooth as a baby's. "I think maybe you are, Kenny," I said quietly.

For a second I saw fear stir deep in his eyes, but he pulled it away somewhere and swallowed hard. "It don't matter none," he said. "You-all will drive them Yankees back, won't you . . . won't you, Jess?" He laid his cold hand on my forearm.

I looked deep into his fading eyes and lied like a dog. "We will, Kenny. You know we will." He coughed up a trickle of blood and smiled. I felt him try to squeeze my arm, but there was nothing left. He'd slipped too far into that dark tunnel.

"God bless Dixie," he whispered, and I watched his eyes glaze over as peace soothed his tortured brow. As I brushed his eyes closed I remember thinking of something my pa always said when somebody died: "He's gone off to dance with the angels."

Floyd bowed his head as Parker stirred in his sleep. Behind me Jack Smith grunted as I began standing up slowly, taking Kenny's hand from my arm. "Should've finished him off last night; we could've been halfway to Missouri by now," said Jack.

I never pulled iron as fast in my life as I did swinging around toward "Quiet" Jack that morning.

I swung the ten-inch barrel of my forty-four up into his balls as hard as I could, damn near lifting him off the ground. He hit the mud facedown and rolled up like a bale of cotton. Splattering out into the woods, I leaned against a pine tree and breathed as deep as I could, hoping the damp, cold air would cleanse me.

I could not square myself to having trained that poor boy to fight and die for something I didn't believe in any more than a hog believed in Christmas. This war was not personal enough for me. I felt no sacrifice on my part. I had no right to share Kenny Ellworth's last seconds of life. I was a fraud, I thought, unworthy kin to the likes of that brave young man. I felt lower than a snake, and commenced shaking deep in my chest. For a long time, nearly till daylight, I hung there against that ancient pine, and though I ought not admit it, I wept until my tears ran dry.

When I walked back to the fire that morning, Jack was lurching around like a cripple, gathering his gear. Beside him was a pool of sickness he had spit up. Floyd and Parker were already mounted and waiting for me to join them. Kenny's body was wrapped in a gray blanket laying beneath the tree where he died.

Jack limped over and struggled up the side of his horse. Seeing his difficulty, I shouldered him under the rump and pushed. When he sank in his saddle still bowed over at the waist, I stepped back and spoke up to him. "Jack, I didn't mean to hurt you, hitting you in the nuts the way I did."

Jack looked puzzled and shook his head. He glanced painfully at the others, then back to me. Floyd and Parker pulled down their hat brims and stifled their laughter. "You didn't mean to hurt me? Well, I'm goddamn glad you didn't mean to hurt me, cause if you had, I guess I would've spit my balls out on the ground."

I was just shy of laying my hand on my pistol when Jack looked at Floyd and Parker and shook his head. "Hear that? He hits a man in the rack with a ten-inch shooting iron, then says he didn't mean to hurt him. I'll be goddamned!"

I knew it was over when all three of them laughed. I took a razzing for what I said. But Jack never held a grudge over it, and he never let me live it down.

7

"It's a pardon, goddamn it," "Little" Billy Clinton said, "and they ain't likely to offer it very long." After hiding back and forth between Rock Ledge and Piney Creek for three weeks, we'd met up with Clinton, "Skillet" Meeks, and Deek Fulton in the woods outside of Clay County. We sat around a low flame, wrapped in wool blankets against the cold, foggy night, cooking shoush on the ends of our knifes.

"Then take it," "Quiet" Jack said. "Nobody will think the less of you. But we're staying till the last dog's hung, right?" He nodded to me.

"I don't know," I said. "I'm just crawling through it one day at a time. But like Jack says, do what you think is best for you. We'll never belittle you for it."

"I don't trust it," Parker Avery said, taking a cut from a canteen of whiskey, then pitching it to "Skillet" Meeks.

"Might not be so bad," Floyd Nix suggested. "Maybe they're honoring us with an act of kindness so this country can put the killing behind it and go on."

"Kindness—shit," Deek Fulton said. The firelight danced in his narrowed eyes and cast an unwholesome glow on the jagged half-moon scar running down his left cheek into his scraggly beard. "They know they'll never beat us, so they've gotta forgive us. Ain't that sumpin." He shook his head and studied the low flames. "I'll die a-fore I pledge honor to a Union flag." He spit a stream into the fire.

"Hey! We're cooking food here, goddamn it," I said, and Deek turned and spit the next stream over his shoulder. "Sorry."

"Well . . . me and Skillet talked it out, and we're going in," "Little" Billy announced. "Reckon you got room for Deek here, doncha?"

I glanced between Parker, Floyd, and "Quiet" Jack. Their eyes showed approval, but I thought about Kenny Ellworth and how I should've sent him home. "Why don't you go on in, Deek?" I asked quietly. "Nobody gave it more than you have."

"Saying you don't want me?"

"That ain't it, Deek, and you know it."

"Then what is?"

"I'm getting tired of running my thumbs down deadmen's eyes."

"Dingus ain't always this cheerful." Jack chuckled. "You just caught him on a good day."

I smiled a tired smile and blew on the end of my glades knife to cool the steaming shoush. "Ease off, Jack. You know why I'm saying it."

"Then he'll ride with you?" Billy asked. I couldn't understand Billy Clinton thinking he had to speak for Deek Fulton. Deek was hard as cold steel—one of the most feared of all the guerrilla fighters.

I shrugged. "Deek knows he's welcome." Then I glanced toward Deek and saw a strange, hollow look in his eyes as he studied the flames. "Just don't spit near the cooking," I said, hoping to lighten the air a little.

"I won't," he said in a low voice. He turned his face to me with a crazy grin, then started chuckling under his breath. "Jesus Christ," he said, as he began to laugh and shake his head. "Woman's dead, both my boys . . . dead." Above his wide grin, his eyes slanted down in pain, like a lost soul begging mercy before the throne of God.

"Lord God, Dingus"—he laughed and sobbed—"what's the point?" I saw his gun slide up from his holster, but I hesitated a split second before making a move. "So long, Dingus," he said behind that crazy broken-hearted grin; and just as my hand went toward his face to stop him, he slipped the barrel into his mouth. His hat spun up in the air as the orange flame belched from the top of his head and his brain exploded in every direction.

"Good Lord—God . . ." I wiped the blood and flecks of meat from my face as I leaned over and pulled him up into my arms. The campfire sizzled and flared; a sickening smell rose in the bellowing, dark smoke.

"Let's move out," Jack yelled, dropping his shoush into the fire. "They heard that shot plumb into Kearney."

"Goddamn it, Deek," I said quietly, beneath the sound of men scrambling to their horses.

I reached to close his blank and hollow eyes, but Little Billy caught my wrist. I looked up and saw tears streaming down his tightened cheeks. "Just go on, Dingus," he whispered, as he slid Deek from my arms and into his. "He's one of my squad . . . I'll close his eyes . . . I'll bury him."

I stood up and put my hand on Little Billy's shoulder as Jack handed me the reins to my mare. Deek's blood ran down my hand and spread onto Billy's shirt. "I know how you feel," I whispered.

Billy sobbed and shook his head, holding Deek to his chest. "I should've seen it coming . . . I should've."

I looked around at Jack and the others. "Skillet" Meeks still sat by the fire, a knife covered with shoush still hanging from his hand. Floyd and Parker were mounted and leaning over "Little" Billy. I looked around at the blood, the gaunt and weary faces, and the ragged blankets left lying on the ground. "We all should've seen it coming," I said, "a long time ago."

I turned and stepped up into the saddle. Drawing my rifle, I spun the mare toward the deep woods. "You heard him, goddamn it!" I yelled, slapping the barrel against my mare's rump. "Move out!"

Three days later, near dark, as we slipped into Jackson County along a creek bank, a shot knocked Floyd Nix out of his saddle and pitched him into the swift water. He just floated off downstream as we dove for cover.

In seconds, the high ridge across the creek blossomed with puffs of orange-gray explosions. My bay mare disappeared down the bank in a hard gallop; Floyd's gray gelding followed. The other two riderless horses circled in confusion as bullets slapped into the mud around them.

Pressed against the mud bank beneath an overhang of tree roots, Jack and I fired back, but our pistol rounds fell short by fifty yards. "They're going to cut up our horses," Parker yelled from ten yards up the bank. "Cover me!"

Before I could tell him to stop, Parker was out in the open. Rifle fire spit all around him. The horses were jumping around like crazy as he snatched at the reins. How he did it I'll never know, but he gathered the reins on both horses and held on long enough to jerk the rifles from the scabbards. Then one horse went down as Parker dove back into the bank. "Shit," he yelled. "Goddamn it!"

"Are you hit?" Jack yelled, hearing Parker cuss. Rifles volleyed again.

"No, I ain't hit." The other horse went down in screams of agony, wallowing in mud. "I forgot something, goddamn it!"

"Oh, no," I said to Jack, "he's going back for his bottle." Jack poked his head out enough to look around toward Parker.

"Throw me a rifle, Parker, I'll cover you," Jack yelled. He looked at me and shrugged. "I mean . . . since he's going anyway."

Parker came out firing at the ridge, diving against the belly of the dead horse just as bullets spit out again. Reaching an arm up over the horse's side, he felt around for the saddlebags. Rounds thumped into the dead animal. "Stay down!" I bellowed.

"Throw me that goddamn rifle," Jack screamed. He looked at me shaking his head. "Damn this shit. Would you *please* tell him to throw us a rifle?" Rounds cut into the roots around us. They were moving down from the ridge line, taking closer position.

Parker lay snug against the dead horse, pulling the cork from a bottle of rye. "Listen to me," I called above the rifle fire. "We need your help here."

"This beats all," Jack said, disgusted. "Parker, if you don't throw us a rifle, I'll empty this pistol into you, I swear to God."

Parker took a deep pull on the bottle, recorked it, and slung a bandoleer across his shoulder. He paid us no mind till he tucked the bottle in his coat pocket. Then he came up quick. "Cover me!"

"No!" I hollered, but he was up running toward us as bullets pounded again. Ten feet away he jerked to a halt as a round tore low into his back. He froze there. I was out and grabbing him, pulling him to the bank as he fell. Another round hit him high in the shoulder as we fell under the tree root.

Jack and I pulled him up against the mud bank between us. Jack stripped the bandoleer from his shoulder and snatched up the rifle. "Thank you," Jack said, wild-eyed and sarcastic. "Thank you very *goddamn* much."

"Ease up, Jack, the man's hurt," I said. Jack mumbled under his breath as he shoved cartridges into the magazine. More rounds slammed around us. My voice trembled. "Why did you do it, Parker, why?"

He groaned and adjusted his back against the bank. Grimacing in pain, he managed a strained laugh under his breath. "Ever needed a drink?" I looked in his eyes close up. They were so much like Cletis's eyes, only bloodshot and yellow-stained. He stunk of cheap rye.

"How bad is it?" I asked. There was no room to look him over.

He squinted, as if considering it. He tapped his coat pocket. "Get that for me, will you?" He was drunk. He hadn't been completely sober in months. "It's bad," he said.

I took the bottle from his pocket and pulled the cork. "Will you make it, if we get you out of here?" He took a long pull on the bottle, then looked at it, gauging what remained. He shook his head, lowered his chin to his chest and stated flatly, "I ain't going nowhere."

Rounds pounded in heavier, but now Jack had wiped the mud off the rifle sights and took a slow, easy aim. He pulled the trigger and a gut-wrenching scream echoed from the ridge. The rifles stopped. We heard rustling in the woods above us. "So there!" Jack yelled.

"We won't leave you here," I said to Parker. He managed a drunken smirk.

"I ain't—by God—going, and that's that," he said. "What I'll do is cover you boys come dark, and you-all get the hell out of here." His voice was dulled by pain and slurred from the whiskey. There was no point arguing.

One sharpshooter with a rifle can hold off a dozen average marksmen. Jack picked his targets by waiting till they fired, then snapped a round at their muzzle flash. Witnessing the deadly accuracy of Jack's strategy, the gunmen weren't nearly as eager to fire in long volleys. They tried the same trick, but we were heavily covered by those big overhanging roots. So far, we had position.

For nearly an hour, Jack held them pinned to the ridge. At the same time, I dug upwards behind us with my glades knife, carving out a two-foot-round tunnel up through the mud and tree roots. Darkness began to set in heavy. Any minute they would creep down the ridge and be straight across from us. That would do it. They could pick our eyes out from there. We figured the best way out was up the bank behind us. I dug like hell.

Three feet back, up around a thick root, I felt wet grass roots tear loose from the surface and felt cool air on my hands. I ripped chunks of sod down from the surface till I had an opening wide enough to squeeze through halfway around the tree.

I dropped back down beside Parker, kicking dirt away with my feet. "That's it," I whispered, "time to go." Parker shook his head. A few rounds slammed into the bank near our feet.

"I said I ain't going."

"By God, I am," Jack whispered. He crawled over Parker and up over me, dropping the rifle against my side.

"Parker," I said, "you've got to come with us. We don't know if they're Yankees or Free Militia out there. If it's Yankees they'll fire in here till there's nothing left. If it's the others . . . well, you know what they'll do." I thought about his brother Cletis.

"Can't go," he said, shaking his head. I started to grab his shoulder and shake him, but I remembered his wounds.

"Why, Parker, damn it?"

"Cause," he answered, letting out a long breath, "I'm out of rye, I've pissed all over myself, and I can't feel a damn thing in my legs."

I took up the rifle. "Then I'm staying too." Parker elbowed me in the chest. I coughed and caught my breath. Across the creek, I heard movement in the brush. The shooting stopped altogether. A bad sign. They were slipping down on us.

"You don't know when to let up on a feller, Dingus." He looked me right in the eyes. "I'm tired and I'm drunk, and I'll die where I damn well please. Now don't fool with me, don't give me no shit."

I waited a second, hearing more movement coming down the ridge. I started to say something. I wanted to say, "Don't do this to me, Parker, not after Cletis," but I lost the words. Parker took my face in his big hand and grinned. He patted me roughly on the jaw, then nudged me away. "Aw . . . get out of here, Dingus. Go see about Jack."

I laid the rifle across his lap and started crawling back, up under the tangled roots toward the surface. Clawing up onto the ground, I bellied a few feet and into some thick brush. I not only felt like a filthy rat leaving Parker there to die, I reckon I looked like one coming up out of the ground that way.

I made it twenty yards up the bank before the shooting started. As I topped the ridge line I looked back. Below me, across the creek, rifle fire blinked on and off like so many fireflies. "So long, Parker," I whispered. I sure owed the Avery boys, first Cletis, now Parker. God love them.

In the pitch darkness I realized I was standing on a dirt road. Squeezing up through that hole, I had lost a boot and packed mud into my pistol. Now, limping and scraping the mud off my person, I got my bearings and headed in the direction my mare had taken. If I could get within wind of her, I knew she would find me.

I was a good quarter-mile down the road before the rifles settled down. Any minute they would see what we'd done and be right on me. In the silence I heard horses coming face at me from a short distance. I don't know why; I just figured it was "Quiet" Jack.

To play it safe I jumped over into the weeds. I waited as the sound came closer, then let out a night-bird whistle.

The horses stopped dead silent. I held my breath waiting, praying. The sound came back to me and I let out a sigh. "Jack," I called out real low. Hearing my voice, my bay mare nickered. I heard the horses start galloping again. In my excitement I bolted straight toward the sound, and in a second, in the darkness I smacked right into my mare. My nose busted like a ripe tomato, and she trampled right over me. I grabbed her hind leg and she went crazy, kicking and bucking right on top of me.

"Whoa-baby! Goddamn it!" I screamed, and took a hoof in the belly that knocked me ten feet end over end.

Now both horses were spooked out of their minds. I heard Jack cuss. Neither of us could see a thing. Dazed, I tried to right myself as I heard them turn and start back for me. Jack meant to save me, but damned if he wouldn't kill me trying to do it. My voice was a breathless rasp. "Stop . . . Jack, please! Goddamn it! Just hold 'em there." I could see myself dying, killed by my own horse, led by one of my own men.

I strained to my feet and staggered forward, groping till I found my mare. Doubled over, my ribs thumping in pain, my nose pouring blood like a pump spigot, I managed to find my saddlehorn and hang there. My mare was settling down some, but pulling away from me, and dragging me with her. Jack couldn't see the shape I was in and I wasn't able to tell him. "We ain't got time for this shit," he yelled, hooking the gray gelding. "I'm gone."

I wanted to plead with him to wait, but I didn't have the breath. As he took off down the road, my mare bolted out behind him with me hanging down her side. Right then I could have killed "Quiet" Jack Smith, but I feared I was dying myself. It was all I could do to hang on and crawl up my mare's side as she galloped away. I just managed to fall over into the saddle as she broke into a full run.

We pounded down the road and veered out across a flatland, depending entirely on our horses in that moonless night. Both of us were blind as bats.

♦❋ 8 ❋♦

I'd had it with the running, the hiding, and the killing. The war was over, I saw no reason to keep fighting it. Jesse and part of the boys were laid up down in the Nations, hiding like animals as far as I knew. Frank, Quantrill, and the rest might have made it to Kentucky, then again they might not have. I didn't know. Most of all I'd had it with "Quiet" Jack Smith. He'd nearly killed me the other night with them horses. I couldn't put it out of my mind.

Next morning, after the ruckus, we'd found a farmhouse over in Jackson County. I was in bad shape, and I knew it. Checking around, seeing the house had been recently abandoned, we hid our animals in the barn and rested three full days thinking over our situation.

Knowing I had busted ribs, Jack had stripped an old bed sheet and bound me up good and tight. My left eye was swollen almost shut, and my nose was broken, swollen twice its size. My left shoulder was so strained I could hardly raise my arm chest high.

Jack had rummaged the farmhouse and come up with a black suit that had a faint skunk smell to it and a pair of high-topped dress shoes. I eased into the shoes, careful of a stone bruise I got from running barefoot along the dark road. With Jack's help, I managed to get my right arm into the suit and he tied a strip of bed sheet into a sling for my left arm. I was still pissed off and blaming him for my condition, but I was in no shape to push the issue. I reckon I knew deep down that it wasn't Jack's fault. I was just sore all over and testy as an ass-shot bear.

Jack sat near the front window keeping an eye on the road while I hobbled around sorting out my gear. I'd made up my mind what I was going to do. I was just looking for a way to tell Jack.

"Jack," I said, "the fighting has about spun itself down, don't you reckon?" Jack glanced over his shoulder, shrugged, and looked back out the window.

"I don't know. We'll have to see what Jesse says. This is his squad, don't forget." I stared at him, wondering just how dumb they raised them in New Jersey.

"Jack, goddamn it," I said, "there ain't no squad. There's just the two of us and I'm beat half to death after that so-called rescue you pulled the other night."

I heard the sarcasm in my voice, but I couldn't hold it back. There was a lot eating at me and Jack was my only target. He glanced at me, and I saw he caught the bite in my tone of voice. Still, he let it pass and stared back out the window. "Yeah, well it didn't go too smooth," he said. He started saying more, but I horned right in before he could.

"Didn't go too smooth?" My voice was weak and strained, but strong enough to be overbearing. "You're the stupidest son of a bitch—"

All I saw was a flash of motion. Jack's forty-four was out, cocked, and pointed at me from less than ten feet. I would have been no more startled had he actually blown a hole through me. I froze, seeing a quick streak of madness shoot across his eyes. Then he caught himself, let the barrel down, and dropped the gun in his holster. He turned back and leaned against the window frame. His hands shook like a man with a fever.

I stood there a few seconds, dumbfounded. He'd come damn near blowing my heart out. "Damn, Jack," I said cautiously. "What the hell was that?" He stared out the window. I wondered if he was going nuts. If he was, maybe I should ease out my gun and drop him while I had a chance, if I had a chance. From what I just saw, I wasn't sure anybody could get the drop on "Quiet" Jack.

"I didn't mean to throw down on you, Jess, but don't ever call me stupid."

"I won't," I said, and I meant it. I stood there watching his back, wondering if it was over. I had hit on some deep place inside him, something that should be left alone.

He studied the road a while longer, then tossed a glance over his shoulder. "Just because a man ain't real smart at some things, that don't make him stupid." His voice was clipped and strong, but there was something in it like a child's. He stared back out the window like he was speaking to the road. "You can't punish a man . . . brow-beat him . . . treat him like he's an animal just because he ain't fancy smart . . . Can you? Can you, goddamn it?"

I backed away toward my gear on the floor. "No, Jack, I reckon not," I said as quietly as possible. The past few weeks had taken a heavy toll on both of us. I saw now that it wasn't me Jack was talking to, it was red demons, them raging little beasts that live inside a man, and breed, and grow, and feed on the scar tissue of his memories. All I had done was open their cage. Now they were out and upon him, dancing on his brain with clawed feet.

"I mean, not everybody can be some . . . you know . . . big-shot lawyer or doctor or something. That don't make him a dumb-brute animal."

"You're right, Jack," I said, dragging my spindle and saddle bag across the floor toward him. He rattled on. "You're right," I repeated. "Goddamn it, you're right!" I stopped five feet behind him, and he turned facing me.

"Just because a man—"

"Hold it, Jack, hold it . . . please," I put up my hands cutting him off. It appeared there would be no end to his raving unless I stopped it myself. "I was wrong saying what I said, I admit it. What happened the other night wasn't your fault. But, Jack, I'm sore plumb to the bone from being mauled by my own horse, and I'm not going to stand here listening to this bullshit. I'm too stove up to fight you, and I know better than to throw down on you, so let's not say no more, all right?"

Jack shrugged. "All right," he said. He looked puzzled, as if he didn't know what had just gone on. He looked at my gear on the floor, then back at me.

"I'm hanging it up, Jack, I'm hanging it up right here. This war has run its course. That's all I should have said in the first place. If you need to hear from Jesse, you're hearing from him right now. He left me in charge, and I say it's over. Go on home."

With my good arm, I hefted my saddlebags up on the table and divested myself of my articles of war. I held the bag upside down, spilling the contents on the table. A thirty-eight revolver, a derringer, loose shotgun and pistol shells, a leather garrote, my glades knife, an oak club filled with lead, and two burlap hoof mufflers; these instruments of battle slid out on the table like serpents sliding from the bowels of hell.

Limping over to my saddle, I unsnapped my sawed-off and pitched it to Jack. I pulled my Colt forty-four from my waist, then I had Jack run a loop of rawhide through the trigger guard, and I dropped the loop around my neck. I let the pistol hang loose down my chest in full view against the white shirt Jack had scrounged out of a closet.

Jack watched, only half-believing what I was doing. "What happens now?" he said. I shook my head, dragging my saddle across the floor. At the door I stopped and took my hat off. "Like I said, Jack, go on home, or do whatever you want."

I took the gold-braided band from my hat and pitched it to Jack. It was the braiding worn by all "The boys." Wearing it now would be like pinning a bull's-eye on my back.

I closed the door and limped out to the barn.

It was a most peculiar thing. I'd been ducking from tree to stump all them months in the middle of the night with soldiers on my neck all the time. But that day, bold as brass, I rode two hours through the burnt section and never come upon a soul till I crossed the Carthage town limits.

All the way there I mulled it over in my mind. The fighting was over except for rounding up the guerrilla forces. I figured wearing a decent suit, even if it did smell of skunk, and bearing no more arms than any other pilgrim, I had a better than fair chance of passing for a civilian. I might be questioned, maybe even detained, but what the hell. I had lied my way out of a hanging during the war; surely I could work up something. Besides, there were no living witnesses to anything I'd done.

I rode right up the middle of the dirt street in Carthage and stopped at a hitching post outside a restaurant. As I swung down from my saddle and slipped my reins around the post, two soldiers took notice of me and started over from across the street. One of them called out, but I ignored him and limped into the restaurant with no plan at all except to get some hot food and coffee. I was prepared for questioning when it came, but right then, I believe I would have killed any son of a bitch who stood between me and a sit-down meal.

As it was, I sat there and ordered without incident. Outside, the two troopers were gathering support. Knowing it, I took my time enjoying hot grits with flapjacks and salt bacon. I reckoned they wouldn't make a move for fear of getting the other two customers killed if I was one of "The boys." They were in no hurry. Hell, there was no way for me to leave except through them, anyway.

The red-haired young woman who served me food came back when I was finished and spoke to me in a near whisper. "They'll be taking you as soon as you leave here." I played dumb.

"Who?" I asked. "Taking me for what?"

She nodded toward the street. "Out there, the soldiers will be waiting for you, you damn fool." I just stared at her wide-eyed. "Look," she said, "I support what you-all are doing. I can get you out of here." Something told me to stay dumb.

"Beg your pardon, ma'am," I said. "I've wronged no one. I'm just in from Nebraska Territory, come to check on my family's farm over in Cass County. I'm of a religion that admonishes violence of any kind."

Her gaze examined my battered face and the pistol hanging down my chest. "I can see why," she said. "Anyway"—she took up my empty plate and wiped the tabletop—"I just want you to know, if you're one of 'The boys,' I wish you Godspeed, and I'll help you any way I can." I dug some money from my pocket and laid it on the table.

"If I was, ma'am, I would thank you wholeheartedly. Since I'm not, I thank you for the food and coffee just the same."

When I stepped through the door onto the boardwalk, I raised my hands in the air before they could say a word. I was ready for it. It was just something I had to do and get it over with.

Immediately I was surrounded by blue uniforms. Strong hands tore the pistol strap from my neck and slammed me against the front of the building. I was neither afraid nor angry. I ached all over, but I wasn't about to let on.

A thick-necked Irish corporal held me by the throat and looked me over. "What the hell happened to your face, lad?"

"Not a goddamn thing," I said. "What happened to yours?"

9

For the next six weeks I lay in a makeshift military jail under heavy guard. I'd thought that since the war was over, I'd be through with it. As it turned out, the war was not nearly through with me. Had I the slightest notion of what the future held that morning riding in, I would have lit out straight for Texas, maybe even Mexico. But I reckon not seeing the future is the very thing that turns a duck's ass into Sunday supper.

The best thing about having a full regiment of Yankees in the area was that it kept a man from being hanged without some kind of trial. Had the Kansas Free Militia been in control at the time, I would have hanged the first day.

After they'd jailed me for questioning, I lay on an army blanket staring at the ceiling. In a way it was real peaceful in that jail cell. I hadn't been able to really let down my guard for so long; I was just enjoying not having to look over my shoulder every few seconds to see who wanted to kill me.

I had begun to doze off when I heard the front door open. Sitting up on the blanket, I prepared to answer a few questions and be on my way. Then I recognized a voice talking to the sergeant of the guards. I heard footsteps coming toward my cell. In seconds, there at my cell door stood Daniel Zanone of the Kansas Free Militia.

If I'd had time to think of it, I would have reached through the bars and choked him to death. I would have done so even as the guards blew my head off. As it was, I just sat there stunned, watching him look me over.

He looked pale and drawn. He should have been dead. There was no way I could see him living through that shotgun blast. But there he was, big and bent, and from the looks of him, still smarting painfully from the run-in at Dant's Mill. I wondered how he had explained that. I didn't have to wonder long.

"That's him," Zanone said, turning to the sergeant, "that's one of the brothers." I had no idea what he meant.

No sooner than he said the words, he turned and left. A few minutes later the sergeant returned with an officer. The officer was an older feller with a pitch-black beard, silver-gray hair, and a red scar down his cheek. He walked with a cane.

Stopping outside my cell door, his voice rolled smooth and deep like God's own thunder. "Are you Jesse Woodson James?" I stood and stared at him speechless. "You sir," he demanded, "are you Jesse Woodson James?"

I don't know if what I heard was only in my mind or if it was something going on outside the jail, out in the street. But it sure sounded to me like somewhere somebody was driving nails, big nails, the kind of nails you would use to build a gallows.

I spent the next week trying to convince Captain Morris Fitch, the officer with the cane, that I was not Jesse James. They were the only truthful words to come out of my mouth and he wouldn't believe it for hell. Everything else I told him he went right along with and it was all a bunch of lies. I couldn't figure the man out.

At our first interrogation session he sat down and laid a battered photograph of Cousin Jesse in front of me. I was taken back at the resemblance between us. When I rode with him and Frank, everybody remarked on it, but I never paid it much attention after that day at the well. I guess it took a picture of him sitting still without his eyes shifting about to make me aware of our similar features.

Captain Fitch made it clear at that first meeting that he would not be bullshitted or misled. I decided to be real careful how I lied to him. He tapped his finger on the picture staring me straight in the face. "Do you deny this is your photograph?" In the picture Jesse was wearing his guerrilla braiding and soldiering clothes. His hat was cocked high and his hand lay on a pistol in his belt.

"That is not me . . . no sir," I said. "I can see a resemblance sure enough, but may God strike me down, that is not my photograph." I might as well been talking to a fence post for all the good it did. After three hours of me denying and him accusing, I was returned to my cell feeling as tired as a man who had split wood all day.

The next meeting was in my cell and he started right in. "Do you know a Captain Daniel Zanone?"

"Yes, I do," I replied boldly. "I know him as a murdering, cowardly dog."

"On May seventeenth last year, were you apprehended by Captain Zanone and his men, while procuring animals and supplies for guerrilla forces at Wilson Morgan's farm near New Hope?"

"No sir," I lied. "But I was beaten and robbed and my uncle was burned to death by Zanone and his men when we stopped to get directions in that area."

For the next hour I told my story, some of it coming straight off the top of my head. Captain Fitch had me tell it again and again while he tried to bore holes in it. The more I told it the better it sounded, till finally I started believing it myself. After three hours I could have told it to God and never batted an eye. When Fitch left my cell that day I was as game as a fighting cock and felt as good as a man who had watched another man split wood all day.

That night the sergeant of the guards stuck a Kansas City newspaper through the bars; he just dropped it on the floor and walked away. I picked it up and looked at it in the thin evening light from my barred window. William Clarke Quantrill had died two days ago in Louisville, Kentucky, from a rifle wound to his spine.

According to the article, Quantrill and three of his closest squad leaders were shot down in a running battle across an open cornfield. The other three died on the spot, but Quantrill lingered on a few days and was taken to Louisville for medical attention. I had no doubt that my cousin Frank was one of the dead, and I spent a sad night thinking about it.

The next morning Captain Fitch had me brought to his office in shackles and leg irons. He was seated behind his desk and holding a quill pen when I arrived. At a smaller desk next to Fitch's, a young corporal sat at attention with a quill pen and writing paper at hand. When I was seated, Captain Fitch started in right where he left off the day before, except this interview seemed more formal and every word I said was written down.

After yesterday's session and after reading about Quantrill's death, I was ready for anything they pitched at me. Since Frank had been with Quantrill, I figured they'd both gone down putting up a fight. To pay them proper respect, I could surely do no less. I sat poker straight in that hard wooden chair and stuck to my story like a gnat on a bull's ass.

"For the record, state your full Christian name," Captain Fitch had said, and there it began. The young corporal commenced writing.

"Miller Crowe," I said, straight-faced. Captain Fitch cleared his throat and shot me a dubious glance. He produced a leather-bound Bible from a drawer and plopped it on his desk before me.

"Mister Miller Crowe," he said, "do you swear on this Bible that the testimony you are about to give is the truth, the whole truth, and nothing but the truth, so help you God?"

I slapped my hand down on the Bible and stared him straight. "Damn right I do."

For the next hour we went over the same subjects as we had discussed the day before, except with no interruptions. When we finished this time, Captain Fitch and I sat stone-still, while the corporal finished scratching with that quill pen. The only sound in the room was the lazy swing of a grandfather clock.

When the corporal had completed the paperwork, he passed it to Fitch, who, without even looking at it, laid it on his desk in front of me. Beside it he laid the quill pen and the dipping bottle. "Read it," Fitch said, "if you find it correct, sign here." He tapped a finger at the bottom of the page. Here's how the paper read:

On May 17th, 1864, my Uncle Moses Crowe and myself were traveling through Cass County, Missouri, for the purpose of buying horses. Being from the Nebraska Territory, we had no knowledge of Order Eleven, that is we did not know it applied to us. We were not familiar with that area and stopped in some woods to wait for a fog to lift. My uncle heard animal sounds from a distance and we decided I would wait there in the woods while he went to see if he could find a farmhouse. After an hour, maybe longer, I decided to go see what was taking him so long. My uncle had been known to have seizures and blackout spells and I feared he had gotten down somewhere in the woods.

As I mounted my horse, I was attacked from the woods by riflemen. My horse was shot and killed—and that horse had cost me fifty dollars. Before I could do a thing, I was sat upon by these men who were led by Mister Daniel Zanone, a man I did not know at that time. I was beaten and my money was taken from me. At no time did I get a chance to defend myself in any way, nor did they ever identify themselves as Kansas Militia.

They dragged my uncle out of the woods. I could tell he'd had a seizure because at that point he didn't have the sense of a goose. They insisted we had more money and that my uncle better tell them where it was. My uncle could not understand them, but they thought he was being belligerent. So they hung him upside down from a tree and burned him up, the way you would do a roasting animal.

They shackled me and forced me to ride with them to a place I am unfamiliar with. These men behaved like heathens and showed no military bearing at all. They said when we got to where we was going, Mister Zanone would use me like I was a woman. They said Mister Zanone did this sort of thing all the time. He is truly a sick and unwholesome human being.

I thought I was a dead man. Then, we rode into an ambush and I was thrown from my horse over the side of the road. I got up and heard fighting on the road. I was going to run away, but Mister Zanone came over the road shooting at me. Another man came behind him and shot him in the back with a shotgun. That man fell and rolled near my feet. He dropped his shotgun and I grabbed it.

For all I knew, these ambushers were no better than Zanone and his men. So, when that man stood up I killed him with his own shotgun, then got away from there. If that man was part of a military group, then I guess I ought to hang for shooting him, although I didn't do so except in what I thought was self-defense. For all I knew that man might have thought I was one of Zanone's.

As I lit out of there I heard somebody call out the name "Jess, Jess," just like that, but I couldn't hear much else except for Mister Zanone whimpering and crying and begging them not to kill him. He is truly a yeller, cowardly dog. I think it should be investigated, what he must have done to keep them from killing him.

So, if the man I killed was a union military man I can only plead guilty, having sworn to tell the truth here, so help me God.

If anybody there was named Jesse Woodson James, I would not know it, nor would I be able to identify anybody there that day, except for Mister Zanone and his murderous group.

I mulled over the letter a few minutes, tapping my chin with the feathered end of the quill pen. This was the biggest mess of lies I'd ever seen, but it would have to do.

"What happens after I sign this?" I asked Fitch.

"One of two things," he said. "If you plead innocent to all charges made by Zanone, you'll be given a civilian trial by jury. If you lose, you'll more than likely hang. If you change your statement and admit to violating Order Eleven, you'll be brought before a military court and sentenced accordingly. If you choose to amend your statement, you may do so now."

"Will I have somebody talking for me at a military trial?"

"You will."

"And that will get me off the hook with Zanone?"

"No, if Zanone can make a military council believe you are Jesse Woodson James, a guerrilla with Quantrill's forces, you could still be sentenced to death, only it would probably be by firing squad." Fitch leaned back in his leather chair. "If you'd like to think it over, you have until noon tomorrow."

People from my part of the country, central Kentucky, that is, are known for doing things on the spur of the moment. I've never known why that is, but it's a fact. Over the past year I had done a few things without giving them much thought. I reckoned one more wouldn't bend a barrel hoop.

"I don't have to think about it," I said. I scrawled my newly acquired name right across the bottom of that letter and slid it to Fitch. "Let's get to a military council and let her rip," I said.

Fitch glanced over the letter and put it away. He gestured for the corporal to leave the room. When the man was gone Fitch gazed at me with a smile of restrained satisfaction. It was the kind of look a cat has when it's got a paw clamped down on a wounded mouse and is deciding whether to play with it or eat it up.

"Let's get something straight between us here and now," Fitch said. Something in his new tone of voice caused my guts to pucker up.

"There is nothing you can do or say that could convince me you're not Jesse Woodson James."

I pointed my finger across his desk and started to protest, but he pointed right back, cutting me off. "You will get a fair and impartial military hearing, but don't think you are shitting me about who you are or what you've been up to."

"Wait a minute," I said. I begin feeling rope burns around my collar line. "You told me I'd have somebody talking for me at that council. I want to meet that man. I want to know what kind of job he's gonna do against you low-life snakes."

Now Fitch leaned forward on his elbows as if to get a better look at my expression as he dropped the words on me. "Mister James," he said, "excuse me, I mean Mister Crowe. I will be your attorney. I will see to it that the truth comes out. After all, that is what you want, isn't it?"

The trouble with a lawyer is you never know what the bastard's thinking. The more they tell you—if they tell you anything at all—the less you understand. As for Fitch, I never have understood what he did before that council.

That evening, the red-haired girl from the restaurant showed up with a plate of fried chicken. I hoped her being here wasn't a bad sign, like a condemned man's last sit-down dinner. She had not been here before. When the sergeant took the plate and slipped it under the door, she stood close to the bars.

"I'll just wait here for the plate," she said. I was surprised when the sergeant walked away and left her there.

No sooner had he left than the red-haired girl raised up her dress and pulled out a pistol. "Quick," she whispered, "come here and take it." I jumped over and snatched the gun through the bars. I stuck it under my shirt and down in my trousers. "Tonight," she said, "around midnight, when you hear a whistle outside your window, be ready to go."

"Why are you doing this?"

"Never mind," she said. "Just listen. When you go before that military board, Zanone has it all rigged up. They're going to see to it you either hang or go before a firing squad."

"How do you know so much?" I asked. I glanced past her, watching for the sergeant.

"Hand me that plate," she said. I grabbed it off my bunk, threw the fried chicken under my blanket, and was back in one step. "You have friends here," she said. "I was trying to help you the other day, but you spun that religious story at me."

"Who is helping me?" I asked. She touched her finger to her lips as I heard the sergeant coming back. She shot me a quick sincere smile. "Good luck," she whispered.

I must've walked five miles that night, back and forth in that eight-foot cell. I studied, figured, scratched, and thought about it all, as far as my mind could stretch.

It was like Zanone to rig that council. Anybody who'd burn an old man to death would do about anything. And I wasn't expecting much of a defense from Fitch, he being convinced I was Jesse James. Something told me to be ready at midnight and make my break. Whoever was helping me by sending me that gun was doing a damn sight more than anybody here was going to do for me.

Near midnight I'd filled up on fried chicken and was waiting for a signal, but I'll be damned if I didn't start getting second thoughts. The one thing I swore back last year was that I'd kill that dog Zanone. I swore it to Cletis's spirit as I rode shackled toward Dant's Mill. I thought Raymond Claire had done him in. Now that I knew he was still alive, I wanted him bad enough that I would kill him at that hearing, if it meant my life. I would get Fitch at the same time, the dirty son of a bitch. He had to be in on the set-up.

At midnight, when I heard a soft whistle outside my window, I was busy picking thread out of my trouser seams. I worked out enough thread to tie that small revolver up into my crotch. They hadn't searched me any of the times they took me to Fitch's office. I was betting they wouldn't search me tomorrow. Three more times I heard the whistle outside my cell. By the time it had stopped, I'd finished up my work and lay on the steel bunk staring up at the dark window. Whoever had come to help me had given up and left. God help me if I'd just thrown away a winning hand.

◆✳ 10 ✳◆

The first thing I did when they seated me was to drop my hands in my lap so it wouldn't look too sudden when I went for the pistol. I was right about them not searching me. I had pulled open a seam in the crotch of my trousers so I could jerk that pistol out quick at just the right second. I meant to pull iron as soon as I sat down, but looking around, I didn't see Zanone anywhere. Killing Fitch would be easy, but it meant nothing if I didn't get Zanone.

Four Yankee officers entered single file and seated themselves at a long polished table beneath a Union flag. No sooner had they sat down than Fitch stepped up to the table and began speaking with them very quietly. They stopped, and Fitch turned around as Zanone came through the door. Had Fitch and Zanone gotten within ten feet of each other, I would have started spitting lead.

As it was, Zanone went to a table on the other side of the room and Fitch came over and sat beside me. It was all I could do to keep from throwing down on them right then, but I held out, knowing that soon enough they would be side by side in front of the officer's table.

After the charges were read, the middle officer summoned Captain Fitch before them. He looked me in the eye as he stood up. With the smile of a mischievous schoolboy, he said, "Watch this, Mister James." I thought it a bad sign, his calling me "Mister James."

"General, sir," Fitch began, "in all fairness to the accused I ask that Mister Zanone be removed from this room until identification is made by the first witness." Zanone came out of his chair on that one. I could only figure they had that little disturbance made up between them to make it look good.

A mealy-looking little captain rose from his chair beside Zanone and commenced protesting Fitch's request. I didn't know his role until then, but he was the prosecuting officer. He was the one who would put the screws to me. He motioned Zanone down in his chair as he spoke to the council. "There is no reason for Mister Zanone to be removed from this part of the trial." Before he could say another word, that big ole general slammed a gavel and Zanone was taken out into a waiting room. Now I was puzzled.

From another room they brought in four hard cases near to my age, shackled and chained, same as me. I didn't see what they had to do with anything unless Zanone and Fitch had it set up so that they were going to say they knew me. That made me boil inside. I felt my hand ease toward my crotch, but again Zanone was out of the room. I waited while they seated two of the young fellers on my right and the others on my left. I tried to look them in the eyes but they all ignored me. The rotten skunk bastards.

"You may now proceed to call the witness," the general said to the prosecutor. The prosecutor called out in a voice I thought just a bit shrill for an army officer.

"Prosecution calls Mister Morgan Wilson of Cass County."

That was the man Cletis and I were to have met that day. I had never laid eyes on him, nor he me.

He came in from a side room, a rough-looking old feller with a gray-red beard. He sat down before he was told, so he had to get back up while they swore him in.

"Mister Wilson," Fitch said, after the prosecutor finished with him, "according to your sworn testimony, on May seventeenth, eighteen sixty-four, you had arranged with a Mister Raymond Claire to have a team of guerrilla riders arrested at your farm in Cass County?"

You could have knocked me out with a hard breath. My neck went chill, plumb down to my shoulder blades. That was why Claire shot Zanone; he thought Zanone might spill it out about the set-up that day. I perked up now, but still kept my gun hand ready.

"That's correct, sir," the old man said. I'll be damned, I thought to myself.

Fitch walked him through the story to the part where he was to identify me. Fitch asked, "Did you accompany Mister Zanone into the woods where the second man waited?"

"I did, sir," was Wilson's reply. I almost jumped up from the table to call him a liar then and there, but I caught myself.

"And how close were you to that person?" Fitch asked.

"Near as I am to you," Wilson said.

"So you would have no trouble identifying that person here today, is that correct?"

"That's correct."

"Good," Fitch said, turning and folding his hands behind his back. "Please point that person out for our record."

Wilson looked back and forth at me and the other men at the table. He began looking puzzled. He hesitated too long. I had my gun ready to come out if he pointed at me. I couldn't get Zanone, but I'd settle for busting a cap on Fitch and Wilson. I had my hand in my trousers and on the verge of coming out of my chair, when Fitch seemed to go crazy all of a sudden. "Tell us, Mister Wilson, isn't it true you never laid eyes on anybody in the woods that day? Isn't it also true you have received payment from Quantrill's forces on many occasions for revealing locations of Union encampments?" Fitch's voice got louder and meaner with every word. I thought he was going to bust Wilson in the head before he finished. "And tell us, Mister Wilson!" he bellowed. "Aren't you being paid to appear here today, and don't you realize what a stiff penalty perjury carries?" Now Wilson came unhinged.

"No," he said, raising half out of his chair, "I mean *no* to all that other. I mean . . . hell yes, I can pick the man out." Wilson pointed a shaking finger at the man two places on my right. He was the only person at my table wearing a gold-braided cord around his hat. "That's him," Wilson said. "That's the man I saw in the woods."

"Are you sure, Mister Wilson?" Fitch asked. He had that strange look of satisfaction I'd seen in his office.

"Yes, I'm sure."

Fitch faced the man with the gold-braid cord and asked him to stand. "Will you identify yourself, sir?" demanded Fitch in a low, serene voice.

The young man had snapped up from his chair. He jerked his hat from his head and stood at attention. "Sir, I am Private Matthew Vincent of the Third Michigan Infantry, sir."

It got stone-quiet in that room for the longest time. During that quiet, I eased down into my crotch and let down the hammer on that pistol, hoping nobody would hear it in the silence.

After that it seemed Fitch had snatched Zanone and the prosecution by the short hairs. I never seen a man act that wild and not be drunk. It was as if he was going into a fistfight.

When they led Wilson out, he was staring over his shoulder like he was fearing a back shot. As a sergeant came and took the shackles from the Union soldiers posing as hard cases, I instinctively held my hands out too, but he just stared at me like something you'd spit up after a bad meal.

When Zanone returned and took the stand, Fitch tore through his story like a double-blade plow. Every time Zanone said something, Fitch would study that letter I signed and turn it all around on him. Everything I had said matched what Zanone said, except that I had put it in a different light. Finally, the prosecutor was at a point where he wouldn't say shit—he just sat there looking stupid while Fitch took control of the room.

"And isn't it also true," Fitch put forth with disgust, "that you ordered a poor, simpleminded, afflicted man to be burned to death over a blazing fire?" Fitch leaned in real close on that one. Zanone squirmed like a crippled rat.

"I object," the prosecutor said, "Mister Zanone is not on trial." He must've figured he had to say something.

"Your objection is so noted, Captain," the general said. "Captain Fitch, address your questions to the charges at hand."

Fitch nodded and continued, using my shooting Raymond Claire as proof that I was not a part of the ambushers. Otherwise, why would I do something like that?

Each time Fitch asked another question he did it in a way that left Zanone looking more and more like a liar, a coward, and finally, this being the last straw, a mind-sick pervert.

"Mister Zanone, is it true, as your own men stated to the accused, that you have on many occasions assaulted men and forced them to perform acts with you that a man would ordinarily perform with a woman?"

That seemed to puzzle Zanone for a second as he worked the words through his mind. "That's hearsay," the prosecutor yelled, but his words went unheard as Zanone finally unraveled what was being said about him. Zanone seemed to swell up and turn redder than a stoked furnace. Just when I thought he was going to burst open, he let out a squall that would curl rope, and he came up swinging his chair like a club. As it whistled past my head, I pounced across the table and into his chest. We slammed onto the wooden floor in a tangle of arms, legs, and chain.

Two guards tried pulling me off Zanone's chest, but I had my shackle chain wrapped around his neck squeezing toward tomorrow. I caught the bridge of his nose between my teeth and felt the bone crunch as I clamped down.

Above the ruckus I heard Fitch yelling without missing a beat, "There again, gentlemen, is an example of a man defending his life under a brutal attack."

I awoke in Fitch's office after the back of my head had exploded. First thing I did was reach between my legs for the pistol, but it was gone. "Looking for this?" Fitch asked. I saw the pistol dangling from his hand as he stood over me. "It fell out and slid across the floor while you were choking Zanone. Nobody saw it but me."

I sat up on the divan and it felt like drums were beating inside my head. Fitch walked over to a cabinet and poured whiskey in a water glass. "You took a hard lick on the head." He brought the whiskey to me and I took a long swallow. Only then did I realize my shackles were gone. Noticing my surprise, Fitch sat down in a chair in front of me. "That's right, Mister James, you're a free man, for now anyway."

"My name is not James," I said. "What do you mean 'for now'? Did we win or not?"

"Oh, yes, we won. Of course you nearly killed Daniel Zanone on the courtroom floor, but overall it went smooth enough."

"I meant to kill him," I said, "and I will, first chance I get."

"Is that what the gun was for?"

"Yeah," I said, "that and other things, if it hadn't gone right."

Fitch nodded and pitched me the gun. "Take some advice?"

"Probably not," I said candidly, "but you're going to give it to me anyway." Fitch smiled and took the empty glass from my hand.

"The war's over," he said. "Quantrill's dead, most of the others are either dead or on the run. It's time for a young man like yourself to go on to something else. Let the old wounds heal."

He had no way of knowing, but that's what I was trying to do when I rode in. As far as wounds, I had none to heal, none that I knew of anyway. But since he'd saved my life I let him run his sermon.

"The prosecutor never saw your picture, I acquired it on my own.

As far as anybody knows, you are Miller Crowe, not Jesse Woodson James. Even if you had admitted your real name, there are no charges against you anyway. From here, you get a chance to start new. I'd like to see you take it."

We both stood up and he walked over and took my Colt .44 Navy from his desk drawer. The cord was still tied to it. He handed it to me butt-first and then took a folded paper from his tunic.

"These are travel papers. You'll have a hard time moving about without them for a while, now that they're mopping up rebels all around. These say you have been investigated and found to have no charges against you. They've been signed by the general, and myself as well."

"I don't know what to say," I told him. He shrugged and put out his hand.

"Nothing to say. Your horse is at the livery stable at the end of town. I can't keep Zanone from coming at you, but I don't think you mind that too much."

I turned and reached for the door, but before leaving I turned around, still holding the doorknob. "Damn it, Captain, I thought you was a no-good son of a bitch, that's why I had that gun. I figured you for another Zanone. Now I've got to know why; why did you help me? You knew I would have killed you without batting an eye, didn't you?"

Fitch nodded. His eyes looked dark and tired. I guess it had been a long day for both of us. "It needed doing," he said, "that's all."

My expression told him that wasn't good enough. He managed a tired smile. The flesh along his scar turned chalk white. It must have hurt him to smile. "I had a son," he said, sipping at the whiskey. "He was just a boy really, not much older than you." He sipped again. "War took him." He sat the glass on his desk and wiped a hand across his mouth. I nodded and tugged at my hat brim.

"I'm sorry," I said. Fitch gave me a curious look, shaking his head slightly.

"I'm not asking sympathy," he said, "I'm simply telling."

"My son was your enemy, but hurting you won't bring him back." He shrugged. "Now that it's over, what have we really done except kill off our children and cut scars in ourselves that will take a hundred years to heal. I came down here to fight for a just cause, not so dogs like Zanone can reap their personal vengeance."

He smiled knowingly. "I think you're Jesse Woodson James, and I think you've done everything Zanone accused you of. But that's the past. From now on you're Miller Crowe. Turn Miller Crowe into a name you can be proud of."

I stood there nodding my head. I only agreed with him out of courtesy for saving my life. His words gave me no explanation for his helping me the way he did. I reckon when I first asked him he had said it best: "It needed doing, that's all."

From the long end of life, looking back, you can sure work up a bucket full of irony if you've a mind to. A man I rode with turned out to be a traitor, and I didn't know it till after I killed him for an entirely different reason. And there was Fitch, a man I would have killed: he knew what I was, he never believed a word I said, yet he fought like a devil to save my life. Why? Because his son had died at the hands of somebody like me. Thinking about it, it could have been me that killed him for all I knew. I wondered if Fitch had considered it. I reckon he did. Maybe that's what he'd tried to say.

Part II
Wildflowers

◆✳ 11 ✳◆

I was a free man, nearly nineteen. I had seven dollars, a fine shooting iron—two in fact, counting the one the red-haired girl had given me—a fine riding mare and an open road in any direction. All I had to do was kill Daniel Zanone and I could light out of there owning the world and owing it nothing.

My intention was to stay in the woods close to town. I wanted to get a fix on Zanone's comings and goings, and figure how to best blow his brains out. I wasn't about to be caught out on the street by any of his men if I could help it. Still, before I left town I thought it only fitting to stop and say thanks to that red-haired girl for her offer of help. I stopped at the livery stable, picked up my mare, and led her over to the restaurant.

The girl looked scared when I first walked in. These were dangerous times for folks in that area; I figured turning down her help might have made her wonder just who I was and what I was up to. Even with the war over, you could get in more trouble in two minutes than you could get out of in a hundred years.

She acted nervous when she served me coffee, and shied away from me till the other customers left.

When the place was empty except for her and me, she eased over to my table. She sounded a bit upset. "What happened last night? Don't you know the risk I took giving you that gun? My friends ain't going to trust me for a long time because of you."

"I'm sorry for that," I said. "I come to thank you, you and your friends. As it turned out, I took a gamble and I won. I'd be glad to meet your friends and square it for you."

She relaxed a bit. "Well," she said, pushing back a strand of red hair, "you're alive, that's the main thing. I'll square myself with my friends, thank you."

I laid money down for the coffee and stood up to leave. "What about Zanone?" she asked. "He'll still be out to get you, you know."

"Then he better get me quick, 'cause I'm heading for Illinois come morning," I lied. I'd learned never to say where I was going or what I was up to.

She looked disappointed. "Oh, you're leaving?"

Even at that age, I'd learned enough to know what a woman says with her eyes. "I planned on it," I said. "I reckon there's no reason for me staying here, is there?"

She shrugged and gave me one of those smiles a man's supposed to guess at. "I've got a room upstairs here," she said. "I live by myself. Had a man, but he got killed over near Shadyville, fighting 'Hawkers."

"I'm sorry to hear it," I said. "I'm on my own, too. I ain't had much time in one place. Maybe I could stay another day or so."

"Meet me tomorrow night," she said. Her words came so quickly I almost stepped back in surprise. "Yes, meet me out at the mill north of town."

The sound of her voice, the way she rushed the words, fanned a fire in my young belly, and just to be sure she wouldn't change her mind, I asked her, "How about tonight? How 'bout right now?"

She looked embarrassed by her forwardness. "No, tomorrow night, and I'll put on my good dress, and you bring me flowers." She gazed away a second as if watching something a long way off. "It don't matter what kind, just flowers."

That afternoon I drew camp twenty yards off the road, built a fire, tied my mare to a tree, and slept like a dead man for more than three hours. I went to sleep thinking about the red-haired girl and I woke up thinking about her. Since I didn't know her name, I lay there staring up through the pines imagining what it might be. Being young and easily stirred by the pictures in my mind, I tried to imagine a lot of things about her, but mostly I tried to imagine her name.

Near dark I pulled some dried shank from my saddlebags. It looked so old I feared eating it, but did so anyway. Afterward I struck out walking, leading my mare across a rise in search of wildflowers. I just wanted to find them tonight. Tomorrow I'd come back and pick them.

I was still thinking about that girl as I neared the top of the rise and heard voices from the valley on the other side. Being used to prowling around unseen, I eased up and peered down at a small farmhouse fifty yards below. In the fading daylight I saw two men pitching camp in the front yard. On the porch, dressed in a flannel nightshirt, wearing a bandage across the bridge of his swollen nose . . . I'll be damned . . . Daniel Zanone! "Lord," I thought. "What have I done to deserve such luck as this?"

My good fortune excited me so much, I had to ease the mare back into the woods and calm down. Figuring quickly, I checked my forty-four and tried to remember the layout of the place before darkness set in. I wrapped my reins loosely around a scrub hickory for a quick ride out and belly-crawled ten yards back to the top of that rise.

By now it was dark except for a dim circle of light around the campfire where the two men lay wrapped in blankets. I watched a lamplight trimmed down next to nothing in a window and the shadow of the nightshirt moved down out of sight. It would be just like Zanone to make his men sleep on the ground while he rolled himself up indoors.

Not wanting to miss another chance at killing that snake, I crawled inch-by-inch, guerrilla style, down into the valley and around to the rear of the house. I forced myself to go slowly and stay clear-headed. I had him. By God, I had him good.

Quiet as a spirit, I eased the horses out of the corral and silently shooed them away. With my forty-four drawn, I crept up against the back of that house and leaned there a long time trying to soak up any sound from inside. The silence of the night was broken only by the sound of my heartbeat. It thumped steadily and deeply like a funeral drum.

Using the beat of that funeral drum I went about my killing as if I had been rehearsing for it all my life. I slipped through the back door and moved around the kitchen close to the wall so as not to make a sound on a loose board. I inched down a short hallway through the musty smell of old wallpaper, my pistol at shoulder level, and cocked. Stopping at the end of the hall, I looked down at the flickering glow seeping beneath the bedroom door, and heard a stirring from a feather mattress on the other side. I stood long enough to brace myself for the ruckus that would come from the front yard once I popped that forty-four, then I squeezed the latch and shouldered the door just enough to make sure it wasn't locked. "Sleep tight in hell," I thought to myself, then I moved in like a raging fire.

One long step and I was at the foot of the bed. I snapped the forty-four out at arm's length and split the darkness in a blue-white blaze right through the center of the pillow. The muzzle flash showed a glimpse of a head. It bounced like an empty gourd as the bullet tore through it.

No sooner than I fired that round, I heard someone squall out behind me. Spinning around, I caught a glimpse of Zanone hurling himself through a closed window, naked as shame. Startled as I was, I still fired once across his naked white ass before he spilled out onto the porch in a spray of broken glass.

Now bullets spit back through the window. Chunks of the walls filled the air with splinters and dust. I was ducking and firing back straight through the thin wall. I had to get out quick, before they had time to start thinking clearly. I'd caught them asleep and had the upper hand, but not for long. By now I figured one of them would be thinking enough to go around back and close my only way out, but I stopped long enough to whip the blanket from the bed. I had to know.

A woman lay there on her side like she was sleeping through the hail of gunfire. Above her ear, blood poured in a widening trickle down across her face. Her body was relaxed, snuggled up like a child. Naked, she looked the way I had imagined she would look . . . all that afternoon.

I can't tell exactly what happened after that. I must've run like hell, firing and ducking out through the back and up to the woods. The truth is, I felt like I just walked out in kind of a daze, pointing and firing but not caring whether I hit anything or not. Nor do I remember caring if I was hit. I caught a graze across my right shoulder, but I didn't even check to see how bad it was. Next thing I can clearly remember, I was punching that mare out across the flatland and feeling a cold breeze pinching my face.

Daylight the next morning, I stepped down from my saddle beside a shallow stream. Taking off my coat and shirt, I lay at the edge of the stream cupping water in my hand and pouring it on my wounded shoulder. Only then did I probe around to see what shape I was in.

The graze clipped me deep, right at the collar bone, deep enough to expose white bone, and deep enough to rack me in pain when the cold water hit it. Other than that and bleeding like a stuck hog, I'd be alright—physically—in a few days. As far as what happened last night, that would require a much longer healing.

There is no worse or more low-down feeling in this world than mistakenly killing the wrong person, unless the wrong person also happens to be a woman. I knew a man once in Kentucky who went off crazy and never came back after he ran down a woman with a freight wagon—and that was an accident. I had gone in there strapped and stoked for the letting of blood. I killed her by mistake, but as my violence was deliberate and voluntary, I could not justify it as accidental.

I wandered around the woods and flatland for two days, hollow-eyed and dark-minded. I didn't eat, didn't want to, couldn't sleep, hell I couldn't close my eyes without seeing that poor red-haired girl dead, with blood filling her ear. I'd killed her for no reason except the blindness of my vengeance. That poor girl lay dead after trying to help me; it cut me . . . cut me deep.

My mind was so torn up, I didn't even want to think that she might've been setting me up for Zanone. My first thought was that she was sleeping with him just to gather information for her friends, maybe even for me. Maybe she would have brought me information the next night; maybe she was doing it to save my life. I tell you, everything I thought made it worse. Maybe she did it with him because she had no choice. He could've been forcing her. I kept hearing her telling me to bring her flowers. I could see me handing her the wildflowers I'd found in the woods. I saw that, and imagined her in her good dress.

Finally, to save my sanity, I made myself think about her setting me up. I felt guilty as a dog for letting it come to my mind, as if she was sitting somewhere watching me and being ashamed of me for thinking that way.

I got down from the mare and let the reins fall to the ground so she could go or stay unfettered. Walking to a low rise overlooking a stretch of wild grass, I sat down and stared out for the longest time, feeling empty as a hollow log. I opened the chamber on the small revolver the girl gave me and let four bullets fall to ground.

I closed the chamber with two bullets inside and took a good long breath. I watched the wind bend lazy circles in the tall grass. There was only one way I could settle up. If she set me up with that gun to get me killed, I'd know in a second. If she gave it to me to save my life, I knew what I had to do.

I pointed the gun straight out across the wild grass and pulled the trigger. It just snapped, same as it would've if it wasn't loaded. I sat there a while examining the pistol, then tossed it away from me and walked back to my mare. Had that first bullet fired, I would have put the second one through my forehead. I'm sure of it. But someone had filed the firing pin down just enough to where it fell short of striking the cartridge. I felt better now, but not much.

◆✳ 12 ✳◆

For the next few days I drifted between Carthage and Roscoe, staying out of sight in the brush and woodlands. Killing that girl had knocked my spirit for a loop. I still had every intention of killing Zanone, but for now I decided that was one pot I best let simmer.

Holding tight rein on my seven dollars, I tripped the back door to a general store in Roscoe, took no more than I needed to stake me and the mare, and drifted up to Springfield with no more direction than a blind rooster. I quartered in a boardinghouse under the name Miller Crowe and went about finding work.

Easy as it would have been to hook up with some of the hard cases that roamed the area, to my own credit, I have to say I was putting forth an effort at going straight. Though I have never been a big drinker, I hung around the local bars and gambling parlors partly out of restlessness and partly to keep an ear out for job prospects. My comings and goings were looked at by others just in terms of what I was, a young man trying to carve something out for myself.

Staying at the boarding house during that same time was James Butler Hickok, later to be known as "Wild Bill." Not a friendly man, Hickok exchanged greetings at the dinner table only in reply. Not being much of a talker myself, we had little to do with one another either at the house or in the parlors where he gambled most evenings.

I spent a lot of time studying the game from my spot at the bar ten feet away. One night when his game wasn't going as well as he would have liked, he excused himself for a minute and came over to me. Blunt as a hoop rivet, he just walked within two feet of me and told me to find something else to stare at.

"I'm only watching the game," I said, "I mean no offense to anyone." I was respectful but firm. He stared at me a second through narrowed lids, and I wasn't sure if he was going to stir a ruckus or what. I stood firm and stared right back. I knew nothing of his growing reputation as a pistol man, but it would've made no difference. I'd done nothing to be called on and wasn't about to step back from this long-necked buzzard.

Whether he decided I was just a dumb young buck or whether he might have realized he was out of line for no reason, I don't know. Whatever his reason, he finally nodded his head and went back to the table. To keep from fanning anything further, I soon drifted down bar to watch a game that seemed a little friendlier.

A few minutes later, all heads turned toward Hickok as he and another player came half out of their chairs cussing and growling. The other feller was holding a gold watch that I'd seen Hickok lay on the table earlier to cover a bet. "You'll get it back," the feller said, "when I get my money. Not a damn minute before."

Hickok stomped across the room and threw his cards out the window, then headed for the door. He stopped and turned around, opening his coat to show a pistol butt. "Don't wear my watch," he warned.

"Bullshit." The man tossed his head in disregard.

Hickok pointed a long finger and said, "If you wear my watch tomorrow, I'll shoot you down like a dog." He backed out the door and left. I don't know why he postponed the incident to the next day, but that's exactly what he said.

When he was gone, the man he'd threatened dropped the watch in his coat pocket and grinned at the crowd. Evidently, he hadn't seen what I saw in Hickok's eyes as he made the threat. Had I been that feller, I think I would have settled then and there or else snuck out the back door and waylaid Hickok as he crossed the alley. I know that don't sound honorable, but as it turned out he would've been better off.

The next morning as I stepped out the door of the boarding house, I heard Hickok's voice boom out from across the street. When I looked around he was standing mid-square calling into a group of men sixty feet away. "Tut," I heard him call into that group. The group parted, and Dave Tut, the man from last night's argument, stood facing Hickok with the gold watch chain looped at his vest.

Straight across from me on the other side of Hickok, I saw four men who spent a lot of time with Tut at the Old Southern Hotel. They stepped into a line two feet apart. I didn't know if Hickok had seen them or not, but there was no doubt in my mind as to their intentions.

This was the first time I ever saw what you would call a "showdown," and it was over so fast, if you blinked, you missed it.

Tut pulled the watch from his vest pocket, turned it about, then smiled and put it away. It was his way of answering the invitation I reckon. He took a step forward, maybe expecting Hickok to do the same. I don't know, nor will anybody ever. Hickok jerked out a forty-four and put a bullet through Tut's heart on the upswing. Tut looked real surprised as if to say, "Wait, we ain't close enough yet," and then he slapped the ground like a bundle of rags.

Hickok stood holding the smoking gun in Tut's direction. On the other side of him, I saw four men ready to throw down. I pulled open my shirt and snatched my pistol. "Hickok!" I yelled. I was not so much concerned for him as I was for myself. If they fired on Hickok, I would surely be hit where I was standing. Hickok swung the barrel toward me and saw my hand on my pistol. In that split second before he pulled the trigger, I nodded past him and he swung facing the four men. Two were already coming out of their holsters; but they froze under the sight of Hickok's forty-four. Facing them, he backed over almost beside me. All I was doing was protecting my own interest; now I seemed to be involved. "All of you lay them shooting irons down, or more men will die here," Hickok said. He glanced at me from the corner of his eye. He seemed puzzled, almost offended that I'd warned him.

By the time two constables arrived, the men had eased their guns from their holsters and laid them on the ground. I was still beside Hickok, grateful it was winding down. "What's going on here?" one constable demanded, pointing a sawed-off shotgun at me and Hickok.

The other constable ran to where Tut lay on the ground. "He's a goner," he yelled back.

"You're under arrest," said the one with the shotgun.

"No, I ain't," Hickok corrected him, "it's a fair shooting." He was still holding the forty-four and it hovered near the constable's chest.

"You'll still have to go to trial," the constable said, giving in. He looked real concerned about Hickok's forty-four pointing at him.

"I understand," Hickok said. He slid the forty-four into his holster. "You let me know when." He just turned and walked away, leaving both constables standing there slack-jawed.

That afternoon I was sitting at an empty card table in the Old Southern Hotel. It was slow that day and I was waiting to meet a freight-line owner about a job. Hickok came in and walked over to my table. He didn't mention the shooting right away. Looking down at me, he tugged at his mustache and studied my face. "You remind me of somebody, but I can't recall who," he said.

I didn't know it then, but I learned later that Jesse and Frank had done Hickok a favor back during the war, even though they were on opposite sides. I reckon he was seeing the resemblance between me and Jesse. I shrugged. "I'm Miller Crowe. I'm not from around here."

Hickok shifted around and gazed toward the ceiling as if embarrassed about something. "What you did out there today," he began, tugging his mustache and avoiding my eyes. "Why'd you do it?"

I shrugged. "I felt like I should. Why're you asking?" I'd never seen anybody have such a hard time saying thanks, if that was what he was trying to do.

Suddenly his eyes snapped from the ceiling and riveted to mine. "I ain't beholding to nobody," he said, almost like a warning. I felt a smile move on my face, but I stopped it. Here was a man whose pride—vanity—would not allow him to thank someone for maybe saving his life.

"And you're not beholding to me," I said. "Where I stood, if they'd thrown down on you, it would've been my ass. I acted in my own interest."

He stared at me a second, chewing the inside of his lip. "That's how you call it?" he finally said.

I nodded and pushed my hat up on my forehead. "That's how I call it."

I saw a trace of a smile move at the corner of his mouth. He nodded his head and pulled out a chair. He dropped a deck of cards on the table and spread them into a fan. "Mister Crowe," he said, "do you mind if I teach you a couple things?"

◆✳ 13 ✳◆

For the next six or eight weeks I teamstered freight between Springfield and Roscoe, sometimes doubling my wages by playing poker there at the Roscoe House. They weren't the class of players that I was used to back in Springfield. At the Old Southern Hotel, I didn't fare nearly as well, but what I learned from Hickok and the others stayed with me, and I got to where I could hold my own with the best of them. It was understood that I wouldn't play in a game Hickok was in at that time. Since he'd taught me a lot of inside moves, I thought it only fair.

"How long will a young man like yourself be satisfied with teamster wages?" Hickok asked me as I unloaded cargo from Roscoe.

"I was raised staring at a mule's ass from behind a plow," I said. "I could teamster till I die of old age. It wouldn't bother me a bit." I'd reached in the wagon for a bag of flour when Hickok's hand came down on it, not hard, but firm.

"You fought that war without a uniform, didn't you?" he asked with a sly expression.

I stared at his hand for a second choosing my words. "I knew some guerrilla soldiers along the border. You'll never hear them admit to anything. I teamster freight for a dollar a day, Mister Hickok. Any more questions?" I turned and looked him straight in the eyes. He understood.

One night, when I was just back from Roscoe, I'd dropped my wagon at the freight station and rode my mare over to the Old Southern. I'd spun my reins around the hitch rail and started in when I heard a voice call my name from the alley beside the hotel. It'd been a while since anybody called me by my real name, so I tensed up as I stepped toward the sound. The voice sounded familiar, but I slipped my hand inside my shirt to my forty-four just in case.

Two men on horseback sat just outside the glow of the street lamp. Seeing my hand in my shirt, one of them spoke above a whisper. "Jess, it's me, Jack Smith."

Recognizing his voice, I stepped into the alley close enough to get a better look. It was "Quiet" Jack and a thin young feller with black hair hanging to his shoulders. Since I didn't recognize him, I kept an eye on him as I spoke to Jack. "My name's Miller Crowe, Jack, don't you remember?" Jack nodded, understanding my position regarding the other man. Jack had no way of knowing I'd changed my name, but he caught on.

"Yeah, I meant to say Miller Crowe," he said. "Anyway, Crowe, this here is Dave Mather. We've come a long way to see you."

I nodded at Mather. He was young, as young as I was. His jaw line was set hard beneath a drooping black mustache. His eyes seemed on the verge of a deep sleep. He returned my nod and his lazy eyes never left me as I spoke to Jack. "Didn't expect to see you again, Jack. How you making out?"

"Neither better nor worse," he said. "I brought you some bad news from downriver. Your cousin Jesse has been shot."

I wasn't at all surprised, but I hated hearing it anyway. "Damn it!" I said. "How bad?"

"It's bad, I expect he's dead by now. If he ain't, he ain't far from it."

"How about Frank? I reckon he went down with Quantrill, didn't he?"

"I ain't heard," Jack said, "but I figured you'd want to know about Jesse."

"I appreciate you telling me," I said, "but how'd you know to find me?" He nodded toward Dave Mather.

" 'Mysterious' Dave knew where to find you, but that's a whole other thing. I think Ma Samuel would want you around."

I didn't even stop by to get my day's pay from the freight company or my belongings from the boardinghouse. I remember as we rode past the front door of the Old Southern, Hickok stepped out on the boardwalk and watched us leave town. Near the end of the street I looked back over my shoulder and he was still standing there, silhouetted in the golden light that spilled from the open door.

How "Quiet" Jack Smith got his nickname I'll never understand. At times he was the talkingest son of a bitch in the world. It couldn't be because he was soft-spoken either, because most times his voice was two notches louder than anyone else's. But at times he wouldn't speak at all for a day or two. I reckon he got it during one of those times and it just stuck with him. On the other hand, it was easy to see how Dave Mather come to be called "Mysterious" Dave. He was truly a puzzling, mysterious, and hard-to-figure piece of work.

I decided I wouldn't ride far with "Quiet" Jack and "Mysterious" Dave until I found out how Mather knew to look for me in Springfield. I'd never laid eyes on him. When Jack told me there in the alley that Mather knowing my whereabouts was a "whole other thing," I knew I better not go very far without finding out why.

After we struck a fire and settled in that first night, I wrapped up in a blanket I got from Jack and propped up on one elbow just as they were going to sleep. Mather lay wrapped in a blanket with his head on his saddle and his hat over the side of his face. "Dave," I said, "how'd you know where to find me?" I had my forty-four laying against my chest. I'd cocked it before lying down.

Without making a rustle, Mather spoke in a voice half-asleep. "An old boy named Zanone, back in Carthage, is real interested in having you killed. He paid me fifty dollars to track you down and do it for him."

Jack sat straight up on his blanket, his eyes wide in surprise. "It's the first I've heard of it," he said. "I swear."

I nodded at Jack, letting him know I believed him, but I had my eyes on Mather all the while. I readied my pistol for a quick move. I wanted to know as much about Zanone as I could find out before shooting Mather. "So Zanone knows where I am?"

"No," Mather replied, "I never went back and told him anything. I came out here looking for you a few weeks back. Didn't know if I was looking for Miller Crowe or Jesse James, but I searched you out just to see if I could."

"Now that you've found me?" I asked.

Mather's voice, muffled beneath his hat, sounded more and more sleepy as he spoke. "If I had wanted to kill you, I could have done it back in Springfield."

"Why didn't you?"

"Couple of reasons, I reckon. First of all I didn't think much of that man, being foolish enough to pay me in advance. Other thing was, I figured anybody with more than one name was more my kind of people than Zanone."

Mather lay as still as stone for a minute, and I didn't know if that was a good sign or not. Then he let out a long breath. "Besides," he said, his voice teetering on the verge of deep sleep, "by the time I found you, I'd already spent the money. It felt like I was working for free."

I thought about it a while. What Mather said made sense to me. Why would he want to throw down on me and take a chance on getting shot for money that was already gone? He had to know Jack would side with me. Strange as it might sound, I decided "Mysterious" Dave Mather was not then, nor ever would be, a threat to me. I felt we were both of the same cut.

"I'm going to sleep now, Dave," I said, letting him know I had settled it in my mind. I let the hammer down on my forty-four as easy as I could, still I heard it uncock and I knew they heard it, too.

"I'm glad to hear it," said Mather. A second later I heard the same sound from his blanket.

The next morning before breaking camp, we sat and drank coffee beside the fire. I was still curious about Zanone. I also wondered if anybody knew about the girl I'd killed. Sipping from the metal cup, I asked Mather, "Did Zanone say why he wanted me killed?" Wind stirred the low flames. Dust licked at our collars and hat brims. Jack had walked over to grain the horses.

"He says you and your brother Frank had him in an ambush downriver. I guess it made him look bad."

"Is that all?" I shook my head. Zanone was still convinced that I was Cousin Jesse.

Mather shrugged. "He thinks it was you who broke in on him and tried to kill him over near Carthage. Says it was too dark to be sure, but he thinks it anyway."

"Well," I lied, "he is damned mistaken. I ain't been near Carthage for the longest time. I lit out the day I got out of jail and came to Springfield."

Mather smiled. "I believe you, but Zanone thinks it was you. He thinks you killed a young woman there, woman by the name of Glenella Zanone."

I stiffened up at Mather's words. "Glenella Zanone?" I asked. "You mean . . . his wife?"

"No," Mather said, "it was his daughter."

I sat there nearly as stunned as I was the day I shot her. I could see that dead girl plain as day. "You mean Zanone was rutting with his own daughter?" No sooner than I said it, I realized I'd made a mistake. Mather grinned like a sly dog.

"I wouldn't know," he said, "I wasn't there."

Jack had untied the horses and thrown his saddle up on his gray gelding. My mare walked to where I sat beside Mather. I stood up, dusting off the seat of my trousers. "Mather, you have a way of getting on a man's nerves, you know that?"

Mather pitched the remainder of his coffee into the fire, got up, and kicked out the fire with his boot. "I mean no harm," he said. "You spoke too quick. Don't blame me for that."

I knew he was right. The information caught me off guard.

The Samuels had moved back to Kearney, over in Clay County. Jack's information had it that Jesse had been taken there by steamboat from Rulo after he'd been shot.

Outside a small supply depot Mather rode in for food while Jack and I stayed in the woods by a creek outside of town. As soon as Mather left, I turned to Jack. "Why the hell didn't you find out more about Mather before you came searching for me?"

Jack looked a little embarrassed. "I didn't know where you were. He said he knew you were in Springfield, so I just went with it. He never mentioned Zanone. You don't have nothing working between you now, do you?"

"That ain't the point, and you know it," I snapped. "You could've found out more about him."

"Look," Jack reasoned, "what if I had asked more questions? You think he would've told me anything he didn't want me to know."

"No, I reckon he wouldn't at that, but what do you know about him, anyway?"

"He says he's from Pennsylvania, but I don't know. I know he's damn good with a gun, and he's damn good with a deck of cards. I think he would steal a blind man's cane. Says he wants to be a lawman."

I squinted at Jack. "A lawman?"

Jack shrugged. "I'm just saying what he told me. You figure him out. He says a lawman can make more money than any thief in the world if he plays it right."

"He must be crazy," I said.

"I figure he might make a good lawman," Jack said. "He did pretty good, getting you to admit you broke in on Zanone."

"I didn't admit a damn thing," I said.

"You come mighty close." Jack laughed. "And you should have seen your face when he cornered you on it."

"Think it's true, that girl being Zanone's daughter?" Again I saw her face with blood running down it.

"What's the difference?" Jack shrugged. A silence passed between us as he stared off into the distance. "Zanone wants your hide," he concluded. "He won't stop till one of you kills the other."

14

Just outside of Kearney near the Samuel place, Dave Mather split off and headed north. It seemed "Mysterious" Dave did not greatly enjoy the company of others, at least not in large numbers. Most good lawmen are like that. They're fairly comfortable with groups of three or four, but with more folk than that they get a little tense. I reckon they like the size crowd they can hold rein on. I say this in no way as a criticism of that cut of person—it just happens to be something I've observed through the years. The better lawmen avoided crowds, and as lawmen go, Mather became one of the best, even if his reputation never equaled that of some others.

A half-mile from the Samuel place we met Payton Jones and Clell Miller. They appeared out of nowhere, and on seeing it was us, they commenced razzing and hooting us all the way there. It was like a welcome-home greeting we all did to each other. Though my jaw was sensitive ever since I got it broke, the first thing Clell Miller did when he rode up was to grab me around the head and mess my hat up. It hurt like hell, but what can you do? We were all like family back then.

After mouthing a few fake threats and insults, I asked Clell, "What's this about Jesse getting shot?" Clell's face turned serious.

"Yeah," he said, "he's been hit bad, but he's starting to come around. Frank and some of the boys are at the house. They'll be glad to see you."

I was surprised to hear that Frank was still alive. I had just figured that when Quantrill went down, Frank had gone down beside him. As it turned out, Frank and a few others took to the woods and slipped away clean, but Quantrill and two of his squad leaders got caught out in the open crossing a grain field. It was like the newspaper said. The two squad leaders fell dead on the spot. Quantrill lay wounded and paralyzed. According to Clell Miller, Frank snuck back that night to bust Quantrill loose, but Quantrill knew he was dying from a bullet in the spine and refused to go along with him.

The four of us raced the last quarter-mile. Jack Smith, not knowing this bunch as well as I did, made the mistake of showing off his gray gelding. I held my mare back just enough to show a respectable run, but not enough to draw interest in her. With this bunch, if you had a favorite riding animal, one of them would steal it sure as hell, just to piss you off. If you blew up over it, they enjoyed it that much more. Since I was partial to the mare, I thought it best not to let on. Jack would have to learn the hard way.

Riding into the Samuels' front yard was like riding into an army camp. Three tents stood in the yard and a tripod of rifles near the front porch. Either sitting or milling about the porch and yard was as unwholesome a bunch of swags as ever graced a wanted poster. They were killers and robbers to the man, but as I said, they were like family.

Among others from the old Quantrill bunch there were Clell's brother, Ed, my other cousins, Cole and Jim Younger, Wood and Clarence Hite, "Cock-eyed" Charlie Pitts, Olly Shepherd, Andy "The Snake" McGuire, and old "Bloody" Arch Clements. Seeing them all together let me know right off that something was brewing. I didn't care what it was; I was only there to see about Jesse.

Hearing us ride in fast, Frank and Ma Samuel came out of the house, and when Ma saw it was me, I barely made it out of my saddle before she ran from the porch and threw her arms around me. She was so glad to see me her voice cracked some when she spoke. "Now all my boys are home," she said.

Jack rode over to one of the tents and hefted up a jug of whiskey. With our arms around each other, Ma and I walked up on the porch where Frank stood nursing a fresh pipe. Frank nodded. "Cousin," he said. He looked me up and down the way you'd size a man up for a new suit. "How've you fared, since I saw you last?"

"Neither better nor worse," I said. "I heard about Jesse—how is he?" Frank nodded over his shoulder and I walked into the house.

Inside the kitchen I stopped like a man struck senseless. At the table kneading dough was the slap-down prettiest woman I ever saw in my life. When she looked up at me and pushed a lock of dark hair from her face, I stood dumbstruck. In the heat of the kitchen her gingham dress was unbuttoned at the throat and lay open just above her breasts. I gawked as she raised a delicate hand and righted her dress. She glanced at me, then away with a coy smile. I yanked my hat from my head and held it before me.

Another young woman spoke to me as she walked in from the bedroom carrying a serving tray, but I only heard her speak the way a man hears things after he's been hit on the head by an oak bucket. I could hear her, but not really hear her. "You must be Jeston Nash, Jesse's cousin," she said. I was staring back and forth between them, mostly at the one by the table.

"I'm Zerelda Mimms, Jesse's cousin from Kansas City. This is my friend, Jeanine Wilcox, of the Kansas City Wilcoxes."

The sight of that woman had me so rattled I must've forgot I was among family for a second because I introduced myself as Miller Crowe. "Oh," Zerelda said, "pardon me, but you look so much like Jesse, and I've heard he and his cousin Jeston Nash favor—"

"I am," I said, cutting her off. "That is . . . I'm Jeston Nash."

From the bedroom I heard Jesse's voice, weak and faltering. "He don't know who the hell he is. Come on in here, Dingus."

Both women looked surprised. Jeanine Wilcox giggled under her breath and turned her eyes from me as I walked to the bedroom still looking back over my shoulder.

It was plumb eerie seeing Jesse propped on pillows in that feather-bed. In the four months since I'd seen him, I had filled out a little from handling mule teams and eating regularly. He, having been shot and falling off some, especially around his face, put us at about the same size. Standing there looking at him was looking in a mirror. Except for the lump on my left jaw, you could hardly tell us apart.

I went right to his bedside and took hold of his extended hand. His hand was moist and cool, the way a man's hands get after a bad fever. His nightshirt was open at the chest, exposing a large healing scab. Pus seeped from the edge and trickled down his side. He saw me looking at the terrible wound and glanced down at it himself. "Almost three months, and it's just now starting to close up." He turned my hand loose and I took a chair near the bedside.

"I'd of been here sooner, Jesse, but I just heard about it last week."

He waved my words away with a thin hand. "Can you believe it," he said, "you go riding into Carthage armed to the teeth, 'fessing up to nothing, and get a set of walking papers. I ride in trying to give myself up under a white flag, and they near shot my heart out." He smiled and coughed. "You ought to think about being a preacher, Cousin."

"I'm giving it thought," I kidded. "How you holding up?"

"Much better now," he answered. "Now that I got that lovely woman here tending me."

At first my heart sank, thinking he meant Jeanine Wilcox, but when his cousin Zerelda came in carrying a poultice dressing, I saw how their eyes met. There would be many who'd say if it hadn't been for her, Jesse would've curled up and died that summer.

Watching how she handled Jesse as if he was a newborn calf made it clear that we'd be seeing a lot of Cousin Zerelda from then on. I sat there a while knowing they didn't even realize I was still in the room. Finally, after she'd finished applying the poultice and left, Jesse looked back at me like he was surprised I was there. "How is life treating you, 'Mister Crowe'?" Jesse smiled.

"Hard but fair," I said. "I've been teamstering, bucking freight out of Springfield the past few months. That's where Jack Smith found me and told me about you. I'm damned sorry to hear it."

"I heard you covered up for us at that Yankee trial."

I didn't even ask how he knew about it. I reckon the wind had ears in those days. "I did what I could," I said. "They didn't press too hard." I didn't want him to feel he owed me anything for keeping quiet. He would have done the same for me.

"Fact is," Jesse said, "they couldn't have done anything to us anyway. Me and Frank both got pardoned, but we're both obliged to you just the same."

I acknowledged his thanks with a nod. "What now for you?" I asked.

"Well, we're clean as snow. We can leave it like it is if we want to. Frank acts like he's interested in doing some serious farming, but who can tell. This damn bullet has taken a lot from me. I don't know yet if I owe them Yankees anything for it or not."

"Leave it lay," I said all of a sudden. I surprised myself saying that to Jesse. "I mean it, Jesse. I know you boys have a lot harder feelings about the war than I do, and I got no right to say it, but leave it lay, Jesse. Start all over from here."

Jesse studied my words for a second, as if actually considering them, then he smiled. "You are taking up preaching, ain't you?" I just shook my head and returned his smile.

He nodded toward the window. "Listen to that bunch out there. Without Quantrill or Anderson around, they're going to be pressing me to take over. They've been settled in here since they heard I was still alive."

"You don't have to take it up. You can tell them to go their own way."

"Listen to you. We're going to have to start calling you 'deacon' if you keep talking like that." He reached a hand under the mattress and drew out a blue medicine bottle. After struggling with the cork, he finally cussed and pitched it to me. "I ain't even got the strength to handle my own damn medicine."

"You'll get it back," I said, "it just takes time." I pulled the cork and handed him the bottle. He took a swig as if it were whiskey. "Damn, Jesse, that must be some good stuff. What is it?"

He smiled and relaxed back onto the pillow as if anticipating a long, lovely dream. "Blue River," he said with a smile, "finest stuff twixt heaven and hell."

◆✳ 15 ✳◆

Over the next few weeks as Jesse's health improved, I laid around the Samuel place sniffing out Jeanine Wilcox of "The Kansas City Wilcoxes" and managed to get close to her every chance I could. There was no question she was the most refined and elegant woman I'd ever seen. Her manners and bearing were pure polish and finishing school. I couldn't believe none of this bunch had made a move on her, but then I reckon they all saw that she was way over our heads.

Whatever made me think I could reach her has been a mystery to me my whole life. But despite her sophistication, her elegance and charm, I saw a fire in them emerald eyes of hers and sensed a hunger about her that begged—demanded—to be fed. Once I'd stripped off the poise and pretense and looked behind the veil of her proper breeding, I could see clear as a bell: Jeanine Wilcox was the kind of young woman who would hand-pat a rattlesnake.

One hot summer morning I had just flat-ironed my clean white shirt and was shoving it down into my open trousers when Jeanine walked through the tenant-house door. "Excuse me," she said with a gasp of surprise. She threw her fingers to her lips, but I noticed she didn't turn away.

"Good morning," I said, going about adjusting my clothes as if her presence made no difference to me. "Did you get a good night's sleep?" I finished buttoning my trousers and slipped my shoulders under my suspenders.

Seeing my lack of modesty toward her, she faced me with the firm expression of a woman not to be intimidated. I saw right then she was no wallflower. "No," she said, fixing her warm emeralds on me. "Indeed, I don't see how anyone sleeps in this infernal heat. How about you, Mister Crowe, how do you do it?" Her lips turned in an ever-so-slight suggestion.

"It's Jeston Nash," I corrected her. "I sleep just fine in this heat. There's a trick to it you know."

"Why no, *Jeston Nash*," she said playfully, "I'm sure I don't know."

I dipped my hands in the wash pan and combed my fingers back through my hair. "Simple," I said. "During the hottest part of the day you ride out across the flatland into the woods where there's no one around, and you lie in the sun."

"And that somehow keeps a person cool of a night?"

I shrugged. "Sure helps me."

"I really don't see how boiling in the hot sun . . ."

"You live in town, don't you? Kansas City?"

"Yes, on my family's estate."

"Well, it's different out here. Out here you do what you have to, to stay cool." I saw a flash of excitement as she watched me drop my pistol loop around my neck and slip the forty-four under my shirt. "Take off all your clothes," I said.

Her eyes widened in flushed surprise. "I beg your pardon!"

I stepped toward her buttoning my shirt. I smiled and deliberately ran my eyes up and down her. She stood firm.

"Out there," I nodded over my shoulder. "Out in the woods where no one's around. You take off all your clothes and bathe in the hot sun. Try it sometime." I stepped closer. This time she stepped back, but not far. "During the hottest part of the day you get plenty of heat on your bottom, and of a night the rest of you will cool right down." I saw a spark of interest glow deep in her eyes, and I knew . . . I knew.

Jeanine sensed the outlaw quality about me: It fired her juices to the boiling point, and I played to that tune like a fine-strung guitar. I told her stories about the war and my guerrilla adventures, and everything I told her was a damn lie. There was no way I could tell her real stories, like the one about Kenny Ellworth dying that night in the rain, or poor old Cletis Avery burning till he fell off the bone. She didn't want that anyway. She wanted adventure and excitement. I had it by the ton.

"Do you think I'm a wanton, shameless woman?" Jeanine's voice was playful.

We had spent the day making love on the banks of a spring-fed pond deep in the woods beneath a cliff overhang. Near evening I had dropped my mare's saddle and led her deep into the cool water to wash her before heading back to the farm. Jeanine walked into the pond naked and slid up on the mare. She stretched out along the mare's back and gazed up at the evening sky.

Still naked myself, I stood chest deep in the pond, washing the mare with my hands. "Will you take offense if I say you're wanton?"

Jeanine's long, dark hair lay glistening wet against the mare's mane. "I might take offense if you say I'm not," she answered, laughing.

"In that case, Jeanine Wilcox, you are a wanton shameless woman."

Jeanine closed her eyes and ran her hands slowly from her thighs up her wet body, pushing her breasts into high firm mounds. Even words could arouse her. She arched her back slightly then relaxed with a sigh as the mare's flesh quivered beneath her. "Oh God," she said, "you trained this horse to do that, didn't you?"

Watching Jeanine and hearing her voice turn breathless with passion, I felt myself warming all over. "No, I didn't," I said, "but it's worth an extra bag of grain if she'll do it for the next hour."

I slid up on top of Jeanine and felt her burning hot beneath me. The sun, the passion, Jeanine's wetness, and the heat from the mare melted around me like honey and pepper. "Do me hard and deep," she gasped. And I went up into her all at once, tight and aching, and felt her clamp around me and explode.

Just after dark we rode back into the front yard. I sat behind the saddle, bare-chested, and nearly asleep. Jeanine sat backwards in the saddle sleeping against me. Her dress was unbuttoned to her navel and her breasts, moist with perspiration, pressed against me.

On the ride back, as tired and drained as we were, we had tasted each other once more right there on horseback. Afterward, I reckon we just passed out from exhaustion, for neither of us had bothered to attend to ourselves. Jeanine's dress was up across her lap, her pale inner thighs pressed against the saddle, and I lay exposed at the waist.

Going into the barn, I saw "Quiet" Jack come trotting up within ten feet of us, and I waved him away. I didn't want him seeing Jeanine this way; me neither for that matter. Jack stopped and stared with his mouth hanging open. "Lord God," he said in a hushed voice. "You're gonna fuck each other to death!"

"Go away, Jack," I said quietly.

"It can happen, you know." He laughed under his breath as he walked away.

As I lowered Jeanine from the saddle into my arms, she stirred against me. "What can happen?" She whispered near my ear, a child's voice from within a dream. I held her against me, felt the warmth of her move through me once again—

"Mercy," I thought to myself, breathing in the scent of her hair. Jack's right. It could happen.

"Hmm?" She whispered.

"Nothing." I smiled. "Just a crazy thought."

But knowing that soon she would go back to "The Wilcoxes of Kansas City," I wanted all of Jeanine Wilcox I could get, and she felt the same toward me. Over the following weeks, it was all we could do to keep our hands to ourselves in public. I would wake up at night aching for her, and she for me. Many nights we didn't even bother going into the house. Instead, we lay naked in the hayloft till first light, then she would slip inside before anybody stirred. Still, everybody saw what was going on. There was too much heat not to notice.

One morning, Frank walked up beside me as I brushed my mare. I'd been expecting him to say something. I knew Jesse was too stuck on Cousin Zerelda to see anything between me and Jeanine. I also figured Ma Samuel had said something to Frank. I reckon she felt it wasn't right, Jeanine and I carrying on that way.

"If I'm out of line," said Frank, "I beg your pardon. But I'd like to know your intentions toward that young Wilcox woman."

I knew better than to come back real strong at Frank's words. Still, I soured a little and he must've sensed it. "I don't like asking you, Cousin," he said, "but I told Ma I would talk to you about it."

"Why's that?" My voice sounded a little testy. "We've kept out of sight. We've offended no one."

Frank shook his head. "That ain't the thing of it. Ma feels responsible for that young woman as long as she's staying here."

"You saying I'm taking advantage of Jeanine?" I knew I was getting riled at the wrong person, but I felt he was crowding me. Frank stared at me, and I could see he was wondering how to carry on the conversation without turning it into a fight. He put his hand on my shoulder. "Listen to me, Cousin, listen close. I don't want this to go the direction it's headed. We don't even know the Wilcoxes, and we don't owe them a damn thing. I don't give a damn what you and that young woman do. If you're having a good time, that tickles me to death. But Ma wants to know that you ain't taking advantage. Do you understand me?"

I cooled down and took a deep breath. In a way it was funny, I thought. Frank was asking if I was taking advantage of Jeanine when at that very second I was sore to the bone from her sitting atop me all night and riding me like a hundred-dollar stallion. "I understand, Frank. Believe me I'm not doing nothing Jeanine don't want done, and that's all I have to say about it."

Frank smiled and dropped his hand from my shoulder. "You know I don't like talking this kind of shit, don't you?"

I nodded and went back to brushing my mare. Frank started out the door, then turned and stopped. "You know, Cousin, it's one thing to take what's offered from a woman. It's another thing if you tell them you love them just to loosen their undergarments."

I glanced over my shoulder at Frank. He raised his hand and backed out the door with a devilish grin before I could say another word. It was just like Frank to say enough to get my wheels turning, then leave. That's probably all he had meant to do anyway, because I spent the rest of the day running his words through my mind.

That night after Jeanine and I spent ourselves in the hayloft, we lay naked on a blanket in the soft hay. Moonlight spilled through the loft door and washed Jeanine's body in a soft golden glow. Outside the loft door, a rope hung from a squeaking pulley, and swayed in the night breeze. Jeanine moved up atop me, raised my hands to her breasts and moved them down to her warm patch of fur. She swayed back and forth gently, brushing her warmth against me. "What's on your mind, Mister Crowe?" she teased.

I looked up at her sitting there on me and gently closed my hands against her moist thighs. She closed her eyes and pressed down against my hands. "Run it up me again," she whispered, and her voice caused my loins to stir. But I relaxed my hands and gazed out through the loft door.

"Jeanie," I said, "I have to ask you something, something serious."

She'd reached beneath her warm thighs and stroked my rising member. "You mean right now," she moaned, "right this minute?" I took her hands away and pressed them together at my chest. "Yes, right now." I let out a breath, resisting the urge to slip inside her. My thoughts had rattled around in my head all day, and now I was just a little irritated that she wasn't interested in hearing me. "I need to know something from you, and I want you to be honest about it."

Now she turned loose of my hands and sat up atop me. She pushed her hair back behind her shoulders and looked down at me in earnest. "Of course," she said. "What's wrong?"

I raised slightly up on my elbows and placed my hands on her legs straddling me. "Nothing's wrong. It's just that we've been doing a lot of this, and, well, I've been wondering." I picked a piece of blanket lint from her knee and studied it as I spoke. "Have I misled you or led you on in any way?"

"What?" Her voice had a trace of disbelief. "What do you mean?"

"I mean, well, I've never promised you anything."

"And neither have I," she said. Her voice turned crisp. "Now what is it you're trying to say?" She sprang up from me and stepped away toward her clothes. I sat up and reached for her arm but she pulled away.

"Look," I said, "I just didn't want you thinking the wrong thing, is all. I've never said I love you. I've made no promises."

"Well, so you haven't," she snapped. She snatched up her pantaloons. "Dear, dear," she said in a frilly voice, "I guess I'll just wilt up and die. Because some two-bit outlaw doesn't love poor little me."

"Goddamn Frank," I thought, this was all because of his bullshit. I jumped to my feet and grabbed Jeanine by the wrist.

"Take your hands off me, you bastard," she hissed. She jerked back and kicked at my exposed groin. I threw one leg in front of the other just in time to deflect her. It was close enough to make me turn her loose and instinctively drop my hands in front of myself.

"This ain't working out at all, Jeanine. I just wanted to be honest with you." I pointed my finger at her. "But don't you try that shit again."

Jeanine ran her hand through her hair and tossed the loose ringlets back over her shoulder. I'd never seen such fire in a woman. It surprised, angered, and excited me at the same time. Standing there naked as sin and barely missing a kick in the rack, I stared speechless for a second, then dropped my hand. "I have really read something wrong here," I said, "and I'm damned sorry for it."

Jeanine had dropped her pantaloons and now gazed down at them lying in the straw. She reached out her foot and kicked them away. She stepped toward me, her green eyes sparkled like flames in the moonlight. "Don't tell me you're sorry, you bastard. You haven't hurt me. All I wanted was to feel a man inside me," she said. "It could have been any one of you. You just happened to be the one wearing a clean shirt. If I was looking for love and flowers and courtship, I wouldn't have even slowed down on my way past you, Mister Miller Crowe."

I must've looked like somebody had slapped me with a razorstrap. She stepped forward and took me in her hand, stroking me, squeezing so tight I ached with pain and pleasure, and flexed myself against her grip. "This is all I want from you," her voice was cruel and seductive. Stepping against me, she pressed me between her burning thighs. "And this is all you want from me. Let's not pretend. I want all the war, the wildness, the killing, and the excitement that's beating in your blood. I want to squeeze it from you as badly as you want to spill it into me. So fill me with it." She pressed against me and bit into my lips till I tasted blood. "Outlaw," she gasped, "I want your love no more than I want a snakebite." She licked the trickle of blood from my mouth; smeared it across my chin. "You'll die tasting blood, we both know it." She dug her nails deep into my neck. Skin broke. I shoved her away.

She slammed against the loft post. I saw my blood on her cheek. Her words sent a dark chill up my spine, and in that second I saw everything she wanted from me, and everything I wanted from her.

My mind swirled in a picture of blood and gunfire, of raging bonfires and burning flesh. Passion boiled in my groin; I strained against it. I saw silver goblets raised by jeweled and manicured hands, fine tapestries, and polished balustrades. I heard the screams of dying horses and men. A sea of money and sparkling gold coins washed across marble fountains set in trimmed green lawns. A hemp rope jerked tight under a heavy weight and creaked back and forth. A glades knife slashed across that rope just as I felt my breath choke shut in my throat.

"You rich little slut, don't ever talk like that to me. You're a spoiled little bitch behind a mountain of money." I grabbed her as she lunged against me, clawing my chest, and we fell to the straw, fighting, clawing, and screaming like wildcats in heat.

When we had used each other up, when there was nothing left, we carried the blanket with us and rode naked on my mare out into the warm night wind. I felt like a man who'd been whipped with barbed wire.

Near dawn, as the wind cooled across the flatland, I drew Jeanine around from behind me and cradled her across my lap. I threw the blanket around us and we basked in the heat of our bodies and that of the mare's. We kissed deeply, carefully, our mouths and bodies tender and healing from last night's fury. That morning, while our passion simmered like spent candle wax, we watched a red sun creep up in the east, and a quietness of spirit surrounded us.

"Good thing we cleared the air, ain't it," I whispered. My voice sounded strange in the silence of morning. Jeanine snuggled against me. She bit me gently on the chest, and we gazed up at the sunrise till the mare finally turned on her own and walked back through the wild grass and broom sage.

✦✳ 16 ✳✦

It was late August when I had arrived at the Samuels' and Jesse didn't get to where he could get out and around until mid-November. As soon as he was able, he and the rest of us started spending nights in Liberty, a town less than fifteen miles from the farm.

I was so wrapped up in Jeanine, all I could think about was keeping us both naked and wet; but as Jesse and the rest of us begin making runs into Liberty, I began playing up to the local women who came around just for the excitement of our group. To tell the truth, I started fearing that Jeanine Wilcox was making me crazy. I'd gotten to where all I wanted was to feel her against me, and to ride naked with her. I even wondered if my mare might go swayback from packing us both around day and night. I tell you, if we weren't in love we were damned sure possessed by each other.

Though I hadn't actually lay with any of the girls in Liberty, I had played a lot of pinch and giggle. Somehow, though Jeanine and I clearly held no strings on each other, I began feeling guilty about spending so much time away.

One frosted November morning, after making love all night in the bough of an old willow tree, above a crackling camp fire, I turned to Jeanine and asked her flat out if it bothered her that I was spending so much time in town. "What you want to know is if I'm jealous of you sleeping with other women? Isn't that right?"

"No," I said, "because I ain't slept with nobody else since I met you. Hell, I wouldn't have the strength."

"Good." She smiled. She moved against me, fondling me. "Because if there's anything left of you, anything at all, you let me know. I want it all, right up till it's time to leave. Then you can take it to whoever you want. I'll be back in Kansas City being a proper lady."

I leaned back far enough to look at her face. Lord, she was the most beautiful woman on earth, then or since. Her green eyes haunted me night and day. Her hair, black as a desert night, spilled in long ringlets that glistened in the slightest light. August had warmed her to a dark, rich tan. Now, in the gentle sun of autumn, her skin turned a soft cream, and the sprinkling of freckles across her cheeks turned a whisper of brown. When the wind tossed her hair across her face and she smiled at me through that raven veil, I thought my heart would stop.

"You are the prettiest woman I've ever seen, Jeanine. When I'm not inside you, all I can think of is being inside you."

"Then get inside me," she whispered, using her hands on me like warm satin gloves. "And if you find something you like better in Liberty, it won't bother me a bit."

In mid-November I traveled to the Valley of the Ozarks to pick up a string of horses. Jesse and Frank had worked up a plan that involved fresh mounts, so I didn't even have to wonder what was going on, nor did I ask. For handling the horses I would make a hundred and fifty dollars, clean and simple. I was determined to go straight.

I'll never forget the week before Christmas, Jeanine met me in the Samuels' barn one night after telling me at supper that we needed to talk. From that time on I've never known it to be a good sign when a woman says "We need to talk."

Jesse, Frank, and the rest had rode into Liberty and left me to tend to the new horses. I had finished graining them when Jeanine came into the barn wrapped in a heavy wool coat. She held the coat collar tight at the throat. Her eyes looked worried.

Without working up to it in any way, she walked to where I was saddling my mare and looked me right in the eye. "I'm carrying your child," she said. Then as if I wouldn't understand it right away, she added, "I'm going to have your baby."

I turned from her and fooled with the cinch, avoiding her eyes as long as I could. I had no idea what to say, do, or think. I didn't love her nor did she love me. Leastwise, we'd never made mention of it after that strange night in the barn loft. I reckon we both knew our worlds were too far apart, and we hadn't dared get any closer than satisfying each other's physical needs. Now, it seemed our worlds would be drawn together whether we wanted it to happen or not.

Drawing the cinch tight, I realized what a mistake we had made, and I didn't know a damn thing to do about it. I felt low, dirty, and sick. She must've sensed it.

"I'm not asking you for anything," she said, "I just felt you should know." I still couldn't face her. I stared across the saddle into a dark stall.

"I'll be going home soon. If you want me to, I'll write and tell you about the baby."

"No," I said, without turning around. "I've shamed you, and I'm sorry, but let's leave it at that."

I felt her hand on my shoulder and I tensed up, then her hand went away and I heard her footsteps moving away across the straw-covered floor. "Jeanine, wait," I said, and I turned, taking her by the arm and turning her toward me. A tear trickled down her cheek. I started to reach out and wipe it away, but she pulled her face back.

She looked up at me with fear in her eyes, yet she managed a proud stand. "You haven't shamed me," she said. "I wanted you, and I've had you. It was my choice as well as yours. Do you think I'm some mindless creature with no will of my own?"

"No," I said, "I don't think that at all. But I don't know what's the right thing to do or say. This is not supposed to happen."

She offered a tired smile and pushed back a lock of hair. "I know." She sighed. "We should have known better." She closed her eyes. I saw her struggle against a flood of tears, and I pulled her to me. At first she tried to push away, then she swayed against me and came undone. "Jeston," she sobbed, "what will I do? My family will disown me. How will I take care of a baby?"

"We'll think of something," I said, soothing her. I stroked her long, dark hair and gazed up at the rafters. I had as much business being a father as a hog had stacking wood. Little babies were something I always saw stuck to other people's hips. I never pictured one stuck to mine.

"I'm sorry, Dingus," Clell Miller told me, "but it's a matter of arithmetic, pure and simple." I sat atop my bay mare and fanned through the ninety dollars in my hand.

Earlier that day, I'd talked to Clell and his brother Ed and mentioned that I'd taken a job with the Boughman Logging Company, starting the following Monday. "Good thing today is Friday," Clell had said. "We've got the weekend to try and teach you the logging business."

"I want this job, Clell," I'd said. "Jeanie and I are getting married... I know what I'm doing."

"The trick to the logging business," he said, ignoring me, "is to get them working for you, instead of you working for them." He motioned me toward him with his finger. "Come on with us, I want to show you something."

"No," I said, "I know what I'm doing."

"Aw—come on, Dingus. It's Friday, it's a pretty day... We'll pick up some of Dutch's homemade beer." I hesitated a second, leaning on my saddlehorn. "Come on," he said with a shrug. "Just look at something."

An hour later, Clell and I sat inside the woods line sipping beer and looking down at the logging company in the clearing below. Ed had ridden down, tied his horse to a hitch rail, and gone inside the office shack where I'd been looking for work the day before. "He ain't going to do something stupid, I hope."

"Naw," Clell said, throwing back a swig of beer and wiping his hand across his mouth, "you worry too much."

" 'Cause I really want this job."

"Relax."

"I mean, I've got responsibilities—"

"Here he comes now," Clell said, and we watched as Ed rode up at an easy gallop. "Look at him grin. Ed *knows* the logging trade."

"What went on, Ed?" I smiled at his funny expression. "What did you say, down there?"

He turned his wide silly grin toward Clell, let out a belch, then grinned at me. "I said..." He laughed and pointed his finger in my face. "Stick 'em up!"

I started to laugh, but my jaw dropped as I realized what he'd said. "Oh no, Ed, goddamn it... you didn't!"

"Yee-hiii," Clell yelled, snatching out his rifle as a man came running out of the shack with a rope dangling from his wrist. "Ed knows this logging business!"

"Goddamn it!" I yelled, swinging my mare so sharply that she reared up as she turned. Clell laughed and let go with a round toward the clearing. I saw dust explode at the man's feet.

"There they go," the man bellowed as another came stumbling out with a shotgun. We tore out through the woods, with me cussing, and Clell and Ed laughing like lunatics.

Back at the Samuel farm, I folded the money and stuffed it in my shirt. "See, it just don't add up the way you were going to go about it," Clell said.

"That wasn't a damn bit funny," I snapped. "I'm trying to go straight." But by then I was smiling about it. "I really did want that job."

"Shit," Ed said, "logging is hard dirty work. You're lucky we showed you the right end of it."

"Look at it this way," Clell said. "We paid for our beer and made ninety a piece. Logging pays at best, what . . . a dollar a day? You just logged five minutes and got paid three months in advance."

"Yeah," Ed went on, "you could log free for three months if you had to, and not feel bad about it."

Clell laughed. "You can buy Miss Jeanine a pretty dress, buy you a new gun, get drunk, and go rob some other business."

Ed: "Yeah, it ain't just logging. There's other businesses you can go into."

"Diversify!" Clell hooted and slapped his leg.

"Don't limit yourself." Ed doubled up, holding his stomach and slinging his head.

"You damned idiots," I said, turning up a swig of beer from a canteen.

"Make your money work for *you!*" Clell screamed.

Sitting in the parlor with Jeanine that evening, I took her hand and we gazed into the fire. One thing Clell had said made sense. I could buy Jeanine a pretty dress with the money I'd made today. How long would I have had to save up for it on logging wages? "I know you're used to a lot, Jeanie, and I just ain't got a lot," I said, feeling ashamed.

She leaned against my shoulder and sighed. "And all this time, I've been after you for your money."

"Don't kid around," I said. "I want to do what's right here, and there's an ocean of difference between your life and mine. I thought about it today when I was discussing some . . . business with Clell and Ed. I can't give you what I know you're used to, and it worries me, it shames me." I felt low, knowing that all I could do to make big money was steal it from others. Aside from fighting and killing, I was a dollar-a-day man, and I feared I would be all my life.

After our talk in the barn that day, Jeanine became steady, calm, and resolved. I reckon she just needed to get the crying behind her and get a grip on the situation. Now I was the one who went around spun tighter than new rope.

Jeanine relaxed against me. I drew my arm up around her shoulders, felt her hair against my cheek, and breathed in the scent of it. I was amazed at her strength and calmness through all this. "Who the hell ever called women the 'weaker sex'?" I smiled, leaning my face into her hair. "I'm coming apart in all this and you're getting stronger every day."

"I don't know who started it," she said with a quiet sigh, "but I promise you, it was a man."

Part III
Devil's Deal

◆✳ 17 ✳◆

February 14, 1866. For me, riding into Liberty that cold morning was a relief from all that had been pressing on my mind. Wondering and worrying about Jeanine and the baby had borne heavy on me lately. It felt good to be riding the way I did in the old guerrilla days. Now that Jeanine was back with her family, I had made up my mind to pull this one job. With the baby coming, I needed money. It was that simple.

Our wedding had been sad and secretive, not at all what a fine woman like Jeanine deserved. I had to threaten and bribe a drunken preacher into backdating a Bible register so it looked like we were married six months earlier. At first he refused—seems he'd been in jail on the date we requested. But after asking Jeanine to step outside, I cuffed him around a little and stuffed twenty extra dollars into his shirt pocket. That took care of the paperwork.

We rode straight from the preacher's shack into Kearney. I kissed Jeanine on the cheek and put her on a coach to Kansas City.

While we waited for the coach, Jeanine had reached up and placed her fingertips to my lips. "Jeston, I'm sorry if what I said yesterday hurt you. I just want to be honest about this."

I shrugged and felt embarrassed. The day before, I had gotten carried away and started seeing myself as a husband and a father. I had looked at Jeanine and seen how peaceful and loving she looked, and I reckon everything went to my head. "No, Jeanine, you didn't hurt my feelings," I told her. "I just said those things because I thought you might want to hear them, I mean, your condition and all."

"Good," she said with resolve. "I appreciate your concern." She let her hand fall from my cheek and rest on my chest. "Don't worry, I'll be fine, and so will the baby."

"I know you will. It was foolish of me saying the things I said."

"But it was sweet." She poked her finger against my stomach. "Just promise me you won't get yourself killed until after you come to Kansas City and make an appearance before my family."

I never liked joking that way, but I let it pass. "I promise to stay alive long enough to convince your family that we're a real man and wife. After that, I'll blow out of Kansas City like a bad wind."

Jeanine's smile faded. Her voice took on a worried tone. "Oh, Jeston, do you think this is going to work, I mean do you really?"

I swept my hat from my head and stepped around her as if posing for a photograph. I pointed at our reflection in a dusty store window. "Just look there, Jeanie. How could anybody not believe that to be the most perfect couple in the world?"

I didn't say it, but something inside me wished we could be like that couple standing arm in arm looking back at us from that dirty, cracked window. Jeanine in her fine traveling clothes, me in my white shirt holding my hat against my chest, we looked like the ideal young American family. Soon there would be a baby there to make the picture complete. "It's only our reflection," I reminded myself, "don't start thinking it could ever really happen."

"What are you thinking?"

"Nothing." I shrugged, reached around and patted my hat on her behind. "I'm going to miss you, baby." The coachman pitched Jeanine's bags up and opened the doors.

Jeanine stepped close to me as I kissed her cheek. Her hand brushed against me below my belt. "I miss you already," she said, with a teasing smile.

I remember thinking, "Damn, I wish there was more to it than that."

My part in robbing the bank had actually started back when I brought up the horses from the Ozarks. I figured if I was in for a penny I might as well be in for a pound. For the horses I would make a hundred and fifty dollars. For riding on the job, I could make ten times that much.

I had gone to Frank as soon as I found out what they were up to. "Frank," I said, "are you really planning to rob a bank?"

"That's right, Cousin." He laughed. "Ain't it the damndest thing." I had to laugh right along with him.

"Who in hell ever heard of such a thing?" I said.

He chuckled. "It's Jesse's idea. I told him that medicine he's taking must be choking off his brain."

I pushed back my hat. "Well, Frank, I reckon if it works, it works. What do you think about me coming in on it?"

"Aw, hell, Cousin, you don't want no part in this, do you?"

"Yeah, I do, Frank. Fact is, I need the money."

"I bet you do." Frank made a gesture like rocking a baby in his arms. He smiled when he saw me bristle up. "Don't get riled, Cousin, you know there ain't no secrets around here, not for long anyway."

"Frank, we're married, goddamn it, we're man and wife."

"Yeah, I know that, too. I ain't figured yet how you married her two months before you met her. But, by God, if anybody can do it, you can."

I laughed and shook my head. "Just tell me how, Frank, how the hell—"

"I heard it from a drunken preacher with a broken nose."

"I didn't break his nose. I just smacked him around some."

"Don't matter. He ain't gonna say nothing to nobody else."

"Why's that?"

" 'Cause," said Frank, "I told him if he ever opened his mouth about it again, I would hammer a spike into his forehead."

I set "Quiet" Jack up to meet us with the fresh animals ten miles out of town. We figured if we were pursued, we could spend out our mounts on a hard run and have the advantage of swapping them to Jack before we split up. As it turned out, we left the townsfolk of Liberty so stunned, we could've left on foot and had a good lead before they recovered enough to come after us.

At eight o'clock, as the town clock rang out across the square, we hooked our horses and rode straight down the main street shooting and yelling. We had counted on all the ruckus to chase people indoors and numb the town till we took care of business. It was a tactic that served us well during the war and it worked well that morning.

Six of us jolted to a stop outside the bank. Clell and Jim Younger held our horses near the door as Jesse, Frank, Cole, and myself sprang from our saddles and ran inside. The other four rode around yelling and shooting in the middle of the street.

Two cashiers, Greenup Bird and his son, William, had just unlocked the doors when we came spilling in with our guns pointed at them. In spite of the commotion outside, they were so stunned they almost smiled, as if to welcome us in for business. As soon as Jesse yelled for them to get their hands up, it dawned on them they were being robbed and both their faces turned chalk white. Since this was the first civilian bank robbery in the United States, I reckon nobody knew what to expect.

Cole stood on one side of the door and me on the other. I threw Frank an empty feed sack, and he and Jesse forced the two men behind the counter and into the vault. Jesse acted like he had been robbing banks all his life. Frank glanced around and smiled at me and Cole. "Ain't this the damndest," he said, as gold coins and paper money rattled down in the bag.

I heard Cole chuckle and say, "Damned if it ain't." It was as if none of us could believe it was happening.

In what seemed like seconds, we were out the door, up on our horses, and pounding out of town. I remember the look of surprise on everybody's face as we ran out with the bag of money. When I grabbed my reins from Clell and jumped up in the saddle, he had his pistol in the air ready for action. "Is that it?" he asked, dumbfounded. I didn't even answer. "Hadn't I ought to shoot at something?" He was truly stunned.

As I hooked my horse around joining the others, Clell sat there staring at the door like a cat watching a mouse hole. I heard Frank yell with a laugh, "Clell, you better come with us, ain't much going on here."

I have to say, given my state of mind at that time in life, I was prouder than a twenty-dollar rooster. I'd never seen anything go as smooth and easy in my life.

Then, just as I was feeling really good about it, near the edge of town, a young feller went running across the street and somebody behind me put four bullets in his back. Watching that young man fall to the cold ground made my heart sink down into my belly. I swear to God, I felt like stopping and running to him, but there wasn't a damn thing I could do. If I'd known right then who shot him, I believe I'd have killed that person. All I could do now was ride on. From a distance I looked back and saw a little nigra boy standing over the body in the street. The kid stared after us scratching his head.

All the way to our meeting with Jack Smith, I let the shooting fester in my mind. As soon as we dropped down and started swapping our saddles to the fresh horses, Jack sidled up to me. "How did it go?" he asked. Then, seeing I was good and riled up about something, he backed away and asked Jim Younger the same thing. I could feel hot blood pounding in my head as I yanked the cinch on my saddle. I jerked so hard, the horse jumped away, slammed against Cole Younger, and knocked him to the ground.

"Watch out!" Cole yelled. There was a laugh in his voice as he got up, and slapped dirt from his legs.

"Watch out your goddamned self," I bellowed, and in a split second the whole group froze at my words and fell silent as a tomb.

Cussing Cole Younger was as smart as French-kissing a rattlesnake, but I was out of control, just looking for somebody to throw down on. Cole's smile half-disappeared, then stopped. He shook his head a little like he didn't believe his ears. "What's that?" he asked.

I stepped away from the horses and faced Cole. I had my hand thrown out, ready to grab my pistol. "You heard me, goddamn it." I spun around facing the whole group, turning in a slow circle. I must've lost my mind. "Every goddamned one of you heard me."

"Easy, Dingus," I heard Frank caution.

"Take it easy your damned self," I yelled, "and don't call me Dingus, goddamn it! Not ever."

My breath was coming in angry gulps, steaming in the cold air and burning my lungs. "I want the brave son of a bitch who shot that boy to step forward and show me how he did it."

I'd gotten completely out of hand. Everybody, even Frank and "Quiet" Jack, fanned out with their hands near their guns. The whole bunch were my brothers-in-arms, but there wasn't a one there who wasn't ready to put the smoke to me. I had stepped in deep, maybe too deep to get out.

It was Jesse himself who saved me. He stood off to himself, saddled up, and ready to ride. Seeing what was about to happen, he dropped his reins and walked toward me real slow with his hands held before him waist high. "Stay back," I warned, yet he kept on coming slow and easy, till he got four feet from me.

I was cooling out a little, realizing how close I was to dancing with the angels, when Jesse stopped and let his hands down to his sides. Now Cole had circled around before me and I stared at him over

Jesse's shoulder. Jesse gestured with his hand and spoke to Cole without turning around. "Cole, you and Jim feel like helping Jack take them horses to the barn?"

"Not just yet," Cole said. "I want this settled."

Jesse let out a deep breath and shook his head. Speaking to me, real quiet, he said, "Of all people to throw down on, why did you pick him, huh?"

I started getting that sinking feeling you get when you know you've gone too far but can't get turned around. "That feller in Liberty didn't deserve to die. I want the son of a bitch who shot him."

Jesse looked real curious. "You blaming Cole?"

I felt myself waver a little. I was burning mad about the shooting and I didn't want to be talked out of it. "I'm blaming whoever shot him," I said.

"Step away, Jesse," I heard Cole say. Jesse held up a hand, quieting him down.

"You feel so strong about that boy getting shot, you're wanting to take a chance getting shot yourself just to make up for it? Is that it?"

The more Jesse spoke, the more foolish I felt. Still I couldn't turn it loose. "Listen to me," Jesse said, "we ain't riding guerrilla here. What we're doing is robbing. It's too bad about that boy getting shot, but that's part of it. This is the business we're in."

"Step away, Jesse," Cole said. His voice was more determined. Jesse didn't answer him, instead he stepped closer to me.

"I'm running this bunch, Cousin. If you got to blame somebody, looks like I'm the one killed that boy."

I shook my head. "I know you wouldn't do that."

"And you don't know Cole did it," Jesse said. "If you're just looking for a way to die, Cole's the best way to do it. If you're trying to make up for that shooting, there ain't a damn thing you can do to change it. The only thing you can change is from now on. The only way to do that is to ride away from here and not look back."

"I want this shit settled here and now," Cole demanded. "Now damn it, Jesse, step away!"

"You hear him," Jesse said, "I can either stop this thing or let it happen. Tell me what you want."

I took a deep breath and let it out slow. I knew I was wrong and I knew I was crazy for doing it. Yet somebody had to die for that boy in Liberty, either Cole Younger or myself. I didn't care which. I must have picked Cole because I knew he was the best gunman of the bunch. I was a damned fool. "Step away, Jesse," I said, real quiet-like.

Jesse stepped out from between us and I stared at Cole from twenty feet. We were too close for either of us to take a chance. Like as not, at this distance both of us were buzzard meat.

About that time I heard Clell Miller say, "Hold it, Cole, I'm the one shot that boy." He stepped over almost between me and Cole. I turned slightly toward him.

"No, you didn't," Jim Younger said, "I did." Then next to him Frank pulled back his duster and laid his hand on his pistol. "You're both lying," Frank said. "I did it."

Jesse drew his bottle of morphine from his coat pocket and took a drink. He looked back over my shoulder toward Jack Smith. I reckon Jesse saw I wanted out of this, but he knew I was too proud to turn it loose. He held the bottle up and gauged the remains before putting it away. He clamped his hand against his chest near the old wound. It bothered him all the time. "I really feel like shit, Cousin," he said, "and you're just too damned aggravating." He leaned, looking past me again. "Jack, since you're the only one who didn't shoot that feller, would you mind busting Cousin in the back of the head, so we can go on?"

I saw Frank and the rest of them smile. Clell Miller even laughed. Everybody sort of eased down at the humor of Jesse's words and I let out a breath, thankful that it was over. But then, no sooner had I relaxed my gun hand, the last I remember was hearing a loud *thwang.* And I'll be damned if Jack Smith hadn't snuck up and whacked me across the back of my neck with a goddamn rifle barrel.

When I first woke, the whole world was bloodred. After a few minutes I remembered everything that happened, and I looked across the camp fire at "Quiet" Jack Smith. The pain in my neck pounded as if my spine was being used for an anvil.

"Finally woke up, huh?" Jack asked. "I reckon you're wondering why I knocked the shit out of you?"

"Yeah, Jack," I said as quietly as possible. "I . . . really would like to know." I raised my hand to the back of my neck. Pain flashed.

"Well," he said, coming toward me with a plate of beans, "I figured Cole would've killed you even after everybody else settled down. See? Then I would've had to throw down on Cole, which I've been wanting to do anyway—we don't like each other." He smiled. "Then, that would've led to something else, and pretty soon we all would've been shooting each other."

"Jack, I don't know what to say." I tried to shake my head, but couldn't. Stiffness had set in.

"So, I think I did the right thing, don't you?"

"Jack," I said, slow and deliberate, "it was over. Jesse stopped it. He . . . didn't mean . . . for you, to actually knock my goddamned head off. It was . . . over!"

"Well, I say it's always best to play it safe in that kind of situation."

I just sat there and stared at Jack for the longest time.

◆✳ 18 ✳◆

I was lying to myself when I rode away from "Quiet" Jack outside of Clinton County. Heading up to Kansas City, I swore I would steer clear of my cousins and the rest of the bunch, yet I missed them before I was gone three days. When Jack and I split up, I remember him telling me to look for him around Abilene if I changed my mind.

I was three weeks getting to Kansas City because I kept coming up with things I had to do first. I had to play a little poker at Springfield, which was out of my way to begin with, and I had to make a couple horse auctions over in Otterville, out of my way but leaning closer. I knew I was just stalling about facing Jeanine's family. Even though it was only for a short time, just thinking about it tightened my collar down three sizes. Still, I promised Jeanie I'd square things for her, and I would do it if it choked me to death.

In Springfield I showed up at Hickok's table and produced a respectable roll of money. He welcomed me with as friendly a smile as I'd ever seen him muster, but I saw in his eyes he had a pretty good notion as to how I came up so flush all of a sudden. When he'd last seen me, I was teamstering for a dollar a day; now I was trading top riding stock and gambling with the high rollers.

On my second night in town, Hickok and I played poker with a couple of bankers from over in Kansas. The Liberty bank robbery was a running conversation all over town and when they brought it up, Hickok watched me out the corner of his eye. "Imagine the audacity of those scoundrels," one of the bankers said.

"If you ask me," the other offered, "it was a bunch of border trash. They'll have to be dealt with in the strongest manner. Who ever heard of robbing a bank? A bank, for God's sake!"

Hickok chuckled under his breath and dropped ten dollars in the pot. "Just think," he said, "they'll be off spending that bank money on whores and whiskey, right up till they hang." He watched me close and said, "To you, Mister Crowe, if you're staying in the game." Picking up ten dollars, I pitched it in the pot and took a sip of warm bourbon. I stared right back with a devilish grin. "Call," I said, knowing full well that Hickok was talking about a lot more than the card game.

Right then, being a young man with a roll of money, I hadn't a care in the world. I'd gone through a lot—the war, killing that poor girl and such, but trouble has a way of sliding off a young feller's back. My future, though it wasn't all that clear, was at least as bright as the next man's. I had a string of good horses—that meant a lot. Dealing horses was as close as I'd ever come to having a real dream in life, and now with a little luck, I realized it was starting to come true.

But I felt honored somehow, proud that Hickok cautioned me in his roundabout way. I hadn't met many legitimate people since taking up with "The boys," and I reckon it felt good thinking that somebody like Hickok might be a friend.

"You've learned to play a good game," he'd said after all the other players had left, and a pale streak of morning sun crawled beneath the swinging doors. "But you play a little dangerous."

"Dangerous?"

He tugged at his mustache as I poured us both a shot of whiskey. "When you know you've got a good shot at the pot, you jump—too quick, too reckless—without thinking it out." He offered a sly smile and threw back the drink. "It could get you in big trouble someday, if you don't smooth it out."

I shrugged, pretending to think he was talking only about poker. "You taught me to play."

"Not the kind of game you're playing."

I stared him in the eyes. "Maybe I'll smooth it out, once I get used to winning. It's been a rough haul; I'm still making up my losses."

I threw back the shot of whiskey and Hickok poured us another. "Making fast money is habit forming," he said. "It's important to know when to quit."

"What about you, Mister Hickok? You win a lot. How do you know when to quit?"

"I ain't in it for the money. Money is just the scorecard. I play for the sharp edge, the life that comes with it. Win or lose, the game reaches way past the table. . . ."

* * *

My part of the Liberty job came to eleven hundred dollars. It was as much as an average man made in three or four years. From dickering a few horses and playing some up-ended draw and five-card stud, I more than doubled my holdings that week in Springfield.

The morning I left, I stopped at the mercantile and bought a few things before heading out. I bought a used shoulder harness for my forty-four, the kind you could adjust way down to your waist. I took a double-holster belt and a pair of used Colts to go in them. A brand new brass-trimmed repeating rifle caught my eye. I took it, a new glades knife, and a used saddle scabbard, along with a linen riding duster, and a handful of cigars. For a man going out of the robbing business I was sure loading a lot of fresh hardware.

Outside at the hitch rail I loaded fifty pounds of feed on one of my horses and fitted my shooting gear to my bay mare. Hickok showed up as I adjusted my rifle scabbard and slung the holsters across my saddlehorn guerrilla style, butts forward for a riding draw. Glancing at my string of six riding horses and my new supply of shooting irons, he smiled and lowered his brow. "Looks like you've had a good visit here, Young Friend."

"That I have, Mister Hickok. I've fared well at my horse trading—not that I've found any bargains—horses costing what they do these days. But I did get a good string. Take a look at that gray gelding."

Hickok raised his hand. "Hold on," he said, "I ain't in the market for a horse."

I looked at him and smiled. I knew he was curious about what I'd been up to. I was just throwing him off, letting him know that horses would be the only thing we had to talk about. He saw exactly what I was doing and turned bold as brass. "Young Friend, I don't give a damn what your business is. For all I know you could've robbed the bank in Liberty." I saw his eyes checking my response. I tensed up. He couldn't tell it, but I was already judging the distance between my hand and the shoulder holster. "And it wouldn't matter to me if you did," he said, noticing my pistol butt just inside my new duster. "Just wanted to let you know, I'll be leaving here myself in a few days. I'm taking a sheriff job over in Hayes City." He rubbed his chin as if considering something. "You ain't headed that way are you?"

"No," I replied, "I'm heading to Louisville, Kentucky. I said it straight-faced, lying like a dog. He might've seen it or he might not.

It didn't matter to him. He was just telling me in his own way to stay out of Hayes City.

"Good town, Louisville," he said, nodding his head. "You'll like it there. Good horse trading, good poker . . . yes, you'll do well there."

I returned his nod, letting him know I'd gotten his message. Reaching my hand real slow inside my duster, I took out two cigars. I handed him one; he nodded thanks. I stuck the other in my mouth. Biting off the end, I blew it to the ground, and turned toward the hitch rail. Taking the lead rope to my string of horses, I swung up into my saddle and smiled down at Hickok. "If Louisville is that good a town, I reckon you'll never see me around Hayes City."

Hickok tipped the cigar against the brim of his hat as I turned and headed the mare up Main Street.

I thought of the day Hickok put a bullet in Dave Tut over a cheap pocketwatch; and I glanced back at him as I led my string of horses off the main street and through the alley out of town. He stood leaning against the hitch rail, smoking the cigar and tipping his hat to people along the street, like a ringmaster addressing an audience. "It's not the money that's important," he'd said the morning after the game with the bankers. "It's just knowing you're good at it. Like good shooting," he'd said with a strange gleam in his eyes. "Killing is just a way of keeping score."

◆✳ 19 ✳◆

I don't know what I was thinking riding up to the Wilcox mansion the way I did. I could've stopped and barbered down and cleaned up first. Instead, I rode into Kansas City through a hard two-day rain and didn't stop till I reached the Wilcoxes' front door. Hitching my muddy string of horses and my mare beside a fancy carriage, I went to the door smelling wet, dirty, and just a little like bourbon. It was wrong and I knew it. I reckon I was bent on making a bad impression.

Their nigra houseman let me in with a look of uncertainty that eased a little when Jeanine came down the stairs and threw her arms around me. I felt the tiny bulge of her stomach press against me and I pulled back, not to slight her, but out of fear I might hurt her or the baby or something. Hell, I didn't know.

She looked like I'd hurt her feelings, but before I could explain why I did it, her mother showed up. As bad as I looked and smelled, Jeanine stepped beside me and slipped her arm in mine. "Mother," she said, as proudly as she could under the circumstances, "meet my husband, Mister Miller Crowe."

There's no other way to say it. That hawk-nosed, high-bred old bitch declared war on me the minute we met. She smiled the friendliest smile you have ever seen, but there was the gleam of straight razors in her eyes that said, "How goddamn dare you do what you've done to my daughter?"

I breathed a little easier when Jeanine told me her father was out of town on business. He wouldn't be back for a week. I was picturing maybe he'd fall between cars and the train would run him over. Judging the hatred in my mother-in-law's eyes, I dreaded seeing what my father-in-law was going to think.

Over the next week I made myself familiar with the Wilcox stables and busied myself with my horses. Jethro, the nigra houseman, was a good old feller who would take a nip from a jug any time I offered it. And I offered it every chance I got, trying to find out what I could about the Wilcoxes, especially Mister Wilcox and whether or not he carried a gun.

You can find out a lot about a man by inspecting his horses and tack rigging. Mister Wilcox had put a lot of money into fine riding stock. Even the saddle horses and buggy animals—the ones for everyday travel—were of a quality fit for the royalty of Europe. This told me that Wilcox was a man of pride and distinction. Besides the saddle and buggy stock there were sixteen high-bred runners in his stable. Cronin Wilcox had a sporting side to him.

His saddles and bridles were plain and expensive. They were kept to a high shine and stored on clean maple racks all in a row. They told of a man who liked order and control, a man who liked to put his hand down on what he wanted, when he wanted it. On the grounds behind his stables he'd had a circle track built. According to Jethro a lot of money changed hands around that track. That got my interest up. That racetrack told me more about Wilcox than anything else.

One morning Jeanine and I went out to the stables right at daylight. We needed to get together and talk somewhere away from the poison-eyed mother-in-law. I also had a curious hankering to try my mare around the circle track.

Jeanie watched as I saddled my mare. I didn't really know what to say to my wife. Since the day I watched her leave Kearney I had tried to dispel any notion of us having a life together. The night before she left, she made it clear. All she wanted from me was a name for the baby and a pretense to justify it to her family. After that I could drift out of the picture, as far as she was concerned.

So, what was there to talk about? The night before she left, I told her I loved her. I told her I wanted us to build a life together. She drew back from my words the way a person draws back from a biting dog. And that was that. The next day I told her she hadn't hurt my feelings, and that was a lie. She'd hurt me more than I knew. It was like being stabbed by an ice pick: It didn't show on the outside, but inside, the wound was bad.

Jeanine stood there wrapped in a long wool coat, watching me adjust a track saddle to my bay mare. The big bay felt the difference in weight right off and blew her stomach out to keep me from cinching it snug. Instead of kneeing her in the belly the way you do most animals, I rubbed her and talked her down easy-like till she finally let me draw the cinch.

Jeanine laid her hand on my shoulder as I rubbed the strange bridle on the mare's muzzle to get her used to it. "You're really good with horses, you know that?" She said it like she'd never noticed it before. Funny thing was, I never even thought about it. I'd fooled with horses so long I guess it was second nature to me. Most anybody could handle horses, but in my case it went deeper than that. It was as if I shared some silent language with horses.

"Seems like I do better with horses than I do with people," I said, busying myself with the bridle, not facing Jeanine. Her hand dropped from my shoulder. I reckon she sensed a difference in me since that day in Kearney. I had swallowed her rejection the way a man swallows bitter medicine. Since that day the medicine had worked into my system. It cured my illusions.

The bay mare swung her head back and forth, rattling the strange bridle and adjusting to it. I rubbed her muzzle as she gnawed the new bit in her mouth. "No, I mean it," Jeanine said, "you're really good with horses."

I turned, facing her. "I heard you," I said. I wasn't cross or unpleasant. I reckon I just wasn't showing much feeling at all.

She started to touch my arm, but changed her mind. Huddling up in the wool coat, she folded her arms and looked out across the track. "I mean . . . as good as you are with horses, you could do something." She shrugged. "I don't know . . . maybe make a living at it some way."

"I do make a living at it," I said. Now I saw where she was headed and I was ready to cut her off.

"What I mean, Jess, is . . ."

"It's Miller," I said, "remember? I'm Miller Crowe."

"See, see what I mean? Your name is Jess, you go by Miller Crowe, most of your friends call you Dingus."

"Not anymore they don't." I was thinking about the day at the barn outside of Roscoe.

"But you don't have to live that way, is what I'm saying. You're a good man; I see it in you. You're better than that bunch of border trash. You could do something with yourself."

She meant well; I knew she meant well, yet I took offense. "That border trash was good enough for you when you came looking for sport. Now all of a sudden you're better than everybody. Don't forget, we didn't come here and drag you down to Clay County. And as I recall, you kinda fancied the idea of me having a whole string of names. I think it warmed your blood up."

"Jess," she pleaded, "this is not the way I meant it. I'm carrying our baby. I'm scared, scared for us and for you. Don't you understand. I need you with me now. I need you close."

I was leading the mare out of the barn. When Jeanine said those last words, I turned and faced her. Sometimes a man expresses his cruelty by showing no expression at all. My words were smooth and level, but carried the sting of a snake whip. "You made it clear before you left . . . you didn't need me. Remember that night? The night I was talking foolish, the night I said I loved you. That's the night you told me all you needed was a warm body to show up here and play this out for you. I reckon that night I learned where I stood with you. I'm kinda like a handyman. I'm here to clean things up, whitewash the story."

"Please, Jess," she cried softly. "Don't do this. I'm sorry for that night."

"Don't worry," I went on. My voice was still calm, still even, and still drawing blood. "I'm here just like I promised. I'll play this out for you straight up. I'll play it so smooth, you'll have no problem marketing your goods to some respectable young feller after I leave."

I was spun up tight and bitter when I got into the saddle. The mare sensed it through the reins and jolted forward in the direction of the track. Inside the gate she stopped at the red-and-white starting pole. Glancing around, I saw Jeanine standing there watching and I couldn't face her. I was mad at myself for saying what I said, and for some reason madder at her because it seemed like she made me say it.

Hooking the mare once easy with my boot heels, we shot out like a bullet. The big bay took to the track like she'd been a circle runner all her life. We were halfway around the quarter-mile track before I realized how fast she was running. She didn't waver an inch to one side or the other, and I felt her belly down, coming out of the short turn. Then she stretched out without me asking and it felt like we'd hooked onto a comet.

Running on that raked and tended track was like sliding down a ribbon of silk. That mare laid out a stride longer than two hay wagons end to end. I had run her flat out before, but always through dips, valleys, and plug washes, never like this. Knowing she had her footing on a flat, sure surface, she tore the earth apart. I just drew up in the saddle and leaned forward close to her neck, her mane whipping my face like a handful of mad hornets.

Passing the striped pole into the second lap, it came to me that this mare had run a circle track before, somewhere. I'd taken her from a dead Yankee officer because she wore no brand or markings. She must've come from his private stable.

I gave her rein in the second lap and saw we had not wavered more than inches from the hoof prints she made in the first. The wake of dust from the first lap still clouded the track as the mare bore down harder. I squinted against the stinging particles.

She shot through the second lap, then the third. At the end of the third lap I was nearly blind from the lashing of her mane and the fine burning powder. I pulled her up going into the fourth—this big bitch would run straight off the face of the earth if I let her.

I tried reining her toward the gate at a brisk clip, but she fought me like a wildcat. She snorted and bucked sideways back toward the track, still wanting to run.

I sat back hard against the reins, and she reared up thrashing her head wildly. She came down slinging her head, nipping at my boot, and cantering sideways into the track. "To hell with this," I said to myself. I gave her rein and hooked her a quick tap. She tore the track apart on the fourth lap. This mare was a flat-out "mile-runner," born and bred.

Back at the pole the big bay let down on her own. She made another full lap cooling down, and then, as if following instructions, she trotted right through the track gate into the holding yard. For the past year and a half this horse had outrun anything that got near her. That's what had kept her alive—me too for that matter.

All the times I'd run her in and out of fires and gun battles, through Ozark swamp, and up and down rock faces, it'd never dawned on me what I had. For all the horse dealing I'd done, somehow it had slipped past me. All that time without knowing it, I had me a goddamn Thoroughbred.

"Lord God, Almighty!" I cried out. I dropped from the saddle and ran to Jeanine, leading the mare behind me and wiping dirt from my face. "Have you ever seen such a run?" In my excitement, I'd forgotten the cruel words I had let spill out on her.

"Never in my life," she answered. I saw her smiling and I saw tears in her eyes. Her cheeks were blush red from standing there crying, watching me run the mare. I looked at her and my heart came unwound.

This wasn't the proud and willful Jeanine Wilcox I'd known back in Kearney. This wasn't the fiery wanton mistress who had filled my nights with sweet, aching lust. Naw, sir, this was just a young woman in trouble, trouble that bore my name. Her guard was down now, and she was scared and hurting. It didn't matter what she had said back in Kearney. It was all pride and pretense. Now she needed me, and she'd been honest enough to tell me so. And what had I done? I'll be damned; I'd made her hurt worse.

My eyes were already watery from the dust of the track. At least that's what I told myself. I pulled Jeanine to me and just stood there holding her. "I'm so afraid," she said, and she wept like a child. I stroked her hair and held her against my chest. I was careful she didn't see my face. I wanted to tell her that I felt the same way. I was scared and confused and hurting right along with her. I wanted to tell her, but damn it, I dared not say a word right then for fear my voice would betray me. I bit my lip and stared out across the endless green lawn.

After a while we walked to the barn with our arms around each other. Jeanine stayed close as I brushed down the bay mare. Closing the stall, we walked the grounds in the cool morning air as sunlight broke through the treetops. There was so much we didn't know about each other, so much we needed to talk about, and so much more we needed to understand.

It would be spring soon and I wanted to square things between Jeanine and her family before the baby came. Our plan was for me to stay long enough to make our marriage look respectable. I would stay gone—supposedly on business—and in a year or so, I would disappear altogether. I reckon it wasn't the best plan in the world, but it would have to do.

I knew I wouldn't be here through the summer. As much as I wanted to be around when the baby was born, I needed to be out doing something to make a living. Even though we would never be a real family, pride wouldn't let me take from the Wilcoxes. The baby would bear my name—even if it wasn't my real name—and for as long as I could, I'd see to it my child had plenty, no matter what I had to do to get it.

We walked the paths through the narrow strip of woods near the rear of the grounds. With my arm around her shoulder, I studied her features as she looked ahead and spoke. My wife was a beautiful woman; there was no denying it. She had the proud, delicate features of a young lady accustomed to the best in life.

A cool breeze lifted her dark hair and pitched a strand across her face. She raised a hand and brushed it back. Her face was pinched blush red from the chill in the air and her green eyes looked strained from crying. "I must look terrible," she said, smiling up at me. "I don't usually act the way I did back there. Can I blame it on my condition?"

"Jeanie," I said, drawing her closer as we walked along, "I swear to God I'm sorry for what I said back there. I'll never talk to you that way again. Whatever it takes to keep from shaming you and the baby any more than I already have, I promise you I'll do it, and you'll never hear me say a cross word."

"You didn't shame me, Jess," she said quietly. "What you said back there was more true than I want to admit. I was reckless last summer, same as you. I've never known people like you and your cousins. I've led a sheltered life here under my father's rule. It was my first time on my own and it got out of hand."

She stopped on the trail and turned to face me. "I know we only married to give the baby a name and we don't know a lot about each other, but I've thought of you often since I came home. I want to know you, Jess, I want to be your wife, I mean really be your wife. Maybe having your baby inside me is causing me to feel the way I do."

She hesitated a second. "I love you, Jess. I didn't know it back at the Samuels', but now I'm certain of it. I love you and I want you to be my husband."

I stared down at the ground, hoping my words came out the way I meant them. "Jeanie, let's not push things. I don't want to say something just because you want to hear it. We both know what was said before you left Kearney. Maybe our worlds are too far apart. Maybe what you said was right. I didn't want to think it then, but I've come to accept it. I don't want to open an old wound. Let's go with what we've got for now."

I don't know how she took my words because she didn't say anything else that morning. If I could compare our life together to a card game the way Hickok would, it would be like five-card stud. We never had a chance to look at all our cards at once and see what we had. It seemed like life just turned over one card at a time, and we were always waiting to see what came next. I reckon we didn't trust ourselves enough to just play our hand.

✦❋ 20 ❋✦

I took my string of horses into town the next morning and sold four of them for cash money. I traded the other two against a Morgan stud, and picked up a fancy saddle to boot. All day I kept thinking about my bay mare. For all my keen appraisal of quality horseflesh, I couldn't believe I'd missed seeing it all them months. I reckon it just never entered my mind that anybody would have brought such an animal into battle, knowing what she was.

I made up my mind that I would board the mare out somewhere and raise a couple colts from her as soon as I found a good riding animal. Trouble was, how would I ever replace her?

Seeing her here in these fine surroundings was like looking at a different horse altogether. She looked and acted right at home on that smooth circle track. Curried and kept, except for the brush-cuts along her legs and a graze across her rump, she looked as good as anything in the Wilcox stable. I'd only seen her run roughshod and wild the way I'd turned her. Over the past year and a half I'd dragged that animal through pure hell. She bore the scars and the hardship of war right along with me, but she'd never faltered. Now that I saw what she really was, I felt a little strange. It was like I started thinking my own horse was too good for me.

From the auction circle I drifted over to Number Three Missouri Avenue and played the tables till noon. When I saw I'd lost fifty dollars before ever claiming a pot, I cashed in and drifted next door to Landry's Lucky Lady Saloon. There I ran into "Mysterious" Dave Mather, who I hadn't seen since we split off near the Samuel place last fall.

Dave was wearing a constable's badge pinned to the lapel of a well-cut black suit. He packed a brace of thirty-eights in brand-new shoulder holsters. Not knowing what name I was going under, he just tipped his fingertips to his hat brim when I walked up to him at the bar. "If it ain't Dave Mather, my name ain't Miller Crowe," I said, letting him know. Mather smiled from behind drooping eyelids.

"Mister Crowe, how have you been since I seen you?"

"No better, no worse," I replied. "See you got yourself a badge and a new set of iron. Law work must agree with you."

Mather ran his thumb down the lapel of his new suit and smiled. Waving down the bartender, he ordered me a shot glass and poured me a cut from his bottle of rye whiskey. "How'd your cousin ever come out from that chest wound?"

"Real poorly," I lied. Sometimes I wonder how anybody ever knew the truth about anything back then. "Last I heard, they took him back up to Nebraska. I reckon he's died since then."

Mather nodded, not believing a damn word. "Hear about that bank robbery back in Liberty?"

"I heard some talk," I said. "I figured them boys have been caught and hung by now."

"Not yet," Mather said, looking at me straight-faced. "If I was them boys I would sure walk real quiet a while. I hear they killed a college boy, and the sheriff in Liberty has a list of witnesses.

"That a fact?" I threw back a shot of rye and poured another.

"None of them even covered their faces," Mather told me. "Imagine that." His dark eyes honed in on me. "Know what I think?"

"What's that?"

"I think they wanted to be identified. I figure they're going on a bank-busting spree and they killed that boy just to let people know they mean business. I think we'll be hearing a lot more from that bunch."

I hoped Dave hadn't caught the look that must've come across my face. I honestly had not thought of it that way. It made sense. I had mentioned something about wearing masks on the Liberty job, so had Clell Miller. Even "Quiet" Jack Smith had been curious as to why we didn't plan on covering our faces that day. Jesse, Frank, and Cole had planned the job and the rest of us did what we were told. If what Dave said was right, and I believed it was, Jesse wasn't lying when he told me he was responsible for killing that boy. Hell, he might've pulled the trigger himself. Thinking it turned my stomach.

"Is that what the law is thinking?"

Mather shrugged. "I don't know," he said. "That's just my opinion.

But if I'm thinking it, somebody else is probably thinking it, too. The point is, if I was riding with that bunch, I'd make damn sure I knew what I was getting into, 'cause it ain't no temporary thing to whoever is running the gang. He means to make it a career."

Mather was giving me a lot to think about and I believe he knew it. I studied his face wondering just how much more I could find out from him, not just today and not just about the Liberty job. A lawman was a good person to know when it came to getting inside information. I wanted to know just how far I could go with Mather. How far was he willing to step over the line. "What's the law doing about that bunch?"

"Right now, they don't know much to do. They're kinda waiting to see what happens next. Bank robbing is something new. The locals are getting what they can from witnesses, but as far as tracking them down, they gave up after six hours."

"That's interesting," I said. "I believe you're right. Anybody riding with that bunch better keep an ear to the ground."

Mather nodded and leaned in close. "I heard the greenbacks and silver that was taken was old enough they can't be traced. But the gold coins were fresh from the mint and they'll be spotted easy. Now I know a feller down in Texas who buys hot money. He's willing to sit on it a while and run it out a little at a time. I figure that Liberty money is already spoken for. But if I'm right about that bunch hitting more banks, and I knew somebody could get word to them, that man and I would both make some money."

There it was, Mather wanted a part of anything he could get his hands on. From now on anything I needed to know, I'd come to him. I tipped my shot glass toward Mather and tossed down the rye.

"I might know somebody like that," I said.

Mather smiled as I set the empty glass on the bar and turned to leave. "Tell your cousin I hope he gets feeling better real soon."

That afternoon I had coffee at the Star West Hotel on Main Street before heading back to the Wilcox mansion.

I tell you it was like taking a beating every time I walked through that door. Sometime tomorrow evening Jeanine's father would be coming home and that just made me feel worse.

To get a feel for the black Morgan stud, I rode him home leading my bay mare. He was a finely built animal, but headstrong even for a Morgan. Whoever had owned him broke him wrong and let him stray from the reins. Before I got him home, I thought we'd wind up in a fistfight. Finally, I got off and tied a bandanna around his eyes. Lots of times riding an animal blindfolded a few miles will make them tend more to the reins once you take the blinder off. This plug just got worse. I'd been taken on the swap. It would be days of wrestling this big bastard before I could ever make a riding horse of him.

By the time I reached the Wilcox mansion and quartered my horses it was dark and well past dinner time. That suited me fine. I didn't like dressing for dinner and I particularly didn't like sitting at the same table with Jeanine's mother. She must've made up a list of questions she knew a man like me didn't want to answer. She made it a point to ask them every chance she could. Jeanine stayed nervous at those times, but she stuck right along with any story I told. There was a lot to admire in Jeanine Wilcox, more than I even realized.

Old Jethro let me in through the back door and I handed him a half-full bottle of Eagle-Spray rye whiskey. Glancing around, he thanked me and pulled the cork. After he had his drink I nodded behind him toward the dark house. "Is everybody turned in for the night?"

"Miz Wilcox is done gone to bed, but Miz Jeanine is in the sewing room. Want me to fetch you some coffee up there with her?"

I thought about it a second. "Please do, Jethro," I said. "That would be fine."

His face lit up in a wide grin. "I knows you young folks needs some time to ya'selves. I'll fetch up coffee right away." He corked the bottle and turned to stoke up the wood stove. "Ain't my place to say so, Massa Crowe, but Miz Jeanine seem so sad. I hates seeing her so sad."

I went quietly upstairs and to the sewing room at the end of the hall. Stepping silently through the door, I saw Jeanine stitching a border on a small wool blanket. She looked so peaceful and serious there in the glow of the fireplace. She was nothing at all like the fiery young woman I'd known and run wild with at the Samuel place. When she looked up and saw me she seemed a little embarrassed. "How long have you been standing there?"

"Oh, about an hour," I kidded. I think she was getting self-conscious about her stomach starting to round out, yet you really couldn't tell she was pregnant if you didn't already know.

"I know better than that." She smiled, then said, "I heard you through the window when you rode into the stables less than twenty minutes ago."

"You got me there," I said.

I seated myself close to her on a wooden chair and propped a foot on an ottoman. Jethro came in grinning, and served coffee. I pulled out of my dirty boots and pitched them beside the chair. After Jethro left, Jeanine pulled her chair beside mine and held out the half-finished crib blanket. "See," she said, "it's the first one I ever made. Not bad, don't you think?"

"It's pretty, Jeanie, real pretty." I took an edge and examined the fine stitching in the dim firelight. I don't know why, but being around her here, in her world, made me anxious and restless. Maybe this place reminded me what a mistake we'd made. I had stepped way out of line by taking up with Jeanine; these surroundings showed me just how far.

I sat my coffee cup on the chair arm, got up, and walked to the fireplace. Whoever invented fireplaces must've done it so people would have something to stare into when they didn't know what to say. I took the warm poker and stirred around in the ashes. Tiny sparks swirled and drifted up the chimney. For a few seconds I pictured old Cletis Avery hanging upside down over that raging fire back in Cass County. A haunting feeling stirred in me. Anytime I let myself watch sparks swirl in a fire, I could see Cletis dying again . . . still smell him burning. Beyond Cletis and the raging fire, I heard the rifles and the screams of tortured men and wounded horses dying.

I heard Jeanine's voice soft and easy behind me. "What's wrong, Jess?" I shrugged and shook my head, still staring into the fire.

"Did I do something . . . say something?" her voice sounded shaky.

"No, Jeanie," I said, turning to her. "No, baby, you didn't do or say anything." I kneeled beside her taking her hands in mine. "I was just thinking about some things past." In the firelight, her eyes glowed warm and peaceful, and for a second I felt like I could finally give up something inside me, something that needed to be let go.

Suddenly I felt tired plumb to my bones, and I laid my head in her lap and smelled the warmth of her. I felt her hands brush my face. A terrible burden seemed to leave my chest, silencing the rifles and the screams, and softening the smell of burnt flesh. As my eyes closed, fear started to recapture me, but as I tensed up, Jeanine pressed her hand to my face real gentle, stroking and soothing. I drifted. I sensed our tiny baby so close to my face, yet in a place of peace, of silence, away from the struggle, the fear, the pain and the killing. Jeanine lay the soft new crib blanket across my shoulder and brushed my hair back from my face, and I lay there for the longest time.

Later, in my room, I trimmed the lamp low and lay there watching the dim glow flicker on the ceiling. Lying there under the blanket, with one hand under my head and the other on my chest holding the forty-four, I heard the slightest rustle at my door. I closed my eyes feigning sleep and watched through my eyelashes. I was ready to throw iron when I saw Jeanie slip inside the door and ease it shut behind her. I relaxed, letting my hand move away from the gun. "Damn it, baby," I swore, "don't you know how dangerous that is?" She didn't say a word.

She came to the side of my bed and pulled the sash on her cotton gown, letting it fall to the floor. Reaching out my hand I touched it gentle against her stomach, and she seemed to shiver. "You haven't touched me like this since you've been here," she said.

I watched the glow of the lamp flicker on her breasts, "I didn't know if it was the right thing to do—I mean, your condition and all."

She bent down pressing her fingers to my lips, hushing me. Her hair fell against my face. "It's the right thing to do," she whispered. She slipped under the covers beside me. "You won't need this," she said, pushing the gun away.

All the wild lust, all the breathless passionate sex we'd shared at the Samuel place, was nothing, nothing like the peace and the pure spiritual pleasure I felt that night in my Jeanie's arms. Making love in that soft feather bed, with her having that tiny baby growing inside her, was like nothing I'd known in my life.

Back at the Samuels', we were wanton and reckless. We'd burned for one another. Last night was a whole different thing. It was tender and gentle, and the only word to describe it was "sacred." It was as if our spirits joined somewhere high above the struggle and toil of flesh and blood—Jeanie's, that tiny baby's, and mine. Our spirits soared together as one, somewhere far away from ourselves, in some holy place. It was a place I'd always sensed but never seen, and it stirred something deep inside me.

And yet, even as I felt myself giving way to a longing for that peaceful place, I felt a reluctance, a caution, as if I dare not dream of a wife, a child, and a home, for to do so would only bring sorrow, for them . . . and myself. "What are you thinking?" Jeanine had whispered near my ear. But I didn't answer. Instead, I pressed my face to her breasts and felt her heart beat until sleep overcame me.

◆✳ 21 ✳◆

When I got to the Wilcox stables the next morning, I felt better than I'd felt since before the war. I was carrying around more of the war, the killing and running, than I realized. That night, with my head in my wife's lap, I reckon I let some of it go. Funny how you think something's a long way off in the past, then suddenly it jumps right out at you. Of course I didn't realize back then what was bothering me; it takes a man years sometimes to figure out what he's running from. I was just gut-restless and worn-out tired from always keeping my guard up. Jeanie was the only person in the world who'd ever stepped inside.

Like a lot of rich men, Jeanine's father had names for all his horses. I found out from Jethro that a gelding called Star Of Dawn was the fastest horse on the place. I went straight to that horse's stall and led him to the tack room. After I had fitted the saddle and bridle, I rubbed his muzzle a long time and stroked his mane to get him used to me. When I felt like we were ready, I led him out past the stable, mounted, and headed for the track.

After making three hard laps on Star Of Dawn, I trotted him a full lap to cool down and took him back to the stable. There was no question he was one of the fastest horses I'd ever ridden. I tried to compare him to the ride yesterday on my bay mare and it was so close I couldn't judge the difference. If there was any distinction between the two, in strength and speed, it wouldn't show till they split earth side by side. I knew when it came down to it, when neither of them had anything left, I could call on my mare and she'd find something. She would find something if it busted her guts.

It didn't matter that Star Of Dawn was bigger or better trained. It didn't matter that he'd lived on fine grain while my mare had scrounged the range like a common mustang. My mare had the breeding, I saw it now. But it was more than that. Star Of Dawn hadn't been where my mare had been. He'd never run for his life. My mare had learned to run for nothing else. When I hooked my mare she knew what it meant. She'd seen too many fall around her. It wasn't a sporting event and an extra bag of feed for her. She'd felt the devil's breath whistle past her.

Back at the house, Jeanine was up and around, pulling open the curtains and straightening the bed. I stepped right over and caught her by the arm as she reached to fluff up the mattress. "Here," I said, "you shouldn't be doing that." She smiled and tried to pull away. "I mean it," I insisted, "you need to take it easy." I turned her around holding her hands. "You don't have to do a thing around here, so relax. You'll be plenty busy around July when that little feller gets here kicking and cussing."

"What makes you so sure it's going to be a little 'feller'? Little girls get here the same way you know."

I hugged her close to me. "I don't care which it is," I said, "so long as it's all right and looks like its mama."

Jeanine stood there against me real quiet for a few seconds, then she whispered, "Thank you, Jess."

"Thank me for what?" I asked, holding her out where I could look in her eyes. In the early sun her green eyes were the color of a calm sea.

"For coming here," she said. "I wasn't sure you would. I'm glad you did."

"I'd say there were some who would've bet against it"—I laughed—"but I wouldn't miss meeting your folks for the world."

Laying her head against my chest, I felt her chuckle and shake her head. "We sure got ourselves into something, didn't we?"

"Nothing we can't straighten out," I said.

"In a hundred years?"

"Yeah," I said, hugging her close, "about that long."

We must've made a strange-looking pair, me and old Cronin Wilcox. I had just got back from town that evening sporting a scent of rye whiskey and horse musk. It had rained all day around the auction barns. I was soaked across the shoulders of my duster, and the brim of my wet hat sagged down to eyebrow level. I looked like what I was, I reckon, so did Cronin Wilcox.

He was a big suit-full of man, rough cut, but cleaner than a prize bull. I sized him up as a man accustomed to good food, good living, and good whiskey. If his shoulders didn't get that broad from building his fortune, they surely got that way from packing it around. Thrown on the same griddle, the two of us looked like a thin slice of beef jerky beside a full round of prime rib.

When he first got up from behind his desk and came around toward me, I remember thinking that his nose was near as wide as my fist. The first thing I felt like saying when he stopped before me was "Damn, you're a big, ugly son of a bitch." Of course I didn't.

Instead, I stood looking up from under my hat brim while he looked down at me like something he scraped from under his thumbnail.

Remembering my manners, I took off my hat and stuck it under my arm, then reached out my hand toward his. "I'm Mister Miller Crowe," I said. He ignored my hand, turned, walked to his bar, and poured himself a drink. I let my hand fall to my side and wiped it on my duster as he stepped back behind his big oak desk. "I know who you are, and what you are, and I don't like neither."

"Well now," I said flatly. I stared off at the ceiling just nodding my head and considering. I knew Jeanine would never forgive me killing her pa and I wondered just for a second if she would forgive him for killing me. Either way, it would be hard on her.

Finally, I let out a deep breath and flipped open my duster. "Might as well get the old wheels rolling, by God," I said. Snatching out both my pistols, I dropped them on a chair. At first he started to sneer as if to say, "Your guns don't scare me a bit." When he saw them bounce on the chair his expression turned curious.

"Let's don't beat around the goddamn bush and hurt each other's feelings," I said. Crossing the room in two quick steps, I bent down on the way and jerked my ten-inch glades knife from my boot. I slammed it down an inch deep right in the middle of his desk. That big knife quivered back and forth gleaming in the firelight. I jerked right out of my duster and slung it across the room. "Two feet!" I hissed.

He looked at me real puzzled and just a little shocked. "What the hell are you doing, boy?"

I pointed at the floor behind him. "Get back two feet same as me and say when you're ready, goddamn it!"

His voice sounded like he'd lost some of his breath. "You're out of your mind, boy. A knife fight?"

I snatched both my sleeves up past my elbows and half-crouched. "Let's get right on to it," I said.

Wilcox raised his hand in disbelief. "You're not serious?"

"I'll count three," I said. "One!"

"Hold on goddamn it, boy! Listen, I say . . . listen to me!"

"Two!" I had my hands out to my side like I was ready to lunge for the knife. I wasn't really going to unless he did. I didn't figure him for a fighter, not like this anyway. I just wanted to make sure our conversation didn't start off one-sided. I'll say this for him though, there was a couple seconds when it crossed his mind to make a jump for that blade. I saw it in his eyes.

"Hold it, boy, this is crazy." He raised both hands chest high and I knew I'd won.

"You call me 'boy' one more goddamn time and you better be ready to do some cutting and hacking, 'cause only one of us is going to leave this room. They'll take the other out with a mop."

"All right, son, let's just settle down here . . . not do something we'll regret."

I started to tell him I wouldn't regret carving him up a little, but I could see it swinging my way. After all, I was only here to work something out for Jeanine and the baby.

I know what I did was crude and crazy, yet I saw no reason to mull it over too much. If there's to be a confrontation, I say go at it from the first harsh word and get it over with.

Young as I was I'd already earned my share of grit, and in spite of Cronin Wilcox's size and experience I was betting he hadn't rode trails as rough as the ones I'd been on. If he had, it was a long time ago. Few men who work their way to the top of the heap would risk throwing it all away on some two-bit border trash. That's what he thought I was. Had I been wrong in my thinking, I reckon one of us would've died. Luckily, I had figured right.

I let my hands down some and straightened up. "Your call, Mister Wilcox," I said, "I come here in respect to you as the father of my wife, but I'll stand for no man's insults."

He stepped away from the desk and I saw his hands were as calm as my own. He was no coward, he just saw that he'd stepped out of line with the wrong person and I reckon he didn't want to chance dying or killing over a mouthful of bad talk. "How the hell am I supposed to act?" he said. He picked up his glass of bourbon, swigged it empty, and slammed it down on his desk. "You've ruined my only child."

"I have shamed your daughter, Mister Wilcox, and I wish to God I hadn't, but we're married and I'm wanting to do right by her and the baby. That's why I'm here."

"If you want to do what's best for her and the baby, get on your horse and ride out."

"It ain't that simple, Mister Wilcox, and we both know it. If I thought my leaving here would smooth the bumps out of the road for Jeanie and the baby, I would have left days ago. But I can't ride out knowing you'll hack and cow Jeanie and the baby for the rest of their lives, and that's exactly what I figure you're going to do. I shamed her once, but if I leave her here under your thumb without some kind of understanding, you'll shame her from now on."

"Why, you rotten little bastard!" Old Cronin's face swelled up like a red balloon. He glanced toward the knife sunk into his desk top and rubbed his hand against his leg. I knew what went through his mind.

"No offense, Mister Wilcox, I'm just speaking flat-out to you man to man. I'd like to work something out here in a good businesslike manner if we can. If we can't, we can always go to cutting."

I have never seen it fail; when you say the word "business" to a businessman, he'll always perk his ears like a hunting dog. It doesn't matter whether he's interested or not, he's got to sniff at the deal, same as a dog with a full belly still sniffs at a possum.

"Business?" he asked, picking up my word with a look that was both enraged and curious at the same time. "You dare refer to my daughter's future as business?"

"That I do," I said, bold as brass. I knew the word "business" would build a wall between him and that glades knife long enough for me to sell my goods. "Fact is, Mister Wilcox, right now Jeanie is the only business I've got and I ain't budging from your life till my business is settled."

I circled around to the bar and poured a tall water glass full of fine bourbon. Some of it spilled over the top of my hand. I slung it off on the polished floor then licked the back of my hand. Old Cronin stared at me the way a growling dog watches a house cat.

I circled back around him and propped my behind against his desk sipping the tall drink. "See, Mister Wilcox, I ain't used to this high living, course I adjust real easy to anything, always did. The longer I stay here the better I'll come to like it. So, till I know things are square here for Jeanie and the baby, I'll stick here tighter than a fly on a bear's ass. I can keep your barn half full of auction stock, suck up this good bourbon, and make a name for myself around every gambling hall and whorehouse in Kansas City. And just as soon as they say my name, they'll say 'Cronin Wilcox's son-in-law.' You know it as well as I do."

"I'll have you run out of here," he said.

"I know that, but you can't shut me up 'less you kill me."

"If you love my daughter, you couldn't put her through that kind of torment."

"I never said I love your daughter. I said I care what happens to her and the baby, and I do. But I wouldn't be the one putting them through it; I'd put you through it and you'd do the rest. Anyway, if her and I are going to lose, we might as well lose big. 'Course that's only one way it can go."

He cocked a shrewd eye. "Are we getting to the part where you're going to ask for money . . . to get rid of you?"

"No, sir." I shook my head. "Ordinarily there's nothing I care more about than a bag full of warm money. But this has nothing to do with me getting money from you. This is about me giving you money."

He managed a sarcastic grin. "You're going to give me money? Where would somebody like you come up with any money, or should I dare ask?"

"No, you shouldn't," I said, "but here's the deal. I'll give ten thousand dollars now and another ten thousand in a month if you let Jeanine and the baby live here from now on and not cut them out of your estate. That's a fair amount of money for her to raise the child without costing you a dollar. That sends me down the road out of everybody's life forever. Wouldn't you call that a bargain, Mister Wilcox?"

Bad as I hate wasting good bourbon, I took a big sip, wiped my hand across my mouth, and pitched the rest into the fireplace. Old Cronin watched his expensive brew flare up and sizzle. He stared at me real hard, but the wheels were starting to turn.

◆✳ 22 ✳◆

That night I rode into town leaving Cronin Wilcox to ponder my proposition. Like any good businessman he would let me know his answer in a couple of days. Not to be outdone as a businessman myself, I decided to apply a little pressure to his decision. Instead of going to Linley's or the Lady Luck, my usual playing rooms, I rode straight to the Imperial Club on the black Morgan and hitched him between two fancy surreys.

In spite of my appearance, work clothes and slouch hat, the mention of my father-in-law's name got me past the door and into the gaming room. I more or less buffaloed my way into the biggest game in the place. Without making a complete ass of myself, I made sure the message got back to Cronin Wilcox by way of his friends and business associates. His son-in-law, "Mister Miller Crowe," could be as crude as a bed tick.

After four or five reckless hands of draw poker, betting foolishly and throwing up bluffs a schoolboy would've seen through, I left there questioning the honesty of the game. I didn't come right out and call them cheats. Not that night. Like I said, I was just starting to apply pressure. I mumbled under my breath as I gathered my money and spilled a drink on the table when I got up and left. I saw Melvin Bracker, one of Wilcox's bunch, watching me from the bar, and I knew he would bust a gut getting to old Cronin with the story.

Funny, but there among all those big shots, I acted like a trashy bastard. As soon as I got to Linley's I settled down and became as mannered as a gentleman. I reckon it's all in how you want to play it.

I had just about made up what I'd intentionally lost at the Imperial Club when Dave Mather showed up with a feller I'd never seen before. He was a big man wearing a strapped-down forty-four and gold braiding around his hat. Anybody still wearing guerrilla tack now that the war was over I figured to be either plain stupid or looking for trouble. I was right both ways.

Mather caught my eye and nodded me to the bar. I could tell by the way he gestured that it would be something on the sly, so I waited a couple of games before going over. I stood beside him without saying anything till after I ordered a drink. With me standing on one side of Mather and the big feller on the other, we talked between us by watching the mirror. "Frank," Mather said, "this here is Miller Crowe from Nebraska. Crowe, this here is Frank Reno from Indiana. He asked me where he could find a good hand. I thought of you right off." Mather stepped away from the bar and tossed back his shot of rye. He tipped his hat in the mirror and left without saying another word.

"I reckon you've heard of me," Frank Reno began, watching me in the mirror.

"No offense, but no I haven't."

Reno shrugged it off. "No matter, you've heard of some of the work me and my boys have done—stage coaches, payrolls, that kind of thing." I couldn't believe he would say something like that to a stranger, even if Mather had recommended me. Not knowing how to reply, I just nodded my head.

"We mostly work in Kentucky and Indiana, but I got a big job coming up close to here. I need a good horseman; Mather says you're one of the best." I knew Mather had said nothing more than he had to, nothing to cause me any trouble in case this feller was not what he said he was.

"I'm not a horseman." I smiled in the mirror. "I'm a horse-man, there's a big difference." I wanted him knowing right off, I wasn't interested in riding with him. "Horse-man" meant I only gathered horses for the job.

"Either how you say it, I need horses."

"I dicker horses some. What will you need?"

"I'll need six good horses ten miles outside of Gallatin over in Davies County. You know that area?"

"I do," I said. "It's full of troops, has been for a while."

"That's right." He grinned in the mirror and said, "Once a month them troops get paid, all in cash."

"I understand," I said, cutting him off. So far nothing had been said that could land me in jail. If a man wanted to buy horses and have them delivered, that was all I was doing here.

"You interested?" he asked the mirror.

"I dicker horses and I do deliver them, but they won't be cheap."

"How much?"

"The kind of horses you want and the place you want them brought to, we're talking four hundred a piece."

"You work alone?"

"Sometimes I do, sometimes I have a partner." I had already decided if I worked for Reno, I would bring Jack Smith with me. There's no way I'd meet this man and his bunch somewhere in the woods after a robbery. With Jack along they would think twice before a double-cross.

"That's damn high," he said, "especially if it's just you by yourself."

"It ain't that high, considering," I said. "Not that you would, but just suppose you and your boys happen to break a law on the way to get those horses and about the time you-all show up, so does a posse. Four hundred a head sounds real cheap if I'm staring up a rope."

Reno laughed in the mirror, then turned and faced me. I didn't like him talking straight to me, but he'd already started. I glanced around to see who might be watching. "I like your style," he said, as if I would be pleased to hear it. "We'll do a lot of business together." I doubted it. If ever I saw a man destined to do a hemp-waltz, it was Frank Reno. As it turned out later on, I was right. A group of vigilantes busted into jail and hanged him and most of his gang four years later over in Indiana.

"When are you wanting these horses?" I asked. I wanted to finish with him and get on away.

"I say we meet here in three weeks and work it out."

"Two weeks from now I'll start coming here every night for a week. If you don't show I'll figure it went wrong. Fair enough?"

"Oh, I'll be here," he said, "just get some good horses."

I had turned to leave when he said one more thing and caused me to turn back around. "One thing I want to tell you, Crowe," he said. "You know that bank robbery over in Liberty a while back?"

I turned and looked at him with no expression. Right inside my shirt sat the forty-four. I was one second away from ripping buttons and slinging iron. "I heard something about it," I said, feeling the skin on my neck ripple.

He grinned and slapped his tied-down holster. "That's one me and the boys did." I smiled slightly; it was a smile of relief.

"I like your hat," I said. I turned and headed for the door as he raised a shot glass of whiskey high in the air, in a toast. Faces turned toward him from behind their poker hands. I lowered my hat on my forehead, keeping my hand to my face as I left.

"God bless Dixie," I heard him say with a boisterous laugh. The stupid son of a bitch.

◆✳ 23 ✳◆

I started to call off the deal with Reno as soon as I found out "Quiet" Jack Smith was in jail in Abilene, but I was still waiting to hear from old Cronin about our family situation—his "couple of days" was going on two weeks—and I was getting restless, anyway. I decided to see it through.

I got word to Hickok in Hayes City and asked him to forward some money on to Abilene for Jack's fine. Seems Jack had gotten drunk, pistol-whipped an ill-mannered bartender, and emptied a spittoon in his face. Jack was a real stickler about manners, especially when he was drunk.

I sent Hickok's money to him through a teamster line, and sure enough, Jack showed up at the Lucky Lady a week later, ready to work. I spotted him a hundred dollars and told him to stick around till I was able to get things ironed out.

In the meantime, I was getting closer and closer to Jeanie, and with everything else I had going on it was starting to scare me. This was not a good time for me to go falling in love with my wife. Being with her, sharing that warm feather bed and sometimes just holding her and watching her sleep, was pulling on feelings inside me I couldn't deal with right then. What made me even more scared was the way she'd taken to me.

Old Cronin Wilcox was acting more peculiar every day. The message I sent him from the Imperial Club seemed to make him hesitate on my proposition instead of jumping to get rid of me. I noticed him watching every move Jeanine and I made. I didn't know what was going through his mind, but I didn't like it. I even wondered if maybe he had planned to have me killed or something. With everything I had going on right then, I'd gotten jumpy as a squirrel.

About the time I got ready to set up the deal with Reno, Cronin

Wilcox came up behind me one morning while I saddled my Morgan. I was thinking about the payroll job and Cronin's voice startled me. I nearly swung on him before I caught myself. "I've decided to take you up on your offer," he said, "but I have one problem."

"What's that?" I asked.

"How do I know you won't come back anytime you damned well please?"

"Because we'll put it on paper. You have your lawyer write it up and I'll have mine look at it."

Cronin gave me a sarcastic smile. "You have an attorney?"

"When your man gets it drawn up, have him send it to Morris Fitch over in Carthage on my behalf. When Fitch approves it, we've got a deal."

"And the money?"

"I have the first ten thousand already waiting for you. As soon as you sign the agreement that my wife and child have an irrevocable trust set aside for them, I'll drop the money in your hand." Cronin Wilcox looked impressed that I knew enough to talk that way. "You're full of surprises, Crowe. I'm glad we're not leaving this to a gentlemen's agreement."

"There's no such thing when it comes to business, Mister Wilcox." I pitched the saddle up on the Morgan and cinched it. "I think we both agree on that." I turned facing him and shoved my hat back on my head. "Just because you're sitting on top of the hill doesn't make you any better than me. You just got started sooner. Maybe you and your bunch can work among yourself and pretend it's all honorable, but that's just because you've got all the money in the world. I'm the outsider here, same as you'd be if we was dealing with my people."

"No, Crowe. Don't try to compare yourself in any way with 'decent' people. You're dirty water that seeped in while we weren't looking."

"Then I reckon you should've been looking, 'cause I'm here to be dealt with. My blood is your blood ... will be from now on. Whatever decency and goodness you think you know, you better be ready to teach to my child. Whether you like it or not, that's what I'm buying here."

Cronin stepped back as I swung into the saddle. His fists were clinched tight in controlled rage. He knew I spoke the plain truth. "I'll see that your name is never breathed in this household. You'll never lay eyes on your child. You hear me, Crowe!" he bellowed.

I smoothed the reins in my hand and looked down at him. My voice must've sounded resolved, because it seemed to defuse him when I spoke. "Don't you reckon I already know that? Look at me, Mister Wilcox. Look at the life I lead. I doubt I'll be around to see how my child turns out. It won't be long before they'll be pitching sod in my face and you'll be giving Jeanine's hand to some decent feller." I smiled and hooked the Morgan once easy. "Get past it, Mister Wilcox," I said.

Since "Quiet" Jack was living on the hundred dollars I'd spotted him, I had him check around and find out who raced horses with Wilcox. At the same time, I had him passing the word around the auction barn that my black Morgan was one fast son of a bitch. Instead of rein-breaking the Morgan the way I should have, I let him bully and boss me as much as he pleased. As far as I was concerned, this horse was no "keeper" anyway; I could straighten him out later on if I wanted top dollar for him, or I could run him through the auction same as the last owner.

Anybody knows a Morgan is a fine, strong animal with more than just a respectable amount of speed. But as far as racing, putting a Morgan up against a Virginia-bred runner or an English, or a Kentucky slick-back for that matter, was pure foolishness. Still it was just a couple of days before Jack's story about my Morgan came circling back to me at the Lucky Lady.

One evening while I waited to hear from Frank Reno about our deal, Melvin Bracker showed up at the crowded bar with another of Cronin Wilcox's bunch. I knew they were looking for me. They looked as out of place in the Lucky Lady as I'd looked in the Imperial Club. I never let on that I saw them till they worked their way right up next to me.

"Well, look who's here," Bracker said, his voice pitched a notch above the rattle of the piano and the din of a crowded saloon. I turned toward him and nodded respectfully. "Philip," he said to his companion, "I don't think you have met Mister Miller Crowe. Mister Crowe, this is Philip De'Boue."

We exchanged nods and I went back to sipping my rye. I saw how Bracker glanced at De'Boue before speaking to me. "Philip and I were just discussing you and your horseflesh business. Perhaps you can tell us something?" The way he said "horseflesh business" made it sound like something you wouldn't admit to in the presence of Christians, but I let it slide past me.

"Sure," I said, "what's that?"

"Well, Philip tells me that around the auction barns they're saying you have a black Morgan that outruns track horses. I told him that must be a mistake."

"No mistake," I said, bold as brass, then turned with my glass of rye and sipped it looking toward the mirror.

"Come now, Mister Crowe," Philip De'Boue said. "I certainly don't want to dispute your word, but really, a Morgan that outruns racehorses?"

"Hold on," Bracker said to De'Boue. "I won't witness your questioning Mister Crowe's word. If he says it's so, then it is. Right, Mister Crowe?"

It was going to be easier than I thought. These two peckerheads really believed I was too dumb to see they were working a play on me. If they wanted to learn how to work something on somebody, they should've been there the day old Cletis and I worked on Zanone. This was a nursery game to me.

"By God," I swore, banging my empty glass on the bar, "my Morgan is right out front there at the hitch rail. If you doubt what you've heard about him, go get your fastest track runner and bring it on. We'll run from here to Main Street and back, and the winner gets five dollars." I slapped five dollars on the bar like it was a small fortune.

They could hardly keep a straight face. It was a compliment to me that they considered me a simpleton. That was exactly what I wanted. I have always been amazed at how a man with a clean shirt and a pile of money gets to thinking he is the smartest son of a bitch in the world.

"Five dollars?" Bracker scoffed. "It seems hardly worth the effort."

I made myself appear more ruffled. "Ten damned dollars!"

"Hold on, Mister Crowe," De'Boue said. "I would not risk ruining a track runner by racing through the street here. If you want to put your horse against mine, bring it to the track Sunday. I'm sure I can risk ten dollars, if you can."

"Now wait a minute," I said, looking sheepish. "I don't know about running him on a circle track. I've always raced straight out."

"Then I guess you don't know what you're talking about saying a Morgan can beat a racehorse. The only way you could know is by racing on a track." De'Boue looked real pleased with himself and turned to walk away.

"I'm afraid he's right," Bracker said, shrugging. "You should bring the Morgan to the track Sunday and prove yourself." He turned and the two of them walked out looking as if they had set up some ingenious scheme to take my money and make me look a fool.

I slid my glass across the bar and smiled to myself. Glancing in the mirror I noticed Dave Mather looking back at me from a few places down. He tipped his hat and smiled in the mirror as if to say he knew I was getting ready to put the screws to Bracker and De'Boue. I shook my head and laughed.

Later that night, before I headed back to the Wilcoxes, Frank Reno showed up and we laid our plans for the horses he needed on the Gallatin job. I was starting to have what you might call a scheduling problem between the Reno deal, old man Wilcox and the trust for Jeanine and the baby, and the horse-racing scheme I planned for Sunday. It would take some tight moving to take care of everything. For some reason I felt it necessary to do all three as quick as possible.

On the way out of town I stopped by Number Three Missouri Avenue to let "Quiet" Jack Smith know how it was going with Reno. Jack had already gathered the horses we needed. We figured if Reno never showed, we could always run them back through the auction and turn a small profit. What Reno was buying was not just horses, he could've done that on his own. He was hiring me because he wanted someone he could count on to be there waiting no matter how hot the situation. If it went well, they could change horses with all the time in the world; in that case any horse-man would do. The reason Mather had referred me was in case the chase got too close coming out of Gallatin. In a tight spot, I would deliver them horses right through a running shootout if that's what it took. Not that I owed any loyalty to Reno, I just wouldn't get paid otherwise.

I found Jack coming out the door with a whore under each arm. Not wanting to interrupt anything, I laid three fingers down the side of my leg—the guerrilla signal that everything was going as planned—and kept riding.

I rode extra quiet into the barn that night. After feeding the Morgan I trimmed a lantern and walked all the way to the breeding barn, which was nearly a half-mile from the house. Inside the barn Old Jethro sat on a bale of hay with a ten-gauge shotgun across his lap. He started to stand as I walked toward him, but I waved him down with my hand. "How's it been going?" I asked quietly. He nodded and pointed toward a breeding stall.

"They's been at it most'a the afternoon," he said. "If'n he ain't brought her in, she can't be brought in."

I stepped over and held up the lantern. Inside the dark stall my mare nickered and shook out her mane. Beside her, Star Of Dawn looked up at me with a muzzle full of hay, and kept chewing on it as I reached in and rubbed his ears. "Seems a shame, old buddy," I said to the stallion. "After all you've done for her today, she's going to get you on that track Sunday and rip you a new ass."

I walked back to Jethro and handed him fifty dollars. I sat down beside him and took out a pint bottle of Eagle-Spray rye whiskey. He rustled the money a quick count, shoved it into his trousers with one hand, and reached for the bottle with his other.

"Massa Wilcox ever gets wind I bred that stallion out behind his back, he skin me shur's hail."

"I reckon fifty dollars is worth risking a skinning, ain't it?"

Jethro smiled and smacked his lips after taking a cut of rye.

"I brought this old goose-banger like you ast me to," he said.

"Good, let me see it." I checked it over. It hadn't been fired in a long time. I gave it back and handed him two shells from my shirt pocket. "First chance you get, take this thing out, and fire a round through it to make sure it works, alright?"

He shrugged. "Shur."

"Then, Sunday, I want you to be in the woods just behind the track. I'm going to be riding in one of the races. When you see me riding, I want you to wait till I get just past you on the last lap. You understand?"

Jethro nodded. He had a curious look on his face. "You ain't wanting me to do nobody harm, is ya?"

"Nothing like that." I waved my hand. "As soon as I ride past on the last lap, I want you to fire this thing straight up in the air, then light out of there."

Now he looked outright dumbfounded. "Wha the hell fhur, Massa Crowe?"

I fished a roll of money from my pocket and peeled off some bills. "For fifty dollars," I said, "that's what for."

I saw a light come on in his eyes. He didn't reach for the money. "I ast you wha fhur, Massa Crowe." I saw a sly grin creep across his face. I grinned back and peeled off more bills.

"For a hundred dollars, that's what for."

◆✳ 24 ✳◆

"I ain't gonna run him, and that's all there is to it. The horse is bit-sore." I turned as if to walk away.

"I'll be goddamn if you ain't!" "Quiet" Jack growled. He spun me around and slammed me against a stall gate.

Jack cut a striking figure in that silver-gray suit and shiny top hat. Bracker and De'Boue stood ten feet away enjoying every minute of it. Jack held me by my coat lapel, damn near lifting me off the ground. "I wagered two thousand dollars with these gentlemen on your goddamn Morgan. Now you either run him, or I'll reach straight up your ass and jerk your brains out."

I waved my hands and looked like a man facing an alligator. "I swear to God, Mister Smith, the horse's mouth is too bit-sore to run. You rode him yourself—am I lying?"

I had insisted Jack take the Morgan out around the barn in front of Bracker and De'Boue. The big plug wouldn't rein at all. He thrashed at the bit like it was setting his mouth on fire.

Jack turned me loose roughly and rubbed his chin like he was wiping sweat. I was truly impressed. He played his role to the hilt. Breaker and De'Boue loved it.

"Gentlemen," Jack said, "you see the spot I'm in here. What can we do?"

Bracker shrugged. "Come now, Mister Smith, a bet is a bet. If Mister Crowe doesn't race his horse, I'm afraid you will lose by forfeit." He smiled at De'Boue. This was too good.

Jack spun back toward me, his finger pointing like a dagger. "Then you're running that goddamn horse!"

I started to protest, but De'Boue cut me off. "We've seen the horse is clearly bit-sore. I'm afraid racing him would be dangerous for every horse in the race."

"Crowe!" Jack said, playing it so well he was starting to scare me, "you sold me on how good a horse that Morgan is, now I've got my money on the line. You're a goddamn horse dealer. You better come up with a horse that can run that race, right now!" He spun toward Bracker and De'Boue. "I plead with you as gentlemen, to allow us to substitute another horse."

Breaker and De'Boue shot each other a smug glance, then turned toward me. I shrugged and pleaded with Jack. "I don't have anything to run," I said. "You've seen my whole string. They're all auction stock."

Bracker loved seeing me on the spot. Nothing would suit him better than humiliating me in front of Jeanine's family. "Our wager was on the Morgan, but if you can provide another animal, I feel it only fair to allow Mister Smith a sporting chance. What do you say, Mister De'Boue?" They smiled at each other.

De'Boue looked me up and down as if deciding whether or not somebody like me could possibly have anything of value. "I've seen Mister Crowe's stock. I doubt we're actually giving Mister Smith a sporting chance."

Jack looked at me as if he was ready to explode. "Damn you!"

"Now hold on, Mister Smith," I cut in. "I do have one hell of a riding mare, that's as good as—"

"A goddamn riding mare!" Jack shouted. I hoped he didn't get too caught up in his role. You never knew about "Quiet" Jack. "I'm winding up betting two thousand dollars on a riding mare!"

Bracker and De'Boue were straining to keep from laughing out loud. "But don't forget," Bracker said, stifling a laugh, "we're giving you five to one, same as on the Morgan."

"I don't want to do this," I pleaded. I sounded as whipped as possible. Bracker and De'Boue couldn't hold it back any longer. They left the stables laughing and strutting like peacocks. When they were out of sight, Jack leaned toward me and whispered, "How did I do?" I winked, and laid three fingers across my forearm. It was going as planned.

I reckon I was a little ashamed riding out onto the track—not of my bay mare, but of the way I'd treated her. Her fine strong legs bore the scars and cuts of hard months in the brush. Across her rump, a rifle graze stood out coarse and ugly there among those gently kept animals. I patted her neck as she pranced forward. This would be the last I would ever ask of her. Well, that is, after I found me a good riding horse.

Jeanine came up beside me as I rode toward the track. "What's going on here?" she demanded. I leaned down from the saddle.

"What're you talking about?"

"I heard my father and Bracker talking. Why are you and Jack Smith acting like you don't know each other?"

I tried to look as innocent as I could. Jeanine saw right through me. "Damn you, Jess, you didn't have to do this. Why couldn't you just run the race like anybody else?"

I didn't answer. I gigged the mare forward, out onto the track. From where Bracker and De'Boue stood near the rail, I heard laughter, and Bracker's voice above the noise of the crowd. "Look," he said, "he's going to ride the race, himself!"

Beside me, I looked around and saw De'Boue's silver-gray stallion try to bump us. I veered my mare over just in time and glared at the weasel-faced jockey beside me. He spread an evil grin across bad teeth. "Keep that plug out of the way," he sneered, "or I'll run over her."

On my other side, between me and the rail, Star Of Dawn trotted up. His jockey offered a friendly smile. "Pay him no mind," he said, "De'Boue must pay him extra to be an asshole." He gigged Star Of Dawn forward and called over his shoulder, "Good luck."

At the starting line, just for a second, I had some doubts. Of the six horses, my bay mare was the smallest. Of the six jockeys, I was the largest. From the center starting position, I looked around at the fancy horses, riders, and rigging on either side of me and realized for the first time what a total ass I would be if I didn't pull this off. Not only would I embarrass Jeanine in front of her family, I would lose the money and the winnings I was counting on to pay her father.

When I saw the starting pistol raised into the air, I braced myself in the short, drawn saddle and pushed the doubt out of my mind. Jeanine was pissed off about me and Jack working a scheme on Bracker and De'Boue, but she didn't know the half of it. I had Jethro and his goose-gun ready for when I came around the last lap. I knew how quick my mare would bolt at the sound of the blast. I was counting on that for the extra "something" just in case.

I should have been ashamed of myself, doubting my mare like that.

At the crack of the starting pistol, she came off the line like she'd been shot from a cannon. Neck and neck, Star Of Dawn bolted forward on my left from the inside and the silver-gray stallion closed toward me on my right. I saw right off. Star Of Dawn's jockey meant to win the race, the silver-gray meant to beat the shit out of me. To win the money, I only had to beat the silver-gray; to win the race I had to beat them all.

Leveling into the first lap I let the mare drift toward the rail, cutting across the front of two horses with lead to spare. Beside me the silver-gray pounded close, too close I thought. But as surprised as I was the other day when I rode my mare on the empty track, I was even more surprised to see that this girl knew her business when it come to other horses. As the big silver closed in, my mare veered toward him just enough to turn him back, then she pounded in close to Star of Dawn on the rail.

Now that the weasel-faced jockey knew what to expect, he goaded the silver-gray with determination and moved sideways almost into us as my mare scooted forward just in time. Star Of Dawn had the lead by two lengths.

Coming before the crowd at the end of the first lap, I heard booing and yelling rise up like a dark cloud. At first I thought it was directed at me, but out the corner of my eye I saw angry fists shaking and fingers pointing at the silver-gray right behind me. I reckon no matter how little use they had for me, nobody held with the kind of race that little weasel bastard was running.

Into the second lap, I felt my mare belly down a little, but I could tell she was holding back. I gigged her a short tap but it was like she never felt it. She had a pace set and she wouldn't break it. I left it up to her. On the inside, Star Of Dawn had pulled forward another length. For the money, all I had to do was stay in front of the silver-gray. He came forward every few seconds but couldn't hold pace to my mare. Seeing that, his jockey got dirtier.

Each time the silver-gray pulled forward, the jockey veered against us, slamming us almost into the rail before my mare could pull out. I could feel the constant battle wearing down my mare. Going into the third lap, the silver-gray was coming up quicker and staying beside us longer. Star Of Dawn was ahead by five lengths. I had to do something. The crowd was hissing and screaming at him, but the little bastard kept it up. I caught a glimpse of five or six men wrestling

"Quiet" Jack to the ground. His gun waved in the air. Evidently, he meant to shoot the jockey off the silver-gray. In the next second I wished he had.

Halfway around the third lap, I heard a whistling sound beside me and felt the sting of the riding crop across my side. I flinched just as it whistled again, and felt my mare jolt, almost losing stride. The son of a bitch was whipping my mare. That did it. He didn't want to race, he wanted a guerrilla fight. We could do that easy enough.

Over and over, I felt the riding crop cut across me as I slipped my right hand from the reins and clawed at my belt. The son of a bitch was going to make a whole day of whipping me and my mare.

When I had my belt out of my trousers, I swapped ends with it and wrapped the tongue good and tight around my right hand. The weasel was too busy whipping me to see what I was doing. I drew my mare up slightly, just enough to let the silver-gray gain more than he had so far. The jockey was pleased.

Just as he settled in to pass us, just as he faced forward and lowered his riding crop, just as he concentrated on getting ahead, I swung the belt in a high, vicious circle and saw the steel buckle split his face in a long red gash. He started falling from the saddle, knocked cold. Feeling the shift in weight, the silver-gray careened across the track and leaped over the outside rail to keep from crashing through it. At that second, the rider left the saddle, blasted through the fence, and tumbled in a spray of blood, dust, and splinters. Star Of Dawn was six lengths up and bellying down into the fourth.

I had beaten De'Boue's stallion and had won the money. That was the main thing. I dared anybody to claim "foul" after the way the bastard had done me. Now I could ease up and slide in a respectable second. The nearest horse behind me was a good eight lengths back and fading. But my mare had a different idea. With the silver-gray off her side, she bellied down hard.

I tapped her easy to let her know it was her choice, and she fired out of stride, gaining four lengths in what seemed like a split second. Behind us I heard the crowd yelling and applauding us. Above the roar, I heard Jack let out a rebel yell. By God, now we had us a horse race.

Rounding the far turn I saw Jethro over near the trees where I had stationed him. He had a worried look on his face. He shrugged and I saw his hands were empty. Then, I saw Jeanine step out from behind a tree with the goose-gun cradled in her arms. By now we were gaining on Star Of Dawn. Jeanine smiled and yelled as we streaked past. "Go get it, Mister Crowe!"

Laying down deeper on the mare's neck, all I could see was brown dirt flashing beneath me and a flurry of hoofs. It was her race, all I could do was hang on. One length back now, both horses held steady for what seemed like forever. Then slowly, inch by inch, my mare shortened the lead. She was bellied down as far and as fast as I'd ever seen her. For a second I actually closed my eyes. I didn't gig her, I didn't slap her with the reins, I reckon I was just willing her on. And she must've sensed it.

When I opened my eyes we were right beside Star Of Dawn. His jockey glanced over in surprise, then smiled, and leaned down farther, slapping with the crop.

The seconds we spent going down the final stretch were like two men and two horses tangled up in each other's dream. I saw the stir of the crowd, I saw their hands clap and their lips move, but I couldn't hear a thing. There was no sound, no wind, no dust, and no feeling of movement beneath me. I saw the jockey turn loose of the riding crop in midair and let it fly. It seemed to drift and turn lazily in the sunlight overhead. It was down to the horses now. We were only ornaments on their back. Time had stopped. Instead of the horses pounding to the finish line, it was as if the track was a long silk ribbon and the horses were gathering it beneath their hoofs.

Suddenly, the crowd exploded and the world came back to life. A blast of wind hit me in the face as the mare let down into a fast trot. I tasted grit and dust. Beside me, Star Of Dawn snorted and nipped at my mare's muzzle. The jockey raised up in the short drawn stirrups. "Congratulations," he yelled, trotting along with me, "but I'll beat your ass next time."

I returned his smile. Combing my fingers back through my dust-tangled hair, I shook my head. "Naw, sir," I yelled, gesturing toward the crop cuts along my side, "this is too rough a sport for me."

Halfway around the track I stopped my mare beside the rail where Jeanine stood laughing with tears in her eyes. Jethro had taken the goose-gun and disappeared back through the woods. "Except for nearly killing one of the jockeys, I think you ran a pretty clean race."

Reaching down, I swept her up over the rail and onto my lap.

"See," she said, "see what I mean about you and horses? You didn't have to cheat and scheme, all you had to do was trust yourself."

We rode back to the starting line where the crowd stood applauding. Jack came out and helped Jeanine down from the mare. His top hat was busted and flipped up like a stove lid. His shirt was torn and a long scratch cut across his chest. "I would've killed him for you, if that bunch hadn't stopped me. I want you to know that."

"Thanks, Jack," I said. "How is that bastard anyway?"

Jack shrugged and looked disappointed. "Can you believe this shit? That little turd is still alive." He reached inside his shirt and took out a bundle of money. "But here's the good news. I made that goddamn De'Boue pay up the second your nose crossed the finish line."

"Put it away," I whispered, "before Bracker and De'Boue see it."

"Aw, hell, they've crawled out of here looking like two shit-sucking dogs."

Jeanine looked at the money, then glanced up at me. She looked worried. "What's the matter?" I asked. I slipped down from the saddle. Leading my mare with my arm around Jeanine, we walked over to the crowd by the rail. Jeanine's voice sounded truly frightened. "Jess, you can't fool with these people." I started to laugh, but she shook me by the arm. "I mean it. You don't know how my father and his friends are. Don't underestimate them."

At the rail Cronin Wilcox stepped between me and Jeanine and threw his arms around us. "I want all of you to know how proud I am of my son-in-law," he said, holding us there in front of the crowd. I looked at his face close up and never saw a more sincere expression in my life. I couldn't help but smile. The crowd yelled and cheered. His voice rose above the crowd. "This young man not only raises top Thoroughbreds, he can even ride them if he's a mind, too." He hugged me close. "And win!"

"What's the horse's name?" yelled a voice from the crowd. At first I didn't know what to say. I'd never named a horse in my life. The mare stepped up and nudged her muzzle against my shoulder. Trying to think of something, I reached my arm up around her neck. She was sweaty and smeared with dust turning to mud. I looked past the mare and saw Jeanine beaming proudly, and it came to me in a flash. There was no more fitting name than what came to my mind. "Jeanie's Pride," I yelled into the crowd, "her name is Jeanie's Pride."

As the crowd cheered again, I leaned forward glancing around toward Jeanie. She smiled and waved to the crowd. Cronin Wilcox tightened his arms around our shoulders, nodding his approval. My mare smeared mud against his cheek, but Wilcox just laughed and smiled at me. He turned, smiling at Jeanine and she returned his smile. And just for a second as Jeanine's and her father's eyes met, I couldn't help but notice, she looked more worried now than before.

✦❋ 25 ❋✦

"I don't like the feel of this one bit," Jack said, searching the road as far as his eyes could see. I looked at him sitting there atop his gray gelding hunched up in his duster against the fine spring mist.

At ten in the morning it was as dark as late afternoon. The sky was heavily clouded; thunder threatened closer every time it grumbled out of the west. The weather reminded us both too much of the day Kenny Ellworth took a slug through the chest. I reckon we felt a dark premonition that neither one of us wanted to admit.

"We'll give them a little longer," I said. "I don't want to leave without getting paid, and I don't want word to get around that we didn't stick to the job."

Jack spit a long stream of tobacco juice and crossed his arms on his saddlehorn. I'd never seen him so jumpy. "I don't need money this bad, and I don't give a blue damn what them upriver bastards say about me. Far as I'm concerned, we light out of here right now. They ain't going to show." He took out a bottle of morphine-laudanum, the same kind of medicine Cousin Jesse took for his chest pains. Jack took a swig as if it were whiskey. After a minute he settled right down.

"You sick, Jack?" I'd seen him take a drink of the medicine months back at the Samuel place, but just to see what it tasted like.

"Got a tickling in my chest," he said, "nothing to it."

I had to grin at the sight of him. Water dripped from his long oval brim and his duster stuck to his back and shoulders. The tails of his riding duster clung wet to his horse's flanks. I knew I looked as bad. No sooner had Jack calmed down, I heard the sound of hoof beats in the distance. I hooked my mare lightly and circled out onto the muddy road for a better look. When I could clearly make out the Reno gang, I eased back off the road and motioned for Jack to lead the six-horse string back into the woods.

The horses were outfitted with used saddles and reins for a quick change over. In a small clearing, we untied each animal from the lead rope and let them mill about in a circle. I hadn't heard any shooting that would spook the animals and I wanted them roaming free when Reno's bunch arrived. In case there was a double-cross, I wanted Reno to see the animals roaming loose and know that gunfire would send them running.

As the riders broke into the woods, Jack gigged his horse over near the edge of the clearing and whipped his repeating rifle from the saddle scabbard. From his position, if need be, he could drop in behind the trees and pick their eyes out. I stayed in among the horses to make sure that if it came to shooting, nobody would leave there with a fresh mount, which is all they came for anyway. This was all done to let Reno know that it would be easier to pay us our money than to try some far-handed bullshit.

"Here they come," Jack announced, cocking his rifle and propping it straight up from his lap. He was as relaxed as a baby lamb.

I only counted five of the gang riding into the clearing, and judging the look on Frank Reno's face, I knew before asking, something went wrong.

"Where's your sixth man?" I yelled, as they jolted to a halt.

"Dead in the street!" Reno shouted. He looked beat and scared. He and the rest of the gang slid down off their wet saddles and started for the fresh horses. "Hold on," I yelled. "Where's my money? Nobody touches a horse till I get paid, that's the deal!"

"The deal's gone to hell!" Reno yelled, "and we ain't got time to explain it." They all gathered reins and started mounting. Slinging my reins around my saddlehorn real quick, I cross-armed myself beneath my duster. Yanking the .36 caliber from the shoulder holster with my right hand and the Colt .44 from my waist with my left, "Make time!" I bellowed. Out of the corner of my eye, I saw Jack flip the rifle to his shoulder and level down on Frank Reno.

All five of them stopped and raised their hands nearly chest high, looking wet, scared and desperate, like trapped rats. They could either surrender or go for their guns, it was up to Frank Reno to call the play. "Goddamn it," he yelled, "the whole thing went to hell on us. We got no more than a few hundred dollars at best, and Whitmer got blown down carrying the money. We've got to get out of here. They're no more than twenty minutes behind us!"

"What about my money?"

"Damn it, man! We ain't got no money. I'll have to make it up to you next time."

"Either I get paid, right here, right now, or there ain't going to be no 'next time.'"

"Don't crowd me on this," Reno warned. "We'll fight you if we have to. I'm telling you on the square, it went bad and we ain't got no money."

His men had been spreading out slowly as he spoke. He must've been telling the truth. There was no reason for him to waste this much time if he had the money to pay me. At the same time, if the posse was as close as he said, and judging from his expression I believed him, I was wasting too much time myself. It wouldn't benefit anybody but the law if we threw down on each other right now, and from the looks of his bunch that's what would happen if I didn't give in. "Alright, goddamn it! Take the horses and get the hell out of here." I motioned Jack to lower the rifle and jumped the mare forward out of the middle of the horses.

"I won't forget this," Reno said gratefully. "As soon as we get something else lined up, I'll pay you double, I swear it."

"Yeah, goddamn it, sure," I mumbled, and rode over beside Jack.

"I can't believe this shit," Jack said. "They're not smart enough to rob a damn payroll?"

"I reckon not," I said with disgust.

"Think we ought to blast away at them?"

"No," I said, "they've got enough problems without us. Them poor dumb bastards are going to stretch hemp, sure as hell."

"I could shoot just one," Jack said. His eyes were a little glazed. "Just one, right in the back as they ride out."

I looked at Jack and saw he meant it. Reaching my hand over carefully, I eased his rifle barrel up. He watched real close as they grouped and started out of the woods. I heeled my mare forward. "Best we can do is get these horses somewhere, clean them up and try to sell them out to somebody. At least we make something out of this mess."

By the time the Reno bunch disappeared in the distance, the rain was coming down harder and the thunder turned from threat to a full-blown storm. As far as I cared, as soon as we had the tired horses stringed, we could ride them right into Gallatin and sell them off. As long as we stripped their saddles and bridles, there was little chance of anybody recognizing them.

By late evening we arrived in Gallatin, bone-soaked and low in the saddle. After quartering our animals at the livery, we took a room at the Borden Hotel and dried out by hanging our clothes on chairs in front of the fireplace. We sat there in our long-wools, cleaning and oiling our hardware. As miserable as we felt about the day's work, I couldn't help thinking how much worse it turned out for Frank Reno and his bunch. They were pounding through mud and storms with a posse on their heels, and hadn't a damn thing to show for it. I reckoned we were lucky at that.

"You think they didn't press hard enough for the big money?" Jack asked. He held the cleaned forty-four near his ear and listened to action as he clicked it a chamber at a time. Smoke curled up his face from the cigarette in his mouth.

"Who knows," I replied, oiling and rubbing my shoulder holster. "One thing for sure, Reno ain't going to fare well in this part of the country, not robbing banks anyway."

Jack laughed. "Yeah, as many soldiers as there are around here, a man's a damn fool to think he could ride in shooting up the place and ride out with the big money. People don't scare as easy when they know there's a town full of stripe-legs waiting outside the door."

I knew Jack was just making conversation, but what he said sparked an idea in my mind. There was no doubt the Reno bunch rode in whooping and shooting the same way our bunch did over in Liberty. That being the case, the bankers must've balked against handing over the payroll money, knowing with all the soldiers in town the Reno gang didn't have time to bully them out of it. After Liberty, every bank in the country had to be smart enough to work up a plan against the same thing happening to them.

I sat up late that night cutting shots from a bottle of rye and staring into the fire, thinking, while Jack snored like a grizzly from the creaking feather bed.

Next morning by daylight we were settling up at the livery stable. Discounting the grain and stall fees, I dickered a fair price for five of the six horses, keeping a big roan, and signed a phony name on a paper showing they were my legal property to sell. I never saw much point in doing it, but most stable owners thought it did them some good.

Over breakfast I explained to Jack what I had planned last night while he slept, and when I finished telling him, he looked at me like I had gone plumb out of my mind. "You mean you're going in there by yourself, right to the teller, and say, what? 'Excuse me, sir, I want you to give me all the payroll money . . . *please*.'"

I leaned in close, a little put off by his mockery. "Listen goddamn it, there's a bank full of money sitting there. The Reno gang has every lawman in town chasing them. This town is off guard, I'm telling you. The only thing they know to watch for is a gang of whooping, shooting raiders. You said yourself a man's a damn fool to ride in here like that with all those soldiers."

"I say a man's a bigger fool to think he can go in there by himself and squeeze out that payroll. If that gang didn't scare it loose, how you figure one man's going to?"

"Because I'll have all the time in the world, and the banker will know it. Once I walk through them two guards outside the door real peaceful like, he'll know I've got time to pull every tooth in his head with a pair of shoeing tongs if I want to."

Jack stared at his plate, sucked his teeth, and considered it. "I think you dropped too deep into that bottle last night, to tell you the truth." He pushed back his empty plate and scratched at his week-old stubble. "But it's your call. I hope you ain't fixin' to get us hung."

I leaned back in my chair. "Jack, if these soldiers catch us we deserve to be hung. I'd hate to think I couldn't do no better than Frank Reno and his bunch, wouldn't you?"

"That's for sure," he said, then he pointed his finger at me. "But, Jess, I swear to God, much as we're friends, if you ain't there when you ought to be, I'm cutting out on you."

Leaving there, our first stop was the sheriff's office, where we found a note on the locked door. We were going to have Jack report a horse stolen just to size up the situation, but sure enough, the note said the sheriff was out on a posse. Anybody needing help should go to Ben Mudd at Mudd's Mercantile. I grinned at Jack as we headed there.

Inside Mudd's, I went straight to the big feller behind the counter. "Can I help you?" he asked with a smile.

"Yes, sir, I'm John O'Keeffe, and this here is my foreman. I had a string of horses stolen from my place over in Cass County near a week ago. We've tracked the fellers that took them all the way to about five miles from here, then that damn storm washed out their tracks last night and I wanted to ask the sheriff's help."

"Like the note said," Mudd replied, "sheriff and his deputy and half the townsmen are running posse right now, don't know when they'll be back. Over half the army battalion riding with them, too, so I don't 'spect you'll get much help from them either."

"What in the world happened?" I asked, real surprised.

"Whoo-iee!" Mudd shook his head. "You've never seen such as we had here yesterday. Six riders tried to rob the bank of an army payroll deposit. You oughta saw it, two soldiers wounded and one robber shot right through the head."

I glanced, real surprised, from Jack to Mudd. "You don't suppose that's the same bunch we're tracking, do you?"

Mudd shrugged. "I wouldn't be surprised. This was a mean bunch. They've got that one body at the provost officer's station outside of town if you think you can identify him."

"That's a good idea," I said. "We'll ride out there and have a look, later on."

When we left Mudd's we didn't say any more about it. Jack split off and headed for the horses, then left town on his gray gelding, leading the big roan we kept from the livery sale. I took out of town on my bay mare and run her out just a little to loosen her up, and spent the next two hours roaming around near town, letting Jack get to where I needed him to be waiting when I made my run.

At ten o'clock I loose-hitched my mare in the alley behind the bank, stuffed a new rope and some rags down into my saddle bags, and walked a good distance through the alley before going out to the street and heading back toward the bank.

With my bags slung over my shoulder, I tipped my hat as I walked between the two uniformed door guards standing at ease outside the bank. One of them glanced me up and down, but I reckoned they thought nobody would try anything this soon after what happened yesterday. Besides, I was carrying a full saddlebag going in, a thief would've been carrying an empty, and he wouldn't be on foot like I was.

Grinning like a possum, I stepped straight across the wooden floor—"Morning gentlemen"—right through the swinging gate to the president's desk. He and the teller looked surprised, then cautious, then delighted, as I swung the saddlebags down on his desk and said boastfully, "There's three thousand dollars, gold coin, sir. I trust your bank is safe enough to keep it for me?"

Coming out of his surprise, the president stood up tugging at his vest. "Oh, yes, sir," he said, "no question about it."

With only the three of us in the bank, the teller, a young feller, curious to see that much gold at once, came from behind the cage and stood beside the president. "Perhaps I can help, Mister Schaffer," said the young teller. The president shot him a look of disdain, then smiled at me. "Mister Barnes here is new and overeager, you'll have to excuse . . ."

His words froze as my forty-four stared up at him from my waist. "Just keep smiling," I said. "If one of them soldiers looks through the window and figures out what's going on here, you'll both die. So you better smile like your life depends on it."

I glanced back across my shoulder real quick, then back toward the two frightened men. Through the window I saw the back of one soldier's head. His neck muscles were working like he was talking and laughing. "Good," I thought. This was going to go better than I expected.

"Now both you boys know who I am, from yesterday. That was my brother got shot down like a dog in the street. I've come back for that payroll, or for blood vengeance, I don't care which. You-all tell me, you want to give me that money, or die choking on your own guts?" They couldn't have been more helpful.

After tying and gagging the two, I worked quickly, stuffing both sides of my saddlebags so full I couldn't latch them. I crammed both side pockets of my duster full and stuffed more bundles down in my waist. Looking around for something to carry money in, I picked up an old cloth bank bag, but the bottom split when I ran my hand down it, so I dropped it and stuffed more money up under my hat. I needed to get out before someone came in on business and started yelling. I poked five more stacks down inside my shirt and noticed there was still large stacks of money down in that strong box. I couldn't get it all; I had to accept the fact. "Boys, I'm going to hand this to my partners out back and come right back for more. Raise a ruckus and I'll kill you when I get back, you understand?" They nodded vigorously, staring wide-eyed.

I charged out through the back and across the alley to my mare. I was so loaded, packed with money, it took two jumps to get into the saddle. Once up, I hooked her sharp and tore out through the alley and up across the hills in back of town. Once I was on the back road above town, I lay forward and stretched that mare out belly-down, and felt her taking in the road beneath us in thirty-foot strides.

Rounding a turn half a mile out, I come barreling down on two well-dressed fellers riding fancy saddlebreds. They veered to both sides as I charged through, duster tails flapping like angry flags. I must've looked like a crazy man coming on them. I was leaned low into the mare's neck with her mane slapping me in the face. In my right hand I held the reins and my forty-four, my left hand slapped down firm on my slouch hat and greenbacks sticking out like straw from under a scarecrow's hat. Letting out a blood-curdling yell, I pulled off three rounds that sounded like cannon fire, belching smoke and flame between the two horsemen. One horse reared, throwing its rider to the ground while the other bolted from the road into the scrub brush. I tore down the road laughing, yelling and shooting, crazy as a goddamned June bug.

◆❋ 26 ❋◆

"You're early." Jack looked surprised and worried. Seeing me holding my hat down on my head, he demanded, "What happened? Are you hit?"

"Yeah," I said, rolling clumsily out of my saddle under the load of money. "I been hit by a ton of greenbacks, and I ain't likely to recover." Pulling off my hat and shaking my head, money fell everywhere, both loose bills and wrapped bundles.

"Lord God! Thank you, Jesus—thank you, Jesus!" Jack bellowed.

"And thank you, Frank Reno," I added laughing, holding open my duster, showing the money in my waist and jumping up and down. Jack's eyes went wide as silver dollars, seeing the bulges of money all over me. "Lord God, Jess, did you rob the whole town, or the whole goddamned county?"

"By God, it feels like it," I said. "Look at this." I pulled the over-stuffed saddlebags from across my saddle and pitched it to the ground. More money spilled out.

"Holy damn!" Jack yelled. "No wait, wait a minute." He laughed. "It ain't safe carrying this kind of money around. We need to put it in a bank somewhere."

"No way," I said, "not with that Reno bunch prowling around."

Jack coughed and hacked with laughter, and leaned forward slapping his hands on his knees. "Whew," he said, "hold on here. Are you sure that's all of it? I mean, you don't have a loaded wagon sitting back up the road, do you?"

I wiped my eyes and took a deep breath, "That's it," I said, "every last dollar of it, and it was so easy it scared me."

When I said that, it kind of reminded us both not to get too carried away with ourselves. Jack instinctively glanced up and down the road. "Did you get a clean start?" he asked. I saw the look of caution come back to his face.

"Slick as a whistle, but they're on to it by now. We best wrap up here and light out."

"What about all this?" Jack pointed to the money, "what do we do with it?"

"This money is clean enough we could spend it today, if we had a mind to, but I say take a dab of it and bury the rest somewhere deep in the woods for a while. What do you say?"

"That's fine with me," said Jack. "Whatever we're going to do, we better get to doing it, before they get any closer."

Deeper back into the woods, we found a cliff overlooking a creek twenty feet below. While Jack turned over some heavy rocks and dug a hole under them, I spread my duster on the ground and piled the money on it, wrapping it into a large tight bundle. After burying that part of the money and marking our spot, we went fifteen yards upstream and did the same thing with the bulging saddlebags.

Each of us kept seven hundred dollars apiece, choosing the oldest, least identifiable bills we could find. After an hour's ride through deep timber we came to a logging road that looked grown over and deserted. We followed it nearly two miles before coming to a run-down cabin in a small clearing. Riding slowly to the cabin, we were met by a skinny growling hound with one shredded ear and scars that could have only been caused by a bear fight.

"Hello the house," I hollered out, seeing that hound wasn't going to let up till he had somebody's leg in his mouth.

"Hello, yourself," a woman's voice called from inside. "Don't come any closer," she warned. A faded curtain pulled to one side of a window, revealing the dark shine of a double-barreled shotgun.

"We mean no harm," Jack called, "we're travelers in need of food and water, with money to pay for both." At the sound of our voices the hound got more threatening, diving at the horse's legs in short cautious jabs, then pulling back at the last second. "I hate to shoot your dog," Jack said. "Reckon you could call him back?"

"Shoot that dog, and I'll shoot you. Now what are you doing here?"

Jack started to say the same thing over, but I stopped him. "Hold it, Jack," I said. I lunged my mare toward the dog. If I hadn't reined her up she would have stomped his guts out. The dog went yipping across the yard and slid under the porch. "Goddamn it, ma'am, we said we mean no harm. Now pull that goddamn trigger and kill us, or kill that goddamn dog, or kill your goddamn self, we don't give a goddamn!" I jerked the mare around toward the trail. "Come on, Jack, to hell with this."

We turned and headed out when a voice called out behind us. "You don't have to use that kind of language, young man." I smiled and winked at Jack as we turned our horses back around.

She was standing on the porch with the shotgun cradled in her arms. "I never stand for that kind of talk around this house."

We tipped our hats. "And I truly apologize for it, ma'am," I said. "We are tired and hungry and plumb done-in from the road. We will gratefully pay for food and water if you see fit."

She was a strong handsome woman in her late thirties, early forties I guessed, with clean features and large breasts like the women I'd seen in oil paintings. Jack was already out from under his hat and smoothing back his hair against its will. "Maybe we could speak to your husband?" he asked. Hell, I already saw what he was up to.

The hound slipped back out from under the porch and at the sound of Jack's voice, the bear-whipped animal walked back and forth with his hackles up, stiff-legged and growling.

"Fine-looking animal," Jack called, laughing under his breath. I just shook my head and stared off at the woods.

After supper that night, I sat outside whittling with my glades knife, watching the trail with my rifle across my lap. Jack walked up and sat down beside me rubbing his full belly. "You ought to hear the story she just told me," he said.

"You telling each other stories already?"

Jack laughed. "Listen to this, you know she said her husband has been dead over a year, right?"

"I heard her say that," I said.

"Well, the banker that holds a mortgage on this place has been trying to get her on the mattress since before her old man turned blue. Since she won't oblige him, he's coming here tonight to collect the money she owes him, and if she ain't got it, he can have her pitched out."

"Then why don't she give him what he wants. Looks to me like she could stand to wrestle the snake a round or two."

"But you see, Jess, I've got me an interest here."

"That's what I thought," I said.

"Well, think of it a minute. We got money buried near here. Here's this warm-blooded widow woman living here alone, which you've got to admit ain't safe with all the hard cases running loose."

I squinted and shook my head. "You know what I mean, Jess. I don't mean people like us, I mean people who would take advantage of somebody like her."

"She turned us around with a shotgun, don't forget." I stared at him.

"Oh the hell with it," Jack cussed. He stood up to walk away.

"You saying you want to stay here with her a while?"

"Thinking about it," he said. "I got nothing planned except to spend that money when we dig it up. I could stay on here if she'll have me."

"I reckon she'll have you," I said. "How much you talking about spending to pay off the banker?"

"Three hundred is all." He shrugged.

"Well, it's your money; do what you like. I reckon I got time to rob that banker on my way back to Kansas City." I stood up and stretched.

Jack looked real puzzled. "What do you mean, rob him? I'm talking about giving him three hundred dollars."

"Yeah," I said, "and as surely as you give him three hundred when he gets here, I'll take three hundred from him when he leaves." I grinned at Jack and watched his face light up as he got the point.

"I like that, Jess." Jack's face split in a wide smile. "By God . . . I like that a lot."

◆✻ 27 ✻◆

I arrived at Kansas City two weeks later, after stopping over at Springfield long enough to sharpen up my poker skills. The gamblers in Kansas City couldn't hold a candle to the boys around Springfield when it come to white-knuckled draw. I came away losing two hundred and felt privileged to do so. Besides, I had over nine hundred on me—counting the three hundred I'd taken off that banker in the woods—and enough to last a lifetime waiting in the woods with "Quiet" Jack guarding it like a pit bull.

I had decided that all deals were off with old man Wilcox. To hell with him. He'd stalled too long anyway. With the kind of money I had, I could take Jeanie and buy us a spread somewhere. We could make babies, raise babies, and I could keep my lovely wife half out of her pantaloons for the next fifty or so years.

Once a man comes into big money, the world is a whole different place. I had thrown in with Reno for short money—horse money—to scrape up enough to take care of Jeanie and the baby. Now that I had been struck a solid punch of good fortune, I leveled out and did some clear thinking.

I knew Jeanine and I were worlds apart. For that reason, I had been willing to pack it in and disappear from her life like a bad dream. But if an ocean of difference lay between our worlds, I could now build a bridge of greenbacks. Now that I had money, I mean money by the buckets, there wasn't a doubt in my mind. I worshipped that young wife of mine, loved her like God loves sunshine. I wanted to be a part of her world. I wanted to taste and savor the kind of world that created someone as fine and lovely as my Jeanie. With money, love and time, I would be a part of that world, and make her proud to be my wife.

At that point my clear thinking jumped the track a bit. There was a picture running through my mind of Jeanie and me taking a spread in Kentucky. It wasn't a place like the one I grew up on in Grayson County. I was picturing something over near Lexington, something in Thoroughbred country. I had enough money to get us in—and I was convinced I could out-dicker horses with them rich fellers and make enough to keep us there.

The more I thought on it, the more I expanded on the picture. By the time I sprinted to the front door of the Wilcox mansion, I was picturing my being a lawyer, same as ole Morris Fitch. "Miller Crowe," I envisioned, "Esq. Respected pillar of the legal community, and dealer in Thoroughbred horseflesh." From what I'd seen of these rich boys, with a title like that, I could pluck them like a flock of lost geese.

My daydreams had clouded my guerrilla instincts. Reaching for the brass door knocker, I felt a chill run up my spine. My mind skipped back to a few seconds earlier. Riding through the gate past the row of hedges, my mare had twitched her ears, then laid them straight back, in warning. I paid her no mind, then. Now it came to me in a cold flash. "Goddamn!" I yelled, as the realization struck me.

Dropping low as I spun around drawing my forty-four, I heard a balcony door crash open above me. I heard Jeanie scream my name in terror. At the same time, two slugs tore into the door just over my head, and more shots ripped apart flower pots on the porch. A carriage pony went down in a spray of blood. My mare reared high, tearing loose the hitching ring and bolting up onto the porch. Bullets licked at her hoofs as she ran crazy on that wide porch.

I rolled toward her, firing at the rifle smoke in the hedges. Bullets slammed behind me. Leaping up under the mare, I threw my arms and legs around her neck, bulldogging her down. From the balcony, I heard rifle fire, and Jeanie's voice, "I'll cover you!" She must've gotten one of her father's rifles. I caught a glimpse of her leaning across the balcony rail, pumping out shots like a buffalo hunter.

"No!" I screamed. "The baby!" My voice was drowned by the rifle fire. I ripped the sawed-off from my saddle and blew open the front door. I didn't know what waited inside. All I could think of was stopping Jeanie.

The firing shifted up, slamming against the balcony rail. I pulled up the mare. Catching into the saddle, I emptied my revolver toward the hedges as we bolted through the door.

We trampled over one rifleman as he fired. The bullet clipped me under the arm as I caught the barrel and jerked it from his hands. Another feller leveled down on me, but I swung the rifle butt around, slamming it into his face as we tore past him. His shot went past my head, shattering plaster from the high ceiling.

Shots flew in behind us, kicking up furniture and shattering pictures on the walls. As if knowing what I wanted from her, my mare started up the wide winding stairs to the second floor. Halfway up, a gunman appeared on the stairs. He fired once, slamming a round into my left shoulder, then tried to turn and run as the mare plowed into him. He flew over the rail screaming, and I heard a tremendous musical explosion when he landed spread-eagled on a fancy piano below.

At the top of the stairs, rounding the corner, the mare slipped on a long rug. Going down and rolling, she went one direction and I tumbled off in another. Beneath us, riflemen had taken position on the first floor. I slung the rifle barrel over the rail one-handed and pumped a shot straight through a feller's chest. Then shots spit back at me as I scrambled toward Jeanie's bedroom door.

My left shoulder bleeding like a stuck hog's, I pitched into the bedroom and saw Jeanie kneeling against the far wall. Her head was bowed as if in prayer, and her hands clutched her stomach. Crawling to her, I felt the puddle of water around her. "Oh my God," I thought, "not now, not here. It's too soon. Please God!"

"Jeanie," I yelled, grabbing her by the shoulders. "Are you hit? Are you alright?"

She opened her eyes and shoved me away. A piece of rope dangled from her wrist where she had been bound. Blood ran down her hand. She must have broken the skin working herself loose. "I'm alright," she screamed, nearly hysterical. "Get out of here. Go!"

"But the baby."

"We'll be alright. I was scared, I wet myself. Now go!"

With my good hand, I reached around, jerked the feather mattress from the bed, and pitched it over her. "Stay there!" I yelled. I limped out onto the balcony and yelled down, hoping to get the gunmen away from Jeanie. Then I ran to the far end of the balcony and climbed up on the rail. Glancing around for something to land on, I saw my only chance was to jump out into the branches of a large spruce. Beneath me, two riflemen had come out of the house and were taking aim. Just as a round tore splinters from the railing next to my boot heels, I lunged out into the cool breeze.

In the second I lunged, I recognized the face of one rifleman, then spruce needles stung my face and arms as I grabbed, floundered, and slid down the branches. "It can't be," I thought, even as I twisted and bounced down, clawing at limbs to save myself. "But it is," I decided, feeling bullets spin through the needles. "And he has me, sure as hell."

Dazed, I rolled over on my back and stared up at Daniel Zanone's ugly, smiling face. I saw him through a watery half-conscious veil. I was surprised at how the fall hadn't hurt me, and I felt like telling him. Another thought tried to scratch through that veil. It told me to roll away and run, but it just didn't seem that important right then. I couldn't move anyway.

I watched Zanone lower the pistol down close to my forehead. He fanned his hand behind the hammer to keep my skull from splattering in his face. "I've got ya, Mister Jesse—by God—James," he said. "Kiss your ass good-bye."

But then, before he could pull the trigger, as my watery veil lifted, I saw another gun barrel. This one came out of nowhere and leveled right against Zanone's ear. I saw a big thumb cock back the hammer as Zanone's face turned chalk white. I watched Zanone's eyes shift slowly as "Mysterious" Dave Mather leaned in close. Mather had a relaxed smile, but his words cut sharp as a glades knife. "Nobody kills a prisoner of mine, Zanone. Now pitch it away, or I'll dump your slop all over the lawn."

Zanone trembled as he flipped the revolver out of his hand. "When the sheriff gets back, I'll have him fire your ass," Zanone hissed.

"Sure you will," Mather said with a lazy grin. "But for now, I'm in charge, and I ain't standing for this kind of shit. So tell your pig-fucking flunkies to drop their iron. I'm taking this man in for a trial. That's the law."

Staring up, still dazed, I tried to say something to Mather. He leaned down and grabbed me by my collar. "And you, you outlaw son of a bitch. Give me a nickel's worth of shit, and I'll save the county the cost of a hanging." I saw his gun barrel swing back at a high arch. The last I remember, I was thinking, "Aw, hell, ole Dave ain't gonna hit me."

◆✳ 28 ✳◆

"But did you have to hit me with that goddamned pistol?" Mather shrugged, like it was no big deal. "I didn't know what you were apt to say, the shape you were in. Besides, don't you think that made it look good?"

For days my head had been pounding like a parade drum. When Mather managed to slip a bottle of whiskey into my cell, it dulled the pain a little, but the alcohol thinned my blood, causing my shoulder wound to start bleeding again. "What about Jeanie and the baby? What've you heard?"

"Nothing yet, but as soon—"

"Jesus, Dave, I'm going crazy worrying." I pressed my hand against the pain in my wounded shoulder.

"Settle down," Mather said, "I'll find out."

I leaned against the bars. "What's going to happen now? Can they pin that bank in Gallatin on me?"

"Both the president and a teller say they can identify you. They think you're Jesse James. There's also a banker from Roscoe, says you robbed him of three hundred dollars. They'll all be here in two weeks for the trial. You tell me what they'll say."

I frowned at Mather. "Quit fishing around like a lawman," I said, "tell me if I'm going to hang."

Mather tugged at his drooping mustache. "I don't know. I'm working on something."

"What?" I wrapped my hands around the bars.

He smiled, as if some idea of great importance had come to mind.

"Give me time. I'll see what I can do. Meanwhile, rest up and get yourself well. I'll take care of everything."

"I owe you, Dave," I said. "How can I repay you?"

"Like I said"—he smiled and turned from my cell—"I'm working on it."

I watched him walk through the door to the outer office, and wondered just how far I could trust "Mysterious" Dave. Zanone wanted me, wanted me bad, and I wondered just what price it would take to turn Mather's head. Mather was not known to act against his best interest. It had me worried.

Of course, if it hadn't been for Mather, Zanone would have skull-popped me that day at the Wilcoxes'. Also, if Mather hadn't taken care of me, I reckon I wouldn't have made it through the two weeks that followed. He saw to it that I got medical care, and he stayed close by to keep Zanone and his vultures away while I got some of my strength back.

My mind was pulled in a dozen different directions; there was nothing I could do but wait. My greatest concern was for Jeanie and the baby, but there again, what could I do?

When Mather came back the next night with news about Jeanie, his face was gray and solemn. He slipped me a new bottle of whiskey through the bars, and I knew what that meant. I thought I was ready to hear the news, but I reckon there's some things you can't be ready for.

"Your wife lost the baby," he said. Then, like a man ought to do, he left quietly for a few minutes, leaving me to handle my grief. When he came back, he stood silently, watching me through the bars until I nodded my head, telling him I was alright.

"They've taken her to a private sanitarium outside of town. That's why I've had a hard time learning anything. I talked the judge out of charging her with firing on Zanone's posse. Since Zanone showed no proof of who he was, I explained to the judge that your wife thought they were enemies of yours from back during the war."

"Thanks," I said. "How about Jeanie? Is she alright?"

"She's a strong woman," he said. "She'll make it. I found out her father and mother left town the day before Zanone rode in." Mather's expression implied something more than his words were saying. "Old man Wilcox even gave the servants some time off to visit their kin. Seems the only reason your wife was there is because she came over to get some needlework she forgot. She was supposed to be staying over with a friend. When she came back, Zanone's posse was in the house, so they held her there."

"So this was Wilcox's doing," I said. The rage of hatred in my mind toward Cronin Wilcox held balance with the sickness I felt in my stomach for what I had brought home to my wife and baby. My Jeanie didn't deserve this. That innocent baby didn't deserve this. No matter how much I blamed Wilcox and Zanone, I blamed myself even more. My hatred for them boiled in the same pool of hatred I felt for myself.

"It's not my place to say," Mather said. "I'm telling you what I know. How you call it, is up to you. But Zanone and Wilcox are tighter than blades of grass in a pig turd. Zanone is convinced you're Jesse James, so Wilcox probably thinks it, too."

"That means Jesse and Frank are going to catch the blame for the robberies, because Zanone says so."

Mather smiled and shook his head. "It's a crazy world, Mister Crowe, you know that."

I took a long cut from the bottle of whiskey and passed it through the bars. "Drink with me, Dave. It's a bad time to drink alone."

He turned up a quick shot and passed the bottle back. "I've got a rule about blaming myself for stuff," he said, as if reading my mind.

"What's that?" I was only talking to take my mind off the mess I'd made of my life. At that second, I reckon I cared less about hanging than I did about staying alive.

"I only do it when I can't think of somebody else to blame." He smiled and took the bottle through the bars.

"Good rule," I said, "but right now I can't think of another soul."

Mather nodded with a smile. "Yeah, you've pretty well ruined everything but the weather."

"Yeah," I said. "Now I reckon I'll hang and be done with it."

He nodded. "You'll probably hang, but not here, not this time."

I looked up into his dark eyes. "Huh?"

Even though the jail was empty except for the two of us, Mather glanced around before opening his coat and slipping the forty-four between the bars. "You up to breaking out of here, or are you feeling too sorry for yourself?"

I glanced at the dull shine of the revolver he offered, and thought of how good it would feel pressed against Zanone's and Cronin Wilcox's heads. "Yes!" I snatched the revolver. "That is, no, I ain't feeling *too* sorry—"

"I didn't think so," said Mather. "Here's the plan.

"Tomorrow, the sheriff will be back in town. Him and Zanone might work up a scheme between them. Zanone's got enough money to buy the sheriff and drag you out of here on a meat hook. I know, 'cause he offered me the deal."

I shoved the revolver down the back of my trousers. I felt ashamed for ever doubting Mather.

"So while I'm making my constable's rounds tomorrow night, the sheriff will be here alone. Make your break before him and Zanone get their heads together. Tomorrow night might be the only chance you get."

"Dave, I'll be honest. I was worried that you might sell me out. I'm sorry I doubted you . . . you're a friend."

"Think nothing of it," he said tossing a hand. "You'd do the same—"

"No, Dave, I mean it. I owe you a lot for all you've done. How can I repay you?"

"There is one thing." Mather's smile faded away, and his expression turned to stone. "Kill the sheriff for me on your way out." He said it as if asking me to turn out the lights before I left. I studied his eyes. He was dead serious.

"Dave, think what you're asking me to do." He was asking me to commit murder for him, to kill a man I'd never even met, a sheriff to boot. And if I killed him for Mather and made my getaway, what then? My cousin Jesse would get the blame for it, sure as hell.

Mather held up his hand, cutting me off. "I won't ask you twice. I figure if he's dead I'll make sheriff, and we both know I'll be a damn good one. But you've got the gun, you decide, Mister Crowe. Wait till you meet him and then make up your mind. Fair enough?" Mather smiled like a sly land merchant.

He turned to walk away, then stopped at the door to the office. "Oh, I meant to tell you. I sold your mare to a feller by the name of Bracker. He was real eager to get her, already paid me top money. 'Course, I told him he couldn't pick her up till after your trial. She'll be waiting for you in the livery stable on the corner, saddled and ready to go." He smiled again before he disappeared through the door. "I love being a lawman."

I spent most of the night walking the floor, feeling the forty-four pressed against my back. Every now and then, I would take my left arm out of the sling and move it around as much as possible. I needed to get whole, and be ready for tomorrow. No matter how I tried to concentrate on my plans, I kept seeing my Jeanie holding that tiny silent baby. I prayed that somehow, someday she would forgive me. I knew I would never forgive myself.

Were it not for the crazy twisted mess I would leave behind, I would have raised that pistol to my head that night. More than once I considered it. But hell, that was just making it easy on myself. It would just pile more hurt on Jeanie. God knows, she'd had enough. Besides, if there was one thing I was determined to do in life, it was to kill Zanone.

Killing Zanone had been my sworn intention since the day old Cletis rode them licking flames. It seemed the longer I let my promise of vengeance go unattended, the more suffering was heaped upon innocent people.

I had to get out of here. I had to see my Jeanie one last time, and I had to kill Zanone. I could put it off no longer. If the sheriff tried to stop me, I reckoned I would kill him, but not for Mather's sake. I would kill him only if he stood between me and freedom. Otherwise, I would knock him in the head, and apologize to Mather if I ever saw him again. For all of Mather's far-handed scheming, he had saved my life. I had to give him that.

As it turned out, Mather must have been thinking way ahead of the game. Next morning when Sheriff Sheckler stood outside my cell, it was all I could do to keep from killing him on the spot.

"Come over here, boy, let's take a look at you," he said. He was a fat greasy walrus, with deep pits of blackheads formed under swollen bloodshot eyes.

I stepped over by the bars, and he backed off a step looking me up and down. He smelled like sour lard and mildew.

"So you're the scum that caused that Wilcox whore to splatter her bastard kid all over the carpet." He reared back in ugly laughter. I had to run his words across my mind two or three times. I couldn't imagine any human saying such a thing. When I reached the point of believing what my ears had heard, I felt my hand instinctively try to grab for the pistol.

It took such restraint on my part from killing him right there that I shook like a man with a palsy. But I held on, tasting a bitter bile that cramped my jaws and set fire in the back of my throat. I stared at him and tried to control my breathing. I decided to say nothing. I knew that my own words would send me into a blood-letting rage.

"I've watched that little filly for a long time," he said with a dirty, twisted grin. His voice dropped a notch like we would share a secret. "I've always said, I bet that's the sweetest patch of fur a man could ever sink a shank in." He stepped close to the bars, twisting his holster close. I saw the safety strap was unbuckled, and realized he was trying to goad me into reaching for his pistol. I wasn't going to fall for it.

"Yes, sir," he said, "I can just feel her legs wrapped around me, wiping sweat off my ass." I felt a deathly calm sweep over me. Now that I saw what he was up to, I just let it slide past me.

He stepped back in surprise and disappointment. He hooked the safety strap on his holster. "I reckon you're just a cowardly piece of shit," he said. I just stared, feeling a crazy peaceful grin forming at the edge of my mouth. "We're all better off without your little bastard stinking up the town. If I'd been there I would have mashed its head and threw it in the hog lot."

He blew a wad of spit in my face, but I just stood there and let it run down. When he started for the door, I stared after him, almost wanting to thank him. He had just made everything so clear in my mind. It would be no problem killing him. Hell, I would have paid Mather for such an honor. Sheckler didn't know it, but he had just uncomplicated my life. He became a dead man the second he opened his ugly mouth.

That afternoon, in spite of all the torment pressing my mind, I forced myself to sleep. Waking with the last rays of sun stretched in broad stripes across the stone floor, I wiped my sweaty face on the wool blanket and got ready for a busy night.

Mather showed up with a tin plate of grits and gravy. He shoved it under the cell door and smiled as I picked it up and faced him. "What do think of our friend the sheriff?"

Without saying a word, I drew my finger across my throat. "Yeah," said Mather, "I figured you two would hit it off." He reached a hand through the bars and dropped a key in my shirt pocket. "That key has his initial stamped on it. I switched it with him this morning. In case he tried to get in there and punch around on you a little, I filed the other one off just enough so it wouldn't work for him." Mather grinned, tugging at his mustache. "So I reckon you've been safer in there than he's been out here."

I shook my head. "Dave, you're a piece of work," I said.

"One thing more," he said. "I'm surprised you didn't ask, but

Sheckler's the one who told Zanone and Wilcox you were headed this way. He spotted you over in Springfield two days before you got here and wired the information. That's how I got word of it. I had no way to warn you, but I figured if I was there, I could tip your odds a little."

I smiled, reaching my hand through the bars. "Don't worry Dave," I said. "His ass will suck maggots before this night's over." Mather took my hand and we gripped in a firm handshake.

"Watch your back, Mister Crowe, or whoever the hell you are," Mather cautioned, and I watched him slip out through the door to the office. He spoke real friendly to Sheckler on his way out. You would have thought they were blood brothers.

Sheckler must have thought the gates of hell had swung open on him. Laying back in his chair with his feet propped on the desk, his mouth gargled and snored toward the ceiling. I sat patiently for a while on the edge of the desk waiting for him to wake up on his own. I didn't want to startle him and cause him to miss a thing. In what little time he had left, I wanted his full attention.

I know I was crazy that night, for no sane man could stomach what I was about to do.

As Sheckler began to wake up, he dropped his hand down to his crotch to scratch himself. His fingers tapped against the shotgun barrel, and a confused look came over his face. Then, as realization came upon him like a cold hand, his face lost all color. He looked into my eyes. His jaw muscles went slack. When he spoke, he sounded like a man speaking from within a bad dream—the words were guttural and slurred. "Maw—Gawd," he said under his breath.

I had the grin of a blood-thirsty lunatic. "Tell me about your dream, Sheriff. Was you dreaming about my wife? Let's see, how was it you said it? Her legs wrapped around your sweaty ass? I bet your ole ass is sweating sure enough, ain't it? Knowing I'm going to blast your balls off."

"Please—God," he begged. "Don't do it."

"Aw, come on, Sheriff, be a sport about it. You said all that stuff about my wife, and my little dead baby. You know I've got to carve you up a little." I had my wounded left arm in the sling holding the shotgun. With my right hand I slashed the glades knife twice across his stomach as quick as a whip.

His hands slapped against the center of the bloody *X*. I pressed the dull edge of the blade across his throat, cutting off his screams. "I just wish there was two of you, Sheriff." His hands worked frantically, pressing to keep his guts in. "So I could do this twice." I popped one round from the shotgun in his crotch. The explosion slammed him down through the shattered chair in a spray of blood and burnt powder.

His arms flung open. So did his bloated belly. He landed on the floor wallowing in a pile of guts. His hands dipped at the mess as if to gather them up. "When you get to hell, Sheckler, try to say something nice about the devil's wife." I stabbed the glades knife down in the center of the desk and headed out the door. The smell in the office was like the stink of rabbit guts. Nailed to the desk by the glades knife, I'd left a note for Zanone. It said: "Sleep on this, till I come to wake you." Across the bottom I signed it with just two initials—"M.C."

For many years I rode with the James gang. During most of that time, because of the striking resemblance between me and Cousin Jesse, those who didn't know better thought we were one and the same.

Part IV
Far-handed Fiddlers

✦✳ 29 ✳✦

The most lonesome, mournful sound I've ever heard was the night wind brushing through the wild grass as I rode out of Kansas City headed away from Jeanine Wilcox and my dream of being a husband and a father. At times, above the sound of my mare's hooves and the beating of my heart, I swore I heard the distant laughter of an innocent child and the soft wailing of a woman's sorrow.

From atop a low rise ten miles out, I looked back at the raging storm that marked my leaving. Purple-gold clouds twisted and curled from a low dark heaven, lingering on the horizon as if pointing to the spot where I felt my life had ended. Thunder rolled out toward me like a threat from God, coming to banish and torment me and drive me on.

I gigged my bay mare and we pounded down from that low rise with the wind licking at my back. In my mind, I could see my pa's face as clear as spring water and hear his voice as sharp as a grave digger's spade. "Son, you've killed a lawman," he said, "they'll never let up, they'll hunt you like an animal till the day you die." I pictured him stepping back and turning away slowly.

I called aloud to him as my mare stretched out and tore the flatland apart. But Pa just nodded his bowed head as he walked away into my memory.

Earlier that night, after slipping my mare from the stable, I'd tore out to the sanitarium where they'd taken Jeanine. When I got there I forced my way in at gunpoint, snatched a young doctor by the collar, and burrowed my forty-four into his ear. Walking stiff necked and on the sides of his shoe soles, he led me to Jeanine's room straight away.

Dropping the gun beside her on the bed, I took her by the shoulders and leaned my face close to hers in the dim glow of the lamp. "Jeanie," I whispered, "Jeanie, it's me. Can you hear me?" She stirred, barely opening her eyes. She looked pale and weak. Her voice sounded slurred from medication. "Jess," she said with a dreamy smile, "you . . . made . . . it here. You came . . . all . . . the . . . way . . . just to . . . see me."

I snatched up the gun and pointed it straight in the doctor's face, and demanded, "What the hell have you done to her?" His eyes darted away in panic. "Nothing," he pleaded, "I swear, we've only tried to comfort her. She's been through an awful lot . . ."

I turned from him and drew her up against me. "Jeanine, Jeanie, baby, God, I'm so sorry." She sighed and tried to press her fingers to my lips.

"Don't . . . be sorry," she said softly. She was coming around some. "You can't . . . be here, Jess," her voice trailed off into a whisper. "They'll . . . kill you."

"I can't leave you this way," I whispered back, holding her close. She shook her head slowly against my chest.

"We've sure had a time of it, you . . . me, and the baby." She seemed to drift away. I looked around at the doctor.

"She doesn't even know if you're really here," he said. "Please, we've got to let her rest."

Easing her back gently to the pillow, I felt her hand try to hold on to my sleeve, then slip softly away. I had come to see her one last time, to tell her I was sorry, to tell her I loved her, that I would always love her. I wanted to tell her I'd come back for her someday. But standing there, seeing the pain I had caused her, I reckoned it was better to end it this way. I was leaving her marked as a murderer's wife. There was nothing I could do or say to lessen the shame I'd brought her. I slipped away like a thief in the night. That was one thing I knew how to do.

I rode hard for three days, through storms that pounded out from across the Rockies, leaving the land sodden and the sky low and dismal. The morning I arrived at the widow's cabin, the sun had managed to squeeze through and its glitter spread across the wet woodlands. The sunlight at the end of those dark storms reminded me that no matter what had just happened, it was time to pick up the pieces and try to go about the business of staying alive.

Whatever plans I might've had to go straight lay swimming in a pool of blood back in Kansas City. Not just anybody's blood, but the blood of a lawman. The best I could do for now was to take up with "Quiet" Jack and head back to Kearney—to Jesse, Frank, and "The boys." I needed the strength of numbers. Hell, I needed to get back in touch with my world.

The night I left Jeanine at the sanitarium, I had stopped by the Wilcox mansion before leaving town. I had told myself I was there to kill Cronin Wilcox, but that wasn't true. When I got there and saw the place was still empty, I would have rode on had I been there only to draw vengeance. As it was, I caught myself wandering through that big fancy house, just touching things, elegant things, things I knew belonged to Jeanine's world. These were things I could only touch and long for, but never have, never be a part of.

Leaving, I heard the crunch of broken crystal beneath my boots. The place had not been cleaned or repaired since the day of the ruckus. Looking down among the shards of crystal, I saw dried blood and splinters of polished oak from the banister. This was the result of my world brushing up against the world of Jeanine Wilcox, of "The Kansas City Wilcoxes."

I did one more thing before leaving Kansas City that night. I tracked through the alleys as long as I could, watching the streets from the shadows like a creature of prey. I saw no sign of Zanone. Like any low demon, he must've slipped back to hell to report to the devil. I could tarry no longer. A harsh front threatened out of the Rockies. It had busted into a full storm by the time I headed south.

"It's that no-good saddle tramp friend of your'n," I heard the widow say through the window. In a second, Jack was out across the porch and helping me down from the saddle. His eyes were glassy and he looked like a man suffering a bad head cold. Behind him, the shredded-eared hound lay under the porch and growled.

"I'll be damned," Jack said in a thick, slurred voice, "can't you go nowhere without getting shot?" My shoulder wound had broken open from the hard ride. I had made a poncho from an old blanket I'd taken from the livery stable. The front of it was covered with blood.

"It ain't as bad as it looks," I said, "and it's the least of my worries right now."

"What's wrong?" he asked, looking past me as if checking the trail. His hand went instinctively to his gun holster.

"I'm in trouble, big trouble, Jack. It's the kind of trouble you might not want any part of." I hesitated a second and let out a long breath. Jack looped my good arm across his shoulder and led me toward the cabin. "I've killed a lawman."

Inside the cabin I dropped into a wooden chair and flipped back a corner of my poncho. "I hope you ain't expecting me to clean that mess," the widow snapped. Jack snatched up a handful of cornbread and hurled it at her. "Shut your goddamn mouth!" he shouted. I was starting to have second thoughts about coming here. "My friend is hurt. Now get your broad ass busy and boil some water, or get me a knife, or goddamn it, do something!"

"No knife, Jack," I said, waving my hand, "it's a clean flesh wound."

Jack leaned down close to me. "I don't mind cutting right in there. I'll scrape the bone if need be." The thought of it made my stomach a little queasy.

"I know, but thanks," I said.

"Now, what about this trouble you're in." I stared at him a second, thinking maybe he missed what I'd said coming through the door.

"Jack," I said, slow and clear, "I've killed a lawman. I gutted him like a hog and left him wallowing on the floor."

Jack gazed at me through his glassy eyes, as if waiting to hear more. "That's it." I shrugged. "That's the big trouble I'm in."

"Well, shit," he said, letting out a long sigh, "I thought you meant something really bad."

That did it. As tired and hurt as I was, I didn't need this stupid bullshit. I blew up. "Goddamn it, Jack! I killed a lawman, hear me? A lawman!"

"So?" He shrugged again. I was ready to come out of the chair into his face.

"So, they'll hunt me down and hang me!"

"They ought to hang you both," the widow yelled. Jack hurled another lump of cornbread. I heard her yelp.

"I've known you two years," Jack said with a laugh, "and so far I ain't seen you do anything they *won't* hang you for." A piece of cornbread fired past my shoulder and clipped him on the jaw. I relaxed into my chair as a piece of cornbread slapped the back of my head and exploded in a yellow spray before me. "I bet I kill this bitch," Jack said, gathering up hands full of cold cornbread. "Welcome back," I thought to myself.

Three weeks later, we'd joined Jesse and Frank at the Samuel place. Between fights, the widow had done a right good job of nursing my shoulder wound. Though she was crazier than a three-eyed squirrel, I could see that she and Jack didn't make too bad a couple. "You know she killed her husband," Jack said casually, the day we dug up the bank money. He smiled affectionately. "Yep, stabbed him in the heart while he was asleep."

"Does that bother you when you go to bed of a night?" I asked.

"Why should it?" He laughed. "We ain't married!"

I'd told Jesse and Frank about Kansas City, about me killing Sheckler, and about Zanone—and possibly many others—thinking Jesse and I were the same person. Except for a few details, they'd already heard the whole story. Since my killing Sheckler, Clell Miller had made contact with "Mysterious" Dave Mather. Dave told them everything. From now on he would be handling any bank money we couldn't spend right away. I was glad to hear it. Mather was a good man to have on our side. He'd done a lot for me, for a high price, of course.

I also told them about me robbing the banker near the widow's place, and how Jesse might get the blame for it. They got a big kick out of it. As it turned out, Jesse started circulating a story about some poor helpless widow who was being evicted from her land and how he, in an act of kindness, saved the day. Somehow, Jesse wound up looking like a hero for robbing the heartless son of a bitch. I reckon any story is only as good as the man who's telling it.

I never mentioned Jeanine. They knew what had happened, but they respected me enough to leave my private life alone. As far as how I felt about it, I reckon they didn't have to ask. It must've showed on my face.

By the end of that year, we had hit two banks and a railroad. I tell you, with all I was going through, it felt good staying busy. Two or three times during the year, I caught myself ready to ride out and find Zanone, but outside my circle, away from the protection of my friends, I was hotter than a two-peckered billy-goat.

Then, as always, lawmen avenged their own. The name Miller

Crowe must've been whispered like a silent prayer, every morning when they shoved their forty-fours down into their holsters. It didn't matter that Sheckler was a snake. I'd blown the balls off their belief system. My ass was theirs.

Dave Mather finally convinced some of the Missouri lawmen that Jesse and I were not the same person. It helped Jesse. Most local lawmen didn't care how much Northern money Jesse stole, but if he had killed one of their peers, that was a whole other matter. It didn't change my situation at all. At any rate, though I knew I couldn't get at Zanone any time soon, I prayed for the day—and if there was a God in heaven I knew it would come—when I could reach inside his open skull and dabble my fingers in his dying brains.

In the meantime, I seldom left the Samuel place on my own, except to ride over now and then to check on my bay mare. I had boarded her at the Dutch Krugger farm six miles down the road. It was best to keep some distance between her and me. Though she wasn't branded, there was the bullet graze across her hindquarters that could be identified by anybody who happened to have seen the race back in Kansas City. Odds were against that ever happening, but why take a chance. Besides, Ole Dutch was a decent sort and had a fine reputation for taking care of horses. He knew our situation with the law, but like most folks around there, he didn't give a damn. He looked out for "The boys."

Cousin Jesse rode over to Ole Dutch's with me the morning my mare, "Jeanie's Pride," birthed her colt. When I raised the lantern above the rail of that dark stall and saw the gold light spill across my mare and that shining black colt wobbling against her flank, I reckon my heart just stopped for a second and my breath rolled up and turned wet in my throat. I wiped my sleeve across my eyes as I stepped through the rails. My voice trembled like a man witnessing a holy event. "Lord God almighty, Jesse," I whispered, barely containing my feelings, feelings that wrapped around Jeanine Wilcox, the baby we lost, the mare and the colt . . . and me. "Would you just looky here."

Jesse reached over the rail behind me and squeezed my shoulder. "Congratulations," he said quietly. "I'm going to see if Ole Dutch will work us up some coffee. Take your time here."

✦✳ 30 ✳✦

Over the next ten years Jesse and I worked out a plan: I would pull a job with some of the boys while he was somewhere with witnesses two hundred miles away. It was good thinking. If ever Jesse was caught, it would take the court forever to sort out what he did or didn't do. Not only that, it kept the law and the railroad agents from knowing where to expect us next.

So, during those years, while the law ran in circles like a hound chasing its tail, Jesse, Frank, and the rest of us went about marrying, robbing, raising young'uns, and tending to our lives as did everybody else. While I seldom ventured away on my own, there was one summer when Jack and I took a string of horses all the way out to Powder River. It was the nearest the law ever came to capturing Miller Crowe, but that's a whole other thing. It had been Jack's notion that we could sell horses to the army and hit a couple of banks on the way back. "Nothing to it," he'd said, but the whole idea was a disaster. We had it out with Indians, bounty hunters, outlaws, local lawmen, and the U.S. Army. I could've killed Jack, but it taught me one thing; I learned to stay close to my own people.

Our first civilian train robbery was Frank's and my idea. I heard Reno's bunch was doing really well robbing trains. I figured if those dumb bastards could do it, we had to give it a try. I'd taken such a hooting from everybody over the Powder River mess, I needed to come up with a good idea just to save face.

At first I couldn't believe how easy it was when I hopped aboard an engine after blocking the tracks near Shadyville. "This is a holdup," I shouted above the throb of the steam engine. The engineer and the fireman looked at the gun in my hand, then at each other. The fireman looked about a hundred years old. He raised a hand to his ear. "What'd he say?" he shouted at the engineer.

"He said—" The engineer responded in a high-pitched yell.

"I said, it's a goddamn holdup . . . see, see!" I waved my gun in the air before them. I pulled off a round through the ceiling. It was not that loud beneath the heavy pulse of the engine, but they jumped back a step. I reached an arm out the window and waved in Jack, Clell Miller, and the other three. Back at the mail car, Charlie Pitts and Andy McGuire were already busting through the door with a broad axe. The old fireman grinned and pointed a long crooked finger. "Yore him, yore him . . . yore that James boy, ain't cha?"

I just shook my head and pulled the kill lever on the engine. The sound died down with a jolt. My plan had been to first rob the train, then take the bandanna from my face right before we left. Seeing that idea was shot to hell, I jerked down the bandanna and spit lint from my mouth. "Yeah, I am," I said, a little disgusted. "Now let's get back there and get to robbing this train."

The old fireman cut a little jig on the floor, waving his arms and laughing. "I knowed it, I knowed it," he crowed, laughing across empty gums. "I seen your picture. C'mon," he said, motioning back toward the passenger cars. "I want you to meet these folks." He actually tried to grab my arm. I drew back the pistol, threatening him.

"Keep your hands clear," I said, "this ain't no damn social visit."

"I understand," he said with a chuckle.

Inside the passenger car, I saw Jack and the rest starting to take money and valuables and drop them into a feed sack. The passengers looked scared and pissed off. "Listen up," the fireman yelled. He clapped his hands real loud to get their attention. Jack almost spun around and shot him. Everybody, including Jack and "The boys," stared curiously. "This here is Jesse—by God—James, and I want ya'll to give him yore undivided attention." He gestured toward me as if I was to give a speech. The passengers stared with their mouths open.

"Yeah . . . well," I stammered and cleared my throat. "I'm here to rob the train. Now, everybody do what you're told and nobody will get hurt." I looked at them. They looked as if they expected more. I looked at Jack and shrugged. He rolled his eyes above the bandanna mask. "That's all," I said, waving my hand, "thank you, thank you very much."

I couldn't believe it. They started clapping, cheering, and digging deeper into their purses and wallets. A few got up and started at me smiling and reaching out their hands. I nearly started shooting. "Sit them down!" I yelled to Jack and the others. "Get them seated, now!"

"Come on now, folks," I heard Clell say, "Jesse needs your help here." Women were reaching out picking at my sleeves. I pulled away. One big fat feller come up quick with his hand inside his coat, and I damn near blew his head off before I saw the lead pencil in his hand. "Would you write your name here on my hat?" he pleaded. "For my young'uns."

"Get them back, goddamn it!" I yelled.

By the time we got the passengers settled down, I was jumpy as a cricket in a henhouse. While the other passengers had thrashed around in excitement, I noticed two well-dressed fellers halfway back who hadn't made a sound. They sat there watching every move we made out the corners of their eyes. I never let on that I noticed them, but I stayed ready to throw down if they tried anything. I didn't want any shooting in such close quarters.

As we jumped down from the train, the old fireman tried to grab my arm again. "Tell us about that widder woman and the banker," he yelled. I shook loose and dropped to the ground. Clell handed me the reins to my new black gelding.

"Not now, Old Timer," I called back over my shoulder, "maybe next time."

"Hear that?" he called back to the passengers. "He'll be back, he said he would." He waved till we were a hundred yards uphill, heading into the woods.

Clell Miller could be the most aggravating son of a bitch in the world, but he was the kind of person who could piss in your boot and you'd wind up laughing about it. All he cared for was running wild and having fun; you had to like him.

Not long after our first train job, I rode with Clell to a secret meeting at a shack outside of Roscoe. Clell was acting very closed lipped about it, but he insisted I go with him. "I don't like it," I told him, as we spun our reins around the hitching post next to a fine-looking horse and buggy. "You know I've got to keep looking back over my shoulder for Zanone and his men."

"You worry too much about Zanone," he said quietly, reaching for the door. "You have to let go and have some fun." He motioned me toward him with the crook of his finger. "Now just keep quiet and look mean."

"Look mean?" I started to turn back, but Clell stepped inside and pulled me with him.

"Mister James!" a voice boomed, and before my eyes adjusted to dim light, I nearly yanked out a pistol and started firing. "This is truly an honor."

"What is this shit?" I spoke to Clell, my eyes straining into the room. Now I could see the heavyset man in a black suit standing behind a broken table. My hand was on my pistol, but it didn't seem to bother him a bit.

"Relax." Clell laughed and slapped me on the back. Then he said to the man in the suit, "Here he is, just like I promised. Mister Brey, I'd like you to meet Mister Jesse James."

I stared at Clell, wondering if he'd truly lost his mind. Then as the man stepped toward me from around the table with a big smile and his hand extended arm's length, I recognized him from our train robbery. He was the one who'd wanted me to sign his hat for his children. I shook his hand cautiously, glancing at Clell. Clell grinned and motioned to a chair. "What is this?" I whispered through clenched teeth.

"Perhaps you remember me from the train the other day," Brey answered, as Clell all but forced me down into the chair.

"Yeah," I said, and I shoved Clell's hand off my shoulder. "What's going on here?"

Brey circled back behind the table and sat down. "I assure you, this place is quite safe," he waved his hands. "When Sheriff Bratcher here said you agreed to meet with me, he insisted I keep silent about it . . . and I have."

I glanced up at Clell. "Sheriff Bratcher?"

Clell grinned. "Jesse has to be real cautious. I'm sure you understand."

"Oh, of course. I understand, the business you're in. And I have to be very cautious in my business, too."

"Hold it, goddamn it . . . just hold it," I said, raising my hands chest high. "Somebody's got about five seconds to tell me what's going on here."

"Oh . . . I'm sorry, Mister James. Let me come right to the point. I would like your assistance in a matter of great importance, and I'm willing to pay one thousand dollars, in advance, right here today." He took an envelope from his coat pocket and dropped it on the table. "And much, much more on the day we complete our transaction."

I glanced between Brey and Clell. "What business are you in?"

"I'm the President of The Stockman's Bank and Trust." He beamed. "I saw what a smooth and splendid job you did robbing that train, and I would like to hire you to—" He coughed and mumbled his next words.

"What's that?" I leaned closer across the table. "I didn't understand you."

"I would like you to"—he cleared his throat and hesitated—"rob my bank, and let me shoot at you as you leave town."

I just stared at him a second. "Time to go," I said, and started up from my chair.

But Clell shoved me back down. "Don't make me arrest you, Jesse," he said with a chuckle. "Just hear the man out."

That night, Clell and I rode back to Kearney with five hundred a piece shoved down in our pockets. "I'm getting drunker than a hoot owl tonight," said Clell, laughing like a lunatic.

I shook my head. "Reckon it's true what he said, that getting robbed by Jesse James will help his career?" Brey had said that his bank was a subsidiary of a larger bank in Chicago, and this kind of publicity—firing a couple rounds at the James gang—would boost him up to a softer chair. I didn't buy it.

"Aw, sure," Clell said. "You just don't understand the world of business. He'll be a hero to that banking bunch."

"Well . . . there ain't no way I'll go near his bank, that's for damn sure."

"Dingus, you worry too much." Clell was the only one who still called me Dingus. "I'll get Ed and Cole, and we'll pop that bank. It's a piece of cake." Clell laughed. "After all we gave our word, and the man *is* a banker."

I knew why Clell was laughing. Before we'd left the shack, as Brey handed me the money, I'd asked him how he knew he could trust us. "Why, Mister James," he'd said, astonished, "you and I are both businessmen, and after all, Bratcher here *is* a sheriff."

I had to laugh with him as we rode along. "Between you bankers and sheriffs, a poor outlaw ain't got a chance."

"That stupid bastard!" Clell hooted.

*   *   *

But Clell didn't hoot after robbing Brey's bank. As it turned out, Brey not only fired a couple rounds, he put one straight through Clell's shoulder and another in Ed Miller's ass before Cole Younger turned in his saddle and splattered Brey's head all over the front of the building. According to Cole, Ed lost his horse and had to hop out of town on one leg, holding his bloody ass with both hands and screaming like a whipped wildcat.

"I can't figure what went on in his mind," Clell said the next time I saw him. We all sat around a campfire, sipping coffee and watching the low flames.

I had to laugh. "I reckon, he figured if firing a couple rounds would make him a hero, think what killing you sons of bitches would do."

"I don't think it's funny," Clell said, staring down at his boots. His arm was still in a sling. His brother Ed still had to ride lying over his saddle like a sack of grain. The day they'd robbed Brey's bank, Brey was the only one there, and they came out with a bag of scrap paper and metal washers.

"If you don't think *that's* funny," Cole Younger said, "you won't get much of a bang out of this either." He flipped a newspaper from his coat pocket and threw it at Clell's feet. Clell picked it up, read it, and let it slump from his hand.

"I'll be double goddamned," Clell said. The paper reported that eleven thousand dollars had been stolen from Brey's bank. Evidently Brey had skimmed money from his own bank and set up a robbery to cover it up. He must've figured if he killed one or two robbers and the other got away, he would be off the hook and looking like a hero at the same time. The poor scheming bastard. Cole stopped his clock.

"I knowed it was all bullshit from the goddamn git-go," Ed's muffled voice said. He lay facedown on a blanket, the seat of his pants bulging from the heavy bandage.

"Quiet" Jack stood and pitched his coffee in the fire. "What was it you said, Clell?" He laughed. "If it worked, you was going to put an ad in the newspaper, 'Banks robbed, by appointment only, signed Jesse James.'"

"Go to hell, Jack," Clell said, kicking the newspaper away from his feet. "It's assholes like Brey that gives this whole business a bad name."

But even as our laughter roared around the campfire, I leaned over, picked up the newspaper, and saw an article depicting Daniel Zanone as a new force for justice across the West. "Nor will I rest," he was quoted, "until I have eliminated the scoundrels who have stained Missouri with the deplorable title of 'The Outlaw State.'"

I wadded up the paper and threw it into the fire. No matter where I was, Zanone was always close enough to darken my spirit.

"Goddamn it!" Cole reached to grab the paper, but it had already flared in the fire. "There was an article about *me* in there. I wanted to keep it!"

✦❋ 31 ❋✦

When Frank heard about Brey's bank, he just laughed and took it in
stride. "All they have to do is look for a bullet in my ass or Jesse's and
they'd know it wasn't us," he said.

"What about Cole?" I said. "What if they think he was you or
Jesse?"

"I can't speak for Jesse," he said, "but if anybody ever mistakes me
for that frog-legged bastard, I want them to hang me."

The bank robbery was soon forgotten, but as it turned out, robbing
that train had been like opening up a sack full of rattlesnakes. Railroads had all the money in the world and were old hands at forcing
and enforcing their will. Where banks had a hard time figuring out
just how to deal with our new enterprise, the railroads and express
companies jumped on us like a duck on a June bug. Banks were
always careful of their image and kept a close eye on public opinion.
Railroads? Hell, to them we were no different than the buffalo.
They'd get us off their tracks in one bloody heap, image be damned.
We were costing them money, money that could buy back public
opinion once the cold sod hit our faces.

Since law enforcement hadn't sorted out who was who in the robbing
circle, the Reno gang got the blame because they dealt heavy in train
robbery, even though I identified myself as Jesse James that day on
the train and looked dead like him. It turned out that the two well-
dressed fellers on the train were former investigators for the Pinkerton Detective Agency, part of a group old Allen Pinkerton had fired
for God knows what.

They were now a part of a new agency called the Midwest Security and Detection Company—a low-handed bunch of cutthroat pol-
troons—hired to track down the Reno gang. I reckon to justify their

pay they were calling it a Reno job, with Frank Reno trying to lay it on the James brothers. It could get confusing.

When Jesse heard Reno got credit for our first train robbery, he blew up. I couldn't believe he acted the way he did. It was like a child pouting over who'd won a foot race. I went straight to Frank. "What's eating at Jesse?" I asked. "I figured he would be tickled to death we didn't get the call for that train job. Instead he's acting all riled up about it."

Frank shrugged, but I saw a concerned look in his eyes. Then he glanced around the yard and jerked an envelope from inside his coat. "This is a letter Jesse wrote to the newspaper in Springfield. He's actually griping about Reno's bunch getting credit for the train job." He tapped the letter against my chest. "Can you believe this shit?" Frank looked truly worried. "Come here," he said, nodding toward the barn, "I want to show you something else." Inside the barn, he flipped up the lid of a large wooden feed bin. When the lid flipped back I heard the rattle of glass and saw the pile of blue medicine bottles. I knew what it meant.

"Damn, are these Jesse's?"

"Every damn one," he said, letting out a long breath. "That's how much morphine-laudanum he has gone through in the past seven months."

"There must be over a hundred empty bottles here."

"A hundred and seventeen," said Frank, "and I don't know what the hell to do. I know he's having a lot of trouble with that old chest wound, but I fear he's going out of his head on this stuff." Frank hesitated and his voice kicked down a notch. "And Jack Smith ain't helping matters a bit."

I knew Jack nipped at the blue bottles now and then, but I never thought much about it. His eyes had been glassy, off and on, since the day he came to meet me in Kansas City. "You saying Jack is causing Jesse to drink that stuff?"

"I ain't sure what I'm saying." Frank shook his head. "But every time Jack leaves here for two or three days, he comes back rattling like a peddler's wagon."

"Jack's as good a friend as ever I've had," I said. I wanted Frank to realize up front that I would stand for nobody throwing down on "Quiet" Jack.

"I know," Frank said, "that's why he's still alive. Cole has been wanting to kill him for the longest time, but I've refused him."

"What's Cole got against him?"

"Who knows, probably just the fact that Jack's fast with a gun. You know Cole."

"Yeah," I said, "and I'll know him in past tense if he tangles with 'Quiet' Jack. I promise you, Jack will chop him off at the ankles."

"Either way," Frank said, "we've got to do something about Jack, and we've got to do something about Jesse."

Leaving the barn, we walked past the porch and saw the two of them, Jesse and "Quiet" Jack Smith, leaning against the front of the house. They stared down at the porch as if watching the secrets of life unfolding beneath them. They nodded their heads slowly, in unison, as if they were just real pleased about something. "See what I mean," Frank said. I didn't even answer.

"This is pure bullshit," Jack said, staring down through the trees toward the tracks. "There ain't a goddamned thing in or out of Hot Springs but a train load of sick people. What're we gonna do, steal a bucket of yeller spit?" Jack was shaky and spun tighter than new rope. I winked at Clell Miller and Charlie Pitts as Jack raised the blue bottle of morphine to his lips.

"Feeling bad, Jack?" I asked.

"Got a tickling right here," he said, tapping his chest.

As the train rounded the turn a half-mile back, I raised the shotgun from my saddle scabbard. "Here she comes, boys," I said. Jack stuffed the bottle into his shirt and raised his bandanna around his face. Just then, I eased my black gelding forward right behind Jack's bay. At first I just wanted to hit him hard enough to addle him, but as I drew back the shotgun like it was a club, I couldn't help but remember the day he whacked a rifle barrel across my neck. "Good God damn!" Clell shouted, as Jack shot forward over his horse's neck and slapped the ground like a bundle of rags, "you've killed him."

"He's alright," I said. "Let's get him in there and get it over with."

We deposited "Quiet" Jack Smith in the Spring of the Hill Sanitarium, the only place in Hot Springs at that time offering a restraining facility. He was still unconscious when the they slipped him into what we called a "happy jacket," and I cornered a thick-necked Swede orderly before we left. "I want my friend to be well taken care of," I said, stuffing a roll of greenbacks into the feller's shirt pocket. "If anything happens to him, I'll reach back in your pocket and rip your heart out, understand?"

The big Swede looked us over, not a bit put off by our hardware, and smiled as cool as springhouse butter. Evidently, he'd dealt with our type before. I didn't know it just then, but as we dragged Jack into that sanitarium, Frank, Jesse, and Zerelda—Zee, as Jesse started calling her after they'd married—were on their way to a relative's farm in Adairville, Kentucky, so that Jesse could be looked after in much the same manner. I reckon using morphine-laudanum must've been like letting a pet bear scratch your balls. It felt good, but you just never knew when it might get a hold on you.

It's not widely known, nor was it ever talked about much in our circle, but on the way to Adairville, Cousin Jesse went into a dark frame of mind and tried to commit suicide. He'd gotten his hands on sixteen grains of morphine and downed a lethal dose before anybody knew it. Had it not been for Frank, Zee, and an old backwoods physician, Jesse would've gone off dancing with the angels that night.

It wasn't known outside our group till years later, when that old doctor wrote about it in the Kansas City *Journal*. It seemed when all else failed, the only thing that saved Jesse was Frank shaking him and warning him of enemies coming to get him.

According to the old doctor's story, Jesse's instincts as a hunted man proved stronger than the lethal dose of narcotics. He staggered around the room waving his gun with Frank prodding him on anytime he faltered. I reckon Cousin Jesse must've fought hell and the devil that night. By morning he rested in a natural sleep, and by noon he was up and about as if it never happened. Poor ole boy, he had his bad times and weaknesses just like the rest of us.

Resting and drying out for six weeks in that peaceful community did Jesse a lot of good. The next time I saw him, he was as clear-eyed as ever and as game as a fighting cock. I heard him talk many times over the years of the gracious hospitality shown him in Adairville. It always made me proud to be from Kentucky. But even though Adairville treated him well, Jesse, along with Frank, Andy McGuire, and some others, rode through on their way out of town, robbed the bank, and killed its president. You just never knew what "The boys" were apt to do.

During the six weeks Jack spent in the sanitarium, I stayed around the outskirts of Hot Springs. Clell Miller and "Cock-eyed" Charlie Pitts turned surly and restless after the first week and left the very second I convinced them I would have no trouble staying away from the local authorities. To tell the truth, I feared one of them would end up killing somebody if they stayed pinned in one spot too long. Besides, with them gone, it gave me an opportunity to venture out a little and see if I would be noticed. I didn't want to spend my life hiding behind somebody's coattails. Jack and I had plenty of money buried near the Samuel place and eventually I wanted to track off on my own and settle down somewhere.

With Clell and Charlie gone, I wired Dave Mather and had him put out word that Miller Crowe had been seen all the way up in Colorado. After a few days I ventured into Hot Springs real cautious-like and took a room at the Sherare House, less than a mile from where Jack lay sweating out his morphine.

I spent a whole day barbering down and soaking in hot mineral water, then bought a brand new black linen suit, white shirt, and boiler hat. After picking out a pair of well-broken dress shoes from a local undertaker, I suited up in my fresh garments, stored my road gear in my room, and set out to visit the gaming parlors.

✦❈ 32 ❈✦

During the remaining weeks, while Jack sweated it out in the Spring of the Hill Sanitarium, I quietly introduced myself as Jim Beatty and went about squeezing every dollar I could from the gambling crowd. Most of that bunch were either sick people looking for treatment from the mineral springs, or else they were visiting and attending sick kinfolks. Either way, they had more on their minds than making money. It took me about five minutes to see that they were mostly just rich, bored, and worried, and gambling to pass time. Since I'd been holed up so long, I reveled in the action and raked in the cash. Careful to draw no undue attention to myself, I managed to stay forty percent ahead in winnings, and blended into the crowd like a homesick chameleon.

From time to time I rode out to visit Jack, mostly to make sure he was getting over any ill feelings he had about me cracking his head and making him go through treatment. On one of my earlier visits I was busting to tell about my good fortune from the night before. I was so far ahead in winnings I didn't bother counting anymore. I just made sure I lost every third or fourth hand.

"Jack," I said, as soon as I stepped through the restraining-room door, "you ain't gonna believe what a pile of money I've scraped off this bunch. When you get out of here, we'll—"

"I ain't shit in over a week," Jack said, blunt as a hoop rivet. His expression was a total blank. He sat with his hands folded calmly on the table top, wearing a white wool shirt buttoned at the throat. I just stared at him a second, not knowing what he expected me to say.

"It's the truth," he continued. "If I don't shit soon, I'll go bug-eyed."

I shrugged and tossed my hands. "Well, Jack, I don't know what to say . . . I mean . . . I'm sorry, I reckon."

"They say I've drank so much 'blue river' my insides don't know what to do or when to do it."

"Jack, maybe I ought to go get the attendant or something."

He shook his head. "They're all crazy here, you know." He was matter-of-fact about it. "Yeah, this whole goddamned bunch is crazy. If you don't get me outta here I'll be goosing butterflies with a broom handle the rest of my goddamn life."

"Jack, you gotta give it a chance."

"Of a night they shrink up about half their size and run up and down the hall slapping at rats with their underwear."

That did it for me. I eased backwards out the door and went straight to the head man. "Mister Beatty," he said, "I understand your concern for your friend." He was an old feller, bald as a stump, with a white beard that swung nearly down to his navel and spectacles that perched right at the tip of a thin hooked nose. "Believe me, what you're seeing are the results of a lot of powerful medication over a long period of time. He will get better, I assure you."

I tapped the tip of my finger down on his polished oak desk. "If my friend comes out of here babbling like an idiot, I'll spray this place down with a ten-gauge, you first."

He didn't appear the least bit threatened. "What do you know about Mister Smith?"

I tensed up. "What do you mean?" I wasn't about to start telling anything I knew about Jack, and I wondered for a second if Jack himself might have said something, something he shouldn't have.

"I mean, Mister Beatty, what does your friend do, how does he act, does he have blackout spells?"

I eased up a little, now that I saw he was just inquiring about Jack's health. "He works for me, if that's what you mean. As far as how he acts, he acts just fine. And no, I don't reckon I've ever seen him black out, unless you count being drunk." It felt odd talking about Jack, him not being present to answer for himself. "Why do you ask?"

The old doctor reached into his desk and pulled out a stack of drawings. Spreading the stack across his desk he placed his finger on one, motioning me closer. "These are drawings of Mister Smith's skull," he said. "Notice these protrusions of bone, both here and here." His finger jumped from one spot to another. I leaned in and studied what was supposed to be the exact likeness of Jack's knotted head. "This indicates an old fracture that runs from just above the temple area, all the way back to here, just above his ear."

"How old a fracture are we talking about?" I asked, thinking about the other day when I lifted him from the saddle with my shotgun butt.

"Very, very old," he replied, "in fact, I would say these fractures— and I mean more than one—must have happened when he was no more than eight, maybe ten years old."

"So, you're saying he must've been kicked more than once by the same horse?"

"Hardly, Mister Beatty." He took off the spectacles and laid them on the drawings. "Have you ever seen Mister Smith without a shirt on? Ever seen his back?"

I thought about it a second. "Come to think of it, no, I reckon I haven't."

The old doctor folded his hands and gazed down at his desk, shaking his head slowly. "I'm afraid Mister Smith has had a hard life."

"Hell, ain't we all." I grinned until I saw the way the doctor stared at his folded hands, as if in regret for some terrible thing that had happened, as if ashamed for even knowing of it. My grin faded.

"Broken ribs, not just once or twice, but many times, judging from the bone structure. Scars. Whelps so brutal that the swelling hardened into cysts."

"Jesus," I whispered, "who would do something like that to a little young'un?"

The doctor shrugged. "That's why I asked what you knew about him. Apparently someone, a guardian, perhaps a parent, a fiend whoever they were, beat that poor man like an animal before he was even old enough to know why."

I backed two steps from his desk and lowered myself into a wooden chair. The old doctor removed the drawings from his desk, dropping them into a drawer the way you would drop something dirty. "That's also why I asked what he does and how he acts. Usually a person like that is, well, sometimes they're not very bright."

"Hold on now," I said, taking offense. "There ain't a damn thing wrong with Jack. Hell, he ain't what you call fancy smart—"

I stopped in the middle of my words, remembering the day Jack and I holed up in that farmhouse over in Jackson County. That was the day he damn near shot me for calling him stupid. "You can't punish a man . . . brow-beat him . . . treat him like an animal, just because he ain't fancy smart. . . ." Jack's words spilled from my memory like cold, clear water. I just stared at the doctor.

He nodded his head as if he'd seen the realization come upon me. "I'm not saying your friend is an imbecile, in fact, there are some things he probably does that border on brilliant. But from time to time, his mind just gets away from him, kind of like a train jumping track."

I thought of Jack's blazing speed and deadly gun handling. I remembered him working the scheme that day at the race track. I also remembered times when he just flat did not seem to know what was going on around him.

"I reckon that's Jack," I said. "I reckon you called him about right. What'll become of him?"

The doctor picked up the spectacles and hooked them back across his nose. He smiled and spread his hands flat on the desk. "That depends on you, Mister Beatty. Your friend, people like him, have to have someone to follow, to mimic, someone to inform them as to the whens and wheres in life. So," he let out a long breath, "I suppose what happens to Mister Smith depends on you, you and the others."

"What do you mean," I snapped, "me and the others?"

He smiled, a tired patient smile. "I've been around a long time, Mister Beatty. I know a couple of 'The boys' when I see them."

Casually, I raised my hand, rubbed my chin, then let my hand rest against my chest. Under my shirt hung the forty-four. "The boys?" I spoke softly. I was already figuring how to get Jack out of there after I head-popped the doctor. The shape Jack was in, it would be like trying to rope a pile of sand.

"You have nothing to fear from me." The doctor's voice sounded calm, almost weary, as if he was tired from having repeated those same words across his desk a thousand times before. "Anything you say to me is in total confidence. Just consider it part of the treatment."

"I ain't here for any treatment," I said. For some reason I believed him, but I wasn't giving any ground, not yet. "And my mind is sharp as a glades knife." He nodded his head slowly, staring me straight in the eyes.

"Of course. So let me tell you about your friend, or people like him." His voice went soft and even, as if to make me reach for, and attend to, every word he said. "Your friend will recover from the morphine. He may go back to it, he may not. Like others carrying terrible scars, or terrible memories, when he starts hurting he'll reach for something, if not the morphine—'blue river,' as he calls it—then something else." The doctor's voice purred low and steady, like a slow pendulum blade, swinging closer and closer to me with each word. I shifted uncomfortably in the hard wooden chair.

"Like others, he'll more than likely drift from one thing to another—liquor, low women, or like many of 'The boys,' far-handedness, robbing, and killing, anything to keep him on the move. Anything to keep him from facing the pain."

I broke away from his gaze and stared down at the floor, but only for a second. When I looked back up, his gaze hadn't wavered an inch. He smiled. "Tell me, Mister Beatty," he said, almost playfully, "do you drink?"

"No, doc, that is, not enough to . . ." I stopped cold as I caught on to what he was doing. "Wait a goddamn minute," I snapped, "there ain't a thing wrong with me. I got no problems, at least nothing that pouring a little mineral water over is going to help. You can save that shit for your paying customers. I don't need it."

"I understand," he said, nodding. He formed a steeple of his folded fingers and tilted back his head, gazing at me down that long hooked nose.

"You don't understand a goddamn thing," I said, feeling my neck heat up, "not about me. You think I don't see that when you say that shit about Jack, all you're doing is talking about me, except you're doing it from around the corner." I stood up and reached for the door. I was starting to boil. Something told me I didn't have to fear his saying anything about me or Jack; if I thought he would, I reckon I would've dropped him right there.

What he'd said had hit me too close to home. I was angry, rattled, and somehow curious at the same time. I was stuck somewhere between shooting the bastard or dropping back down in the chair and asking him to tell me more. When I slung open the door to leave, I stopped for a second. There was something I wanted to tell that son of a bitch, but I wasn't sure what it was. I reckon I wanted to tell him he had no idea what my life had been. He hadn't traveled the roads I'd been down, and been through the shit I'd been through.

In the back of my mind I heard my pa yell as the rifles tore him apart, smelled ole Cletis burn off the bone and sizzle in the fire, watched life snap shut in Kenny Ellworth's eyes, and pictured a tiny stone somewhere in a Kansas City cemetery where a baby slept forever. I wanted to tell him all this, I wanted to twist my fists into his collar and shout it in his face. But when I spun around and faced him, I couldn't say a damn word. He had to see the madness flare across my eyes. He unfolded his hands and lay them flat on his desk. "I understand," he said again, only this time I believe he meant it.

That night, I was gut-restless and testy as a galled dog. After losing a few hands in a row—hell, I couldn't keep my mind on the game—I drifted back to the Sherare House and slipped quietly into the nearly deserted bar. Alone in the shadows at a corner table, I studied the low flame of a lamp as it flickered soft gold through a bottle of rye whiskey. A picture of Jack Smith kept coming to my mind. This was not "Quiet" Jack Smith the outlaw, but young Jack Smith, a scared little boy hiding in a dark room of a large house, shivering in pain and fear. The picture flashed over and over. I couldn't drink it away. I was a little pissed at the doctor for telling me. Somehow it didn't seem right for me to know all that about Jack.

I remembered one night back during the war while we were holed up near the Valley of the Ozarks. Just to make conversation, I had asked Jack about his folks. He shifted around and stared out at the dark woods, "Got none," he'd said firmly. "My mama left when I was a baby."

"Well," I asked, "what about your pa?"

"My what . . . what's that?" He tossed a glance over his shoulder toward me, then back into the darkness. "Oh . . . my dad." He took a deep breath. "My dear old father." He hesitated a second, then said, "He died when I was fourteen."

"That's too bad." I should've left it alone right there, seeing Jack wasn't too keen on talking about it. But I didn't. "What happened to him?" I coaxed.

Jack stared at the woods and commenced rocking back and forth on the blanket, picking at the sole of his boot. "He was killed," he said, finally, "killed in his sleep." Sitting cross-legged, Indian style, Jack rocked more and more nervously on the blanket.

"They ever catch the person who killed him?"

"I don't know," Jack said. He stopped rocking and turned still as stone, staring out into that black moonless void. "I ran away that night and never went back."

At the time it didn't dawn on me what Jack was really saying. Now, after talking to the old doctor, the pieces of Jack's puzzle snapped together in my mind. As I recalled now, thinking back on it, it was nearly a week after that before Jack said another word.

I visited Jack twice a week and spent the rest of my time raking in greenbacks. But to tell the truth, after that day in the doctor's office, I wasn't relishing my good fortune the way I should have. Like the rest of the crowd, my mind was now on other things—on illness I reckon, partly Jack's, partly my own. I was actually glad the night a skinny feller showed up with the message that Jack would be released the next morning.

◆✳ 33 ✳◆

"A wagon load of water?" I shrugged and tossed my hands in the air. Jack sat holding the reins with his arms crossed, staring straight out past the team of mules. His jaw was set and his mind was made up. I'd argued with him over half an hour, but he wouldn't budge.

"I ain't leaving without it," he concluded, "so there."

I'd slammed my boiler hat to the ground and kicked it, then I'd kicked the wagon wheel. Now, my toe throbbed as I picked up my hat and dusted it against my leg. "This tears it, Jack," I said, "this just . . . plumb . . . goddamn . . . tears it." I leaned against the wagon with one hand and stared at the three barrels of mineral water. "Don't you think if this stuff really cured anything, they'd be selling it in every store in the country."

He stared straight on. "It cured me of blue river," he said, then he turned slowly toward me. His eyes narrowed. "It cured the back of my head, where somebody pot-hooked me with a goddamn shotgun barrel."

What could I say? I had bought two rail tickets to Kearney and already put our horses into freight. I figured we could ride back in style and maybe catch a few hands of poker on the way. Evidently somebody, probably that cool smiling Swede, had convinced Jack that Arkansas spring water could cure anything from common clap to missing limbs. There was no talking him down.

"Yeah," he said as I climbed up beside him and settled into the hard wooden seat. "It'll be a rough ride, but damn well worth it." I noticed a pillow sticking out from under his rump as he slapped the reins, damn near throwing me backwards. "Wish I'd of thought to bring you one of these," he said, "but I reckon I need it worse, after being pot-hooked and fitted to a happy jacket, and all." I thought I caught just a touch of sarcasm in his voice. I knew it would be a long trip.

*   *   *

"Jack, look out!" I yelled. We were four days out of Hot Springs and had stopped for provisions in a supply town called Pearly Point. I'd just hitched the team to a rail.

A small figure in a large, dirty coat came rolling down from the boardwalk, bounced off Jack, and landed at my feet. I jumped back as tiny fingers appeared from the coat sleeve and snatched at the glades knife in my boot. I reached down to grab the hand, but saw the knife coming out in a flash of cold steel. The figure rolled away in a flurry of dust as I snatched the back of the coat and slung whoever it was against the side of our wagon.

The glades knife whistled past my face as I jumped back again. This time I saw a slice of my hat brim fly away, and I grabbed a thin wrist as the big knife came back at me. "It's a little yellow woman," Jack said with laugh, "about to wash your face with your own knife."

"This ain't funny, goddamn it!" I yelled at Jack. I struggled to keep hold on the wrist. From inside the coat it felt as if a bundle of rattlesnakes was lashing out in every direction. From behind me I heard the barroom doors crash open and a voice from the boardwalk.

"Hold that little bitch, right there," the voice demanded. With my free hand I reached into the coat collar and grabbed a handful of black hair and shoved back against the wagon. When I saw it was like Jack said—a little yellow woman—I eased up some and twisted the glades knife from her hand, then slung her away from the wagon. I saw her face long enough to know she'd been smacked around pretty badly before she made it out of the saloon. In spite of the blood on her cheek and her swollen eye, I could see she was young—late teens, early twenties.

She scrambled away in the dust, trying to get to her feet, but the big feller from the bar ran up and crashed a boot into her ribs. She folded up with a groan. "You yeller whore," he growled, picking her up and slinging her over his shoulder like a sack of feed. "Now we'll see which way it runs." He started back toward the saloon.

Jack shot me a curious glance as the big feller walked past me. As much out of curiosity as anything else, I stepped in front of him, and he jerked to a halt. The girl's legs hung down from his shoulders, struggling under the grip of his huge arm. I reckon that kick in the ribs had crushed most of her strength. "What the hell do you want?"

he bellowed. Goddamn he was big. I glanced at Jack. Jack just rolled his eyes, like he knew the shit was about to hit the wind.

"What're you fixin' to do to that little woman?" I asked, bold as brass.

He shrugged. "We're fixin' to have some of her. What the hell's it to you?" Behind me I heard hoots and laughter coming from the saloon, and glanced around at four or five faces peering across the swinging doors. Jack had leaned his elbows on the hitching post as if to enjoy the show. I turned back to the big feller and started to say something else. "Aw, the hell with you," he growled. He swung his free arm sideways, knocking me flat on my ass on the dirt street as he stepped up to the boardwalk and disappeared into the saloon. I sat there trying to catch my breath, my glades knife still hanging from my hand. I felt like I'd been bounced off an oak log. Jack laughed and shook his head, then shot me a curious stare. "Well?" he asked, nodding toward the saloon. I knew what he was getting at. I pointed my finger straight at him.

"No, by God, and I mean no." I stood up slapping dust from the seat of my pants. "I can't afford no trouble and you know it."

Jack shrugged. "I understand."

"That was none of my business and I shouldn't have butted in."

"I understand," he said, with half a grin.

"Jack, I mean it. Whatever they do, it's their business."

Jack gazed off at the sky and rubbed his chin. "He's one big son of a bitch, that's for sure." I saw what he was doing; it was getting to me. I was red-assed from that wagon seat and I'd been pissed at Jack since we left Hot Springs. "He ain't that goddamn big, and I ain't that goddamn little," I snorted, slapping that glades knife against my leg and biting the inside of my lip. "Let's get out of here." From inside the saloon, I heard a scream, a hard slap, and laughter.

"Still," Jack said, wincing at the sound of that slap, "him knocking you down and all, seems like you oughta cut him just a little. Just for the sake of good manners."

We heard sobbing, pleading, then another hard slap. I gritted my teeth at the sound, stared at the swinging doors, and wiped the blade across my pants leg. Stepping onto the boardwalk, I hesitated a second and glanced back at Jack. He smiled and slipped the safety strap from his forty-four.

When I stepped through the swinging doors, Jack eased in behind me and faded off to the side. Inside the tavern, the big feller had ripped away her clothes and thrown her up on the bar. Three other men joined him, gathering like wolves over a wounded dove.

Her naked legs struggled, but they were weak from the beating. She reached up and scratched at the big feller's bearded face, but he laughed and backhanded her so hard, blood flew and splattered on the mirror behind the bar. "Jesus God," I said to myself, gritting my teeth against the sound of rough, calloused hands against tender, tortured flesh.

Instinctively I felt my hand ready to rip open my shirt and grab my gun, but I drew a long breath and walked up to them slow and easy, my glades knife hanging from my hand, my heart beating to the slow, steady, familiar rhythm of a funeral drum.

The bartender was the first to see what was about to happen. He sprinted around the bar and said, "Hey now, these are my customers." He stopped as Jack raised his hand.

"Your business is about to take a plunge." Jack smiled. By the time the "customers" heard the bartender, I was within six feet of them, and the bartender was slipping out the door. They turned facing me, like rats from a warm corpse. "Hell you want now?" the big feller growled. My words kept beating to that drum, slow and even.

"Turn her loose," I said, "or I'll kill you." My voice was a hoarse whisper, a death chant that sounded strange to my ears.

He glanced at the other three, then at me. He curled his lips back like a dog, revealing ragged brown teeth spaced like crooked fence posts. His friends laughed. Jack stood way to the side, unnoticed. "Outa here, you l'il sumbitch," he snarled, and next thing I knew my head had exploded and I was halfway across the room, once again on my ass.

"Lord God, what a lick," Jack said, reaching down, raising me up on my feet. I shook my head and staggered. The room swam before my eyes. At the bar they'd turned back as if I'd never been there. The big feller climbed up on the bar between the girl's legs and loosened his belt. "You reckon you'll ever get his attention long enough to cut him a little?" Jack asked. The drum still beat in my chest.

"This time I will," I heard myself say.

In a second that seemed like an hour, I was across the floor, up on the bar, and swept over his back like a dark spirit. My left hand went over his broad shoulder, grabbing his beard. I yanked his head back exposing his wide throat. He strained against my grip as my glades knife flashed high above his face. His neck tensed like steel cable. I slammed down a vicious stroke through tendons and wind-pipe, then his head snapped back against me, almost off his shoulders. A rush of blood exploded up and splashed down, covering the small naked woman beneath him. I rolled away, ready for his friends, but they froze under Jack's forty-four. The big feller hung there a few seconds, kneeling between her legs, quivering, pumping blood. His head lay way back, his throat wide open toward the ceiling. Then the fountain of blood shut down and he melted off the bar.

"So there you have it, boys," Jack said. "Your friend lost his head over a little piece of tail."

They were tensed and ready, and Jack goaded them. He wanted them to go for their guns. It had gone too far to stop, even if they wanted it stopped. In the shameful act of killing, a beast takes over and rages in man. It screams for blood till its thirst is quenched, then it hides in its own ugliness and justifies itself for its own sake.

I crouched, tense, trembling, waiting for the twitch of nerve that would keep the blood spilling. Cold saliva seeped through my clenched teeth, blood covered my arms from the elbows down. My voice was a hoarse rasp. "Do it!" I hissed, as a gun hand twitched, and I chopped it half off before it cleared the holster.

The other two moved at the same time. Two shots rang almost as one from Jack's forty-four. One man slammed the bar and fell, the other flew over it backwards, taking a rack of shot glasses with him. Blood spewed from the stub of a hand, as the last man standing held his wrist tight, staring in disbelief, wide eyed and screaming. Jack stepped in quick, grabbing him by the shirt and jamming the forty-four into his eye. He pulled the trigger, then jumped away as blood and brains exploded.

We jumped back-to-back in the middle of the smoke and carnage, searching for any movement in that stone silent bar. In a far corner, a man stood backed against the wall. He stared, white as a sheet, a cigar delicately balanced in his gaping mouth.

Outside, footsteps hurried across wooden planks. Jack stared at the man against the wall, spun his pistol around, and slid it into his holster so fast you couldn't tell his hand was empty till his finger pointed straight at the man. "Bang!" Jack said, snapping his thumb down against his empty hand. The man looked as if his heart had stopped.

"That's something new I've been working on," Jack said to the horror-stricken man. Tugging at his shirt cuff, Jack splattered through the blood, glancing around the room. I threw a dirty white tablecloth around the Chinese girl, raised her gently in my arms, and followed Jack out into the street.

A crowd had gathered. They stared at the blood on me, the girl, the tablecloth, and Jack Smith, as we climbed aboard the wagon, scanning the street in every direction. "Nothing to worry about," Jack called out. "Few shots went off accidentally." I felt the familiar sickness welling up in my stomach; it always followed the silence when the funeral drum stopped pounding.

I swallowed hard and tried to put the slaughter out of my mind. "We could've done it different," I told myself. In my mind I heard a volley of rifles and my pa scream. "We could've covered them from the bar." I caught a glimpse of Cletis dropping off the bone and sizzling in the fire. I smelled it. "But the girl didn't deserve what was happening to her." I saw the hooked-nosed old doctor steeple his fingers and smile.

The bartender and two men wearing badges elbowed through the crowd and ran into the saloon. Jack slapped the team reins. Halfway down the street, the bartender and the lawmen ran back out into the street. The bartender pointed at our wagon as they grew smaller in the distance. The lawmen stood there arguing with him, shaking their heads and staring after us. I sat crouched in the back of the wagon against a barrel of Jack's curing water, cradling the Chinese girl in my arms. In my bloody right hand I still held the glades knife. It drew tighter and tighter in my hand as the blood dried.

I stayed riled up at Jack the rest of the trip back to the Samuel place. Every time I swatted flies away from my swollen eye, all I kept thinking was that it should've been him instead of me.

"You are one fighting, scrapping, hard-jawed sumbitch," he would chuckle every now and then, as I bounced around in that rough wagon loaded with curing water. Of course that just riled me up worse.

By the third day, Little China had healed up enough to handle the team. I never saw anybody snap back that quickly from a hard beating. After the swelling went down and she cleaned herself up at a river crossing, I can't deny—tiny though she was—that she was as pretty as a new peach blossom. I reckon if there was any consolation for my black and bloodshot eye, it was the unending gratitude Little China would feel for me the rest of her life.

I ought not admit it, but I had not been with a woman since Jeanine. I'd had the urge many times, but somehow it felt as if I would be doing her wrong, even though I knew I'd never see her again. I reckon if a man truly had a calling to his own mind and spirit, mine would forever be ruled by sadness and the strength of my memories of my precious Jeanine.

For the longest time, well after our trip to the Samuel farm and for a while after that, I refused to allow anything to happen between me and Little China. But it was bound to. Forgive me, Jeanine, but it started out with me watching Little China stirring the campfire and making coffee, and it grew from there. As I watched her move delicately in the flicker of red-gold and shadows, wearing my white shirt open half down the front, her long black hair flowing, glistening in tiny diamonds of light, I remember thinking: "Why did God, if he had any sense at all, put such a fine and beautiful creature on this earth, to be stepped on, scarred and abused by the likes of the rest of us?"

After hauling that "curing" water all the way from Arkansas, when we pulled into the Samuel place, Jack just walked away from the wagon and never looked back. "It's suppose to cure what ails you," I explained to Bob and Jim Younger. They just grinned as they inspected the barrels.

"Makes a helluva chaser," Jack called out over his shoulder. "Help yourselves to it." I could've killed him.

✦❋ 34 ❋✦

Little China never fit in with the rest of the womenfolk. Though Zee, Ma Samuel, and Frank's wife, Anna, went all out to make her feel welcome, there was a difference that would never be overcome. For that reason I took a small piece of land thirty miles from the Samuels', fixed up an old cabin back in the woods, and settled us in. For seven years we lived there quietly, Little China full-time, myself between jobs and roaming the country to find good breeding stock. The Samuel place remained our meeting point over the years, but for security's sake, Frank and Anna took a spread down near Clear Creek, Tennessee, Jesse and Zee stayed on the move, and Jack wandered back and forth between the crazy widow's place and God knows where else.

When I got word that Frank Reno and his bunch were captured and lynched, I figured it wouldn't be long before the law started putting some pieces together. At the same time I was greatly concerned about the way the law brought down the Reno gang. As stupid as that bunch was, I wasn't surprised when they fell—in fact I'd predicted it would happen 'most anytime, but I was startled to learn that the law had managed to sneak a couple of Pinkerton detectives into the gang. That's what got them killed. It worried me. It worried us all.

"I ain't changing a damn thing," Cole Younger said. "We ain't got a man with us tonight that ain't been with us from the start." He stood up and turned slowly, facing every one of us one at a time. "As long as we don't let anybody else in, or any of us out, we ain't got any reason to worry."

Gathered that night in a ramshackle old barn, we stared back and forth among ourselves, our faces shadowed by our upturned coat collars and long oval hats. In the dim glow of the trimmed lanterns we looked like ghouls from a lawman's worst nightmare. Dim light flickered on brass-trimmed revolvers and polished rifle stocks. Outside, a storm raged; claps of thunder repeated and rolled off in the distance.

"I agree with Cole," Frank said, stepping into the lamplight. I hadn't seen him or Jesse in nearly a year. When he pushed back his hat, I was surprised at the strain in his eyes. "But a lot of things are different now," Frank continued. "Before, when we lived together on horseback, we all moved as one, thought as one, and acted as one. All we had to protect was one another's backs." He stopped and turned in a slow circle same as Cole had done. His voice kicked down a notch. "Now there's families, wives, and children to protect. And now the law is acting different. If they catch one, they offer him a pardon and cash money to turn in the rest." I'd never seen Frank look so concerned and serious. His look of desperation was but thinly masked by his quiet resolve.

"There ain't a man here tonight that I wouldn't ride through hell with," Frank said, "but think about what I'm saying. If you're sitting in a jail, and a noose is swinging outside the window, and it only takes a mouthful of names and places to send you home to your family, what will you do?" Again he faced us one at a time. As our eyes met for a second, he must've seen what I was thinking. "That's right," he went on, spinning around, shooting a quick glance about the darkened faces. "I'm tired, I'm too damned tired, and from now on nobody knows a thing about the next job till we're ready to do it."

The group stirred, restless. "Bullshit," Jim Younger argued, "if the Jameses are too tired to run this bunch, it's time Jesse steps down and turns it over to Cole." He threw up his hands in protest. "Where the hell's Jesse, anyway?"

"He's up north," said Frank, raising his voice enough to still the rumblings of the group. "He's right now scouting a big job, may be the biggest we've ever done."

"Where?" Cole demanded.

"That's all I'm saying till we're ready to ride on it."

"How far north?" Clell Miller yelled above a clap of thunder.

Maybe it was the weather, the storm; maybe it reminded me too much of other storms and the dark premonitions they held. Whatever it was, I felt a cold hollowness creep into my bones as Frank held up a hand to settle the questions. "All I'll tell you is that it's far north," he said. Lightning twitched and curled, seeped through the cracks in the barn and flashed purple-ivory across the men and horses. "Up in Minnesota."

That night when the rest of the boys split up, Frank, Jack, and I took lodging at a crossroads inn near Bardstown, Kentucky, before striking out back to Missouri. At a table against a wall in the rear of the barroom we pulled cork from a bottle of Kentucky bourbon and watched rain run down a window. Frank's mood was low and quiet. At first he just rolled a full glass of bourbon back and forth between his hands, as if conjuring up a dark spirit.

When Jack drifted off and worked up a game across the bar with a bored bartender, Frank finally tossed back the full glass and emptied it in one swallow. I leaned on my elbows and studied the flame of a candle as it struggled against the shadows. "Want to tell me what's wrong, Frank?" I prompted, just above a whisper.

"I fear my brother is losing his mind," he said. His voice was different than I'd ever heard it. I shifted my eyes up toward him from beneath my hat brim. He stared at me as he poured another glass. "It's getting worse every day."

"Blue river?" I asked.

"Naw, but that's part of it. Sometimes he just sits and stares, and more than once I've overheard him talking to the dead, to people he killed. He argues with them mostly, sometimes he cusses them. Zee told me less than a month ago, she found him hiding in a corner of the barn, crying and praying, begging them dead men to forgive him."

I bit at the inside of my lip and shook my head. I pictured old Cletis, that poor red-headed girl back in Carthage, and young Kenny Ellworth. "Jesus," I whispered, "that's bad." I caught a glimpse of the bodies Jack and I had left on the floor of that saloon back in Pearly Point, and a hand severed in half, spraying blood. Now I tasted blood inside my lip. I tossed back a shot of bourbon to wash it away.

"It's some frightening shit, Cousin, and I fear it'll soon drive him crazy. I wouldn't say it to nobody but you, but you've known all along I'm the one who makes the plans and sets things up. But the fact is, it's Jesse's strength and force that keeps me going. Without his force of will, I fear I'll spill open and get us all killed."

"Hold on, Frank, this ain't you I hear talking. You've been in the breach a damn sight longer—"

He cut me off, shaking his head. "Cousin, this ain't no badman, desperado bullshit we're talking here. This is guts to guts. If you can't hear it, let's change the subject and talk about the weather."

I stared at him, not knowing what to say. I'd never seen Frank this way. He was always the one with a tight grip around the world. I reckon it shook me to see his hand open.

His eyes dilated, shiny and blank from the rush of alcohol. He stared at me with the look of an animal caught in a steel trap. For the first time since I'd known him, I couldn't understand the meaning of his message. I shifted restlessly under his gaze. "You know, Frank, what you said to us back in the barn tonight, that you'd ride through hell with us. There wasn't a man there who wouldn't do the same for you." He just stared, unmoved, his feelings undiscernible. "I mean it, Frank. We all follow Jesse, hell, in a way we worship the man. But, Frank, there ain't a damn one of us that don't feel the same way about you."

Frank shook his head real slow. "You ain't heard a word, Cousin, not a word. I'm trying to tell you the sky is falling. I'm not trying to gain your sympathy, or your support. I know you would ride through hell for me . . . maybe that's what sickens me."

"Come on, Frank, you're just in a dark mood. Tomorrow you're going to wonder why you said it."

"Dark mood?" His eyes glittered in the candle light. "We've run wild and reckless, and the devil *will* collect his due. Yes, tomorrow I'll regret saying it, but that won't mean I don't mean it tonight. I have to live with knowing that I dragged my kid brother into this hell. Jesse was just one more plow jockey when I rode back from the Southern army. Now look at him. I'm the one got him started, and I realize it every time I hear him cussing the dead."

"Frank," I said, "Jesse was his own man. He could have chose different—"

"Listen to you," he snapped, "a fine one to talk. What were you doing when we brought you along?" He threw back a shot of whiskey and poured another. "Tell me we didn't tempt you into our fold. Tell me how much choice you had. Blood and killing has a powerful pull on a young man. Tell me you didn't catch the fever for it. Now, there's a gun to all our heads, and we'll all die tasting blood."

"Jesus, Frank." I tossed back my whiskey and poured another. Frank had me spooked. I noticed my hand trembled as I sat the bottle back on the table. I'd never heard such talk from Frank James. I didn't know if it was just hearing him talk that way that had me shaking, or if it was the fact that I knew every word he said was the sick and bitter truth. I tossed back the fresh drink and turned toward the window.

I stared out into the black, glittering storm and thought of poor Kenny Ellworth. I thought of the night my fingers searched his cold and dying chest. I saw his glazed and sunken eyes, begging me to keep him alive; and somewhere out in that dark and howling storm his spirit swirled, his and all the others who now danced with the angels. Would he be alive if I had sent him home when the war ended? And if he was, would he be sitting somewhere tonight hiding in the shadows like a hunted animal, staring into the storm and wondering?

"See what I mean," Frank said quietly, as if by studying my face he might somehow read my thoughts. I glanced across his face and away from his eyes. I threw back another shot and sat the glass on the table.

"Damn this rain," I swore. "Reckon it'll ever let up?"

◆✳ 35 ✳◆

It was a long time after our meeting in Kentucky before Jesse set up the big robbery in Minnesota. It seemed like every time we got ready, something came up that made us postpone the job. Aside from the circumstances, I always breathed a little easier each time we put it off. After the strange talk I'd had with Frank that night near Bardstown, I sensed an air of doom about us, and at times depression cut deep into my spirit.

The first postponement came when Cole Younger got the living shit cut out of him down in Texas by Belle Starr's old man, Blue Duck. Cole had been sweet on Belle ever since she was sixteen, back when her name was still Belle Shirley. When she started selling her ass instead of giving it away, Cole went nuts, beat her up, and tried to kill her. Later on, when she married Blue Duck, Cole went to Texas to draw blood on that crazy Indian, but came back looking like an Arkansas road map. In Cole's own words, Duck cut him three ways, "wide, deep, and frequently."

That little carving match put Cole on raw eggs and buttermilk for three months, and it was nearly a year before he could hold down solid food without belching and gagging like a choked goose.

By the time Cole was back to his spiteful, arrogant self and ready to ride, a terrible tragedy struck the Jameses, struck us all for that matter.

A band of detectives threw a bomb through Ma Samuel's window. The explosion ripped her arm off past the elbow and killed poor simple-minded Archie Samuel, Jesse's and Frank's younger step-brother. Every one of us went killing crazy. What kind of lawmen would do such a thing?

I shoved the rifle down in one scabbard and my sawed-off in the other. My brace of Colts hung across the front of my saddle, guerrilla style. I pulled my forty-four out from under my shirt and stuck it in a shoulder holster in plain view. To hell with the law, and to hell with my doubts and apprehensions. This was the cold reality. When someone hurt and killed your own, you drew vengeance; you killed swiftly and mercilessly, with no regard for retribution, even from the fires of hell.

Two old fellers were still patting Archie's grave with their shovels when "Quiet" Jack and I rode past the cemetery. They stopped and watched as Clell and Ed Miller fell in beside us, still wearing their funeral clothes, but with bandoleers draped over their shoulders and shotguns propped straight up from their saddles. Up ahead, Frank and Jesse sat on their mounts in the middle of the road facing us.

Off on the side of the road, Cole Younger leaned against his horse puking whiskey, blood, and yellow pus. He wiped his mouth on a handkerchief and swung up in the saddle. Stopping ten feet from Frank and Jesse, I stared at Frank before they turned toward town. The old gleam of fire was back in his eyes. Before I could say a word, Frank raised his rifle from across his lap and propped the barrel straight up against his shoulder. "Never better, Cousin," he said, spinning his gray stallion with a quick hook of the spur.

It was near dark when we rode straight up the middle of the street, bold as brass and aching to kill. Lanterns turned hastily black in windows as we rode past. Boots and slippers scuffled across boardwalks into doorways, and music stopped as we rode past saloons. Behind us lay a wake of silence, save for the sound of our horses' hooves.

In the twilight ahead, three badges appeared briefly in the middle of the street, then disappeared as we rode forward. Two rifles lay abandoned in the dirt as we rode past that spot and to the front door of the hotel. Just as we spread out in a line across the front of the hotel, three well-dressed fellers came around the corner of the alley laughing, carrying a shiny flask of liquor. They were nearly to the door before they even noticed us in the evening gloom.

One of the fellers had just raised the flask to his mouth when Clell's horse snorted and stomped its hoof. He stopped cold and lowered the flask slowly as his companions' laughter froze in their throats. They looked at us with the look of men who had come to a great revelation. Their jaws went slack. One of them glanced between me and Jesse as if he was seeing double. I saw a flicker of realization sweep across his face as if to say, "That's how they do it, there's more than one of him."

Jesse's voice was soft, molten iron pouring from the bowels of hell. Had I glanced at him right then, I felt I would've seen a serpent's tongue uttering his words, and the scaly hand of Satan clutching his rifle stock. "You've been looking for us," Jesse said, and even the skin on the back of my own neck turned cold and prickly from his words. "Here we are."

Like one short rattle of a snake, this was a quick warning before its deadly strike; shotguns, rifles, and pistols were all cocked at once. A raw-boned hound trotted around the corner of the alley, then, sensing the air of death, slinked down on its belly and crawled back out of sight. "It wasn't a bomb," the man with the flask said. His voice was like the bleating of a dying lamb as he stepped from his companions and spread his arms wide. He would be the first to waltz with the devil; I saw it. "It was only a smoker." He moved by inches that grew into feet as he pleaded. He was ready to run. "I swear to God," he sobbed, "it wasn't a real bomb."

"And these ain't real bullets," Jesse hissed.

From my saddle, I watched him dance a wild limp dance as the flash of fire from our guns cut, sliced, punched, and pounded him against the front of the hotel. The gold blaze cast his shadow in all directions as he twisted and bounced. The constant pounding of bullets and buckshot held him up, would not let him fall, as chunks of bone, meat, and blood flew into the air and mixed with the cloud of smoke. Behind him his shadow mimicked his dance of death, dancing wild among the splinters, washed in blood and glistening in fire. Then, ringing silence.

Ten feet away, the other two crouched, sprayed by blood, guts, and splinters. They rose slowly, taking their hands from their faces and staring at the grisly pulp against the front of the hotel. The mangled corpse lay half-buried in the shattered clapboard siding. Smoke billowed. Blood poured from the boardwalk and dripped like rainwater from the cornice overhang.

"I suppose you two would just as soon call it a night, wouldn't you?" Jesse asked. His voice turned matter-of-fact as he slid cartridges into his rifle. I could barely hear past the ringing in my ears. They just stood there, blood-splattered and shaking.

"Yes, sir," one said, meek and trembling, "I would."

The click of cartridges, the snap of levers, the silence after the reload. "Shut up, Pete, don't give them the satisfaction. Die like a goddamn man." Pete dropped to his knees and the front of his trousers turned dark with urine. The puddle spread around him and mixed with the blood.

"The Lord is my shepherd," he began, in a trembling purr, "I shall not want." I felt a sickness welling inside me. I swallowed back bitter vomit and felt my head swim. "He maketh me to lie down in green pastures." This time I wasn't quick enough to swallow it down. It spilled down the front of my shirt, into my lap, warm and oozing against my crotch.

"You low bunch of swine!" the other one yelled. "May your whore sow of a mother die sucking the devil's ass."

"Yea, though I walk through the valley of the shadow of death—"

"Shoot us! you gutless vermin—" Again, the swell of fire, the flashing shadows, the crazy, twisted dance, and then, again, the ringing silence.

"We want to know where we stand," Bob Ford said. He glanced past his brother for support, then back to "Quiet" Jack and me. "Jesse knows us, and he knows we're all grit. We want in, so where do we stand with the rest of you?"

Jack cocked a drunken eye. "Right now, you're standing where I'm fixin to spit." He hiked up a gob and blew it at Bob's boots. Bob jumped back as Jack laughed and threw back another shot of rye.

"That's real goddamn funny," Bob said, clenching his fists and his jaws. Bob Ford was a mousy little prick with long eyelashes, too ugly to be a woman, too pretty to be a man. "Awright," he hissed, "you want trouble . . . you've got it. There's two you and two us, let's have at it."

"Have at it?" I laughed. I'd been drinking more than usual since killing the detectives.

"There has to be two of you," Jack said. "You're too goddamn stupid for one person." Now Charlie Ford stepped forward and swung open his coat, revealing his pistol.

"You don't know who you're fooling with, Mister Smith. My brother has just challenged you both. You better do what he says."

"Challenged us both?" I laughed again. I was feeling no pain.

"Let's get this straight," Jack said. "You're saying I better get up and kick your brother's ass or else you'll shoot me?"

"That's great," I bawled, banging my hand on the table. I just couldn't get serious.

"That's not what I meant," Charlie said to Jack.

"Stop laughing at us," Bob said, pointing his finger at me.

Ten feet away, Cole Younger and Clell Miller leaned against the bar watching the show. Clell wore his wide grin; Cole looked like a pit bull waiting for the bell. We'd all been acting different since the killing.

"I'm sorry, Bob, goddamn it," I said. "It's just that . . . well . . . if you could just see your sorry little ass standing there, like a tadpole picking at an alligator—"

"That's it!" Bob raged. He tore out of his coat and slung it away. It slapped against a deer's head hanging on the far wall; the head crashed on a table between a skinny whore and her customer, slinging beer all over them. Bob pushed up his sleeves and headed toward me, but the little whore came up screaming, wielding a straight razor.

Wet hair hung down her smeared face. "I'll cut ya, goddamn ya!" she screamed.

Charlie drew his pistol, shot once, missed, and him and Bob went skinning through the door with the razor licking at their backs.

"Stop that whore," her customer yelled, "she's got my money!" He drew a pistol and headed for the door, but the bartender swung up a sawed-off and blew a hole through the ceiling. Everybody froze. "Stop all this goddamn racket," the bartender bellowed.

"I don't know why everybody's getting so tense," Jack muttered under his breath. "Can't even have a few drinks without—"

"You—shut the hell up," Cole Younger said. He glared at Jack, his eyes like the warning label on a bottle of poison. Then he turned slowly toward the bartender. "Don't you ever round out a sawed-off behind my back, or I'll blow your goddamn brains out." The shotgun dropped from the bartender's hands like it was red hot.

"Well, well," Jack said, standing up real slow and slipping the strap from his holster, "now we get to hear from the onion sucker himself." Jack was drunk; his words slurred.

I eased back out of the way. The showdown had been brewing between Cole and Jack for a long time. Clell slipped away from Cole and moved farther down the bar.

"What do you mean by 'onion sucker'?" Cole's voice was low and steady, his hand poised an inch from his gun.

"He means you suck onions, Cole," Jesse said from the door. He stepped inside carrying the whore over his shoulder. Blood dripped from the large welt on her jaw. Jesse hung her across a chairback and let out a long breath. "I won't have this shit," he said.

Jack eased his hand away from his pistol and Cole did the same. "Come on in here," Jesse said over his shoulder, and Bob and Charlie Ford stepped in cautiously.

The whore's customer slipped over and reached inside her dress. When he took his money, the knocked-out whore slid down into the wet sawdust. Jesse glared at him a second, and the man's mouth dropped open. "It's his money, Jesse," I said quietly, "he ain't robbing her."

Jesse glared harder, nodded toward the door, and the man scurried out like a rat.

"These boys came here because I asked them to," Jesse said. "I won't tolerate this kind of insult to my friends."

"They started it," the bartender said. As soon as he blurted it out, Jesse's hand shot across the bar, snatched him by the hair, and slammed his face down on the hard surface. We all winced at the sound. The bartender's arms fell limp across the bar, and he lay there facedown.

Jesse glanced between Cole and "Quiet" Jack. "And I won't stand for you fighting among yourselves. We're a squad here, same as always, and I won't have us falling apart."

"No offense to your *friends,* but I don't trust the weasel-eyed bastards," Cole said. "They ain't a part of us, and they ain't coming in."

"They'll join if I say so. And if anybody wants to buck me on it, step forward and settle with me right here, right now." He glanced past each of us, then fixed his eyes on Cole.

Cole stood tense for a few seconds and you could see him ready to throw down. But he finally eased down and raised his hands to the bar top. "Alright," he said, nodding real slow. He raised a finger toward the Fords. "But when these rat-bastards shoot one of us in the back for the reward money, let it be on your head."

It was near daylight when Jack, Clell, Cole, and I rode away from the Handshake Tavern, headed back to Kearney. Jack and Cole argued most of the way, too drunk to do any serious damage. Cole weaved along behind us, puking blood and rye down his horse's side.

"I'm just saying it ain't right, shooting a man while he's on his knees praying." I shook my head. "It ain't right."

"Yeah, well, I'll tell you something that ain't right, is hitting a whore, like that," Clell said. I just looked at him.

"Clell's right," Jack said, "it's bad luck hitting a whore. Jesse's in for it now."

"It ain't right hitting any woman," I said to Jack.

"Yeah, but it's worse hitting a whore," he said.

"Much worse," Clell said.

"Bad luck." Jack nodded.

"Lord God," Cole pleaded behind us, "would you-all *please* shut up."

"Cole hit Belle Starr"—Jack nodded over his shoulder—"just look at *him.*"

◆✳ 36 ✳◆

Killing the detectives added fuel to the already heated war between the Jameses and the Pinkerton Detective Agency. Knowing what I knew about Jesse after the conversation with Frank back in Kentucky, I tried to lay low and keep to the shadows. If Frank was now shouldering the whole load and Jesse was growing unstable, I feared it only a matter of time before the law found a way to get to us.

Without mentioning it to anybody, not even "Quiet" Jack or Little China, I sought out a spread of land in Kentucky, purchased it under the name of James Beatty, and began shipping some of my quality stock there a little at a time. Though I had money enough to pay cash for my land purchase, for appearance's sake I paid half in cash and put the balance on a mortgage note with a bank we had robbed less than two years back.

Unlike Jack and most of the boys, I held tight rein on my money, stashed it here and there, and kept my mouth shut about it. While the rest of our bunch pissed away money on whores and whiskey, I always kept an eye out for good horseflesh. Through a contact of "Mysterious" Dave Mather, I managed to set up some paperwork and bloodline on "Jeanie's Pride," and renamed her Star Angel. I hated doing it, but with me being a wanted man, even my horse needed an alias.

I hired two local brothers to oversee my Kentucky land and tend arrangements for the reconstruction of the old mansion on the property that had been nearly destroyed during the war. They were good folks, Jules and Herschel Parks, and they took care of my investment in Kentucky as if it was their own.

Far as anybody knew, I was a land surveyor. I traveled a lot. To look the part, I grew a full beard and let my hair grow past my shoulders like a true frontiersman. What time I wasn't off surveying, I dealt and raised horses. This was in case I ran into anybody while

I traveled the racing circuit. It worked fine. When the time came, as I feared more and more it would, I would grab up Little China, Jack too, if he needed a place to go, and we would blow out of Missouri like a bad wind.

By the time we got ready for the big job in Minnesota, I had moved all my top horses over to Kentucky. "Jeanie's Pride"—a.k.a. Star Angel—was heavy with her third colt. I'd bred her to a big, fancy stud out of Atlanta and I was anxious to see what would come of it. Her second colt, a filly that looked dead like her, was rein breaking well. I expected to run her in another year. The first colt, the black stallion out of Cronin Wilcox's Star Of Dawn, turned out to be a crazy son of a bitch, but I loved him like a father loves an only son.

He was a fine and majestic animal, black as a bucket of midnight, with Star Of Dawn's strength and Jeanie's Pride's speed and courage. He could outrun any horse I ever owned including his mama, but the big, ornery bastard loved to fight and hated to race. So, what could I do? As soon as he was old enough I held him at stud. The rest of the time he was my personal riding stallion. I called him Buck, and all he would ever be any good for was to fight, fuck, and rob banks. I reckon he fitted right in with most of "The boys."

I'd finished shoeing Buck when Clell Miller showed up at my place one afternoon. "Frank is at the Samuel place," he said, without getting down from his saddle, "he wants to see you, says it's important."

I slipped out of my leather apron and hung it next to my smithing bench. Something told me it would be a while before I used my tools again, so I dropped my nails and nail pouch into a wooden keg and rolled it under the bench.

Clell looked around at my empty corral. "Your spread's looking a little sparse," he observed. "You hurting for money?" It was Clell's way of offering.

"Thanks," I said, "but I reckon I'll make out till Minnesota."

Clell didn't have any money, anyway. He never did. I had money, but I never let it show. In the past year Jack and I had pulled a couple small payrolls and one good bank, all on our own. Jesse and Frank knew about it, but we hadn't talked about it to anybody else.

"I know I'm damn ready for it," Clell said, watching me saddle Buck. "This is going to be my last bank, you know."

I smiled and shook my head as I swung up on Buck. "Sure," I said, "mine, too."

Clell laughed and ran his finger across his chest. "Cross my heart, this is my last." He smiled his broad country-boy smile, and something told me to remember the way he looked sitting there in the evening sunlight. A dark feeling shot through me as we turned and headed for the Samuel place, but I dismissed it. I'd been doing too much thinking lately; I reckoned things were just piling up on me.

A mile from the Samuel place, Cousin Frank just appeared beside us from out of the woods. "Over here," he said, and we slipped into the woods quiet as ghosts. A quarter of a mile in, we came upon Jesse mounted on a big roan, shifting his eyes back and forth, from one of us to the other. "How have you fared since I seen you last, Cousin?" he asked with a tired smile.

I reined up beside him and shook his hand. "Neither better nor worse," I replied. "And yourself?"

Jesse nodded. Now that we'd showed up, he holstered his forty-four, swung the rifle from across his lap, and slid it into his saddle scabbard. He let out what sounded like a tense breath. "I hear you're a hell of a horse-man," he said solemnly, then slowly his expression changed. His eyes were lit with a devilish gleam. The excitement and anticipation of the big job had begun to set in. We all looked at each other and smiled knowingly. Frank cut a chunk of tobacco and stuck it in his jaw.

"Yes sir," I said, "I dicker horses some, and I do deliver them, at a price, of course." Jesse laughed and slapped my hat from my head. I hadn't seen him or Frank much since the night we gunned down the detectives. I'd missed them; I hadn't realized how much.

Frank broke into laughter in the middle of a spit and had to wipe tobacco juice from the front of his shirt. I reared back in laughter and slapped my thigh. Minnesota was *on*.

"Yee-hiii!" Clell shouted, spinning his horse in a quick circle. He pulled out a bottle of Eagle-Spray rye whiskey and pitched it to me. I caught it, pulled the cork, took a long cut, and passed it on. We laughed like fools as the bottle went from hand to hand and the fiery liquid soothed away any doubt and apprehension.

There in the shelter of the woods, each of us in our own way shed the trappings of our personal lives, our lives of hiding and deception, of tending land and raising families, of dealing with our devils on our own. We slipped from that world like restless moths shedding heavy cocoons—it was a world that would never be whole or completely real for us. This was us; this was our time and place. And we were here now, our hands never as steady, our eyes never as clear, and our laughter never as bold. We were "The boys," getting ready to do what we knew we did best.

Here were Frank and Jesse, brave and reckless squad leaders from the Quantrill days, and big ole Clell Miller, a broad-faced country boy, yet wild as a desert wind. Soon others would shed their worlds and slip in beside us. They would let go of whatever doubts and apprehensions they had, and once banded together we would be as strong as an army. And there I was right in the midst, James Beatty, or Miller Crowe, or from somewhere a long ways back, Jeston Nash, as good a horse-man as ever split earth.

"It's about goddamn time," Clell said with a laugh. "I've got whores hocking jewelry and praying for my return." He tossed me the bottle again. This time I tipped it toward him like a salute, then I turned it up and finished it.

The next morning, back at my place, I held Little China close to me and watched the sunlight climb slowly across the window ledge. I brushed my hand down her flowing hair until finally she stirred from sleep and looked up from my chest. She read something in my eyes that caused her to lean up and glance about the room. Near the door "Quiet" Jack Smith lay rolled up in a blanket, his saddle beneath his head, his rifle and saddlebags leaned against the wall within quick reach. She sighed and lay her head back on my chest.

"It won't be for long," I whispered, "as soon as I get back . . ." I felt her hand brush across my beard, her fingertips stopped on my lips, silencing me. "No say," she whispered, her voice was almost a soft pleading, "no say . . ."

After breakfast Jack and I rolled our spindles and saddled up for the trek north. At last night's meeting it went without saying that Jack would be my backup with the horses. We would gather a string on our way up to Minnesota, one or two at a time in case anybody happened to notice us. Pinkertons were everywhere and growing bolder every day. And now that the Reno gang was feeding worms, the Midwest Security and Detection Agency had committed their forces to bringing down the James gang.

There was big money on all our heads. In my case, I wasn't so much wanted as a member of the gang but I was wanted by every lawman in the world for killing Sheckler back in Kansas City. Of course over the years, the name Miller Crowe had cooled off some. Still, I walked real softly, especially when I traveled outside of Missouri and Kentucky. The only one of our bunch that wasn't sporting a price on his head was Jack, and that fact puzzled me all my life.

For some reason, "Quiet" Jack was an invisible man. I'd never seen anything like it. For all the killing, robbing, and far-handed shit he'd pulled in his life—and I mean in the open, bold as brass—nobody could've picked him out of a flock of geese. He could've walked back in a bank twenty minutes after robbing it and I believe the son of a bitch could open an account.

Three miles out that morning, I turned to Jack and asked, "How's things going with the widder woman?" I hadn't seen Jack in months. I figured we oughta catch up.

Jack shook his head. "I'm starting to think that bitch is just a little bit crazy."

"No shit," I said. I'd known that after being around her five minutes. "Why do you think it?"

"Remember me telling you she killed her husband? Stabbed him to death in his sleep?"

"Yeah, I remember you saying something about it."

"Well, a few weeks back, I woke up in the middle of the night feeling like the roof caved in on me. I looked up and there she was sitting on my chest, holding that butcher knife with both hands, ready to jar down on me."

"Lord God! Jack, why?"

"That's what I asked her," Jack answered, chuckling, "and listen to this. That crazy bitch said I was doing her the same way her husband did her. Said I wasn't paying her no attention."

"What the hell did you do?"

Jack shrugged and laughed. "What the hell could I do? I just slapped the shit out of her and went on back to sleep."

I stopped my horse and stared at Jack. He was serious. "Yeah," he said, "now tell the truth. Ain't that something only a crazy person would do?"

I scratched my beard and tried to answer. I tried two or three times to say something, but each time I opened my mouth, my words just tangled up in knots.

I struck camp thirty miles from Kansas City and waited four days in the woods while Jack, my invisible friend, rode in and did some snooping around. We hadn't heard from "Mysterious" Dave Mather in over a year. I decided to find out why. To tell the truth, I was hoping Jack might come back with some word about Jeanine Wilcox, though I didn't mention it to him.

Jack said he would be back in three days, so on the fourth day I started getting a little jumpy. I had started readying my six-horse string for a move farther into the woods when Jack came riding in leading two more horses. He smelled like the upstairs of the Lucky Lady saloon.

"I hope you didn't hurry back here on my goddamn account," I snapped as soon as he reined up. His eyes were bloodshot and he was shaking like a hound passing peach seeds. I could tell he was hungover sick.

"Don't give me no shit," he said, trying to laugh but close to gagging. "I might've fooled around a little, but it was all in the course of gathering information."

I followed him to the coffee pot on the campfire. "What information is that?" His hand shook so bad he had to sit the cup on the ground and used both hands to hit it with an unsteady stream of coffee. "What's happened to Mather? Any word on Zanone? Did you happen to hear anything about the Wilcoxes?"

Jack held the cup with both hands and lowered his face to it. "You do carry on a lot, you know that?" I heard his belly growl like a cougar screaming for help as the hot coffee went down. I let out a breath and walked over to the new horses. There's no talking to a hangover.

In a few minutes Jack came up and leaned on a horse's rump as I inspected its hooves. "They run Mather out of town over a year ago. He's plumb over in Arizona working for the Earp brothers."

"Well," I said, "I reckon we'll hear from him sooner or later. He ain't gonna make much working for the Earps. From what I know of them, they're tighter than a young whore's bedsprings." I'd come across the Earp brothers over the years. I couldn't see Mather and Wyatt hitting it off.

I ran my hands up the horse's legs feeling for any lumps or weakness. "Any other news?" I tried to sound casual. I wasn't going to mention the Wilcoxes again, but I was hoping.

"Yeah," he said, "and you ain't gonna like it. Daniel Zanone is now the sole owner of the Midwest Security and Detection Agency."

I dropped my hand from the horse and turned to Jack. "I'll be goddamned," I said. "How'd you come by that?" Now I understood why that bunch was so keen on bringing down the James gang. It wasn't just the reward. This was Zanone's way of coming after me.

"I learned it from our old buddy Melvin Bracker." Jack grinned. "He never put it together that I was in with you on that racing scheme. We drank together, played a little poker, just like we was old friends. 'Course he was mostly just seeing if I knew anything about you. I told him what a no-good skunk bastard I thought you was, and that I heard you got killed and skinned at Powder River."

"Reckon he believed it?"

"Probably not, but it's no matter. I went ahead and killed him before I left town. I figured since he was there, and I was there, and we was getting along real good, I might as well pop his head for you." Jack chuckled and shook his head. "He seemed real surprised."

"I bet," I said. I had fostered no grudge against that poor silly bastard, but I wasn't sorry to hear of his death. "I hope you didn't draw any heat by killing him. We got enough going on right now."

"Naw, hell, I made it look like suicide. We was sitting in his office drinking whiskey and I walked around and put a gun to the side of his head, that was that. Nobody will think nothing of it, 'cause there's a suicide epidemic going around, anyways."

I cocked my head. "A suicide epidemic?"

"Old man Wilcox," Jack said flatly, "hung himself less than a year ago. According to Bracker they found him hanging from a rafter in his breeding barn, deader than a stump."

"Jesus," I said, scratching my beard. I was glad to hear he was dead, but I worried about the grief it must've caused Jeanine. I felt a sudden urge to go to her, but I knew it couldn't be. "Did you hear anything about Jeanie?" I asked quietly, "I mean, how she's doing and all?" I busied myself with the horse's mane, combing through it with my fingers.

"Yeah," Jack said, slipping a bottle of rye from his pocket. He pitched me the bottle, and I knew what that meant. But I just held the bottle unopened and gazed at him quizzically. "She's married," he said, "got a husband and a child. I found that out from an old nigra feller who used to work for the Wilcoxes. He's the one sold me the bottle of rye."

I turned and walked to the campfire, sat down, and pulled the cork from the bottle. My voice sounded bitter, even though I knew it was the best thing for her. "Wonder how the hell she managed that. Best I remember she's still my wife, on paper anyway."

"Then by God," Jack said, "maybe you oughta ride in there and explain all this shit to a judge." He waved his hand in the air. "Jesus Christ, if I had known you was going to act so small about this."

"Let up, Jack," I warned him. "These are scars that ain't healed. I reckon I wasn't ready to hear it. It just don't set right." I took a long pull from the bottle. "She's still my legal wife."

"And all these years while she's been your wife, you've been living with Little China, so there."

"It ain't the same thing, goddamn it!" I yelled.

"There ain't a bit of difference!" he yelled right back. He pointed his finger straight at me. "You've got half an hour and a pint of rye to work this shit out in your mind, 'cause I ain't riding up north with an ass-kicking hangover and watching you sulk around like a love-struck cowboy."

I took another long pull on the bottle and watched the low flames dance in the breeze. Behind me I heard Buck nicker and stomp, threatening the new horses. Jack sat down and reached across the fire, taking the bottle from my hand. "I feel like shit," he said, taking a long pull on the bottle. After a few seconds he let out a deep, gurgling belch. A few seconds later I heard him chuckle, "You know, as whores go, Kansas City has been overblessed." It was his way of changing the subject.

I looked at Jack and offered a weak smile. It wasn't often that he made any sense at all, but when he was right, he was right beyond question. It was good that Jeanine had carved out a life for herself. It just hurt that it wasn't with me.

"So, you think the widder woman is crazy because she was going to stab you with a butcher knife?"

Jack stood up, dusting the seat of his trousers, and said, "Yep, that's the way I see it. What do you think?"

I stood up and put out the fire with my boot, spreading the ashes around on the moist ground. Behind me Buck was stomping and tugging at his reins, trying to get at the new horses. One of the new horses snorted back and stomped like a bull. Judging the size of the animal, Buck might be taking on more than he could handle.

A breeze moved in from the direction of Kansas City, a soft, soothing breeze. For just a second, I imagined Jeanine's hand brushing my face and I could still recall the feel and the smell of her. "So, what do you think?" Jack asked wistfully. I had drifted away, to a warm peaceful memory, to a place in the past. I shook my head.

"About what?"

"About the widder woman, do you think she's crazy for trying to stab me?"

"No," I said, with a laugh as we turned toward the horses. "I think she's crazy 'cause she didn't finish the job."

◆✳ 37 ✳◆

"We've got big trouble coming," Jack said, staring through the field lens, "look at this."

I was across the dry creek bed in three steps and up the bank where Jack lay covered by underbrush. He held the telescope in place as I slid down beside him. "Aw, shit," I whispered, gazing through the wavering glass, "it's gone to hell."

At a thousand yards I saw four riders rounding a bend from behind a low rise. Then in seconds, two hundred yards behind them and closing, I saw over a dozen other riders. Jesse led the four riders at a hard run. Right behind him Frank had his gray stallion bellied down, and holding to the reins of Clell Miller's horse as it pounded beside him. Clell wobbled in the saddle like a drunken man. Ten yards back, Cole and Jim Younger rode double. Jim hung against Cole's back like a fading shadow. Even through the fogged lens I could see they were shot to pieces. "They've had it," Jack said. I slapped the lens shut and ran to the creek bed. Jesse would be expecting us to catch up to them on the run. He wouldn't break for cover till he spotted us coming.

"We've all had it," I yelled. "Cut out the best five and turn the others loose." Jack had already started chopping the lead rope with his glades knife as the horses jumped and pulled against him. We had brought in a ten-horse string, exactly the number we needed. From what I saw through the lens, half our gang was either dead or captured. From the looks of Clell Miller and Jim Younger, they wouldn't last long.

I grabbed the reins of two horses as I jumped into the saddle and drew my rifle. Buck sensed the tension and reared up. I spun him toward Jack. Jack gathered three horses and shooed the other five away. At that second I realized: we were all going to die in the flatlands of Minnesota.

I leaned out to Jack as he swung up in his saddle. "Maybe you oughta wait here," I shouted. Jack rolled his eyes and tightened his hat. It was a death trap. I knew Jack wouldn't stay behind, but I thought I should offer. "Alright," I said, "but if I go down, don't stop for me."

"I'm not planning to," Jack answered, hooking his horse right along with me, "so watch your ass." We tore up the middle of the creek bed for twenty yards, then veered up over the bank onto the flatland. This kind of job was a horse-man's nightmare. We all knew it could happen and we always planned for it, but we all prayed against it.

For all Jesse knew we might've seen the chase and lit out. If that was the case there was no reason for him to stop for fresh horses, unless he saw he was done for and decided to make a stand. He would be waiting for us to show ourselves, if we were still around. Then he and the gang would break for the cover of the woods. There we could fight long enough to switch horses and light out before they had time to surround us. It was tricky, a delivery on the run. We hadn't done it since the war.

When we hit the flatland in full view, Buck sprang past Jack's big bay by four or five yards. Jesse and the boys were three hundred yards away and running parallel to us, with the posse closing hard. Between us lay nothing but a flat, bare stretch of land. On the other side of Jesse and the boys lay a maple forest twenty yards up a low rise. Frank and Jesse saw us tearing across the flatland and cut sharp for the woods. At the same time, the posse saw what we were trying to do and six riders split off toward us. All we could do was cut straight for the woods as rifle fire spit past us.

Jack and I were like tin ducks at a county fair. I swung my rifle across the front of me and pulled off a round, but it was like a fart turning a tornado. A volley of shots concentrated on me and I felt a graze slap across my back like the crack of a bullwhip. A tip of Buck's ear disappeared and blood sprayed me in the face. He screamed as he ran. A volley honed in on Jack right behind me. I heard him scream and I glanced back just in time to see him and the four horses tumbling end over end in a tangle of limbs, hooves, and chunks of dirt.

Instinctively I cut a sharp left and circled back for him; the two-horse string nearly pulled me from the saddle. Jack staggered to his feet in the midst of the thrashing animals. His face was covered with blood. He fired his pistol blind and wildly.

A volley of shots cut into the horses as they struggled to stand. Blood and chunks of horseflesh exploded into the air as I jolted to a halt, swinging the two-horse string around between me and Jack. "Grab on!" I bellowed, leaning out across one horse's back. Jack groped at the horse's mane as I snatched him by his bloody head and pulled up. "Goddamn it, Jack, grab something!"

More rounds whistled in as Jack rolled up on the horse's back. I felt a white flash of pain slap into my hip and saw Jack's shirt puff out in front as a bullet tore through his shoulder. Then he grunted as a bullet slapped into his side.

As if running slowly through a bad dream, we pounded across the flatland, Jack clinging to one of the two horses, me leading them at a hard run. Out of the corner of my eye I saw the six riders lined up and taking a slow, steady aim. Up ahead and fifty yards to our left, the rest of the posse had dropped down and taken position in a plug wash beside the road facing the woods.

I figured the next volley of fire would be the last we would ever hear. I gritted my teeth against the sting of death. Then I saw puffs of smoke and heard the sound of rifles from the woods line, and I heard a scream from the riders. "The boys" had taken position; they'd covered us.

The suddenness and accuracy of the rifles from the woods stunned the posse for a second, but only a second. I heard another scream from behind us as we topped the road and pounded into the woods. Now rifles and pistols spit through the leaves and snapped branches. I shoved Jack from his horse and dove to the ground beside him. Buck and the other two horses ran on through the woods. They stopped as gloved hands reached from within a grove of maples and caught their reins.

I crawled toward the shelter of the trees, dragging Jack beside me. Blood spread across my back and down my hip, but I knew I wasn't hit bad. Jack had taken a bad one through the shoulder, and another in the side. I didn't know what had hit him before the fall.

Near the grove, when the firing let up a second, Jesse came running out in a crouch. With his rifle pointing from his right hand, he reached down and pulled Jack with his left. I saw the spread of blood on Jesse's chest. "Are you hit?" It could be that his old wound had broken open.

"No," he said, as we collapsed into the shelter of the trees, "but everybody else is."

Another volley of rounds spit through the woods, then a voice cursed in the distance, "Hold your fire, goddamn it!"

The scene in that tiny clearing was one of tortured demons straight out of hell. Rifle smoke lay heavy in a slow drifting cloud and wide trails of blood ran in all directions. Frank held the reins of Buck and the two fresh horses in his good hand and leaned against a tree. Blood ran down his other hand and dripped steady to the ground. The spent horses milled in the clearing, carefully stepping among the wounded and dying.

"Jesus Christ," I mumbled, limping to Cole and helping him as he dragged himself away to a pile of downed timber. Jesse had propped Jack against a tree trunk and laid a rifle across his lap. "Leave him alone," Frank growled, "can't you see he's dead?"

"No!" I yelled. "Not Jack." I dropped from my bad leg and crawled to him quickly. I shook him. "Jack, damn it, Jack, you ain't dead."

Jack's eyes barely opened. He shook his head weakly. I dropped him back against the tree. "See, by God, don't start calling us dead till we are dead."

"Aw, shit," Jack groaned, "I've been hit by a freight train."

"Can you shoot?" Jesse asked, leaning in close to Jack's bloody face.

Frank spun the horse's reins around a tree limb with his good hand and jumped over against Jesse, knocking him to the ground. "He's dying, goddamn it!" yelled Frank. "Leave him be!"

Jesse rolled among the horse's hooves. He clutched his chest and crawled back to Frank. He grabbed Frank by his trouser legs and tried to pull himself up. "See," Jesse gasped, "you're no help. None at all."

Frank reached down and helped Jesse to his feet. From among the horse's hooves, Clell Miller let out a gut-ripping scream. "Keep him quiet," Frank said, and I limped between the horses and helped Clell to the pile of timber next to Cole.

In a few seconds we had the wounded against the downed timber. Cole propped himself up on his shoulder and stared at the woods like a trapped and wounded panther. Blood and saliva ran down and dripped from his chin in a long, stringy froth. Beside him, his brother Jim lay flat. His legs jerked and quivered. He'd been shot straight through the face. The bullet left his cheekbone split open in a large bloody welt and tore a hole through his neck right at his collar. "Somebody finish me," he babbled, "please, please shoot me."

Jack sat holding the rifle across his lap and pressing his hat against his shoulder wound. "Why don't somebody shoot him, so he'll shut— the hell—up?"

Cole drug his pistol from his holster with all his effort and flopped it on his lap. "Go for my brother," he wheezed, "and I'll drop you like a gob of snot."

Jack shook his head and managed a weak grin. "Good timing, Cole."

I took a bottle of whiskey from Clell's saddlebags and cradled his head in my lap as he drank it. He was shot once through the chest and once down low in his belly. There was no stopping the bleeding. I poured whiskey down his throat and half of it surged back up. It spilled down his face mixed with dark blood. "Oh, Lord, Dingus," he sobbed, "nothing ever hurt this bad."

"I know," I whispered, "but we're here with you. You'll be alright." I looked up at Frank and shook my head. "Try to keep this down, Clell," I whispered, and I poured more whiskey.

"Look at this shit," Jesse said, all of a sudden. Frank spun around and the two of them stared out into the woods.

I stayed with Clell. "What is it?" I whispered.

Jesse chuckled. "Some dumb-ass is waving a white handkerchief."

Cole laughed and choked. "It's about time they surrendered. They must've just realized, we've got the badass James boys and Mister 'Hot-shot' Smith in here."

Jack and Cole stared at each other like two pit bulls. "Listen up," Jesse said. A voice called up from down near the road.

"You're trapped in there. There's no way out. If you give it up, we promise not to kill you."

Jesse glanced around at each of us with a curious smile. "Can you imagine, the nerve." Then he yelled to the posse, "If you-all drop your guns and back away, we promise you the same courtesy."

Muffled laughter came back from the woods. "We know you're shot up awfully bad in there; you better think it over."

"You, too," Jesse called. More laughter from the woods.

"That's good," the voice said. "Who's in there anyway? Is that Jesse and Frank James?"

"Rotten assholes," Cole growled, under his breath.

Clell ripped at his belly wound with both hands. "God, Dingus, I can see the devil. He's running his fingers in my guts and dragging me down."

"Hang on Clell," I whispered.

"See him? See him? Here he comes." I poured another shot of whiskey in his mouth, and he swallowed hard. "Aw, Lord God, Mama!" he gasped, as his eyes started to glaze. His body bucked like a man sliding down a rocky surface. "Tell Jesse I'm sorry—" He dropped both hands to the ground and clawed into the moist dirt as if to keep from flying off the earth. I smelled a terrible stench as his bowels emptied, and I slipped from beneath his head and limped between the horses. Our friend Clell danced with the angels.

"Come in and see who's here," Jesse yelled.

"We will, if you don't surrender in a few minutes."

"How many minutes?" Jesse yelled. He glanced toward me and winked.

"Ten minutes?" came a reply. They weren't eager.

"It's Cole Younger," Cole shouted from behind us. We jerked around and stared at him. The strain of yelling caused him to gag and spit up more blood. He smeared it across his shirt sleeve, looked straight at Jesse and nodded his head solemnly. "That's right," he said.

"You sure about this?" Jesse asked.

"You bet your ass," Cole hissed. "And Jim Younger," Cole shouted to the woods. He glanced at Clell's body and shook his head. "And Clell Miller," he shouted. Then to Jesse, he said, "Look at these." He pointed from one bullet hole to the next. "One here, another here and here, and one here," his voice droned. "All these bullet holes. More than the James brothers put together, I bet."

Jesse stepped toward him with the rifle hanging from his hand. "What're you saying, Cole?"

Cole grinned sarcastically. "I'm saying there ain't one of you bastards I want with me in prison. Now get out of here. I'm tired of looking at you."

I switched the blood-soaked saddle and bridle from poor Clell's horse and hastily slapped it on one of the fresh ones as Frank and Jesse bent down to Cole. Man and animal were pressed together in that small space. Mosquitoes hummed in our faces. Sweat poured. I led Buck and the other horse carefully over Cole and Jim, rolled Jack up, and tied him to the saddle. Jesse leaned in close to Cole and I heard him say, "You know I wouldn't have this happen for—"

"Yeah, I know," Cole cut him off.

"I would sooner it be me lying there."

"I know, I know, goddamn it!" Cole hissed. Blood spewed at his lips and he spit it to the ground. "Just get the hell away."

"Five minutes?" called a voice from the woods. They weren't too keen on charging in if they could avoid it. They knew who was in here, knew it clear as day. They had cornered "The boys." It was kind of like grabbing a wildcat by the ass.

Jesse crept past me, brushing flies from his bloody chest, and took the reins to one of the fresh horses. Frank took the other in his good hand. When we mounted, Jesse motioned for me and Jack to ride southwest toward Mankato. Evening was running out of color. Crickets chirped from deep in the woods. I glanced one last time around that tiny clearing. It smelled of smoke, blood, sweat, shit, and sickness. Clell's face and hands were already turning blue.

As Jesse and Frank slipped into the woods like ghosts, I watched Cole stare after them like an old man watching a shooting star. His eyes clung to them long after they were gone.

I led Buck and Jack's horse quietly through the woods. Jack lay on his horse silent as stone. Forty yards out, I heard a voice call into the clearing, "Your time's up, we're coming in."

"Better give us just a few more minutes," I heard Cole reply from the clearing. He was buying us time; the game son of a bitch was defiant to the end. There was silence for a few seconds, then the voice said, "Alright."

Part V
Dark Redemption

◆✳ 38 ✳◆

For three full days we stuck to the creek beds and plug washes and worked our way southwest. From woodland to woodland, crossing the flatland only of a night, we slipped past or laid still and avoided the bands of riders—bounty hunters and posses—who roamed the area like bloodthirsty hounds. By the third evening Jack's face was yellow as parchment, and I knew if I didn't get him some help he would die strapped to the back of his horse. He was too weak to argue as I led his horse to the front gate of a farmhouse somewhere past Mankato.

I had watched the house for over an hour. There was an old man, a younger woman, and a young boy. When I figured they had settled in for supper, I'd decided to take a chance. "Hello the house," I called out from the gate, and in a few seconds the old man stepped on the porch holding a shotgun. Through the window I saw the barrel of a rifle.

"We don't want no trouble here," the old man called, "we've heard who you are."

I was bone-tired and weak from hunger. The graze across my back had dried my shirt to my skin. Flies swarmed. Jack hadn't stirred for the longest time. He might've been dead for all I knew. "I don't want trouble either," I said, "I could've killed you an hour ago from the woods if I wanted to. I just need some help here, that's all." I reached over and brushed the flies away from Jack's face. A scalp wound had scabbed over above his ear in a tangled mat of hair and dark blood.

"Is that your brother Frank?" the woman's voice called from the window. As tired and hurt and hungry as I was, I still couldn't help but smile. "Here we go again," I thought.

"But you don't look at all like your picture."

"Well, Flora," Jack said, propped up on a large pillow, "you know how pictures lie." I almost laughed out loud when she nodded in agreement and held out another spoonful of soup.

"But you do," said ole Henry, staring at me from across the wooden table, "except for the long hair and the beard. I never seen a picture of you with a beard. Not that I would try to identify you later on." He still wasn't convinced that we wouldn't kill them all before we left. We'd holed up with them for over two weeks. I was getting restless. I scratched at my beard and tapped my finger on the newspaper in front of me.

Three days before I'd sent the young boy into town to get the paper. Before he left I told him we would kill his mother and grandpa if he didn't do as he was told. It was a terrible thing to say. I'd apologized to ole Henry later on, but I reckon he was still concerned.

According to the newspaper, Charlie Pitts, Clarence Hite, and Clell Miller were all dead. We later learned that Bob Younger was still alive and had been captured in Northfield. Cole and Jim Younger had surrendered to the posse and were taken back to Northfield for medical attention. Cole denied that Frank and Jesse James had any involvement in the raid, but the paper and the local authorities claimed otherwise. Members of the posse said that Frank, Jesse, and two unnamed members of the gang had slipped through a circle of deputies and made a getaway. Jesse and Frank had been spotted in four other states and as far south as Georgia within three days of the raid. I figured by now they were actually holed up somewhere near Kearney.

In another part of the paper, it referred to Cole Younger as "The Gentleman Bandit." With eleven bullets in him, that arrogant bastard stood up in the wagon and tipped his hat to the ladies as they hauled him into town. I reckon it was his way of showing us he would go out in style. He knew we would read about it.

By the time Jack was up and around, we'd been hiding out with the Fiederman family for near a month. The day we rode out, Flora stood by Jack's horse for nearly half an hour, moony-eyed as a schoolgirl. I reckon she lived out the rest of her life thinking she'd had a love affair with Frank James. I'd called ole Henry to the side, and though he argued against it, I made him take three hundred dollars for providing us refuge. "You boys have been gentlemen," he said. I think he was truly surprised we didn't kill them.

The young boy, Kendall, came up and asked me to sign the newspaper for him. It was probably ole Henry's idea. I ruffled his hair and told him it might not be a good idea, but then I gave him a three-inch pocket knife and that seemed to satisfy him. With a bag of food and three bottles of homemade wine, we rode off into the woods.

That night we risked a small fire deep in the woods and sat down to a plate of beans and hot coffee. The hunt for the James gang had died down, but we would have to worry about bounty hunters and local lawmen all the way back to Missouri.

"What do you think will become of us now?" Jack asked, referring to the gang. He chewed slowly on a mouthful of beans and stared into the fire. He looked thin and drawn from his wounds. Luckily there were no bullets left inside him, but he was still a long way from being well.

"I don't know," I said softly. "With so many dead or in jail, I figure Jesse is going to have to let down and take in some new faces. And I don't like that a bit."

Jack sucked his teeth and studied for a minute. "Well, there's the Ballard brothers from down in Arkansas, and the Fords, they're assholes, but at least Jesse knows them." I couldn't believe Jack was already scheming to stay in the game.

"Jack, you ever thought about getting out?"

"Naw, it ain't likely we'll ever get out. What the hell would we do?"

"Do?" I said. "Shit, we could do whatever we want. I've got horses, we've both got money stashed—"

"Not me," he said, "I ain't got shit stashed away."

I couldn't believe it. "You mean you've run through all the money we've made over the years?"

"Every dime of it," he replied with a laugh that was still shallow and weak.

"What the hell have you spent it on?"

"This, that and the other." He shrugged. "Hell, it's bad luck to hang on to money. You oughta know that."

"No, I don't know that. It's bad luck not to."

"Suit yourself," he said, reaching over for a blanket. "Only money we ever have is through far-handedness. It's bad luck to hang on to that kind of money. You're supposed to spend it as quick as you make it." He wrapped the blanket around himself and leaned back against his saddle. "Besides, don't you think it would look awful puny, quitting Jesse right now, after Northfield going sour on us?"

I pitched the rest of my beans into the fire and sipped at a cup of coffee. Lately I was finding myself agreeing with Jack a little too often. It made me wonder about myself. But the fact was, Northfield was the only job we'd ever done that'd gone wrong. In a way Jack was right. How would it look if we pulled out now, now that Jesse needed people around him he could trust.

While Jack slept, I sat wrapped in a blanket and stared into the low flames. There, a long way from home, healing from my wounds, and hidden among those tall northwestern pines, I did some deep and solemn thinking with both my mind and my heart as well. It was time I faced up to what I really was, and try to find a way to change it. No matter how I colored the picture, beneath the trimmings, I was a hunted, wanted man, a murderer, thief, and far-handed desperado. I was reaching way down to admit it.

There was nothing to justify my being in this world—killing and robbing, and watching men die. The voice I heard from the posse was the voice of a plain dirt farmer, no different than my pa. That's why they hadn't charged in on us. They had no taste for blood, no craving for the taking of lives. They were there protecting what little they'd scraped together by the sweat of their backs. We were there to steal it, plain and simple. I felt low.

Back in Missouri I had a decent spread, a woman who loved me, and more money laid up than any of that posse would see in a lifetime. At least poor ole Clell and the others were there because they needed the money, that was honest enough in a backhanded sort of way. I wasn't even honest with my own kind.

In Kentucky I owned as fine a spread of horse country as a man could dream of, and I'd kept it a secret even from my friends, even from Jack, even from Little China. In Kentucky I was Jim Beatty. I reckon Jim Beatty was better than "The boys," though he'd gathered his trappings at the end of a gun, no different than the rest. He wouldn't spit on the likes of Miller Crowe, yet here sat Miller Crowe, feeding into the charade that kept both men alive. "Jesus Christ," I thought, or maybe I'd even said it out loud. Who the hell was I? And what the hell was I doing, stealing money, spilling blood, and tearing innocent lives apart?

◆✳ 39 ✳◆

"You're awfully goddamn quiet lately," Jack said. We had followed the Platte over into Nebraska, then trekked south across Kansas, into Abilene. We could lose ourselves in the scores of faceless drovers—wild-eyed cattlemen—who filed back and forth steadily between Texas and Kansas City. We would drop down from Abilene into the Indian Nations. From there we would drift into Missouri through the "back door."

"I'm working this shit out in my mind," I murmured. A quarter mile out, dust billowed in the wake of a large herd. The air was thick with cattle musk.

"What shit is that?" Jack laughed. I squinted at him, then turned away. Buck tossed his head restlessly against the reins. The tip of his left ear healed an inch shorter than the other.

"Just life, I reckon."

"Good luck," Jack said. Now that he'd been away from Flora a while, he started getting his color back and healing up. "I worked all that out a long time ago."

"I bet," I said. I really didn't want to get him started.

"Aw, yeah. See I figure it like this. The less a man has, the less he has to lose. The more he steals from one, the more he can pass on to others. Hell, most of them would never do it on their own. In a way, it's kinda Christian, what we do."

"Is that a fact," I said flatly. "What about all the innocent people, the decent folk we hurt, the ones that die?"

"Well, there again. If they're innocent, decent folks, they know life is supposed to be a struggle. When we hurt them, we're just helping them along. If one of 'em dies, they go straight to heaven. Ain't that what they're all reaching for anyway?"

I just shook my head and stared off at the horizon. Northfield had done something to me, but I wasn't sure what. Actually, I hadn't been the same since the day Jack came back from Kansas City and told me about Jeanine, her being married and having a child. I reckon that day, even the thinnest flicker of hope had died.

Although I'd denied it to myself for years, there must've been a spark of a prayer that someday, somehow, I would be near her again. Sometimes, at night, I would still feel her warm against me and still imagine her arms around me in the hours before dawn. I would look into her eyes and let hell and the devil flee from my spirit. Somehow, Jeanine could've changed all this. I felt I could've walked away with her and never looked back. But it was water under the bridge, I reckoned.

"And that's your whole problem," Jack said. He'd been rattling on. I hadn't heard a word.

"What is?"

"You"—he laughed—"you spend all your time wanting to be whatever the hell it is you think you ain't."

I smiled. "You better let me work on that one a while."

That night, after traveling near the herd all day, we rode into the cattle camp at supper time and tied our horses near the string of cow ponies. Though it was a custom among the drovers to feed any wayfarers at the evening meal, out of courtesy Jack and I walked over to the trail boss before taking our plates from our saddlebags. When we approached the circle of cowhands sprawled around the campfire, an older feller, stocky as an oak stump, pushed up to his feet and slapped dust from his trousers. "You the boys who've been riding south of us all day?" The cowboys just nodded at us, too tired to care.

"That's us," I said. "I'm Bob Kelly, this here is Callahan." Jack tipped his hat.

The trail boss looked us over with a glance. "Is that your first or last name?" he asked Jack. Jack smiled politely.

"That's my whole name," said Jack. "First name Calla, last name Hand." That drew a chuckle from the cowboys.

"I'll be damned," said the trail boss, good-naturedly. "I'm Rhodes Blanchard. Draw off some of them beans and join us."

"Much obliged," I said. Jack tipped his hat. We walked back to our horses, got our eating utensils, and returned to the campfire.

"How has your drive been?" I asked, just making conversation as

I sat down and spooned up some beans. Jack eased down a few feet away.

"Hard but fair," Blanchard said. He stared at me with a curious look on his face. "Have I seen you before, Mister Kelly?" I sucked some warm gruel from my finger and chewed on a mouthful of beans. The herd lowed in the near distance. Two riders reined in, and I heard the rattle of tin plates.

"Not that I recall," I said. "We're from Arkansas, been up in Colorado looking at some land."

"Umm," he said, "mighty pretty country up there," then he looked close at me again. "Damned if you don't remind me of somebody, but I can't say who." He turned to one of the cowboys. "Shank, don't he look familiar as hell?" The long-jawed cowboy glanced over his shoulder at me, then the whole group looked my way. I chewed on the beans and tried to be calm about it.

"He shore does," the cowboy said. His Texas drawl was as long as a hay wagon. He stared with his mouth dropped open. The rest of the bunch shifted around and stared as if trying to place a name to a face.

"It's Jesse James," Jack said, laughing, and I nearly snatched my pistol before I realized it was his voice. "I always say he looks just like Jesse James." Jack spooned up some beans. " 'Course he don't like me saying it."

Blanchard slapped his knee. "I'm damned if he don't look like ole Jesse, don't he, Shank?" The whole group conferred among themselves, nodding their heads.

"Shore does," said Long-Jaw, his long neck bobbing slower than any human's I'd ever seen. "He damned shore does."

"By God, it is Jesse James!" Jack yelled, real quick like. He slapped his holster as if to draw. The cowboys jerked in surprise; then seeing he was joking, they hooted and laughed as Jack reached over and tugged my hat down on my forehead. "But I tell you, he gets real salty when you kid him about it."

I tipped my hat back and shook my head, still chewing on beans. "You're full of shit, Calla," I said with a chuckle. Long-Jaw twisted his neck slowly and stretched out a mouthful of words.

"Why, by God, that ain't nothing a man oughta be ashamed of. You oughta consider it a compliment."

I talked through a mouthful of beans. "You're sure right about that," I said. "I ain't ashamed of it at all."

"Naw, sir," said Long-Jaw, twisting his neck. His Adam's apple looked like it was the size of a saddlehorn.

"Who ain't ashamed of what?" snapped a young feller's voice as the two latecomers stepped in among us. They stood above us spooning up beans.

Blanchard gestured a stubby finger toward the young man and announced, "This here's my boy, Gant." Then he waved his finger past us. "This is Bob Kelly and Calla Hand."

The young feller grunted with no show of manners at all.

"We just was'a talking bout how much Kelly here looks like Jesse James," Long-Jaw offered, "don't you think?"

"Not a bit," the young feller said, glancing at me with a hard expression, then back to his plate. "Jesse James is clean faced and well barbered, anybody knows that."

"Son," Blanchard said, "we was just making talk about it, that's all." Blanchard sounded like a man used to holding rein on a hothead son. I slid a quick glance past Jack and finished the last of my beans.

"What ever become of that bunch?" Jack asked, smacking his lips, "last we heard they'd been shot to pieces robbing a bank up north."

"That's true," Blanchard said, "we heard of it on our turn-around trip from Kansas City. A group of detectives rode in searching for the James boys and a couple other fellers. They wanted me to round in my whole crew so they could look them over. I told them to go kiss their sisters. I didn't have time for that shit, besides, far as I care, the James boys ain't done a thing that I wouldn't do myself if I was a younger man."

"Pa rode with them back in the war, didn't you, Pa?" young Gant Blanchard offered.

Rhodes Blanchard shrugged and looked embarrassed. "Well, kind of. You know how it is in a war. You ride with fellers for a while, then you go on."

Jack and I nodded respectfully. "Sure do," I said, "back then everybody knew everybody else, I reckon." Blanchard wasn't the first father to pass along war stories to his son.

"I would ride with them today, just like Pa did, if I knew how to join up with them," young Blanchard said.

"Hush up," his father said, "you've plenty to do right here."

"Was that the Pinkerton detectives?" I asked, trying to find out what I could without seeming too concerned.

"Naw, this was Dan Zanone and his bunch. Sons of bitches. I wouldn't piss in his ear if his brains were blazing. He told Shank here to put the word out that he was gunning for the James boys and especially their horse-man, Miller Crowe."

"I've heard of him," I said, "But I heard he got skinned and gutted over in Powder River." I heard Jack chuckle beside me.

"I've heard that Crowe feller was a no-good bastard," Jack said, just to devil me. "I heard he would shit in a clean kitchen."

"Aw, yeah?" young Blanchard flared up. "And I think it takes a dirty cowardly bastard to bad-mouth any of 'The boys.'"

A hush fell over the bantering cowboys. "No offense intended," Jack said quietly. Hell, he couldn't come out and explain that Miller Crowe was sitting right beside him.

"How do we know you two ain't more of them goddamned detectives sneaking around here?" young Blanchard prodded.

"Easy now, young man," Jack cautioned.

I leaned toward Rhodes Blanchard and stared deep in his eyes. "We're the wrong kind of people for your boy to cut his teeth on," I said, barely above a whisper. I lay three fingers to my forearm and nodded, "Know what I'm saying?" A realization swept across Rhodes Blanchard's face.

He'd raised his son on stories of horseshit and gun powder; now his stories had come to life and were staring him in the face. Here sat two characters straight out of his tall tales, and we weren't the fair-haired heroes he'd lied to his son about. We weren't to be idolized, and we damned sure weren't to be fucked with. Blanchard's face twisted as he tried to sort through the irony. His son was teetering on the edge of eternity, ready to die by the hands of the very ones whose honor he thought he'd defended. Jack would close that kid's eyes like a nickel novel. The old man saw it, and he knew he'd brought it on, not today, but throughout his son's life.

"Gant!" Blanchard said firmly, "stop right now, and get on out of here. Hear me, son? Do you hear me?" Gant Blanchard ignored him.

Jack finished his coffee in a long gulp, not taking his eyes off Gant Blanchard for a second. "Please, son, listen to me," old man Blanchard pleaded, "you don't know what you're fooling with here."

The young feller reached out a boot and tapped his toe against Jack's holster. I saw a flash of white madness streak across Jack's face. "That's a thirty-six-caliber La Faucheux, ain't it?" Young Blanchard's voice had a belligerent tone. Jack shot me a glance as he stood slowly and dusted his trousers. I knew he was going out of his way to avoid a fight when he turned his back on the boy and looked out across the herd.

"Yes, it is," Jack said. He had taken the fancy gun from his saddle-bags and started wearing it after losing his forty-four back at North-field. He'd only used it for practice. He called it his drawing pistol.

"Only gunslingers, bounty hunters, and railroad detectives carry that kind of gun. Which are you?" young Blanchard asked.

"Neither," Jack said softly, still staring away.

"You're a goddamn liar," Blanchard said, and I felt my guts tighten, ready for the ring of thunder in my ears.

"No! No!" old man Blanchard shouted, ready to jump between Jack and his son. I held out my hand, stopping him. Since Jack hadn't already killed the kid I thought there was a good chance he wouldn't. "Let's go," I said to Jack real quiet-like, and we started toward the horses, Jack with his back to young Blanchard, and I, kind of walking sideways with my arms spread in a cautious show of peace.

"I'm calling you a yellow liar!" Gant Blanchard called.

"I've been called worse," Jack mumbled under his breath.

"Turn around, goddamn it!" the boy shouted.

"Keep walking," I whispered.

"Turn and face me or I'll blow the back of your head off."

"I'll have to kill him, you know," Jack whispered out the corner of his mouth as we stepped closer to our horses. "When I hear that gun cock, I'll have to drop him."

"Don't do it," I whispered back, walking a little quicker.

"I'll try not," Jack said. "Let's see how it goes."

Four more yards and we would have made it to our horses. But just as I saw the pistol start out of the holster, before I could even warn Jack, he heard the sound.

Quick as a hornet, Jack's gun flashed as he spun around and fired two rounds almost as one.

"Goddamn!" I yelled, startled by the suddenness of his move. Young Blanchard stood still as stone, his face white and bloodless, his eyes bulged out like a stomped frog. Beside him his pistol lay broken in the dirt. Blood poured back his raised arm and ran in a stream from his elbow to the ground. His hat hit the ground ten yards behind him and spun like a lopsided top. Jack holstered his pistol, stepped over to the horses, and swung up in the saddle.

"Get him, boys!" young Blanchard screamed as I swung up on Buck.

"Bullshit," said one of the cowboys, "get him your damn self! Do we look crazy?"

"Daddy, he tore my gun up." Now his voice sounded more like what he was, just a kid, playing a dangerous game, a game his father had taught him all his life without realizing it. "And my hat . . . my hand! . . . Daddy, goddamn it! Look at my hand!"

"Daddy, goddamn it!" one of the cowboys mocked in a shrill voice, as I trotted Buck cautiously over to Rhodes Blanchard. I kept the cowboys and young Blanchard in the corner of my eye as I spoke down to the old man. "I'm sorry this rolled out of control, I truly am. We rode in here with the most honest intentions." I felt terrible about it. It was getting to where we couldn't even be around ordinary folk without trouble flaring up. It wasn't that we started it; it seemed like we just drew it, the way darkness draws the devil.

The old man's voice trembled as he said, "I just thank you, Mister Kelly or whoever you are, thank you both, for not killing him." I watched his eyes fill and he tried to keep the tears from spilling.

Over to the side, two of the cowhands wrapped a bandanna around young Blanchard's hand and led him toward the wagon. He stared back over his shoulder at Jack. Jack sat with his arms crossed on his saddlehorn. His face was blank. "I'll kill you!" the kid sobbed. "Hear me, you bastard? I'll . . . kill . . . you!"

I leaned down to old man Blanchard. "Turn him around, Mister Blanchard," I said quietly and seriously. "Get the bullshit out of his head and turn him around while there's still time." I waved an arm between Jack and myself, "Or this is what you'll raise."

"Lord God," he breathed.

"How'd you ever get so good with a gun?" I asked, staring into the low flame of our campfire. Out in the darkness a panther let out a long and mournful scream, like a lonesome demon trapped on the road to hell.

Jack's voice was quiet and serious, with an almost bitter tone to it. "When you only know one thing, you better get *damned* good at it." He glanced up from beneath his hat brim with a tired smile. Flames danced in his eyes. Smoke from his cigarette curled up around his face. "How'd you get so good with a glades knife?"

I thought about Sheckler back in Kansas City and the big feller over in Pearly Point. I thought about the first time I'd slipped up behind a Yankee guard. I'd reached around and opened his heart with one swift stroke, then with my hand over his mouth, I sank with him to the ground and felt him quiver as he gave in to death's cold embrace.

I shivered and drew the blanket around me. "I don't remember," I said, trying to wipe away the picture. I thought back to a time when I walked behind a plow and watched dark, rich earth roll over beneath my feet. For some reason it was like looking back on somebody else's life, someone I only knew briefly, a long time ago. From the distance, the panther let out another cry and was answered from even farther away. Jack's tired smile faded from the glow of the fire and sank into the shadows as he lay back against his saddle. He drew his hat down over his eyes. "Neither do I," he said.

◆❋ 40 ❋◆

I was a year or more getting over what happened in Northfield, even longer getting over Jeanine. I should say getting over her again, since I'd gone for years accepting the fact that she was lost to me forever. Cousin Jesse always had his chest wound that never completely healed; I reckoned my love for Jeanie was sort of like that.

No sooner than we got back from Minnesota, I moved Little China and our belongings twenty miles deeper into the woods. At first I started to move over to my spread in Kentucky, but as long as Zanone was alive, I figured he would stay on my trail. When I made the move to my horse farm I wanted no ill wind blowing at my back. Besides, I'd sworn to kill him, I just hadn't yet found the chance.

When China and I went deeper in the woods, I gave my old spread to Jack and the crazy widow woman. I only did it out of friendship, because I knew that like myself, Jack needed a place to put down some kind of roots. As it turned out, giving Jack the house and land was one of the smartest things I ever did. When Zanone's men finally found out about the place, they showed up ready to draw blood, but since nobody ever recognized Jack Smith from anything he'd ever done, he pointed them all the way to Crede, Colorado, in search of Miller Crowe. It worked.

Though Zanone never showed up face to face, he actually sent Jack a letter thanking him for his cooperation. I never saw anything like it. I asked Jack if maybe he thought he oughta run for sheriff. Of course I was only joking.

Jack laughed. "Naw, sir," he said, "still too many of you badasses running loose."

One badass that would never run loose again was Cole Younger. The judge gave him a bunch of years up in Stillwater State Penitentiary. According to a Minnesota newspaper, when the judge asked

Cole if he had anything to say, Cole just smiled and thanked him for his "time."

At first we were all surprised they didn't try to hang ole Cole, but when we saw he had a chance at staying alive, we sent money to his lawyer to help him out. I always thought some of the money found its way to the judge, because Cole never told them a damned thing to implicate the rest of us, yet leniency was granted based on his cooperation. Bullshit. Cole's lawyer told us that when they asked him about Jesse and Frank, he told them the James boys never was tough enough to ride with the Youngers. They asked about Miller Crowe. Cole just laughed and said, "I heard he got skinned and gutted over in Powder River."

I reckon a lot of people heard that story and believed it. I played cards one night with two judges and a federal marshal while I visited my spread in Kentucky. We'd been talking about "The boys," and whatever had become of them. Mostly, I listened for any information that I might need to pass along to Frank and Jesse. But all at once one of the judges said straight out, "Marshal Thomerson here was actually present the day four Indians flayed and disemboweled Miller Crowe over at Powder River."

"Is that a fact?" I asked, appearing to be impressed plumb out of my dress shoes. I thought it funny how in this circle "skinned and gutted" became "flayed and disemboweled."

"I wasn't actually present when it happened," Thomerson said, clearing his throat, "or I would have stopped it, of course."

"Of course," I agreed.

"But, I did chase away the Indians—killed two of them—and cut Crowe's body from the tree. Poor bastard was still barely alive."

"No?" I gasped.

"Yep," Thomerson grunted, "died at my feet with his guts hanging out, the same way he'd done ole Sheckler over in Kansas City."

"I'll be damned," I whispered softly, as if in awe of some higher force of justice. "What-so-ever a man soweth, that shall he reap." I managed to keep a straight face.

"Amen," said one of the judges, raising his whiskey glass in a toast.

But Zanone never believed that rumor, not for a minute.

"You must think a lot of that animal, brushing him like that while you're on the trail."

Holding Buck's reins in one hand, I ran the brush down his neck with my other. "This ole boy is like family to me." I smiled. Buck nipped gently at my hand. "He's like the son I never had."

I heard a low, dark laugh behind me and the rattle of a metal bucket. "That's real touching," the stranger's voice said. "I promise I'll take good care of him . . . *Mister Crowe.*"

I froze, feeling a flash of cold lightning streak up my spine. "God-damn it," I thought, as I turned around slowly, "it's always the ones you never suspect." I should've known.

"My name's Beatty," I said facing him, my hands chest high, still holding Buck's reins. "You're making a mistake."

He was dressed like a banker in a dark suit and silk-rolled tie. He'd rode up in a fine buggy, asking directions. Now he stepped down from his seat with a forty-four aimed at me, and pitched the bucket on the ground between us. "That's what they always say." He grinned.

"You a lawman?" I was just stalling, looking for a break. My rifle leaned against a tree ten yards away; my only pistol was the forty-four under my shirt. I wouldn't be quick enough, not at twenty feet. He had me.

"Bounty-man," he said. Once he'd said it, I saw it written in his eyes.

"You're going to a lot of trouble for nothing," I said, still wondering what move to make. My best chance was the glades knife in my boot. I needed a second, maybe two, out from under his forty-four. "I ain't Crowe, and you'll put in a lot of time and expense taking me in just to find out. Besides, everybody knows Crowe died over at—"

"Shut up, Crowe, I know who you are." He cocked the pistol.

"Look . . . mister, I've got money. How much bounty are we talking about?" I tried to ease my hands down. "I can match it, more than match it." But he tensed up and took a step forward. "Think of it. You won't even have to bother taking me to jail."

"You ain't going to jail, Crowe. This is a personal job, for Big Dan Zanone. And I'll have no expenses." He nodded down. "That's what the bucket is for."

"Bucket . . . for what?" I saw there was one chance in a thousand to get to my knife. I knew what I would have to do, and God, how I hated it.

"I'm going to pack your head in a bucket of mud, and go sit it on Zanone's desk," he said. Then he laughed, he actually laughed!

I can't explain what his words and laughter did to my mind, but something dark and ugly exploded inside me. I would kill the son of a bitch, even with a bullet through my heart. I'd rip his throat out with my teeth—

I dropped straight down and kicked backwards, rolling under Buck and snatching my knife from my boot. The first shot went off just as I dropped. Buck screamed pitifully; there was nothing I could do. He was falling against me as I sprang up on his other side. The second shot tore into Buck's neck as I drew back my arm and snapped it forward like a whip. I hurled the big knife right across my dying horse's back, saw it plunge into the bounty-man's shoulder, then dove over Buck, screaming like a crazed devil.

The thrust of the knife sent his gun spinning through the air, and I was in his chest with both feet. "Kill . . . my horse!" He tried to roll; but my first kick came up full in his face and flipped him backwards. His left hand came up with a derringer from out of nowhere, but I kicked it away as it fired, and kept kicking.

"Pack . . . my head . . . in a bucket of mud!" I saw his front teeth fly away; blood spewed from his mouth like a long twisting snake. I'd lost all control.

Dragging him to his feet, I pulled him to a double-boughed tree and threw him into the fork of it. "Goddamn . . . you!" I snatched up a rock and ranted, "Kill . . . my horse!" I jumped around the tree and grabbed him by the hair. He moaned as the blood poured. "Pack . . . my head! . . . Kill my horse!" I screamed, cried, and beat his head with the rock till I lost track of time.

I'd leaned forward on my hands and knees, puking into the creek and gasping for air, when I saw Jack's boots step up beside me. "I saw ole 'Three-Finger' Ferguson's brains sliding down that tree trunk. Whoo-ie, that *had* to hurt." Jack chuckled.

"You knew him?" I said, still gasping and running my bloody hand across my eyes and mouth.

"I recognized his hand. You didn't leave much else."

I gagged again and spit into the creek. "He killed . . . Buck."

"I know," he said quietly, "and I'm sorry. Ferguson was a bad son of a bitch. You're lucky to be alive."

I dipped water in my hands and washed my face. Dark blood grew thin in the water and swirled away. "He was going to cut my head off . . . and pack it in mud."

"No shit?" Jack chuckled. "I saw the bucket. Reckon it would've fit?"

"Jack, this ain't funny," I said. "I'm sick of this miserable life. That son of a bitch killed Buck and was going to . . . pack my head—" I couldn't finish my words. I just shook my head and felt tears cloud my eyes. I stared at the ground and swallowed back more sickness.

"Zanone?" Jack bent down beside me, took my knife from the ground and started washing it in the creek.

I couldn't answer; I just nodded and breathed deeply. I was sick of this life, sick of the hiding, the blood and the killing. There was no end to it, it seemed; it would torment me forever.

"You're right," Jack said, reaching over and sliding the knife down in my boot. He took me by the arm and helped me to my feet. "This shit ain't funny anymore."

41

"Dick Liddell, 'Whiskey' Ed Ryan, Charlie and Bob Ford, and Frank and myself," Jesse said, "and you and Jack handling the horses." I scratched at my beard and kicked a rock across the yard. I would have felt better if Frank had come with him, but Frank had stayed in Tennessee, as he had been doing more and more lately.

"Damn it, Jesse," I said, "let's look at what you've got. Dick Liddell is a drunk and a braggart. 'Whiskey' Ed is plumb out of his mind and has been since he got shot through the head, and I wouldn't trust the Ford brothers with a pet rattlesnake."

Jesse grinned and narrowed his eyes. "This is big, awfully big, Cousin. They're gonna talk about this for a long time."

It bothered me that for the past couple years, Jesse talked more and more about doing something "big"—something *they* would "talk about for a long time." Hell, we always had our own reasons for doing what we did, but I never remembered it being for publicity. Jesse had gotten to where he was constantly writing articles to the newspapers, to tell his side of the story. I didn't understand it and I didn't like it one bit. Now, staring up at Jesse atop his big chestnut stud, I felt the same way I felt back when Clell brought me word about Northfield. Something told me to remember Jesse the way he looked today, with a wide smile, and with sunlight dancing in his shifting eyes.

"It ain't feeling right," I said. "It didn't feel right at Northfield and ain't feeling right today."

Jesse's smile faded. "You still holding Northfield against me?" His voice turned harsh and cold.

"I never have held Northfield against you, Jesse. This just don't feel . . ."

"Naw, naw, naw." He shook his head and wagged his finger back and forth. "That's it, you're holding it over me just like everybody

272

else. One goddamn time it goes wrong and nobody lets me live it down." I saw he was going into a dark mood and I feared pressing, but I wasn't going to give in.

"That ain't it, Jesse." I shook my head.

"Then why is it you haven't rode with us since then?"

"You haven't done nothing that big since Northfield, nothing that required me and Jack setting up horses."

"I see, you think I can't handle something big, something without the Youngers and the Millers?"

"No, goddamn it!" I yelled. "You're not giving me a chance—"

"Don't cuss me," Jesse hissed. His right hand slapped firm around his pistol. With his left hand he pointed down at me. His eyes stopped shifting and stared straight into mine. I knew I was awfully close to signing my name on an angel's dance card. I brought my hands chest high and spoke calm and evenly.

"Jesse, I didn't mean to cuss you, I swear to God." I didn't understand what had come over him—we'd talked that way to each other all through the years. "I truly apologize, if I've offended you."

He stared at me, breathing in quick angry gulps. I saw that his knuckles were white on his pistol butt. If he drew, I'd have to try and throw down on him, for whatever good it would do me. Finally he eased up a little and his eyes began shifting about.

"This is it for you, Cousin," he said, a little more in control. "Miss this one, and you better never show your face around 'The boys' again." He swung his horse violently and pounded out into the woods. I stood there letting go of a long tense breath before swinging up on my red gelding and heading in the other direction.

"What boys?" I thought to myself. There was nobody left from our old gang except Frank, Jesse, Jack, and myself. The rest were either dead, had disappeared, or were pulling time in prison. I thought about the meeting in the woods before Northfield, how we'd passed the bottle and formed a bond between us. At that time I would have rode over the edge of the earth with Jesse, Frank, and "The boys." Now, I just felt sad, and a little sick. Was this how Jesse had to put together a gang these days, by cussing and threatening? It was the first time he and I ever had a cross word.

I went around with a lot on my mind for the next couple of weeks. I hated turning Jesse down. If something went wrong on the job, especially if it involved horses, I would never be able to live with myself. At the same time, I could no longer justify taking money from people who needed it a damn sight more than I did.

After Northfield I'd decided to drop out of the robbing business. I had a good string of horses at any time and could make more than just a living traveling the auction circuit—and that didn't include my racing stock, nor the money I still had stashed in a dozen different places. Robbing no longer made sense.

I stopped by Frank's place in Clear Creek, Tennessee, on my way back from the big Nashville auction. Frank looked past my shoulder real cautious as he asked me into his house, and all the while I was there, he seemed anxious and preoccupied. This wasn't the Frank James I'd known over the years. When I told him about my confrontation with Jesse, he shook his head and stared at the floor as if ashamed for his brother's action. "I'm real sorry for that," he said, "and Jesse will be too, once he comes to his senses." Frank shrugged. "Lately he has gone plumb out of his mind."

"The bad dreams again?" I asked. "The dead men?"

Frank nodded. "Only it's worse now. There's times he thinks some of his old enemies are still alive and out there undermining everything he tries to do."

"Ain't there some way you can talk him out of this big job he's wanting to pull?"

"I've tried, believe me, he won't listen. If I press a little too hard, he claims I'm turning against him." Frank's eyes looked fatigued from worry. "Besides, judging the bunch he's wanting to ride with him, if I don't go along, I figure he's a dead man. So I reckon I'm in whether I like it or not."

I studied Frank's face a long time. I knew he wouldn't ask, since he knew I'd already decided against the big job, but I also knew he wanted me along. With Jack and I working with him, Frank must've figured we could at least keep an eye on the new men. There was big reward money on both Frank and Jesse, enough to tempt somebody like Dick Liddell, or the Ford brothers. What could I do? I couldn't turn Frank down and I couldn't just stand back and watch him or Jesse die, not after all these years together.

"Well, I reckon you can count me and 'Quiet' Jack in," I said. I tried to throw on a reckless smile like in the old days, but I think it must've looked a little frayed around the edges.

Frank gave me a look that was almost a warning. "You sure, Cousin?"

"Hell, yes, I'm sure." I tossed my hands in the air. "Look, I don't know what's been bothering me, but if Jesse ain't too pissed off to let me, you know I'm going along. I always have."

Frank stepped over to a cabinet and returned with a bottle of whiskey. He pulled the cork, took a drink, and handed it to me. I smiled as I raised the bottle to my lips and took a modest sip. I almost looked around for someone to pitch it to, but I caught myself and passed it back to Frank. The room was still except for the lazy swing of a grandfather clock. There was no hooting or joking, no remarks about whores. There was just the two us and the steady sound of that clock.

Frank cleared his throat. "I'll be putting out more corn come next spring, that's if the price still holds."

I looked about the room and chewed the inside of my lip. "That's good, Frank, that's real good."

My first night back home, as I lay in bed staring at the ceiling, Little China came across the room in her white cotton gown and slipped atop me. She had a strange and pleasant look on her face. Taking my hands in hers, she ran them up under her gown, placing them firmly against her warm stomach. I smiled at her, then looked back toward the ceiling. "Not right now," I said quietly, "I'm thinking about something."

She shook my hands firmly and rubbed them around on her stomach, forming a circle. I looked at her again and saw the warm glow in her eyes and about her cheeks, the same glow Jeanine had so many years ago. I held my hands real still as the realization set in. "A baby?" I whispered. My voice sounded reverent and astonished.

China smiled and slipped down beside me. Lying beside me, her face close to mine, she folded my hands in hers and held them to her face. "You hoppy?"

I chuckled and squeezed her hands gently. She'd never learned to speak much English, and I'd done no better at learning Chinese. Between us, we spoke sort of a mimic question-and-answer language, a guessing game that kept each of us repeating the other's words until we figured it out. "Am I hoppy? Hoppy? Oh yes, China, I'm very happy."

In our years together, China and I never knew each other the way most couples would, but maybe we knew each other in the ways that counted most. What we couldn't learn through words we made up for in intuition. We knew one another like a blind person comes to know a precious stone, by touch and by aura. Since we shared nothing of our pasts, we knew each other only in the present, moment by moment. If what we had was "love," then I reckon our love was like soft footsteps through a quiet forest. We were only visitors to one another's spirit, so we walked gently and left the flora undisturbed.

"Just tell him I'm going along," I said to Jack. "I'll meet him at the Samuel place and work out the details." Jack nodded and swung his horse toward St. Joseph, three miles down the road. "And, Jack," I called out as an afterthought as he neared the edge of the woods, "don't leave me sitting here all goddamn day. I told China I'll be back by Tuesday." Jack waved over his shoulder and disappeared out of the woods.

I hadn't liked the idea of this "big job" of Jesse's from the outset. Now that I'd learned I was about to become a father, I liked it even less. I reckon some old memories of Jeanine and the baby we lost had something to do with my bad feelings. Whatever it was, I couldn't shake it, and I damn near prayed that something would come up to cause Jesse to change his mind. But I'd told Frank I would go along, so that was that.

I sat on a stump in a small clearing with my horse tied beside me and a long-barreled shotgun across my lap. For over an hour I listened to the sound of children fishing a creek that lay a quarter of a mile down from me. Though these children sounded much younger, I thought back to the weeks on the Samuels' farm when Frank, Jesse, and I fished for mudcats along Giddle Creek. We hadn't thought of ourselves as children then, but looking back I realized that was all we were.

We were kids in a troubled time. There were Frank and Jesse, guerrilla fighters. To the enemy, they were bad-to-the-bone killers, but beside Giddle Creek they were like schoolboys on a day off. I was a clear-browed country boy who had the misfortune of killing a young soldier in what at any other time would have been no more than a playground scuffle.

It had been an argument over a horse swap, no different than a hundred other arguments before or since, but the violence and the tension of the times had taken hold. Two boys went head to head like young raging bulls, prodded by an underlying hatred fueled by war, a war we couldn't have possibly understood, at least not the core of its terrible nature.

One boy died that long ago day. Time stopped for him in the muddy streets of a strange town, far from his home. The other ran off into the dark woods, too young and too frightened to realize that the woods would only get darker and deeper with each hunted step.

Now, suddenly it came to me. I sat there dressed in a black linen suit, wearing a finely made boiler hat and a silk tie. I wore a doeskin duster and boots cut from the best leather and gloves that would've cost a man more than six months' pay. I was dressed to suit affairs of state, yet I sat on a stump in the woods with a loaded gun on my lap and two more concealed on my person. For whatever I thought I'd become in life, I realized it was of no matter. From the second the last breath left that young soldier's body, I'd been running and hiding, deeper and deeper, losing myself in the darkened woods.

I stood up that evening as Jack rode silently into the woods. His expression was strained, guarded, as if the devil had met him on the road and given him a message, and he was trying to remember the message word for word.

At first I thought he'd been shot, and I readied my shotgun before me, searching the woods in all directions. I called out quietly at ten yards, "Jack, are you alright?" He nodded his head and drifted on in. Something in his strange stare caused me to lower the gun as he rode up close. I'd never seen such a look on his face, and for some reason I just sat back down on the stump and let the gun barrel rest against the ground.

The strangest thing happened that day in the woods. I did something I'd never done before nor will likely ever do again. But as I sat there looking up at "Quiet" Jack Smith, I swear to God, as his lips moved, though I didn't know from word to word what he was saying, I could've spoke the words right along with him. It was as if our thoughts had tangled together and spilled out at the same time.

In his words, I saw old women dressed in black and men removing their hats as their black string ties fluttered in the wind. Behind me, the sound of the water and the children playing in the distance became a lonesome hymn, a song in remembrance to something passing.

"Jesse's dead," Jack said.

I gazed up, saw a gray dove flutter in the breeze high atop the gently swaying forest, and I heard leaves rustle at my feet as the butt of my shotgun fell softly to the ground.

Part VI
Angels Only Dance

◆*42*◆

"It was a real nice thing," Jack said, "I think Jesse would be proud." Fog swirled in a heavy mist. "Quiet" Jack, "Whiskey" Ed Ryan, and I sat atop our horses beside the crossroad inn in Kentucky and watched the road disappear into the gray veil.

"I'm just sorry I couldn't attend," I said softly. The solemn figure moved closer from out of the fog, his horse's hooves rang low and lonesome against the cobblestone.

"Best you didn't," Jack said, his voice hushed as if to keep from disturbing the night. "I spotted three of Zanone's men hanging around like vultures." At the sight of us gathered in the shadows, the rider stopped in the middle of the road and his horse tossed its head and nickered low. I made the sound of a night bird, and the rider coaxed his horse toward us.

"Who is Daniel—by God damn—Zanone?" blurted "Whiskey" Ed, his voice too loud and assaulting in the thick silence. We both hushed him with a sharp look as the rider moved into the shadows beside us. "Well, by God," Ed mumbled, "I've as much of this as I do of another." In the five or six years I'd known Ed Ryan, I'd yet to hear him make any sense at all. His skull had stopped a forty-four slug years back, and a bald spot on the side of his head pulsed like a soft spot on a newborn baby.

"Howdy, Frank," I whispered, as he reined his horse up beside us. I extended my hand. Frank squeezed my hand as if reaching for strength.

The inn was empty except for the bartender and an old man with a white beard. They both looked around at us, then the old man turned his attention back to a leather dice cup on the bar. "Nobody here but us chickens," the bartender said with a nervous laugh. He'd served us before over the years, and we'd always been respectful to his place. Still, his voice lost some of its depth when we came to visit.

When we were seated at a table in the shadows of a far corner, Jack brought a bottle of rye and four glasses from the bar, and he and Ed stood beside the table holding their rifles as I poured Frank a drink. He studied the glass of rye as I poured three more and passed two of them to "Quiet" Jack and "Whiskey" Ed. "I've got to know one thing," I said, looking Frank straight in the eyes, "did Jesse die holding any ill feelings toward me?"

Frank offered a tired, sad smile. "Jesse was pleased, and proud as a rooster, when I told him you'd changed your mind and were coming with us. You're family, Cousin, always was, always will be."

I tossed back the shot of rye and stared at the empty glass on the table. "Thanks, Frank, that helps . . . a lot."

"Here's to him, goddamn it!" Ed blurted out. His right eye remained steady and fixed, but his left eye roamed as it pleased, as if searching for whatever that slug had taken away. "And every goddamned body else!" He reared his head in a loud, crazy laugh, then dropped it, silent as a stone.

We stared at Ed as he nodded, mumbled, and argued with some unseen entity. Frank glanced away, shook his head, and let out a long breath. I looked up at Jack and nodded toward the stock room behind him. "Come here," Jack said to Ed, "I want to show you something." On their way into the stock room, Jack reached over and picked up a heavy iron poker from against the wall.

"How's Ma and Zee and the kids holding up?" I asked, as we heard a quick slap and a heavy thud from the stock room.

"As well as they can," Frank replied. "It ain't helping that Bob Ford is bragging about the details to any damn newspaper that'll listen."

"Son of a bitch," I said, gripping the glass like it was Bob Ford's throat. "I swear to you, Frank, he won't brag after I lift him up my glades knife." Jack stepped out of the stock room and pitched the bent poker over on the wood pile in the corner.

"No," Frank said, "I don't want you making a move on Bob Ford, that's why I called us together tonight. We need to talk about some things."

Hearing Frank's words, Jack turned to walk toward the bar. Ordinarily, Jack would not have been included in this kind of conversation. "Hold up, Jack," Frank said, "this concerns you as well."

"I'm sorry for 'Whiskey' Ed," Jack said as he pulled out a chair, "he wasn't acting that bad when he met up with us, and since Jesse had brought him in, well . . . I just figured, well, you know."

"I understand," Frank said, "it's just that kind of decision on Jesse's part that got him killed, as far as I'm concerned. He'd taken to drawing in people from outside our circle." Frank shook his head. "No matter now, I reckon." Jack and I glanced at each other and sipped at the rye while Frank studied the tabletop.

After a few awkward seconds of silence, Frank looked up between me and Jack and took a deep breath. "There's no point in me beating around the bush," he said, "I'm going in. I've had my lawyer talking to the governor for me, and I'm turning myself in next week." He sat still as stone staring back and forth between us.

"What about Ford?" Jack asked. "We can't let it lay."

"For now we can. Jesse's dead and Ford will keep, till the time comes. Right now, I need the scummy bastard doing just what he's doing, shooting off his mouth. That's worth more public sympathy than I could buy for a million dollars. But if he dies they'll swear it's coming from me, and that could swing folks the other way."

"I want him awfully bad," Jack warned.

"So do I," I joined in. "Frank, are you sure about this?"

"I've thought it out," he said, "and I need you to go along with me on this. After I'm sentenced or released, he'll die, that's a fact."

"Sentenced or released? Hell, Frank, they've got enough to hang you."

"I don't think so, neither does my lawyer." Frank leaned in close. "Now listen, you might not like what you'll hear in the papers. My lawyer is going to play it like I was just a blind follower, Jesse's weak-willed older brother that just didn't realize when the war was over. I've got a good record of service in the Regular Southern forces, back before I ever joined up with Quantrill. We're going to make my surrender look like the last tired soldier coming in from the battle."

"Jesus, Frank," I whispered, there in the shadows as he took Jack's hand and mine at the same time, "that's exactly what it is."

We sat atop our horses and watched Frank James slip back into the fog as if it had all been a dream. "Whiskey" Ed sat slumped in the saddle, as Jack and I listened to the steady clatter of hooves fade into an echo, then an echo of an echo, then a ringing silence.

"I want you both to know," Frank had said, solemn and proud, "you two are the last of 'The boys.' I'll never forget you or the times we've had together. It's been the honor of my life to ride with you." He faced us one at a time, holding our hands in a firm grip, like some retiring general addressing his troops. "God bless you, Jack Smith," he'd whispered, then he turned to me and let my hand slip from his. "And God bless you, Jeston Nash." It was the first and only time Frank had called me by my real name.

As much as I hate to say it, Jesse's death lifted a heavy burden that had been shackled to my spirit for a long time. I know if Frank had asked me to, I would have rode on with him till we were killed or caught, but the fact is, I'd wanted out. Now that Frank had decided to turn himself in, my days of outlawing were over, and it wasn't a matter of me letting anybody down. "The boys," what was left of us, had just come apart by Frank's own choosing. I was free.

Except for Zanone and his bunch, everybody had pretty much written Miller Crowe off like a bad debt. I couldn't go announcing myself from the rooftops, but I could slip a little farther out of the shadows now that nobody would be mistaking me for Jesse James.

I worked it over in my mind while Jack and I rode back across Arkansas. It was time for me to take Little China and clear out to Kentucky. I wanted to see our baby born in a new place, a bright and cheerful place where sunlight spilled through the window of a morning, and we would never again worry about waking to the sound of rifles. I wanted time, free untroubled time, where I could play with my baby and love Little China, without fearing that it might all end at any second.

When we reached the crossroad that led back to Jack's place, it was well past midnight and I still had another twenty miles to go. "So, Frank is hanging it up, and so are you." Jack smiled. I could see he was a little disappointed.

"Jack, you're welcome to come along, and bring the widow with you."

He gazed up at the moon. "We really were something, you know?"

"I reckon so," I said quietly. I gazed up with him. "I hope Frank knows what he's doing."

"He always has," Jack said. "I hope you know what you're doing."

"What do you mean?"

"Zanone." Jack turned and looked at me seriously. "He'll never give up till one of you kills the other."

"That's probably true, but I've got to chance it. Now that Jesse is dead and Frank is going in, I'm going to try and let things end. If Zanone don't come looking, maybe I can give up killing him." I turned my horse slowly and started down the road. I knew I would be breaking my sworn oath to ole Cletis Avery's spirit by giving up my vengeance on Zanone, but if I was to ever find peace, I would have to stop and change all of a sudden. There's no tapering off when it comes to taking on a new life—you either do it or you don't. I hoped old Cletis would understand.

I stopped a half mile from the house and took the box of candy and the bottle of lilac ambrosia perfume from my saddlebags. I wiped the road dust from the box of candy and rubbed the little purple perfume bottle on my duster sleeve to make it shine.

Part of my changing would be the way I was going to treat Little China from now on. I'd always treated her well, but I'm ashamed to admit that I'd never treated her the way a man should treat a special woman. I reckon because she'd never required the attention of a proper lady, I'd never gone out of my way to show it to her.

I stopped at the edge of the woods overlooking our cabin in the valley. I sat there a few minutes with the presents on my lap, watching a lazy sliver of smoke curl in the silver mist of dawn. As much as I looked forward to our new lives in Kentucky, this little spread would always hold a warm and special place inside me.

I heeled my horse forward down the trail into the valley. China would be sleeping; I would slip in quietly and under the covers. . . .

I jerked my horse to a halt and sat still as stone at the sight of something stirring near the front door. I strained my eyes against the silver haze, then relaxed with a sigh as I saw a chicken rise up and ruffle its feathers on the porch. I smiled and heeled forward again. It would be good to finally let down my guard after all these years.

Halfway across the front yard I caught sight of the water bucket lying empty in the dirt beside the well, and again I froze. This time when I stared at the porch, closer up, I saw another chicken, and another, and my God! they were drifting in and out through the open door.

There are times when a person feels the world stop suddenly, as if some mighty and unseen force clamps a powerful hand around life and spins it off in an opposite direction. At such times the wind runs out of breath and the sky disappears from between man and eternity. Time loses its ability to separate the past from the present, and reality is reshuffled like a worn deck of playing cards.

I remember sliding silently from the saddle and drawing my rifle from the scabbard. Had someone been waiting inside for me, they would've started firing as I crossed the yard. Somewhere in my mind I knew what awaited me inside the house. I must've crept slowly in order to prepare myself for it.

I recall my hands trembling and my knees being numb and weak as I stepped up on the porch. "Hold on, just hold on," I repeated to myself, trying to brace against what I would find beyond the open door. But nothing could've prepared me for the sight of Little China hanging from the rafters with the glades knife stuck through her heart.

"And in as much as flesh doth turn to spirit . . ." The preacher's voice rolled across me like soft thunder and echoed quietly through the sunlit meadow. As the coffin lid lowered slowly, I stared straight across it and into Jack's dark and hollow eyes.

"Now let us bow our heads and pray," instructed the preacher; but I'd never felt less like praying and more like killing than I did at that second. I just stared at Jack as the preacher droned on, and I remembered the broken box of candy and the tiny bottle of perfume that lay in the dirt outside the home I shared with Little China. Jack nodded his head slightly. He held his boiler hat chest high and twisted the brim back and forth between his fingers. "Amen," the preacher said.

Jack had seen Little China before the widow woman washed her and dressed her in a white cotton gown. He saw how she'd been beaten and used, and how finally when there was nothing left of her, the glades knife had been sunk and twisted into her heart. Like myself, Jack could only imagine how China had begged for her life, hers and the baby's.

Later that evening I was back beside her grave, only now I was out of my black linen suit and boiler hat. I'd gone straight home and changed into my riding clothes. I'd picked a handful of fresh wildflowers and brought them back. I laid them carefully on the fresh mound of dirt as if not to disturb my sleeping angel and our unborn child. There in the quiet of evening, for the first time since I'd let her tortured body down gently from the rafters, I felt a soft breeze caress my face, and my sorrow overcame me. As I tried to whisper something to her, something that could be heard between us across the plains of heaven, I felt a rush of tears and sank to my knees on the loamy mound of earth.

Only when I heard "Quiet" Jack's horse nicker behind me did I wipe my bandanna across my eyes and let out a deep, painful breath. I leaned forward on my knees and stared down at the wildflowers. This was all I could do for Little China, for now or forever. She and the baby were gone from my life as if they'd never been.

Standing behind me, Jack reached out and pitched the glades knife on the fresh mound of dirt. He'd washed it clean of China's blood and now I recognized it as it glistened in the evening sun. It had been my knife years ago. It was taken from me when I was captured back in Kansas City. I'd left it covered with blood and sticking in the sheriff's desk, with a note to Daniel Zanone.

"Zanone," I whispered, and my voice sounded like a demon uttering an ancient curse. "Zanone," I whispered again, as if stricken by the revelation. But I already knew it was him. What other low devil would do such a thing?

◆✳ 43 ✳◆

A dark and evil energy had consumed my spirit as I swung into the saddle and reined my horse toward Liberty. An air of death must've hung above us like a storm cloud. Near the cemetery, I saw a young woman run from the porch and grab up two children playing in the yard as we rode by, as if something terrible would surely follow in our wake.

I'd strapped a pair of black-handled Walker Colts across my saddle, butts forward in guerrilla fashion for a riding draw. Under my shirt I wore my old forty-four held by a leather strap, and a brass-framed, custom-made Lang & Thompson hung in a shoulder holster nearly to my waist. I carried a repeating rifle in my scabbard and a ten-gauge hog leg wrapped in my sleeping roll behind my saddle. Two bandoleers of ammunition swung from my saddlehorn as we pounded out across the flatland, our duster tails slapping in the wind.

Thunder clouds growled and gathered in the west the night we rode toward Liberty; a storm raged by the time we crossed the city limits. "Wait here," I said to Jack, as I swung down from the wet saddle. Water poured from my hat when I tipped my head forward and drew the ten-gauge from my bedroll. Jack sat atop his silver-gray mare with his rifle propped up from his saddle, scanning the empty streets.

I stepped through the door of the Midwest Security office with the ten-gauge cocked and hanging from my hand. Behind me, day was as dark as night and lightning glittered across the shotgun as I stood in the open door. "Can I help you?" said a cautious voice from behind a battered oak desk. The stocky, bearded man stood up slowly, leaning one hand on the desk and letting the other fall out of sight.

"Zanone," I said, as thunder exploded behind me, jarring the building.

"Mister Zanone has gone back to our Kansas City office. Can I offer my assistance?" His smile wasn't working. I could tell he'd seen enough posters of Jesse James and heard enough from Zanone to know who I was. I knew that behind his desk, his hand was close to a gun; if it wasn't he was a damn fool.

"I'm Miller Crowe," I said flatly, removing any need for pretense on his part or mine. Lightning twisted and curled.

"That's impossible." He smiled nervously, his hand drifting ever so slowly toward a desk drawer. "Miller Crowe has been dead for years." I just nodded my head. Surely he didn't think he could talk past what was coming to him. He knew what they'd done to Little China. If he hadn't been there, he'd heard of it. "Perhaps you would like to leave Mister Zanone a message." His hand drifted more. I wondered if he realized I was watching, or if he just figured he had nothing to lose. I was going to kill him; we both knew it.

"Yeah," I said, "here's the message," and I watched his face explode in a red and yellow spray as the ten-gauge bucked in my hand.

I took my time pouring the contents from a lamp all about the room, as I heard a voice yell out in the distance. "It came from across the street," said the voice. Thundered rolled in and erupted overhead. I struck a match and dropped it to the floor. Fire raced in jagged lines following the fuel oil, as I walked out the door, took my reins from Jack's hand, and swung up in the saddle.

A pot-bellied sheriff ran around the corner of an alley with his pistol drawn, then skidded to a stop when Jack leveled the rifle toward his chest. He let the pistol drop to the boardwalk and waved his hands chest high. "Don't shoot!" he blurted out. "I know what they did. I don't condone it."

I reined over to him and looked down. "Then you know I'm Miller Crowe? You know Zanone killed my woman and my baby?"

"Everybody knows it," he said in a rush of words. "His men have bragged about it. They're all killers, no lawman condones that kind of shit." He saw me nod to Jack and saw the rifle raise up and uncock. He let out a sigh. "I didn't think you were still alive, though," he said, letting his hands down just an inch. "I heard you'd been skinned and—"

"Yeah, I know," I cut in. "Tell Zanone, if he did it to draw me out in the open, it worked."

Smoke billowed from the office. I backed my horse away from the boardwalk as voices called out in the distance, "It's on fire!"

"Tell him I'll be in the open till one of us dies."

"I won't be seeing that lousy dog," said the sheriff, "unless it's to bar him from this town." Jack reined up beside me and we splashed our way down the muddy street.

For four days and nights we prowled the woods along the road between Liberty and Kansas City watching for Zanone or any of his men. I knew when he heard what I did in Liberty, he would have to come see for himself. After that I figured he would be combing the countryside looking for me. I had cooled down just enough to realize that riding into Kansas City with guns blazing was exactly what Zanone would expect me to do. As bent as I was on vengeance, I refused to play into his hands.

"Riders coming," Jack said in a lowered voice. I moved into the underbrush beside him and scanned the road. In seconds two riders turned the bend and came down the road in an easy gallop. They checked the woods in all directions as they rode past us. "You were right," Jack whispered. "He's heading to Liberty to see the damage." The two riders would be Zanone's front scouts. If we made a move on them, Zanone would duck away. If we let them pass, he would be along shortly.

"Are you sure they're Zanone's men?" I whispered, eager to blast them out of their saddles.

"I guarantee it," Jack replied. "The one with the red beard came around asking about you over a year ago."

From our cover I studied the riders' faces. The one with the red beard bore three slashes beneath his right eye. In my mind I could imagine Little China striking out with her fingernails as he assaulted her, and it took all my effort to keep from blasting him out of his saddle then and there. Jack must've read my face. "If you want Zanone, you better hold on a few minutes longer."

I nodded and drew a deep breath to silence the funeral drum that'd started to pound in my head. Five minutes later the sound of hooves grew closer from around the bend, and in another minute when three riders appeared, my heart nearly stopped cold in my chest.

They came around the bend suddenly, riding at a steady gait, three abreast. The ones on either side carried rifles across their saddles, studying the woods carefully. In the middle, bold as brass and looking like the devil himself, straight out of hell, sat Daniel Zanone. "Easy," Jack whispered, placing his hand on my shoulder as I started to spring up from the underbrush and empty my shotgun in Zanone's face. I felt the drum starting to pound, and this time I didn't want to stop it. I had the son of a bitch. This time I had him good. Jack crawled quickly back to the horses as I edged closer. I would wait till I heard shooting farther up the road, that would be Jack taking out the front riders. When Zanone and his two guards lit out back toward Kansas City, I would be here waiting.

Sure enough, within minutes I heard the bark of gunfire in the distance, and shortly behind it the sound of horses' hooves. I crawled out of the underbrush and into a shallow ditch alongside the road.

The funeral drum pounded in my brain as I waited till the last second and sprang to the middle of the road just as the horses started around the bend. I threw the shotgun to my shoulder. There would be no hesitation or warning. When Zanone came into sight, I would throw down with both barrels, then go for my pistol to finish off the other two.

"Drop the gun!" a voice boomed from behind me, and I knew I was surrounded. Somehow Zanone had outfoxed us.

I started to swing my gun toward the voice, but I realized that in a split second Zanone would round the bend. I would kill him as the rest of his bunch cut me to ribbons. I'd just started to squeeze the trigger when the riders appeared into sight. But it wasn't Zanone and his two guards, it was the two front riders, and in that second my heart sank, for I knew that "Quiet" Jack Smith lay dead somewhere along the road. "Drop it now!" the voice demanded. This time I swung toward the voice and felt a hard slap on my shoulder as the woods exploded.

"After all this time, I finally have you by the ass," Zanone gloated. He stood above me with his rifle lowered an inch from my face. "I hope you like the taste of blood, Mister Miller Crowe, because you're fixin' to choke on it." He kicked me hard in the stomach and I rolled into a ball. I never made a sound; I would die first.

"Get him to his feet," Zanone ordered, and hands pulled me roughly from the ground. Blood ran in a steady stream from my shoulder and dripped from my fingertips. "What about his friend?"

Zanone turned and faced the man with the red beard and the slashes on his face.

"One shot," the red beard replied with a dark smile, "right through the heart." I felt sick hearing it.

"Good work," Zanone said in a low voice. "Now go build a fire under that tree limb over there. Let's cook this bastard to a cinder."

I made a lunge at Zanone's ugly face, hoping to throw him off balance while I snatched the forty-four from under my shirt. But two pair of hands caught me. Zanone stepped in and slammed the rifle butt into my stomach, and I doubled over. He stepped back and laughed as I felt my hands jerked behind my back and a rope drawn tight around them. As soon as I caught my breath, I would lunge at him again. I would fight till they killed me on the ground. I would do anything to keep from burning to death like ole Cletis.

In seconds I heard the crackling flames and saw the fiery glow deeper in the woods. "I've been keeping a running score over the years," Zanone said, "and you've done real poorly. Let's see, there was that old man I cooked up for you back in Cass County. There was those other fellers, one that went drifting downstream and the other you left stuck in a mud bank along the creek." I hadn't known till that minute that it was Zanone's men who'd ambushed us and killed Floyd Nix and Parker Avery. I gritted my teeth and strained against the rope.

"And of course there was that little yellow bitch everybody fucked the other day. I kinda hated killing her. I believe she was enjoying it till that baby started kicking."

I lunged again, screaming. This time I dragged both men with me as I snapped at Zanone's throat like a vicious dog. I had a piece of his coat collar in my teeth as they pulled me away. Zanone backhanded me across the mouth and laughed. "And what have you managed? Sheriff Sheckler and that flunky in Liberty the other day. I'm kind of disappointed now that it's over. I thought you would have done much better."

I knew I was dead and nothing could change it. But I saw a chance to keep from burning over the fire and I jumped at it. "There's one more," I hissed, hoping my words would draw me a quick bullet in the head. "Don't forget your slut daughter. Don't forget how I splattered her brains all over the pillow the night you had her spread out like a two-dollar whore." I hated saying it, but I hated the thought of roasting alive even worse.

Zanone's face swelled red and trembled. His whole body shook violently till blood trickled from his nose and spread between his lips. He dropped the rifle and clenched his fists till I thought his fingers would split open. "I reckon she looked good showing up in hell with her ass still wet—"

"Nooo!" he screamed. His voice sounded as if it was full of torn pieces of his guts and soul. He jerked so hard at his pistol that the safety strap tore loose and flew in the air. I knew it was over for me as the two men dove away, and I clenched my teeth when I saw the belch of fire jump into my chest.

The impact knocked me backwards and I seemed to travel slowly up off my feet and drift in the air. I remember thinking that death didn't feel anything like I'd always imagined it would. It didn't hurt, getting shot to death; at least it couldn't be as bad as burning like some roasting animal.

I saw another belch of fire as I drifted back into the arms of death. This time I felt it hit me in the head, and I could've almost laughed. There was no pain, no sound, and no worry. I'd started down the dark tunnel, that tunnel I'd dreaded all my life, and there was nothing to fear. Dancing with the angels was nothing to fear. Once on the floor, all you had to do was dance.

But something about being dead had me a little confused. I'd rolled through the dark tunnel with my hands outstretched for the first waltz. I'd expected to drop out the other end and find either a golden billowy cloud or a yawning furnace of fire. There was neither. Either God or the devil must've forgotten to make the pickup, for right after my death I still lay on the ground like a stomped frog. After floating into a vast darkness behind a shimmering veil, the veil had lifted slowly and everything was the same as I'd left it. Surely there was more to eternity than this.

"Dig a grave," I heard Zanone say through the watery veil, "and throw him in it. Wrap a blanket around him in case anybody needs to come back to identify him. Since we can't watch him wiggle in the fire, we might as well do it right."

"Hell, Captain, 'most everybody thinks the son of a bitch died over at Powder River."

"Do it anyway," Zanone barked, "just in case."

I felt nothing. My body was an empty shell with a tiny bit of something still rattling around in it, waiting for whatever eternity was going to do. After a while, I sensed myself being rolled into a wool blanket and pitched into a narrow, shallow split of earth. Maybe this was where it started. Maybe after they buried me, I would rise up through the dirt and begin my long journey. "That must be it," I thought, and I relaxed into a warm darkness as the sound of shoveling grew distant above me.

◆✳ 44 ✳◆

"Welcome home, son," said my pa. I'd never seen him look so young and happy. Then I saw my ma step in beside him, and I realized Pa had found the peace his spirit had so greatly craved. Ma was as lovely as I remembered her, back before the fever had taken its toll. She wore a flowered dress with a white apron tied at her waist, and as I fell into her arms, I smelled warm cornbread and the scent of honest toil. Pa's hand felt warm and strong against my back. "I told you he would be along directly," Pa said, his voice shaking with joy and tears.

Hugging my ma and pa, I stared out behind them, at the old house. It looked bright and newly painted. Beyond it was a field of corn so plush and green it seemed too heavy to stand; and the ears of corn seemed to burst from the shucks and glistened like pure gold in the sunlight. "It's heaven," I cried, "this is heaven."

"No, son," Ma whispered, holding me close and soothing my head against her breast, "this is home, just home." Then I remembered my wounds and I pulled back to arm's length.

"But I'm dead, Ma, look at me."

"No," Pa said, "you're just tired. You've come to rest a while."

"You mean I've got to go back?"

"Only for a while," said Pa.

"And we'll be right here waiting when you come back," Ma said, smiling peacefully.

"But I don't want to go back," I cried. "I want to stay here, I want to help you with the fields, and be at peace."

I looked deep into Pa's eyes as he nodded his head. "Son," he said, "your friends are waiting for you, you have to go back."

"My friends are all dead," I said, "every last one."

"No, son," said Pa, pointing out across my shoulder. "They're all here, and they'll wait till you're rested up and ready to ride."

"Holy shit," I whispered, as I turned and looked past Pa's pointing finger. There, a short distance out, on a low rise beneath an old oak tree, stood Jesse, Clell, ole Cletis and Parker Avery, and Floyd Nix, and Kenny Ellworth, the whole bunch looking as reckless and free as ever I'd seen them. "I reckon this ain't heaven after all." I laughed.

"No," Pa laughed and then stared into Ma's eyes, and I saw the peace and the love that flowed between them, "but it's as close as we'll ever get."

I waved up to Jesse and the bunch atop the low rise. "I'm gonna rest here for a-spell." From somewhere a fiddler struck up a bright and snappy tune and they begin clapping their hands, laughing, hooting, and dancing to the music.

"Take your time," Jesse yelled. I'd never heard him sound so happy.

For the longest time I rested with Ma and Pa while the ring of the fiddler's tune drifted through my window and filled my heart with deep joy. I couldn't wait to join Jesse and Clell and the rest of "The boys," but I was concerned that Jack wasn't with them. I remember drifting to sleep wondering about "Quiet" Jack Smith, worrying that if he wasn't here, where in hell was he?

"Don't worry about me," Jack said through the gray veil, as if hearing my thoughts. "Heaven's full of Mormons and hell wouldn't have me." His laugh sounded weak. "I've got my own place not far from here."

Beside him stood the most beautiful woman I'd ever seen. I needed to say something to her, but as she lay her hand on Jack's shoulder, she leaned in close to my face. "He needs to rest, let him rest," she said, and I drifted away beneath her soft, quiet voice.

The next time I saw Jack Smith, he must've crept out of his own place in hell—he was sitting perched up beside me. He tapped a finger against the bandage on his chest. "That lying stack of shit missed my heart by a good two inches. Can you believe that? I heard him tell Zanone he killed me. If I couldn't shoot any better than that—"

"What?" I said suddenly. My ears popped and in a second I heard Jack's voice full volume. The veil had lifted. I glanced around the strange yet somehow familiar room. I didn't know if I had slipped back to life or if this was just one more drifting level of death. "What?" I said again, just to see if my words sounded of flesh or spirit. I raised my hand to my throbbing forehead and felt the large white bandage covering my right eye.

"I said," Jack went on as if nothing had happened, "if I couldn't shoot no better than that, I would take up teaching school."

"What? What? What!" Each word I said sounded more and more real in my ears, and each sound came from deeper and deeper in my throat. "Son of a bitch," I thought, "I ain't dead." I felt almost disappointed. I'd longed to stay with Ma and Pa; I'd longed to join Jesse and the rest on that low rise and dance to that strange and joyous fiddle music.

I lay staring at the ornate ceiling. My chest felt as if it were missing, as if someone had mercifully cut away the skin and bones, and with them the pain. I dared not lay my hand there, for fear it would fall against my exposed innards. Why, if God knew anything of mercy, would he drag me from that pleasant place of love and joy and sunlight, to this, a bed of pain and sickness and suffering?

I heard a door swing open, and a woman's voice. "I heard something," said the voice, sounding concerned and hopeful. "Is he awake?" It was a familiar voice, but in my state of wandering between life and death, I dared not hope. "Is he coming around?" I tried to raise my head as the voice moved around beside me, but I couldn't move, and the bandage over my eye wouldn't allow me to see.

A hand reached across me and I reached my hand up and held it weakly. "It can't be," I thought to myself, "God, let it be," and as I pulled her into view, I thought, "now I can live, now I can live."

"Yeah," I heard Jack say behind her, "he's alive, but he's an idiot. He just keeps saying the same thing over and over."

"Jeanine," I tried to whisper, but I knew the word had not passed my lips. "What?" I heard myself say.

"See what I mean," Jack said, "his mind is going to be like a ball of soft dough. He'll never know midnight from Sunday morning. One little bullet in the head and he just fell plumb apart."

I lay gazing into Jeanine's eyes and felt a spark of strength deep inside me. "I must live," I told myself, "I will live," I vowed. Jeanine's eyes glistened with tears, and she touched her fingertips to my lips as if she knew what I wanted to say.

"Yeah," Jack said, "it'll be oatmeal and a lap shawl from now on—"

"Shut up, Jack," Jeanine said, her voice sounded relieved, as if a prayer had been answered. "Just shut up."

"Thank you, Jeanie," I thought. "Thank you, Jesus."

* * *

Digging a body out of a grave to see if it's alive goes beyond anything I'd ever heard of in my life. To understand why Jack did it would be to understand the inner workings of his mind, and that was something I'd given up on a long time ago. Still I had to ask him, once I was strong enough to sit up in bed. "Hell," he said, "if you was alive, it was the smartest thing in the world to do, and if you wasn't, nobody would ever know about it but me."

I sipped at the glass of water, swallowing slowly and painfully. "But you were shot to pieces yourself. Why didn't you just crawl off and try to find some help?"

"Well," he said, reaching out and taking a piece of bread from my breakfast tray, "I figured in that kind of situation, two heads were better than one, don't you think?" I just blinked my eyes and gazed out through the window. There was no use trying to figure it out, and the fact that I was alive made it worth doing, I reckoned.

"What made you bring me here, of all places?"

"This was closest," he said. "Neither one of us would've made it back to Liberty, and Zanone would've probably been there anyway. So I just rounded up a horse and brought us here. Was that alright?"

"Yeah," I said, "you did real good." I remembered the pain I'd felt the day I heard Jeanine had married and had a child. Now that I was getting my strength back, and my senses, I realized I would have to go through it all again. I thanked God for being alive just to see her once more, but reality was setting in. As soon as I was able, I would have to disappear from her life once more. I didn't want to think about it right then. "How're you healing?" I asked Jack, just to get my mind on something else.

"I'm coming right along. I've got a room over at the Lucky Lady, and them whores have taken to me like I'm a little lost lamb."

I laughed and felt the pain deep in my chest. Luckily the bullet had deflected off my forty-four, but the impact had splintered the cylinder and lodged two pieces of metal in my breastbone. Jeanine had brought in a doctor and it took him two hours of chiseling to get the metal out of my chest. My chest was the color of overripe fruit. "Why didn't you stay here?" I asked.

"I did for nearly three weeks," Jack said, "but you know me, once up, I was on my way."

I raised a hand to the bandage covering my right eye. The bullet had grazed me deep as I fell back, shattering the bone just above my right eye. A splinter of bone had torn through my pupil. It was doubtful the eye would ever heal proper. Other than that, being down to one eye, and being buried alive, I was getting over a terrible concussion, cracked ribs, and had lost a dangerous amount of blood from my shoulder wound. "Where's Jeanine?" I asked, trying to shift my legs off the side of the bed. "And what about her husband and kid?"

"She lit out yesterday evening," Jack replied, lifting my legs up and dropping them back on the bed. "She asked me to make sure you stay here till she gets back. So I'm doing it."

"Goddamn it, Jack," I groaned, as pain jarred through my chest and shoulder, "all you had to do was say so. It ain't like I'm apt to go shinnying down the drain pipe."

"Sorry," said Jack, "but I'm a little sore myself, and I ain't much of a nurse maid."

I leaned back against the pillows and watched Jack cough and hack and press his hand to his chest. Seeing the pain he was in caused me to raise my hand to my own chest, but it was too bruised and sore to stand the pressure. We looked like two dogs who'd been through a bear fight, and I couldn't help but break into a weak laugh at our spent and sorry condition. Jack pressed his chest and laughed in response, a kind of choking, wheezing laugh. "What is it we're laughing about?" he asked between coughs.

I squeezed the mattress against the pain in my chest and shook my head. "Because we're alive, goddamn it, can you believe it?"

Jack shook his head and bent over laughing. "By God, that is kinda funny, ain't it."

That night, long after Jack had left and the maid had retired to her quarters, I lay staring at the dark ceiling when I heard something stir quietly in the hall outside my door. I tensed and listened closely. I was a little uneasy about being here in another man's house to begin with. I didn't know him, and I had no idea when he might come through the door. "Where the hell is Jeanine?" I thought to myself, as I heard the sound again.

I was in no shape for confrontation. Jack had left a forty-four under my pillow and a rifle leaning against the night stand. I hoped I wasn't about to throw down on a man in his own home.

I eased up from the bed with the forty-four hanging from my hand, and using the rifle as a crutch, I limped softly toward the door. Standing there with my back flat against the wall beside the door, I listened to the pressure of silent footsteps on the wood floor. As the door knob twisted slowly, I felt the funeral drum begin to throb in my head. I tried to silence it as the door crept open inch by inch.

"Jeanine's husband?" I thought. "Zanone? No, not Zanone." I felt my thumb press against the trigger as I watched a hand push against the door. "It wouldn't be Jeanine, she knew better." Now a man's head slipped between the crack in the door.

I'd already started making my move as I heard a voice from farther down the hall. "Lane! no, don't," and I grabbed the shoulder and slung him to the floor as I heard Jeanine scream.

"No, Jess, no!" Jeanine's voice rang shrill throughout the Wilcox mansion. I stood over him with the hammer cocked, my wounded right shoulder straining from the weight of the gun and my left hand supporting it. The drum pounded; my finger pressed the trigger. I was too weak to stand much longer; my finger pressed harder. "No," she screamed again, or was it the same scream? as she twisted up the wick on the lamp behind me, and my shadow, and the shadow of my gun fell across the frightened face of the young man at my feet. "Don't shoot! It's your son!"

I swayed, gasping for breath as Jeanine fell past me and cradled the young man against her. Cold sweat slapped at my forehead. The room spun around beneath me and my feet struggled to stay on the floor. I dropped the gun to my side, too weak to let down the hammer, and afraid to drop it for fear of it going off. I felt my back jar against the wall, and it started me breathing again. "He— just— wanted— to see his father," Jeanine sobbed, pressing his head against her breast.

"Oh . . . God," I gasped, staring down at Jeanine and the baby I thought we'd lost so many years ago. I felt myself sliding down the wall. I saw the fine wool rug gather at my feet like furrows on the brow of God. He stared wide-eyed from behind his mother's hands. I tried to smile; it was the grimace of a smitten lunatic.

Blood spread across my chest and shoulder; I felt warm urine spread through my white cotton night-shirt. The bloody bandage on my right eye grew heavier and heavier till I could no longer hold it up.

"What an impression," I thought, as I heard my head thump against the floor and watched the gun go sliding past them.

◆✳ 45 ✳◆

"Jack even heard it from an old feller the last time we were through here." I lay propped up in bed. My shoulder wound had broken open, and the wounds in my chest as well. It was the next evening before I regained consciousness, and my head pounded mercilessly. "He told Jack you had a husband and a child."

"Of course," Jeanine said, raising a hand to her forehead. "You're my husband, you've always been." Her eyes glistened with tears. She sat on the side of my bed, holding my hand in her lap.

"For years I waited and prayed you would come back. I kept telling Lanefred about his father, that you were away on business. And we waited, and I prayed. Then four years ago I heard you'd been killed out near Powder River. At first I didn't believe it, I refused to believe it, but when your cousin Cole said it during his trial, I had to accept it. I just told Lanefred you wouldn't be coming back." She turned her face away and cried quietly.

I stared at the ceiling and felt like the biggest fool in the world. For years I'd had a son and didn't know it. Cronin Wilcox had sworn my son would never lay eyes on me; until now he'd made good his threat. "This was all your father's doings," I whispered, "that old son of a bitch."

"I warned you not to underestimate him," Jeanine said. "He must've bought the doctor and started the rumor that I'd lost the baby. All these years, I thought you knew you were a father. I thought you stayed away because of the law and because you thought you'd shamed me."

"That much is true," I said, "but if I'd of known we had a son, nothing would've kept me from seeing him."

"I know," she whispered, holding my hand to her face, "I know."

* * *

We spent the night talking, putting our lives back together like two people carefully fitting the pieces of a shattered but irreplaceable vase. I felt as if I'd been living someone else's life all these years, while my own life waited for me back in Kansas City.

I told Jeanine about Little China. I felt I should. But I never asked if there had been anyone else in her life. If there were others, and she felt I should know, she would tell me, otherwise I would leave it alone. There would always be a special place in my heart for Little China. It was her death that brought me out of hiding to look for Zanone, and in a roundabout way brought me back into Jeanine's life, back to my family.

"So, for years, you've been the widow of the outlaw Miller Crowe?" I regretted having brought her such shame. It must've shown on my face.

"Listen to me," she said, squeezing my hand, "nobody forced me to wait for you, and nobody made me keep your name. It was my choice, and I'm glad I made it. For years I fought with my parents over it, even after I heard of your death. But I never gave in, and I've never been ashamed of what happened. My father was ashamed, but it was his own doing." She gazed down at her lap. "He couldn't face the public because of what happened, yet deep down he knew he'd brought it on himself."

"And he ended up hanging himself," I said quietly.

Jeanine nodded and turned back toward me. "Three weeks after Mother passed away. His business was failing, his investments were down, and I think he always regretted not having a son to help shoulder the load." Jeanine sighed. "All he had was me, a daughter. What good was I?

"He walked out to the breeder's barn one morning without saying a word, and they found him hanging from a rafter."

"It must've been hard on you and the boy," I said.

"Lane and his grandfather were never close," she said with a sigh. "We've lived here, but we've lived alone. I think Father only tolerated us because he feared someday you would come back for vengeance."

"I thought about it many times," I said. "The only reason I didn't was because I knew it would just hurt you."

"I don't think he saw a minute's peace until the day we heard of your death," Jeanine said. "By then, Mother was ill and she asked me to take care of her." Jeanine shook her head slowly and continued, "When she died, Father just gave up on life. He didn't even realize that just as I took care of Mother, I had also begun taking care of his business. I turned his business around, wrestled the stock market, and made him a fortune, but he died without being able to see it. Or maybe . . . he did see it and died ashamed of it."

I gazed at Jeanine and realized, while men like her father, Jesse, Frank, and myself were busing carving life into meaningless pieces, it was people like her and Jesse's wife, Zee, and Frank's wife, Anna, who pulled life back together, nurtured and cleansed and made things whole. And through it all she'd waited, as they'd all waited until the last flicker of hope had died. And even then, she'd gone on with life, not bitter or ashamed, but in a strong way that showed more guts, grit, and determination than a thousand of us mindless desperados.

"Jeanine," I said, drawing her closer with my good hand, "the day Zanone ambushed me on the front porch, I was coming back for you. I'd planned on us leaving here that day and taking a place over in Kentucky before the baby was born. That's the truth, I swear it."

She lay her head gently on the pillow close to mine and pressed her fingers to my lips, silencing me. After all that had happened, after risking her life the day she took up a rifle against my captors, after facing the shame I'd bequeathed to her and my son, after waiting all this time and tending to a life I'd given up on years ago—considering all she might have said, or asked, or held me accountable for—she simply smiled from a woman's deep well of strength and wisdom. "Rest," she whispered, "tomorrow's a brand-new day."

"But Uncle Jack said you were one of the quickest *you-know-whats* he's ever seen with a glades knife."

"Uncle Jack?" I murmured under my breath. I gazed off at the sky and scratched at my beard. I wasn't going to have this kind of shit going on around my family. "Son," I said quietly, "you can't listen to a lot of what 'Uncle' Jack says." I'd made up my mind, "Uncle" and I were going to have a long talk.

"What's a glades knife, Father?" Lane asked. "And what does he mean about you being quick with it?" We stopped along the path beside the circle track. I had not fully regained my sense of balance, partly due to the concussion, and partly because I was getting used to just having one eye. I leaned my left arm on my son's shoulder, and steadied myself on the right with a hickory cane.

"What he meant," I cleared my throat, "is that back when he and I were living in the wilds, I could clean and carve up a deer real quick. See, a glades knife is kind of a hunting knife—"

Looking down at the upturned face of my son, Jeston Lanefred Crowe, was like looking at a picture of myself as a boy. His face was innocent and searching. I was the father he'd never known, and he needed so much to know me, and I him. But how could I tell him the truth? How could I explain to his young mind the killing and robbing and far-handedness that had been my life? Jeanine had sheltered him from the truth about me. I felt like a low and shameful fraud as I looked into his eyes and tried to lie.

"Actually," I said quietly, "a glades knife is more of a weapon. I was in the war along the border before you were born. We did some terrible things back then, some things I ain't very proud of."

"I see," he said with a nod, a little disappointed, but trying not to show it. "You would rather not talk about it."

"It's not that I don't want you to know about it, it's just that I don't want you to know about it all at once. I reckon I'm afraid of what you'll think of me."

"Mother always says, it's not what you've done in the past that counts, but what you do in the future."

He smiled up at me as we started on down the path. "Does she now?" I said with a smile. It was a tight smile, a small dam that struggled against a high tide of feelings.

"Yep," he said, as we ambled slowly back toward the house, he supporting my left side and I steadying myself with the cane.

I had asked Jack to check around and see if he could learn the whereabouts of Daniel Zanone without drawing any attention. During the meantime, Jeanine and I had begun making our plans to move to Kentucky. My spread was not as fancy or elegant as the Wilcox mansion, but it presented itself proudly in the midst of fine Thoroughbred country. It was a good place to raise a boy and, in time, get to know one another the way we should. It was also a good place to start over for me and Jeanine, a place to create good memories and forget the past.

Jeanine stood on the front porch watching me teach our son how to make a rope harness and plait a leadline, when Jack Smith appeared on the hedge-lined path from the main road. She folded her arms and watched him ride in slowly. I busied myself with the harness and glanced up now and then until he reached the front yard. "Hello, Uncle Jack," Lane called out, as Jack swung out of the saddle and walked toward us.

"Howdy, young feller," Jack said, then in a sweeping gesture he removed his hat and bowed graciously toward Jeanine. "And a good evening to you, fair Jeanine."

Jeanine smiled and nodded toward Jack, but I could sense her concern. Jack had been away a few days, and seeing him ride in wearing a thin layer of trail dust with a pair of Colts slung over his saddle made her realize something was in the works. She didn't let on. "I'm sure you wouldn't refuse a tall glass of bourbon?" Jeanine smiled.

"Not while there's breath in this body," Jack postured. Lately I'd noticed Jack was becoming more and more the Kansas City gentleman. I slipped the finished rope harness on Lane's colt. I'd let him pick the colt himself from a livery corral after teaching him what to look for. I was surprised how well he'd done.

"Want to take her to the stall and brush her down?" I asked, handing Lane the lead rope. He took the rope eagerly and trotted off. Jack slapped the animal on the rump as it went past him.

"You're going to turn him into a good horseman, I can see that."

I nodded and glanced toward the house. "What did you find out?" I asked in a low voice, anxious to hear from him before Jeanine returned from the house.

"Zanone is at his main office in Chicago," Jack said, "but his crew of flunkies are holed up in a railcamp near Hopewell."

"All of them?" When I made my move, I didn't want to leave anyone out. It was his regular men that had raped and beaten Little China, but my thinking was not only of vengeance. As long as Zanone or any of his bunch were alive, I knew my family would never be safe.

"The whole bunch." Jack's face twisted in a cruel smile. "Even that ole boy with the red beard and the scratches on his face."

"Good," I said, imagining Little China fighting for her life, hers and the baby's. I felt a bitter chill crawl across my shoulders. "We'll leave in the morning."

Jack coughed, rolled his eyes, and looked away. I took him by the arm. "I mean it, Jack, I'm not coming back till they're all dead." I couldn't understand Jack turning away, then I heard the glass fall to ground behind me and I turned quickly.

Jeanine looked stunned, her hand poised as if still holding the glass of whiskey. She shook her head slowly as if refusing to believe her ears. "No," she gasped. "Oh God no!" She backed away slowly as if afraid to turn her back on us.

"Jeanine, honey, goddamn it, listen to me." I tried to reach out to her, but she backed farther away. "This ain't like you think. This is something you don't understa—"

She turned and ran into the house before I could stop her. Jack looked down at the spilled bourbon. "Does this mean I don't get a drink?"

"Damn it," I said under my breath, running into the house behind her. I felt my shoulder wound rip open as I caught her by her arm before she started up the stairs. "Jeanie, wait, please listen to me. You don't know Zanone. If I don't kill him, we'll never live in peace."

She spun toward me with tears streaming down her face. "He buried you, Jeston, he thinks you're dead."

"I know, I know, but if he ever gets wind that I'm alive. If he ever dreams that I still walk this earth, he'll hunt us down like we're animals. And it ain't me he'll kill first, it's you and Lane, he'll do that just to torture me. Can't you understand? It ain't me I'm thinking of, it's you and our boy."

She stared down at the floor and regained her composure. "No," she said, "it's not us you're thinking of. I won't pretend I know who or what it is you're thinking of, but it's not us, it's not our life together."

"Jeanie, I swear to God . . ."

"No, don't do this." She held up her hands. "Jeston, I feel like my whole life has been one long *wait*. Every time we get close to having a life together, something tears it apart. Look at me, Jeston, I'm not a starry-eyed young girl anymore. I'm a woman past thirty and still waiting for life to begin. And look at my son, our son. He has grown up without a father. Only since you've been here has he learned anything about being a man. I've had to shelter him from the outside world, protect him against his father's reputation."

"Jeanine," I whispered, "I'm so sorry." I reached out to pull her against my chest. She leaned toward me, then stopped herself and pushed me away.

"Listen to me, Jeston," she said. "If you truly are going to change, it has to be right now, and it has to be completely. Zanone has forgotten about you, you have no excuse for riding out of here looking for blood, other than the fact that you like killing. And if that's the case, maybe you should go, go and never come back."

I saw there was no changing her mind. I saw there was no amount of reasoning that could make her understand. She came from a different world than I, and she could not see past the surface and into the dark level of blood vengeance. To her this was a dark and sinister game, and all I needed to do was stop, and everybody else would follow suit. I envied her, her world of trust and illusion, and I saw I would have to accept it and somehow make it work.

I took a deep breath and let it out slowly. "Jeanine, I want you and my son more than anything on earth. And you're right, I have to forget about Zanone and the past and start looking toward the future."

She studied my eyes until she saw I meant it. "It's the truth," I said, "I swear to you, and I swear to God, I'll not raise a hand toward Zanone, now or ever. I reckon I just got a little crazy for a minute."

"Please mean it," she said, reaching out a hand and brushing my hair back. "He did a terrible thing to you, but nothing you can do will change it."

"You're right," I said, "and I do mean it. I'm going to tell Jack to ride on without me, and tomorrow I'm heading for Kentucky. The sooner we're out of here, the better."

Jeanine smiled and took my hand. "Ever since I've known you, you've had only two enemies, Zanone and yourself. It's time you called a truce with both."

At first Jack was struck speechless when I told him my decision. After my words sunk in and he saw how serious I was about it, he seemed to understand and even seemed a little relieved. "You really mean it this time, don't you?"

"Yes, Jack, I do. I'm through killing, now and forever. If Zanone ever comes looking for me, I'll deal with it best I can. Until then, I'm not even going to think about it."

I'd never seen Jack so touched by anything. His eyes almost got misty and he had to blink a few times before he could speak. "Jeanine," he said sincerely, "I don't know what you've done to him, but whatever it is, keep on doing it." Jeanine smiled and slipped her arm around my waist. Jack turned to me and shook hands in a firm grip. "All the time I've known you," he said, "I've never been as proud of you as I am today. I hope I'll be welcome at your place in Kentucky, once you get settled in."

"Jack, you're always welcome at our place, it goes without saying." I smiled. "I'm heading out in the morning, and I'm sending for Jeanie and the boy in a few weeks. If you don't come see us real soon, our feelings will be hurt."

Jack slipped up into his saddle, tipped three fingers to his hat, and in minutes we watched him disappear out on the main road.

Daylight spun silver and gold through the morning mist as Jack and I met early and turned our horses north toward Hopewell. I felt like a low dog, lying to Jeanine, but I knew I was right in what I'd said. As long as Zanone was alive, I could see no peace.

Jeanine didn't understand killing, hatred, and vengeance. The only evil to have tracked through her life had been on my heels, years ago. I would rather die now, by Zanone's hand, than live in fear that his foul breath would someday blow near my wife and son.

"Don't you think we pulled it off pretty good?" Jack laughed.

"I don't want to talk about it," I snapped. "She's right and I know she's right . . . in her own way."

He laughed again. "I liked the part where you said, 'If you don't come see us real soon our feelings will be—' "

"Leave me alone, Jack. I'm doing wrong and I know it. I'm a dirty bastard sneaking out this way."

"Well, it ain't like you're being unfaithful to her. All you doing is going to kill a son of a—"

"Jack! Please! Goddamn it! Let's not talk, okay?"

He chuckled under his breath. "This beats it all. I never heard of a man needing his wife's permission to go kill a son of a bitch." He gazed off and shook his head. "And where did she ever come up with a name like Lanefred, for Christ's sake?"

"That's it, Jack! I mean it! Shut—the hell—up!"

◆✳ 46 ✳◆

The Hopewell railcamp was a mud strip of a town thrown together by the railroad as an inspection point halfway between Peoria and Chicago. Back when the Texas herds pushed into Kansas City, then separated out by rail in Chicago, Hopewell served a purpose. Now, with rail lines reaching in all directions, the railroad had abandoned its investment and left the railcamp to finish out its days as a gathering spot for riff-raff, drunken riverboat men, and railroad flunkies. There was no law in Hopewell except for the railroad detectives and Zanone's bunch. No lawman with any self-respect would muddy his boots in such a shit hole.

We rode our horses quietly through the black slime of Front Street. At near midnight, the street lay deserted except for a drunk hacking up his guts at the corner of an alley, and two hogs grunting and sleeping in the middle of the street. Up ahead, we heard the sound of an out-of-tune piano coming from a tavern door. "Lord God," Jack said, fanning his hand before his face, "can we please kill these bastards quick and get out of this rotten place?" The street smelled of urine and sour beer mixed with puke, overcoated with pig shit. Moonlight glittered on a swirl of mosquitoes.

I drew a shiny new sawed-off from behind my saddle as we reined into an alley thirty feet from the tavern door. "I wouldn't have come if I'd known it was this bad," Jack said, slipping carefully from his saddle and tiptoeing through the slop and broken whiskey bottles. I tried to keep my mouth shut and breathe as little of the foul smell as possible.

The steady beat of the funeral drum was growing clearer in my head. I took the forty-four from my belt and clamped it under my left arm as we walked quietly to the door. As soon as I emptied both barrels of the sawed-off, I would snatch the pistol and keep on working. I carried another forty-four shoved down in the back of my belt. Jack had his forty-four hanging casually from one hand and the La Faucheux from his other. We stepped back from the glow of light to the edge of the boardwalk and looked in through the swinging doors. One door hung broken from its top hinge.

Through a haze of smoke, we counted four of Zanone's men sitting at a card table in the middle of the floor. At the bar, the man with the red beard stood swilling a mug of beer. Beside him stood two others I recognized from the ambush, and next to them, three drunks wearing boatmen's caps stood arguing among themselves. Jack nudged me with his elbow and nodded towards the boatmen. "Not if we can help it," I whispered. The drum beat louder.

"Throw down," Jack ordered, and I slammed through the door with the sawed-off leveled at the bar. Jack jumped in beside me and four feet to my left. I expected the piano player to stop as we crashed in, but no one heard us above the rattle of the music, and not one head turned toward us through the haze of smoke. They just kept on with their drinking and talking, as if we weren't there.

I shot Jack a quick glance. Holding both guns at his waist, he shrugged and rolled his eyes. "Ain't this some shit?"

I whistled as loud as I could and tightened my grip ready to fire as they turned toward us. They didn't even hear it. "Aw, goddamn it!" Jack swore, "I want out of this scum hole." He raised the forty-four and slammed a round past the piano player's head. Dust and splinters exploded from the piano and the room fell silent as a tomb.

"This is a holdup!" I yelled in my excitement, from force of habit. The drum was starting to pound hard. My voice sounded strained and distant to me.

"No, it ain't, goddamn it!" Jack bellowed. Out the corner of my good eye I saw him shake his head in disgust and I corrected myself.

"No, it ain't!" I said, flashing the shotgun back and forth from the bar to the table.

Zanone's men stared at us, bleary-eyed. The red beard had turned facing us slowly and his eyes widened as recognition took hold. "I'll be damned," he breathed softly.

"Anybody who ain't with Zanone's bunch better hit the floor now," I yelled. Two of the drunken boatmen dropped into the wet, stinking sawdust like a bundle of rags, but the third stood wavering defiantly, holding on to the bar with one hand. "Right now!" I demanded. "Hit the floor!"

"Go to hell," he said in a drunken slur, gesturing toward the floor. "Look at this filth. I ain't laying in it. Lay in it your goddamn self."

"Get down here, Max," coaxed one of the boatmen at his feet.

I kept the shotgun flashing back and forth. Zanone's men were coming out of their stupor. Any second they would make a move.

"I'll have to shoot you," Jack warned, leveling the cocked forty-four at the drunk's chest. Zanone's men were looking more and more clear eyed.

The drunk staggered toward Jack with his arms spread. "Then go on, shoot me. I ain't laying in this shit, would you?"

Jack took a step to the side. "Naw, I reckon not," he chuckled, waving his gun toward the door. "Go on, get the hell out."

"What about us?" came another drunken voice from the floor.

At the bar, the red beard began to realize he wasn't seeing two ghosts. I watched his gun hand tense up. "We ain't got time for this shit!" I said. The drum beat harder and faster.

"Alright," Jack said, "hurry up, get the hell out."

The two boatmen crawled and staggered to their feet. I heard a chair leg squeak against the floor and I flashed the gun toward it. Zanone's men were ready to make a move.

"Look at this," one of the boatmen mumbled as they staggered past us. They were covered with wet, slimy sawdust. They smelled of puke and tobacco juice. "Why didn't you just tell us to leave in the first place?"

"Yeah," grumbled the other, "you asshole, ya."

"So you cowards are going to shoot us without giving us a sporting chance," the red beard said. I watched the slightest twitch of his gun hand. The scratches on his face had healed, but one left a scar from his temple to his chin.

"This ain't no sporting event," I said, taking aim down the short barrel. There was no reason to talk; we were there only to kill.

"I never touched her!" yelled a trembling voice from the table, as Jack's guns moved slowly out beside me, casting long shadows on the wall in the dim light.

"Then this truly ain't your lucky day," Jack said. And the small tavern rocked with explosions and screams. Blood flew and splattered against the walls and ceiling. Shadows danced wildly in the bursts of bright fire. Then silence rang as torn bodies adjusted themselves in the positions of death.

We backed out of the tavern choking and gagging from the thick, hot cloud of burnt powder. Our eyes and noses ran in streams. I blew my nose hard into my bandanna as I hung against a post and gasped for air. Jack staggered about, coughing and trying to catch his breath. As we turned and staggered to our horses, the three drunks stood wobbling in the street. "Rotten bastards!" yelled one.

"Look at this shit!" yelled another. "You didn't have to make us lay in that shit."

"Yeah, who the hell do you think you are . . . Jesse James?"

"We'll kick your gad-dang asses!" A bottle broke against the wall behind us as we rounded the corner of the alley to our horses.

"I don't blame them," Jack said, still choking on the smoke and stepping carefully through the slimy mud.

"Sorry," I yelled, as we hooked our horses through the debris-swollen alley.

"Sorry, your ass," came a distant reply.

✦❊ 47 ❊✦

"This is more to my liking," Jack said, staring out the window as we ate ham and eggs and sipped hot coffee. We'd stopped at the next town with a train depot. After selling our horses, we'd soaked and barbered and suited up in new dress clothes, complete with vests, and neckties.

I took on a black high-collar frock coat, a black, wide-brimmed slouch hat and a black silk kerchief for an eye patch. Jack wore a gray boiler and tan riding duster. We'd taken the next express straight into Chicago. "One of these days," he said, waving his fork for emphasis, "everybody will travel by train. There will be no more horses, mark my words."

"Yeah, right," I said as I poured honey across a hot biscuit.

"This is the truth," he prophesied, from behind a mouthful of ham and eggs. "We might not live to see it, but one day everybody will have their own private little train. It won't be over five or six feet long, but it will be right outside their house and they'll just hop on it and go about their business."

"Is that right?"

He shrugged. "It has to be. Pretty soon there will be too many people, and if we all travel by horse there'll be piles of horseshit as high as the Rockies. So, there'll be little trains, everybody will have one, and there'll be tracks everywhere, I'm talking *every* damn where." He waved his arms.

I studied him a few seconds, just wondering if maybe everybody from New Jersey acted and thought this way. I wondered if maybe there was too much silt in their water source. Finally, I glanced out the window at the billowing black smoke from the engine stack. "What about all the smoke?" I asked. Jack stared at me curiously. "From all those little trains, won't that be a lot of smoke?"

Jack dismissed it with a wave of a hand. "Naw, that shit will just go up in the air, and that's the end of it."

"That's a lot of smoke," I cautioned with a smile.

"Take your pick," he said, "clouds of smoke or mountains of horse shit?"

"What about all them tracks running everywhere? What will keep people from running into each other?"

Jack picked his teeth with his fingernail and gazed out the window. "I ain't figured that part out yet," he said. He shrugged. "Besides, I ain't no goddamn conductor."

A chill wind slapped at our faces as we stepped down from the carriage outside the Stockman's Building near the rail pens in Chicago. Jack paid the driver and we quickly stepped around into an alley beside the building. I kept reminding myself to stay completely calm. Zanone had gotten past me too many times. This time I had him, and I didn't want him slipping past me because I was overeager.

"Are you sure this is it?" I asked in a hushed voice.

"I guarantee it," Jack said. Ever since we'd arrived at the station, Jack had grown more and more quiet. His face had become pale and his eyes had turned grim and expressionless.

We climbed the stairs up the side of the building. I watched the alley and street below as Jack pried open a door with a glades knife. Once inside, Jack closed the door gently as I looked around the office. Across the office on a glass door, I saw the name Daniel Zanone, President, only the words read backwards from where we stood, and I heard a woman's voice from the office beyond the door.

"How did you know this?" I whispered up close to Jack's ear. Until that second, I reckon I never truly realized we would be standing in Zanone's office. Without even looking at me, Jack handed me a wrinkled piece of paper from his pocket as we slipped toward a closet door across the room. It was a sketch of the office.

Evening shadows stretched long across the red wool rug as we slipped into the coat closet and closed the door behind us. I strained to get a look at the office as the door shut.

It was an expensive layout with a large polished desk and a matched set of leather high-topped chairs. Polished book shelves lined the walls. An expensive vase, three feet tall, stood in a corner next to a gun cabinet full of rifles and fancy pistols.

We waited there like two wolves, listening to every sound from the outer office, and breathing as quietly as possible, as if our every breath resounded like a gust from a blacksmith's bellows.

In an hour, perhaps longer, I heard the door to the outer office open and close. From the outer office, though muffled by the walls between us, Zanone's voice sent a sharp chill across my shoulders, and I nudged Jack with my elbow to make sure he'd also heard it. Jack stood still as stone, and I wondered, "God, surely he hasn't gone to sleep." But even in his silence I sensed a dark and raging tension about him.

"That will be all, Miss Amstead," Zanone said. "Please lock the door when you leave."

"Yes, sir," came a timid reply, and a desk drawer closed, and a chair squeaked in the outer office, and we listened breathlessly as Zanone's office door opened and closed, and his heavy footsteps crossed the floor just in front of the closet where we lay in wait like demons for the letting of his blood.

We stood as silent as death until we heard the outer office door close and lock behind her, then more minutes passed as we listened to Zanone settle into the leather chair behind his desk and pour a drink. The funeral drum tried to beat, but I shook it away. I would not hear the beating of the drum. I would slip out of the closet as cool as springhouse butter, put one round between his eyes, and go home to my family. That was that.

I turned the knob ever so slightly and pressed forward. The door was halfway open before it made a sound. By the time it did, I had Zanone in full view as he looked up from behind the glow of the lamp. The pen dropped from his hand as he stared wide eyed at my dark figure stepping from his closet.

I cocked my pistol and held it arm's length without the slightest tremor. My arm, my mind, and my whole body was still and quiet. His hands lay on his desk in full view. I watched a realization set in, as his eyes shrank back to normal and he let out a low sigh of regret. He seemed to relax down into the large chair. This time there would be no ambush, no surprise, and for him, no reprieve. This time we both knew; I had him, thank God, I had him good.

"You're not dead," he said, as if I'd tried to trick him.

"No," I said, as I felt my finger calmly press against the trigger, "but you are."

He resolved himself to his fate. He sat gazing with an expression that said there was no cause or purpose in discussing the matter. I watched his eyes grow more and more resolved as I felt my finger draw tighter on the trigger. But just before I knew the hammer would fall, I saw his eyes widen again. This time as they stared past me—this time in a boiling rage of madness and disbelief—I saw his eyes become a fire of hatred as I heard "Quiet" Jack Smith step out behind me and chuckle low under his breath.

Zanone's hands rolled into tight fists atop his desk and quaked as if he would go into a fit. *"Jack Zanone,"* he growled, his words ascending from the lowest level of hell.

I knew my ears had misinformed me and I eased off the trigger just long enough to clear this up. Jack stepped beside me with the La Faucheux held waist high pointing in no particular direction. I grinned, or I think I grinned, and started to say, "Did you hear that, he called you—"

Jack shot me a strange glance, something between a threat and an apology, then faced Zanone and eased forward a step. "Howdy Uncle Dan," Jack said between gritted teeth, "you lousy horse's ass."

"Uncle Dan?" I said. I felt as if the room had soared high in the air and landed with a thud. My mind and body were suddenly constructed of spare parts and they all dangled loose and in no coordination with one another. "Uncle Dan?" I repeated, staring back and forth between the two.

Zanone leaned both hands on his desk as if to pounce across it like a cougar. His face was a shadowed mask in the glow of the lamp. His eyes became dark circled. "I should've figured you low vermin would meet up somewhere on the road to hell."

"I've waited a long time to watch you die," Jack said, his voice almost soothing, as if addressing a sick person.

"What do you mean, 'Uncle Dan'?" I asked again. A crawling feeling in my guts told me to start pulling the trigger, or once again Zanone would get past me.

"It's a whole other thing," Jack answered, glancing at me, then back to Zanone. "It's something me and ole Uncle here have been brewing up for a long time."

I felt betrayed. "Why the hell did you never tell me he's your uncle?"

Jack smiled. "You never asked."

"Goddamn it, Jack!" I growled.

Zanone leaned closer across his desk, perched on his hands. "There's no excuse for the likes of you," he said to Jack. "Crowe here is trash, always has been. But you came up from decent people. Your father did his best to turn you into something."

"If we had time, I'd raise my shirt and show you what my father turned me into," Jack whispered. Of a sudden, it was as if I wasn't even in the room. Jack cocked the La Faucheux and leveled it at Zanone's face.

Something strange worked inside me. I couldn't let Jack pull that trigger, not after all Zanone had done to me. I eased a step closer to Jack with the forty-four pointed near his stomach. "You've lied to me all these years," I said. Jack raised his free hand, quieting me.

"Don't push on this," Jack cautioned, "I've waited too long for the chance to kill this bastard. I lied to you. Maybe I should've told you back when I joined 'The boys,' but I was hiding from him then, and I was afraid to take a chance. I had nowhere to go till Jesse and Frank took me in. All because this son of a bitch was hounding me."

"You killed my only brother," Zanone bellowed, banging a fist on his desk, "your own father!"

"I killed an animal," Jack said softly, "and because of it, I've killed many people since. He set me on this road, and you kept me on it."

"If he's your uncle, that means I killed your cousin," I said in a low voice. It crossed my mind that there could be more vengeance at work here than what I had expected. Jack had kept it to himself about Daniel Zanone. Was he keeping something to himself about me killing Glenella Zanone, also?

"Poor precious Glenella," Jack said. For a second his voice trembled. "Yes, you killed her. But after what her father here had turned her into, I figure your shooting her was kind of like shooting a snake-bit dog. You did her a favor."

"You scum," Zanone hissed. "How dare either of you mention her name. That was my daughter, damn you both!"

"And you turned her into your slut." Jack's voice and hand shook.

"I had my rights as a father!" Zanone bellowed.

"You have a right to this," Jack said. His hand tensed on the La Faucheux.

"You ain't killing him," I blurted out all of a sudden. "That's one satisfaction nobody is denying me, not even you."

"Sorry, my friend." Jack's voice was strong in his determination.

"I mean it," I warned, "I'll stop you if I have to." I extended the gun toward Jack.

"Look at you," Zanone hissed, leaning forward on his desk. "You're jackals, low-life, blood-sucking dogs." Zanone's voice took on a strained and breathless tone.

Jack turned slowly toward me. His expression was grim and distant. I stared into his eyes, realizing that I faced the one and only man on this earth that I truly feared if it came to a shoot-out. Not only did I fear him as a gunman, by God, I loved him like a brother. Yet, at that second, I believe I was ready to kill him like a dog. "You telling me I can't shoot my own goddamn uncle?"

"You could've been straight up with me all these years," I said, "but you wasn't. I'm killing him, and that's a fact."

"It ain't likely," Jack said, shaking his head real slow. Our gun barrels were inches from each other. Now it was as if Zanone was no longer in the room. I sensed Jack's finger tighten on the trigger and felt mine do the same. At this distance neither of us would live. It flashed through my mind that our hatred for Zanone was about to destroy us both. I wanted to tell that to Jack, to let him know what we were about to do, but I knew it had gone too far.

In the split second before we would kill one another—and perhaps it was our friendship, our years together against the rest of the world that bought us both that split second—there came a loud thump from Zanone's desk, and we both swung our guns in his direction.

Zanone had fallen facedown on the hard polished desk, his arms spread before him, his hands hanging over the edge toward us. He just lay there, deader than a box of rocks.

"Careful, Jack," I cautioned as he stepped forward and took Zanone's wrist, "it could be a trick." I took a step forward, but kept the pistol arm's length between me and Zanone, and pointed at the top of his head.

Holding Zanone's wrist between his fingers and thumb, Jack looked disappointed and shook his head. In a few seconds Jack let go and Zanone's arm thumped down against the desk. "If dying is a trick, I'd say old Uncle here has perfected it." He let down the hammer on the La Faucheux and plopped down on the desk beside Zanone. He sighed.

"God damn it!" I slung my new hat to the floor and kicked it across the room. Then I kicked the corner of the desk. *"God damn it!"*

Jack just sat there, studying the floor and shaking his head. I walked over, jerked my hat from the floor, and walked back. Dropping into a high-backed leather chair, I sank down and let out a long breath. My arms hung over the chair arms. My hat hung from one hand and my pistol from the other. After a full ten minutes of silence, Jack brought his eyes up from the floor and stared at me as if ashamed. He opened the La Faucheux and let the bullets fall into his hand. I watched as he stepped over, drew open the gun cabinet, and hung the fancy pistol on an empty peg. It fit perfectly. When he walked back and sat on the edge of Zanone's desk, I just stared at him with my one good eye for the longest time.

Finally, I got up and walked to the door. As I reached for the knob, I looked back over my shoulder. Jack lay his hand on Zanone's back, and tapped his fingers as if thinking of something to say. He let out a little puff of breath and shook his head. "Sorry." He shrugged. He must've thought I was leaving without him; I'd considered it. But as I turned the knob, I felt a smile tug at my solemn expression, and I nodded him toward the door. He stood up, tugged at his cuff, and adjusted his suit coat.

I chuckled under my breath and shook my head as he walked to the door beside me. "What's funny?" He smiled curiously and brushed a hand across his face. I swung open the door, still shaking my head, and let out a long breath. "I never . . . *asked?*"

◆✳ 48 ✳◆

That night, I left Chicago and traveled by rail all the way to Louisville, Kentucky. From there I took a horse and buggy to my spread over in Fayette County. For the longest time, while I waited for Jeanine and Lane to join me, I couldn't help but get a hollow feeling inside me. I reckoned knowing Zanone was dead was kind of like getting rid of a sore and rotten tooth that'd plagued me for years. Now that the torment was over, my mind touched on the empty spot where the soreness used to be. There was no pain, and I would have to get used to the newness of it.

When I had switched trains in Kansas City that night, I sat watching the darkness of the flatland drift past my window. I can't explain most of what went through my mind that night. I reckon a person's inner thoughts are like a submerged log in a settled pond. If only a twig sticks above the surface, maybe it's better to leave it alone, and let the surface lay like polished glass around it. Raising the log only stirs up the water, and with it the dark and murky substance that time has settled to the bottom. Near midnight, I had to shake my head to come away from that quiet pond, or fear staying lost in it forever.

I walked back to the smoker car to watch a game of poker. I didn't want to play; I just wanted to see movement and hear people go about the business of living.

As soon as I stepped through the door, I saw "Mysterious" Dave Mather seated at a card table with three other well-dressed fellers. Two of them glanced over their shoulder as I entered, then turned back to their game. The third man's face was shadowed beneath a wide-brimmed hat, but as I crossed the floor to the bar, I recognized Wyatt Earp's sharp features in the flicker of the lamp.

I hadn't seen Mather in years and I didn't know if he would recognize me or not—Earp either, for that matter. Since I couldn't just turn and walk out, I seated myself at the small bar, poured a glass of bourbon, and tried to go unnoticed.

After a few minutes of silence, except for the occasional grunt and clatter of chips against the felt-top table, Mather laughed under his breath. "Wyatt," he said. His eyes slid across me on their way to Earp, and immediately I felt a chill jolt through my spine. "Did I ever tell you about that son of a bitch, Miller Crowe?" He chuckled and my shoulders stiffened. The three men glanced among themselves patiently. Without looking up from his cards, Mather flipped two chips in the pot. I hadn't seen Wyatt Earp or his brothers in years. I doubted if they would recognize me. But Mather might have, and if he did, I wondered where he was headed with it.

"I've heard of him," Earp said. "A real slippery fellow." He dropped chips in the pot without looking up. "I heard he kept ole Hickok from getting back-shot over in Springfield, years ago."

"Hickok always said he never thought Crowe was near as bad as everybody made him out to be." Again Mather's eyes slid past me. "He even lent him money once to get a friend of his out of jail. Said he never thought he'd see that money again, but Crowe paid him back in no time."

Earp looked up from his cards as if a spark of remembrance came to his mind. "Yeah, I heard about that," he said, glancing at Mather. "I read something about him a while back. Something about Dan Zanone's detectives killing him over near Liberty."

"Yeah," Mather replied, "I read that, too, but that was bullshit." I felt the hair raise on the back of my neck, but for some reason my hand didn't ease down to the forty-four in my waist belt.

Mather's lazy eyes slid across me once more as he spread his cards on the table. The other players groaned and pitched in their hands.

"Well," Earp said, "that's it for me." He stood up and folded his loose tie as Mather raked in the chips.

"Yeah," Mather said, "they didn't kill Crowe in Kansas City."

"That's interesting," Earp said. I watched him adjust the long-barrelled pistol hanging from his hip as he picked up a small stack of dollar bills and shoved them in his vest pocket. He stepped away from the game as Mather shuffled the cards. "Real interesting," Earp went on, "considering he carried ten thousand on his head, dead or alive." Earp adjusted his flat-brimmed hat and smoothed it. "That's a heap of money."

Mather's eyes sparkled as he shuffled the cards with a sly grin. "You're telling me."

"What was the story on him, anyway?" asked another player. "Didn't he ride with the James bunch?"

"That's right," Mather said, "but I never figured him for a desperado . . . not really. I always felt like he was just a young country boy that got in over his head and couldn't get out."

"That can happen," said Earp. "Still . . . ten thousand."

Mather rapped the deck on the table. "Yeah, I know." He stopped for a second as if considering something of great importance, then turned slowly to me. "Looks like the game is a man short." His hands lay still on the table on either side of the deck. "You, sir." He nodded, and his eyes fixed on me. I have never been certain if he recognized me or not with the patch over one eye and many years between us. "It's gotten late on us." He smiled, perhaps in a sly, or was it a wise, fashion? "You look tired. Are you too tired to play the game?"

I watched his eyes a few seconds, wondering what he was really asking. Mather was a lawman and a snake. I couldn't imagine him cutting slack for anybody where money was involved. If he'd recognized me, surely he would have thrown down on me then and there, especially with Wyatt Earp backing him. Yet I felt no instinct to go for my gun or even let my hand drift toward it. Finally, I raised my glass slowly and emptied it without taking my eye off Mather. Earp and the others watched as if they sensed something between us, or maybe it was all in my mind. "Yes, sir," I said softly. I thought I heard a slight quiver in my voice. "I reckon I am awfully tired."

I saw Mather's hands relax on the table when I stood up and walked quietly to the door. As I turned the handle, I heard Mather say in a voice that may or may not have been intended for me to hear, "But the fact is, Crowe died years ago at Powder River. Anybody ever asks you-all, tell 'em I said so. I saw his body. They gutted him." Mather chuckled in a low voice. "Skinned and gutted that poor bastard."

I hesitated a second, glanced back over my shoulder, and thought I saw the two of them exchange something in their eyes. Then Mather turned back to the game as Earp stepped to the bar and poured a glass of water from a pitcher. The room was dim except for the glow of the lamp above the table. Amid the golden glow, the players watched with interest as Mather reshuffled the cards.

I started to say something, but stopped myself. As far as they were concerned, I'd already left. Feeling the cool wind rush in from across the flatland, I nodded my head slowly, stepped through the door, and closed it firmly behind me.

◆✱ Epilogue ✱◆

I'll always think of "The boys" now and then, what we were and what became of us. Cousin Frank gained his pardon, just as he said he would, by laying everything on his brother Jesse. Jesse would've gotten a kick out of it, and history? . . . Well, what history doesn't know ain't gonna bend a barrel hoop.

As for the rest of our bunch, they just drifted off over time. Cole spent most of his life in Stillwater Penitentiary. When he gained a pardon, I managed to send him some money without him knowing where it came from. I never liked the son of a bitch, but he was one of us. They say he was a model prisoner; I don't know.

Poor Bob Younger died in prison. Jim Younger made parole, drifted around a while selling tombstones and insurance, and fell in love with a young woman from a respectable family. Her daddy pitched a fit about her seeing Jim, and when she broke off their romance, Jim went home, drank a bottle of whiskey and blew his brains out with a forty-four. You just never know.

Nobody knows what become of "Mysterious" Dave Mather. He disappeared after screwing the Earp brothers out of every dollar he could, and was last spotted up in Lone Pine Nebraska. Some say he took to preaching and studying the art of counterfeiting money. I'd never known his artistic side.

As for me, I have fared well for a one-eyed man with a cloudy past. After lying for years about being a surveyor, I was approached by the government through a friend of a friend, and asked to head up an expedition into northern Montana. Rather than look foolish, I hired a good surveying crew and sort of learned as I went. Between my surveying business and my Thoroughbred stock, I have never had to unearth the caches of money I'd hidden years ago. It's laying where I left it, wrapped in time, and secrecy.

For years I regretted Daniel Zanone falling over dead before Jack or I, either one, got a chance to kill him. But I suppose it turned out for the best. In a backhanded sort of way, I'd kept my promise to Jeanine not to kill him. Still, I can't help but feel I avenged the death of my precious Little China, and once and for all, removed forever any threat of Zanone or his bunch ever harming my family.

Over the years, a little at a time, I've told my son everything about me, everything I can talk about, that is. I cannot describe to him the smell of burning flesh, or the screams of wounded men and horses dying. I've simply told him that war and killing begets war and killing, and that it will twist a man's mind and spirit for a long time to come. He understands. He knows that Jeston Nash was a victim of the war, and that Miller Crowe was a product of it.

I've not raised my son on bravado bullshit, nor have I tried to instill false virtue in him at the end of a whip. I reckon there's a day coming when my life will pass like warm breath on a cold windowpane. When my son steps into the dark woods on his own, I hope our time together will have given him direction. Since I've never known a thing about raising a child, I've had to make do with what's instinctive to me. I've taught him to set his own pace, and I've given him plenty of lead. I hope I've touched his life gently the way sunlight touches a young spring morning.

"What about the rumor that Miller Crowe was skinned and gutted at Powder River?" he asked. "Have you ever even been to Powder River?"

"Yeah," I said, "your Uncle Jack and I spent a summer there trying to deal horses to the army." I smiled, ready to change the subject. "But that was a whole other thing."

"Tell me what happened."

"Aw, it was nothing, really," I said. The summer at Powder River was one story I'd never told him. He was still young, and Powder River would take a lot of understanding.

He smiled patiently, as if hearing my thoughts. "Dad, I'll soon be finishing college."

I studied his face for a second. Soon I could tell him the whole story, but not until I'd resolved it in my own mind. "We went to deal horses," I said, "but we ended up in a misunderstanding with the cavalry, and a bunch of outlaws, and Red Cloud's warriors, and a couple of bounty hunters, and a few local lawmen."

"You call that *nothing?*" He laughed. "I can't imagine you and Senator Zanone ever doing something like that."

"It's Uncle Jack, to you," Jeanine corrected, as she stepped out on the balcony in the morning sunlight. "You know how the Senator feels about being a part of this family. He'll be here soon, so you better start calling him Uncle Jack again."

" 'Quiet' Jack Smith," I whispered under my breath. I hadn't seen him since last May, the day one of my horses had finished second in the big race at Louisville. No matter what anybody else called him, he would always be "Quiet" Jack to me.

The night I left Chicago, Jack had stayed at Zanone's office. When he knew I was well on my way, he walked down to the street bold as brass, and told a local constable that his poor uncle had just dropped over dead. As the last of the Zanones, Jack inherited everything, his uncle's estate, and the estate of his father which had gone to Daniel Zanone when no other relative could be found. I never seen anything like it. Daniel Zanone's business and political contacts took to Jack like lint to a blue suit, and from there, well, I reckon it goes without saying. . . .

Of a morning, at this time of year, sunlight blossoms in a golden haze and washes across the meadow and pastureland below. It turns the autumn grass a fiery orange and glistens in the frost on the leaves of the oak and sumac. And I, from the balcony, like to feel the first bite of the crisp morning and hear night vanish softly from the woodlands like a thief fleeing a broken latch. I ought not admit it—not being a religious man, and all—but I have thanked God many times over the years. In some quiet spot, I have gotten on my knees and thanked God with tears in my eyes, for Jeanine, for my son, Lane, and for the chance to be just a part of the circle of ordinary life. And this morning I sat watching my son, and my wife, and in my mind I thank God in passing as a new day begins. I thank God even for the worst of it, for it has brought about the best. I thank him for the best of it, for now the worst is far behind. I reckon I thank him most for all of it as one, the good and the bad, the bitter and sweet, for I've come to know that it is all sacred. Somehow it all works together to season the flesh and temper the spirit. There is no clear cut, no straight and narrow for mortal man. There is only the struggle, and by grace, the turning.

This I know. For I have struggled and turned, and tasted sweat and tears. But through it all, above all else, I have lived—*yes, lived!* . . . in flesh and blood, in spite of hell, on this earth, while angels dance.